The
Thorn of
Dentonhill

MARSHALL RYAN
MARESCA

The Thorn of Dentonhill

DAW BOOKS, INC.
DONALD A. WOLLHEIM, FOUNDER
375 Hudson Street, New York, NY 10014

ELIZABETH R. WOLLHEIM
SHEILA E. GILBERT
PUBLISHERS
www.dawbooks.com

First Printing, February 2015
1 2 3 4 5 6 7 8 9

DAW TRADEMARK REGISTERED
U.S. PAT. AND TM. OFF. AND FOREIGN COUNTRIES
—MARCA REGISTRADA
HECHO EN U.S.A.

PRINTED IN THE U.S.A.

Acknowledgments

This book would not exist without the assistance of quite a few people.

First of all, there is my amazing and incredibly patient wife, Deidre Kateri Aragon. She has been an anchor in my life for the past fifteen years, giving me the ability to pound away at a keyboard day after day to make this book happen. But, more importantly, she got me on task in the first place, moving me from being that guy who just talked about "writing a book at some point" to actually making writing a real focus in my life. She and my son Nicholas have been a source of constant support and strength through the process of becoming a novelist.

No less important to thank are my parents, Louis and Nancy Maresca, and my mother-in-law, Kateri Aragon. My mother, especially, read an early draft and gave it a solid critique and line edit.

Next, there are the many people who read versions and drafts of *Thorn*, and gave useful advice that helped shape it into a stronger, better work. This includes Kimberly Frost and Julie Kenner, as well as Miriam Robinson Gould, and the Bat City Novelocracy crew: Kevin Jewell, Abby Goldsmith, Ellen Van Hensbergen, Leigh Berggren, Nicole Duson and Amanda Downum.

A huge portion of thanks has to go to Stina Leicht, who has been running the ArmadilloCon Writers Workshop for many years, and after I had attended it several times, brought me on board to run it with her. Stina has been a friend, a mentor, a sympathetic ear, and a good source for the occasional much-needed whap upside the head, which is exactly what every writer needs.

I can't emphasize enough how much is owed to my agent, Mike Kabongo. He's handled with grace and humor the arduous task of dealing with my constant harassment while shopping my work. He deserves extra accolades for taking an interest in a manuscript that was not ready or sellable, but filled with potential. He really shepherded that work, which eventually became this novel.

Further thanks are owed to my editor, Sheila Gilbert, as well as everyone else at DAW. I am deeply grateful for all the hard work they've done to make this the best book it can possibly be.

Finally, there is my dear friend Daniel J. Fawcett, who has been my sounding board and bent ear on everything creative I've done since the seventh grade. Nothing in this book would be what it is without his influence. I wouldn't be who I am today without his friendship.

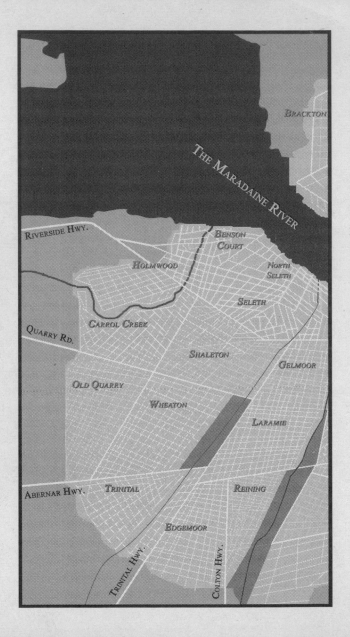

THE MARADAINE RIVER

BRACKTON

RIVERSIDE HWY.

BENSON
COURT

HOLMWOOD

NORTH
SELETH

SELETH

CARROL CREEK

QUARRY RD.

SHALETON

GELMOOR

OLD QUARRY

WHEATON

LARAMIE

ABERNAR HWY.

TRINITAL

REINING

EDGEMOOR

TRINITAL HWY.

COLTON HWY.

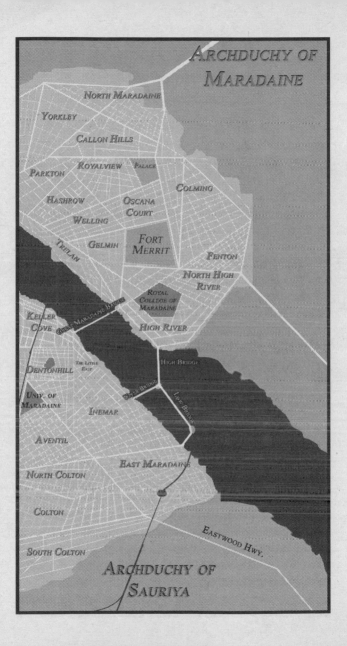

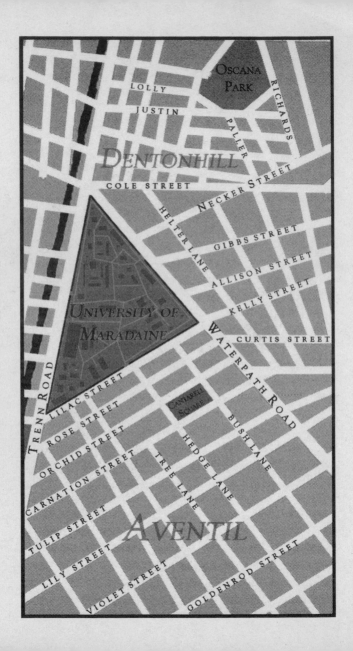

Chapter 1

"**T**HIEF!" a heavy voice shouted from the door.

That's rich, one of them calling me thief, Veranix Calbert thought. He had arrived only seconds before. He hadn't had the chance to steal anything yet.

The man at the door was large, a good foot taller than Veranix, all muscle and bone. Gray wool vest, white shirtsleeves, thin rapier at his belt. Pretenses of a man of substance.

Veranix flashed a grin at the man. "If you think there's a thief, you should call the constables."

"Oh, no, whelp. We won't be needing them." The man drew the sword and edged closer.

There wasn't supposed to be anyone here. Veranix had scouted the place for the past three days. This office above the fish cannery was used only as a drop spot. No one stayed here, no one kept watch. The point of it was to avoid notice.

"Are you sure?" Veranix asked, tensing his legs. "I hear they are awfully friendly."

The man charged in, blade swinging. "I'll show you friendly!"

Veranix jumped out of the way and rolled to the side, landing back on his feet by the desk in the corner. He was grateful that, while the man had a sword, he didn't know how to use it: all muscle, no finesse. Whoever this guy was, he wasn't a guard. Veranix could handle him. Veranix wished he hadn't left his weapons behind, but he had another advantage over the guy.

"Really, chap, that's not friendly at all," he said. His gaze flashed over the desk, taking in the scraps of paper and parchment covering it. The room was too dark to know if the information he wanted was there.

"Not to you," the man said as he turned back around to face Veranix. "But I've got friends. Oy!" Three more men, dressed and armed the same as their friend, appeared at the door.

"That's really not fair," Veranix said. He grabbed a handful of papers blindly and shoved them into the pocket of his cloak.

"You think you're going to take those?" the first man said. They all stood there, looking quite pleased with themselves.

Veranix conceded they had good reason. They blocked the door and the window, and they were four muscular men with swords. From what they saw, he was an unarmed, scrawny-looking young man, barely fully grown. They certainly thought they had him trapped.

"If you don't mind terribly," Veranix said.

"'Fraid we do, mate. Either put them back, or we make you."

"Tempting offer," Veranix said. As unthreatening as he must have appeared to them, they held back, hands resting on their sheathed swords. They clearly wanted to avoid a fight. That gave him a chance. Even so, without weapons, he knew he wasn't strong enough to last in a fair brawl with one of these guys, let alone four.

Good thing he wasn't interested in a fair brawl.

With the few seconds he had, Veranix drew as much *numina* as he could. He didn't shape it much. He didn't have time, and he didn't want them to realize what he was doing. He channeled the magic energy out in a quick, hard blast in front of him. He didn't give it enough raw force to hurt any of them, that wasn't the point. The papers on the desk scattered, filling the air. All the men jumped back in surprise, and Veranix darted for the door.

Quick and dirty, he drew in more *numina* and released it out again. In a flash, the floor under the men was covered in a thin sheen of grease. Veranix braced himself and knocked headfirst into the man in the middle. The man lost his footing and fell over. Veranix slid out into the hallway, overlooking the cannery floor. Not slowing down, he launched himself over the railing.

Right below the railing was a bin filled with dead fish and half-melted ice, too big to avoid. Veranix crashed into it, the cold more jarring than the impact. It wasn't an ideal landing, but it was good enough to escape.

"Get him!" a voice called from above. Doing two bits of fast magic had left Veranix winded and woozy, but he didn't have time to catch his breath. He rolled forward, tossing himself onto the floor of the shop. The men were getting to the top of the stairs, still stumbling and slipping from his grease trick. He tried to push over the bin of ice to block their path, but it was too heavy for him. With a shrug and a grin, he bounded over the cleaning tables toward the door.

4 Marshall Ryan Maresca

"Never leave your gear behind, no matter how small the window," he muttered to himself as he ran out into the street. If he hadn't left his weapons on the opposite roof, he could have escaped without resorting to magic.

He didn't have time to be subtle. With wild desperation, he pulled in all the *numina* he could and channeled it to his legs.

He jumped up, leaping high from the dusty cobblestone road to the top of the roof across the street. He almost fell short, landing chest-first on the eaves. He scrambled over and fell flat onto the rooftop. His whole body screamed with exhaustion, barely able to move.

He cursed himself for being careless, doing magic badly. The jump was messy, all the magic he just did was messy, using more *numina* than he needed. That much, all at once, was more than his body could handle. Sloppy work. Magic like that made big ripples of *numina* that other mages would notice, could trace. Someone might start poking his nose around. If that led back to him, still Uncircled, still at school . . . he'd almost rather take his chances fighting Fenmere's goons.

"The blazes is he?" he heard a voice in the street below.

"Couldn't have gone far," another said.

"Anyone get a good look at him?"

"Skinny kid, maroon cloak. That's about it."

"What did he take?"

"Don't know, but Fenmere will hide us if we don't find him."

Rapid footsteps went off in different directions. He didn't hear any of the men go into the building. They probably wouldn't come up and find him. They'd have no reason to look up, no reason to think he could make it to the roof as fast as he did. Head still spinning from the magic burn, he grabbed his bow, arrows, staff, and pack, right where he had left them. He glanced across the street, back at the office window. From up here, it did look too small to squeeze through with his equipment. In retrospect, he could have done it. He shook his head, deciding not to leave anything behind again unless it was necessary.

If nothing else, with the white moon nearly full and hanging low on the horizon, the view of the city up on the roof was spectacular. The wide sprawl of Maradaine spread out before him. The thick clusters of gray brick of Dentonhill; past that, the densely packed streets and old white stone of Inemar, the true central neighborhood of the city. Beyond that, the wide stretch of dark water that was the Maradaine River. Lamps from sailed ships dotted the river, as well as lighting up the bridges to the north side of the city. Far across the river, the marble towers of the North Maradaine neighborhoods and the gleaming dome of the Parliament shone in the moonlight.

He glanced around the roof. There was a drying line with clothes hung on it, a few chairs and a table, a door giving entry into the building. He tried the door, finding it unlocked, and a dark staircase leading down. It looked like a hallway, not direct access to an apartment. Sighing, he slunk inside. Normally he would have magicked his way down to the ground, or from roof to roof, to get back home. Right now, he couldn't muster enough magic to lift a bug.

He wrapped the bow in his cloak, and hid it in his pack with his arrows and the papers he had stolen. He didn't want to risk the undue attention he would get walking through the streets armed. The staff he'd have to chance, as there was no way of hiding it. Given how his body ached, he might have to actually use it to walk. Luckily, the thugs hadn't seen him with it before.

He went down one flight of stairs, leading to a dank, moldy landing with doors for four apartments. He had only taken one step down the next flight when one of the doors opened.

Veranix froze.

A young man, shabby hair and dull eyes, poked his head out the door. It took a moment before his eyes focused on Veranix, but then he smiled and nodded.

"Hey," he said, calm and friendly.

"Hey," Veranix returned.

"Who is it?" another man's voiced hissed from inside the apartment.

"Just some guy," the man at the door said.

"Is he buying?"

The man at the door turned back to Veranix. "You here to buy a 'vi'?"

The words were asked casually, but they hit Veranix hard. They were selling *effitte*. He knew he should say no. He was spent, head spinning, he needed to get back home. He should just walk away.

"Tell him to roll his own hand if he's not buying!"

Veranix took a step off the stairs back onto the landing. "You're selling?"

"If you've got coin," the man inside called back. Veranix took a tick out of his pocket, and showed it to the doorman.

"You're not a stick, are you?"

"Do I look like a stick?"

The skinny guy at the door chuckled. "Nah. Like they come up here anyway, except to buy."

He let Veranix step into the flop. It was exactly what he expected from an *effitte* den. A few low-burning lamps sat on cracked wooden tables. A floor riddled with clothes, dirt, and other filth. An iron stove sat in the middle of the room, and a few bedrolls huddled around it. The fishy reek of the cannery filled the air, though Veranix realized that was probably his own scent after falling in the ice bin.

One older man, wearing just a stained vest and ripped pants, crouched by the stove, rubbing blackened hands together in front of the open grate. "You buying, kid?" He was obviously the boss in here. One other person, a young girl wrapped in a blanket, maybe fourteen or fifteen, sat against the far wall, staring blankly into empty space.

Veranix held up the coin. "If you've got it to sell."

"Half-crown for a vial."

Veranix nodded. He reached into his pocket, and pushing a small amount of magic through his fingers, made the sound of several coins jingling. "How much for the whole stash?"

"Whole stash?" The man laughed, dry and mirthless. "Funny guy you are."

"I'll pay you fair."

The man squinted at Veranix. "Why don't you buy one, and come back in the morning for more?"

"Sure," Veranix said. He took some coins out of his pocket, slapped them all on one of the tables. The girl startled at the sound, but then went back to her blank stare.

The older man opened up his vest and took a thin vial out of a small pocket. Veranix spotted at least ten more inside the vest. The man handed the vial over and bent to pick up the coins.

Veranix only let it stay in his hand for a second. That was all he could stand. Rage fueling every muscle, pushing thorough the swirling fatigue, he hurled the vial of *effitte* into the stove.

"What?" The seller turned around, still crouched over the table. Veranix swung his staff around hard, cracking the man across the skull. The man fell forward, catching his hands on the hot stove. He screamed.

The other two stared at Veranix in confusion.

"Hey, what are you—" the other man said, reaching out to Veranix. Veranix spun around and knocked him with the staff, once, twice, three times, until he dropped. The man was already *effitte*-dosed; he didn't put up a fight.

Veranix turned to the girl. She did nothing but trace her fingers in the empty air.

Veranix gave his attention to the seller. He pulled the man back up, so he was standing, and tore the vest off his body.

"Is this all?" he snarled.

"All what?" The man was dazed and weeping, looking around the room as if there were something he could see that would make everything that just happened make sense.

"All the *effitte*?"

"Yeah, yeah."

Veranix threw the vest into the fire.

"No more anywhere? Lockbox of cash?"

"Cash is in the bedroll." Tears were streaming down

the man's face. Veranix wanted to laugh; this guy had given such tough talk before. Then he thought of all the *effitte* the guy had peddled. He grabbed the guy by the hair and slammed his head against the stove, and dropped him to the ground. The guy didn't get up.

"Are you the boss?" the girl slurred.

"You should get out of here," Veranix said. He knocked over the bedroll and found a sack of coins. He grabbed it and stormed out of the apartment.

He got down two more flights of stairs before the rush of anger faded, and his head started spinning. Even only using a little magic back there, he was still weak.

He slumped down onto the stairs. With a chuckle to himself, he considered that the night wasn't a total waste. He had destroyed some *effitte*, taken care of a few sellers. That was something.

He took out the stolen papers. As spent as he was, he had to know if he had gotten the information he needed, anything on Fenmere's *effitte* delivery schedules. With that, he could start cutting off the drug at the source, no longer just hitting street dealers. Then he could really make a difference.

It was too dark to read in the stairwell. Annoyed, he shoved the papers back in his pocket.

He let his eyes close, just for a moment.

Church bells rang in the distance. Was it seven bells? How long had he been sitting in the stairwell? Slivers of sunlight came under the door. Had he fallen asleep and not realized it? Panic fueled his body, and he forced himself to move. He couldn't waste any more time.

He left the building and headed west on Necker. It was a major road, with tightly packed dirty gray stone buildings, looming six or seven stories high. Windows were covered with black iron grates. The street bustled with early morning activity. Shopkeepers opened up their iron-grated doors. Horsecarts slowly rolled along. Snuffers put out the streetlamps that hadn't burned out during the night.

Veranix slipped in with a group dressed for work in heavy, brown smocks, headed toward the Dentonhill Slaughterhouse. The scent of blood and the squawking of hundreds of doomed birds filled the air. Veranix was pleased to have a small crowd to blend into. Even if Fenmere's thugs spotted him and recognized him, they probably wouldn't try to grab him where there would be witnesses.

Maybe not.

This was Dentonhill, after all. Fenmere's neighborhood. Any possible witnesses would be people Fenmere could buy or intimidate to keep quiet. Any constables in the neighborhood were likely to be deep in his pocket.

Veranix just had to make it three blocks to Waterpath, and he'd be out of Dentonhill and somewhat safer. At least he'd be out of Fenmere's direct influence.

By the time Veranix reached Waterpath, the sun was peeking over the buildings, casting long shadows across the road. Waterpath was a major roadway, wide enough for four carriages side-by-side, and at this hour plenty of drovers were taking full advantage of that. The street crawled with merchant wagons and horse carriages, while three-wheeled pedalcarts darted through the gaps. Veranix crossed out from the Dentonhill side, sitting like a great gray cliff behind him, and wove between the carts and wagons until he reached the bright green tree line of the University of Maradaine.

There were plenty of people about on the street, but no one seemed to notice as he went behind a wide-leafed tree and climbed up a few branches. His strength had returned for the most part, though he still felt drained. From this vantage point, he could jump onto the back wall of the University. The low wall was there to mark the border of the campus, rather than actually keep people out. He scrambled onto the rough stone and dropped onto the soft grass.

He relaxed a little after entering the campus. It was a stark change from Dentonhill: the green of the campus lawn, the bright white buildings, the paved walkways all lined with banners, statues, and fresh-scented blooming trees, and the open view of the sky.

No one was in sight, and no one cried out that they saw him. Veranix said a quick prayer of thanks to Saint Senea. Now he just had to get back to quarters. That was going to be a challenge. The back doors to Almers Hall were locked, and prefects watched the front doors. If they caught him out of quarters now, carrying a pack and a staff, there would be a lot of questions about what he was up to, possibly an official inquiry. That would mean demerits and reprimands, if not outright expulsion. He didn't need that any more than he needed to be caught by the thugs. He had left a window open on the third floor, but it was too light out now to climb to it. He'd be easily seen. He'd probably be spotted shortly anyway. He made a quick dash for the carriage house.

Veranix went up to one window near the back end of it, and tapped on the glass.

"Kai!" he whispered. "Kai!" After a moment, the window opened.

"Don't tell me you're just getting here," Kaiana said, scowling at him. Her dark eyes were wide and alert. She had already woken up for the day, dressed in her loose canvas pullover and slacks. Veranix cursed himself for losing track of time. She stepped back and let him scramble into the window. "It's nearly eight bells!"

"Nearly got caught, and I burned myself out getting away. And then I stumbled into a den."

"You reek of fish, you know," she said, her flat nose crinkling in disgust. Kaiana Nell was a dark-haired, brown-skinned girl. Ruder people would call her a Napa: half Druth, half Napolic. She was a soldier's daughter, born out on the tropical islands during the Fifty Year War.

Ruder people would call Veranix a Dirty Quin if his Racquin heritage were as clear on his face. Of course, Racquin were only a little darker than "regular" Druthalians. They just kept to the roads and kept to their own, for the most part. Though Veranix, like Kaiana, was only half. His father was a "regular" Druth, born and raised in Maradaine, just blocks away from the University. Veranix had inherited his father's fair skin and green eyes, and could speak in his father's Aventil neighborhood accent. Even his last name, Calbert, was pure Druth. Only his given name gave any hint that he was anything but a local.

"I landed in a bin full of them," he said. "It wasn't fun."

"You got careless out there, didn't you?"

"No."

"You 'stumbled' into a den?"

"Really, I did. Well, I found it was there, and I couldn't just ignore—"

"I get it," she said. Her eyes narrowed. "Did you destroy their stash?"

"Fifteen, maybe twenty vials."

"Not much stash."

He took out the pouch of coins. "Plus this. Keep them from getting more."

"You count it?"

"Of course not." He tossed it over to her. "Can you drop that at Saint Julian's?"

"Yeah," she said, putting the sack under her bed.

He took off his leather vest and linen tunic as if they were one piece. "I'm going to hide my gear here today."

"Gear, yes. Not those clothes."

"Kai, if I get caught in these clothes . . ."

"If that fish smell brings Master Jolen searching here, he'll find all your gear. Then I'll be out on the street." Master Jolen was the head groundskeeper of the campus. Veranix knew that he, at best, tolerated Kaiana's presence on his staff, and would probably use any excuse to kick her out.

"You have my spare uniform?" he asked.

"No, Veranix," she said. "I told you, I hid those in the Spinner Run."

"Why did you do that?"

"Again, if Jolen finds a student's uniform in here, he'll throw me out. After he beats me for being a 'wanton trollop.'"

"He wouldn't dare," Veranix said.

"Oh, I think he would," she said. "I think he'd like it." Kaiana was the only female on the grounds staff, so Jolen had her sleep in the carriage house, while the rest lived in one of the staff barracks. Jolen was constantly threatening her with beatings if she stepped out of line, but he hadn't ever followed through, as far as Veranix knew.

"All right," Veranix said. He rummaged through his pack and took out the stolen papers.

"Are those what you wanted?" she asked.

"Don't know. Haven't gotten a chance to look at them." He glanced at the sheets in his hands.

"You don't have time now!"

"Nearly eight bells already?"

"If not past."

"Fine, fine." Grudgingly, Veranix stuck the papers in the crease of his pants.

"Ridiculous," she muttered, shoving his pack and staff under her bed. "Now, get." He opened her door a crack. No one was out there. With a last wink at her, he dashed out to the stables.

The Spinner Run was an abandoned underground passage that ran from one of the stables of the carriage house to Holtman Hall, where the students' dining hall was. Veranix had no idea what its original purpose had been, but as far as he knew the only ones who still used it, other than Kaiana and himself, were rats and spiders.

He pulled open the trapdoor and dropped into the Run. It was completely dark, but he didn't care. He had enough of his strength back to make a small glowing ball appear. The ball hung in the air, providing enough light to find the hole in the wall, a space where the bricks had been chipped out of the mortar, down near the dirt floor. Reaching in, he pulled out his spare school uniform. Taking the papers out and putting them to the side, he stripped off the dark wool pants he was wearing, and shoved all his fishy clothes into the hole. He'd have to deal with those later.

Not knowing how much time he had, he raced to put on his uniform. He never liked wearing it. The wool of the dark blue pants and jacket was scratchy and stiff. He couldn't move, couldn't stretch, while wearing it. The worst parts of the whole thing were the cap and scarf. Every time he put them on he felt foolish, even though every other student wore the same thing. His were striped red and gray, which marked him as a magic student.

He folded up the stolen papers and shoved them in the jacket pocket. Wiping off the bits of loose mortar from his jacket, he dashed down the passageway, reaching the other end in less than a minute. Other students in his House would be arriving shortly in Holtman for breakfast. If his luck held, no one would notice that he hadn't come from Almers.

He climbed up through the trapdoor, emerging in one of Holtman's storerooms. As usual, no one was there. He snuck from the room, went down the hall, and joined in with the uniformed students from Almers who were heading toward the dining hall.

He felt a tap on his shoulder.

"Where have you been?"

"Water closet," he said. He turned to see Delmin Sarren, who shared sleeping quarters with him in Almers. Delmin was tall and rail-thin, with stringy, light-colored hair that never stayed contained under his cap, which had the same red and gray trim as Veranix's.

Delmin chuckled. "Don't treat me stupid. Your bed wasn't slept in."

"Sure it was."

"Please. I won't tell the prefects or anything. But if you get caught, you're going to be in trouble."

"Caught?" Veranix asked in his best innocent voice.

Delmin wrapped an arm around him and whispered conspiratorially. "Look, mate. That dark girl is a pretty one, so I don't blame you for sneaking into her bed. But you can't be staying with her until dawn, no matter how good it is."

"You're right," Veranix replied. "Thanks."

Delmin sniffed at Veranix. "Also, you need to give yourself time to clean up. You smell like a freshly rolled doxy."

"I'll keep that in mind," Veranix said. He bit his lip to keep from laughing. "What's our course today?"

"We've got lecture with Alimen today."

Veranix sighed. Alimen on no sleep would be a challenge. He went into the dining hall, hoping for some very strong tea.

Chapter 2

THREE CUPS OF TEA and two bowls of porridge later, Veranix stumbled behind Delmin as they went to the Western Lecture Halls. Bells up in the High University Tower rang out the time. It was already nine bells. Delmin broke into a run. Veranix realized that they were about to be late for lecture and bolted after Delmin. The two of them skidded into the hall just as the ninth bell rang.

"Well, Mister Calbert. Mister Sarren. You managed to make it to lecture on time." Professor Alimen stood at the slate board, looking stately in his blue professorial robe. He was an older man, though fit and lean. He kept his gray hair and beard cropped short, and his green eyes had very few lines around them for his age. The sleeves of his robe were rolled up, revealing his strong forearms and the tattoo on his left arm. The tattoo, of the letters L and P surrounded by flame, showed his membership in Lord Preston's Circle.

"We don't want to miss a minute, Professor," Veranix said.

"Surely," Alimen said. "Upper gallery, gentlemen."

Veranix and Delmin went up the narrow spiral stairs to the gallery above the lecture floor, joining the score of students already standing there. Many of them were specifically Third-Year Magic students, like Veranix and Delmin, but several were students of other disciplines, taking Alimen's Advanced Mystical Theory lecture to round out their education. The University Board insisted that all students take several lectures outside of their field of Mastery.

"Very good, then," Professor Alimen said. "As the bells have rung, and we are all assembled, let us begin. Today we will start a new chapter, as laid out in your texts, exploring the mystical nature of . . ."

Veranix looked at the assembly standing in the upper gallery, taking in the wide variety of caps and scarves. He was always amazed that so many students who couldn't do magic would want to learn about magic theory. Theory was a waste of his time, and Alimen's lectures were dry and dull. Despite that, Veranix attended every lecture dutifully. He owed Professor Alimen too much to do otherwise.

He slipped his hand inside his jacket pocket, feeling for the stolen papers. He was getting anxious to know just what he had. As his fingers touched the sheets, they made a slight crinkling sound. Delmin glanced over at him.

"What're you doing?" he whispered.

"Nothing," Veranix said, pulling his hand out. "Had an itch."

"Scratch later," someone on Veranix's other side hissed at him.

Veranix sighed. He'd have to wait.

Professor Alimen droned on.

Two more hours of this. He leaned against the support beam and did his best to keep his focus on the lecture.

"Mister Calbert!"

Veranix snapped out of his doze. His face was uncomfortably pressed against the support beam. There was no hiding that he had fallen asleep.

"Yes, Professor Alimen?" he asked. Blinking to clear his eyes, he looked down to the lecture floor. Alimen was glaring up at him, holding a small rock in his hand. Veranix had the idea that the professor was of the mind to throw it at his head.

"Perhaps you would care to help me demonstrate?"

"Yes, of course, Professor," Veranix said.

"Come down here, then, Mister Calbert."

Veranix pushed his way through the other students on the upper gallery to get to the stairs. Each step creaked and groaned as he went down. He suddenly had the wild urge to jump down from the balcony. He could have done it easily, managing a double or even a triple flip before making a perfect landing, bringing gasps of amazement and thunderous applause from the crowd. He missed those sounds sometimes. He quickly stifled the urge. It was best that no one knew he could do that, as they would surely ask where he'd learned it.

Veranix wracked his brain to think of what he was about to help demonstrate. What was the lecture about again? Something about minerals and mystic properties. He stepped out onto the floor, very aware of all the eyes on him.

Professor Alimen was smiling far too broadly for

Veranix's comfort. "Excellent, Mister Calbert. Now, if you could just take the dalmatium."

Veranix took the rock. It was heavier than he expected, cool to the touch. It was a chunk of metal, not stone.

"Now, Mister Calbert, you get to fulfill the fantasy of many, many students who have passed through these halls. You have permission to blast me."

"Sir?" Veranix asked.

"Whatever form of magic blast or jinx you prefer, Mister Calbert. Hit me, full strength." Veranix was still feeling tired and drained, now even more than before. He wasn't sure how much strength he could even muster.

"Are you certain, sir?" Veranix asked. "I wouldn't want to hurt you."

"Now, Mister Calbert."

The students above chuckled nervously. Veranix was sure all of them were glad they weren't down here.

"All right, Professor." Veranix drew in the *numina* from around him. He raised his hand to release the energy, but it was already gone. Nothing happened. He tried again, but the *numina* was gone. He couldn't make any magic.

Professor Alimen nodded and looked up at the crowd. "As you see, the dalmatium effectively absorbs *numina* energy, making any magic all but impossible." He took the rock away from Veranix and put it back on the table. "Thank you, Mister Calbert. Back up top, and try to stay awake."

Veranix slunk back up the stairs as Alimen continued the lecture.

"Now, also unlike napranium, dalmatium is a hard

metal, and it does not lose its properties when alloyed with iron. In fact, our city's constabulary has special shackles for mages that are made with dalmatium. Mister Calbert has some idea now what it would be like to wear them."

Veranix stepped back into place next to Delmin. Every student with red and gray trim looked at him with sympathy and fear.

"How did it feel?" Delmin whispered to him.

"Strange. Like I was leaking."

"Teach you to doze off in lecture," Delmin said.

"Shh," Veranix said. "I don't want to miss any more."

"Next lecture we'll start going over crystals," Alimen continued. He put the rock in a small box, latching it shut. "I'll have more samples to demonstrate at that class. Good day, all."

"More samples?" Veranix asked Delmin. "What did that mean?"

"Oh, the dalmatium was the only thing he had to show today," Delmin said, gathering his notes while other students filed out of the hall. "The other metals, napranlum, theralium, and so on are too rare for him to get."

"Mister Calbert!" Alimen's voice boomed across the lecture hall. Veranix and Delmin both stopped in their tracks. Veranix turned to see Alimen approaching, arms full of boxes and charts.

"Yes, Professor?" Veranix held out his arms, offering to take some of the professor's burden.

Alimen gave him a dismissive shake of the head, refusing the help. "Please note that you have a practical course with me tomorrow at nine bells. I will demand both your punctuality and full attention." Despite the harsh tone, Alimen's face was cheerful and bright. "Mister Sarren, yours is at eleven bells. Though I know you need no prodding."

"We could switch, Professor," Veranix suggested.

"Absolutely not, Veranix," Alimen said with a chuckle and a shake of his head. "I want to have you done with so I can enjoy the rest of my day." He winked after this comment, and went out of the hall.

Delmin knocked Veranix's arm as they followed. "We could switch? Nine bells is all yours, my friend. Come on, let's beat the crowd to lunch."

"I'm going to skip it," Veranix said. "I need some real sleep."

"Your choice." Delmin dashed off across the lawn to Holmwood, leaving Veranix to trudge alone to Almers Hall.

Almers was several hundred years old, having been built when the University of Maradaine was just the Great High College of Maradaine, and Veranix was certain that very few changes had been made to the building in all that time. The building was stone, mortared and plastered and painted white. In every room the paint had dirtied to a dull gray, the plaster crumbling and mortar cracking. A boring lump of a building, filled with drafts and moldy dampness. Veranix had happily called it home for the last three years, the only home he had ever had that didn't have wheels on it.

"Heard you fell asleep in your lecture today, Veranix," someone said from behind him. Veranix could tell just by the looming presence, a full head and a half taller than him, it was Rellings, one of the Almers prefects.

"Is that story already going around?"

"Word travels fast," Rellings said, looking down his hawk nose at Veranix. "Now, why were you so tired, kish?" Veranix scowled. He hated whenever anyone called him "kish." It was a nickname final year students, especially prefects, used for underclassmen. It was a bit of slang on campus so old no one even knew where it came from anymore, but its use persisted. Veranix swore that when he reached final year, he wouldn't use it at all. Not that it would make a difference. The kind of guys who would use it were the kind of guys who became prefects.

"One of those mornings," Veranix said. As he approached the door to Almers. Rellings stepped ahead and blocked Veranix's entrance.

"A morning where you didn't sleep all night?"

"Nightmares kept me up," Veranix said, staring hard at Rellings. "That happens with mages, you know."

Rellings stepped back. Veranix knew he was easily spooked by magic, even just the idle threat of it. "Right. I didn't note you this morning, but Sarren said you were around. Don't think I'm not paying attention to you."

"Glad to hear it," Veranix said. Delmin was actively covering for him. Veranix appreciated that, but wondered if Delmin would make the effort if he knew what was really happening. "I'm going in now." Rellings sneered but let him pass. Veranix went up to the third floor common room.

The common room was a chaotic mess of threadbare chairs and cracked wooden tables, grouped around the central fireplace. The winters in Almers were brutal. Even now, as spring was well into warm bloom, the place had a heavy chill. The bare stone floor didn't help. Several students were huddled about the fireplace, reading, writing, and arguing. Veranix slipped his way between the chairs. He wanted to get in his room, read through the papers, and take a nap.

"Veranix!" someone called to him. He was a first- or second-year whose name Veranix had completely forgotten. "Thank Saint Hespin you're here."

"Prens!" his companion said. "Watch the blasphemy." He tapped his knuckle to his forehead and then kissed it in benediction. His accent and his act of devotion stood out. He was from the southern Archduchy of Scaloi. There couldn't be more than ten Scallics on campus. Despite that, Veranix couldn't remember his name.

"It's not blas—never mind," Prens said. "Veranix, sweet Saint Veran, please. Really, help us out."

Veranix stopped. They were invoking the sainted version of his name. This must be serious. He only hoped this would be quick. "What's the problem?"

"We've got a Basic Mystical Theory exam in the afternoon," said Prens. "We're dying here." Prens and his pious friend both wore brown and green scarves. They weren't magic students. What was brown and green? Theology? That was it. It was coming back to him. These two were the preseminary students at the end of the hallway.

Veranix shook his head. "You've got the wrong man. You want to talk theory, find Delmin."

"We did last night," Prens said. "I didn't understand half of what he said."

"You did pass Basic Mystical Theory, yes?" his friend

asked. Veranix struggled with his name. Owens? Oads? Oaks, that was it.

"Yes, I passed," Veranix said. "I just . . . look, I'm tired, I came back to take a nap, and . . ." He looked at the two of them, their faces filled with panic. He sat down. "All right, what are you not getting?"

"Everything," Prens moaned.

"Can you narrow it down to something I can answer in five minutes?"

"The five hundred and five rule," Oaks said.

Veranix nodded. This was one of the few things he actually understood. "One out of every five hundred people is born with the basic, raw ability to channel *numina*."

"To do magic," Prens said.

"Not exactly. *Numina* is just the energy that powers magic. Channeling the energy is meaningless if you can't do something with it. That's the other part. Of those one in five hundred, only one in five also have the ability to shape *numina* in any sort of useful way."

"Why does that matter?"

"Well, that's how you do magic. Channel the *numina* through yourself, and shape it how you want it."

"But if you can channel it, then . . ." Oaks trailed off, looking more confused.

"This is how I got it," Veranix said. "Imagine *numina* is like water under the ground. Doing magic is like digging a well."

"I've helped dig a well," Prens said.

"So the one in five hundred, that's like a spot where the water level is high enough that it's worth digging a well."

"Where you can actually get the water." Prens nodded.

"But it doesn't do you any good unless you have bucket or a pump or something to bring up the water."

"And that's the one in five," Oaks said.

Prens looked troubled. "So why is it that only one person in twenty-five hundred can actually do magic? Why do just a few people have the ability?"

"God decides," Oaks said.

Prens ignored him. "And where does *numina* come from?"

"God makes it."

"That's your answer for everything you don't get!" Prens rubbed his temples and sighed. "Even in theology class, it won't be the right answer!"

"There are a lot of theories about both questions," Veranix said, "but the truth is no one really knows. Or, at least, I don't think so. These are questions for Delmin. Anyway, *numina* just is." He pulled a little bit into his body and shaped it into sparkling lights that he let jump from one hand to the other. "It exists everywhere, always flowing, like the wind. I can feel it, but I can't explain it."

"See, I was right," Oaks said. "God makes it."

"That doesn't mean—"

"Give me another—"

"I don't have to give you another—"

"All right, all right," Veranix said, getting up from the chair. "Five minutes are up. Good luck to you both. Delmin is in the lunch hall. I'm going now." The two of them were still arguing when he went into his bedchamber.

The chamber was narrow and cramped. There were two thin beds, two small writing desks, and one wardrobe, all made from raw, unpainted wood, graying and cracked with age. Unlit candles sat on each desk, as well as several books and loose papers. Two unlit oil lamps hung over the beds. A small window on one wall let in a trickle of sunlight. The window had been designed to open only a crack, and there were iron bars covering it. Veranix had spent a fair amount of time fiddling and magicking with the window and bars so he could get out that way, while making it look like they were still intact.

Veranix stripped off his jacket and boots and dropped onto his bed. He lay there for a moment, and then sat back up. He fished out the papers he had stolen the night before. As ready as he was to sleep, he was more anxious to find out what he had, and if it was useful.

Most of the papers were documents about the cannery: payroll, inventory, and money owed to Fenmere. Legitimate money, at least. Nothing about *effitte* or other illegal activities. Veranix grumbled to himself. Waste of time, the whole thing. He might as well just keep knocking over street dealers.

Veranix thumbed through them all again. On one receipt, he noticed something scratched on the side with a charcoal pencil. It was smudged, but it was still mostly legible.

Pellistar Dock 12, Maritan 8th, two bells past midnight. Interesting. Anything that arrived at the docks at that hour had to be illegal. Most likely an *effitte* shipment. That was something worth checking into.

Tonight was the eighth of Maritan. It was going to be another long night. Veranix wanted to sleep until night-time, but he couldn't allow himself more than two hours. There were still afternoon lectures to attend.

Chapter 3

THE SUN WAS hanging low when Veranix came out of the lecture hall. As good as his nap had been, a Rhetoric lecture undid it all, leaving him drained and weary. He was also famished from skipping lunch. The call for dinner service wouldn't ring for another hour.

A pair of hands gripped Veranix's shoulders. His whole body tensed. He was about to strike out blindly at the owner of the hands before he caught a glimpse of the gangly body behind him.

"Still awake after that one?" Delmin asked him.

"Barely." Veranix relaxed as he turned to his friend.

"You hungry?"

"Always."

"I have it on very good authority that tonight's meal at Holmwood is fish stew." The last two words were ominous.

Veranix shuddered. "Oh, that won't rutting do at all." Fish stew at Holmwood was notoriously awful. Common wisdom among the students was that the noxious concoction was the kitchen's method of clearing out rotting food from their stores. Veranix had had enough of fish for quite some time.

"I don't know about you," Delmin said, "but I can definitely spare a few ticks tonight for a real meal."

"Agreed," Veranix said. "Blazes, I'll spend half a crown to avoid fish stew." They walked across the campus lawn to the south gate.

The south campus lawn was a wide, open field of lush greenery, with trees shading the walkways between the buildings. Several young men had stripped off their coats and rolled up their shirtsleeves to play a spirited game of tetchball. Some girls from the women's college, housed on the north side of campus, had come to watch. Their uniforms matched the boys', but with long wool skirts and high-collared blouses, though most of them did not keep them buttoned as primly as their headmistress would have liked.

"Hey, Calbert!" one of the tetch players, blond and muscled, called. "Get over here!"

"Not today," Veranix called back. "Next time!"

The player—Veranix recognized him as Tosler, rich son of a Lacanjan shipping merchant, biding time in school until the father figured he was ready to run some business—came halfway over to Veranix and Delmin. He spoke with the slow drawl of the coastal archduchy. "Listen up, Calbert. We're putting together a tetch squad, see . . ."

"I can't be on a squad, Toss," Veranix said.

"Neither of us," Delmin added. The rules about magic students playing in any official sporting squad were detailed and explicit. "Potential unfair advantage" was the language used. In Delmin's case, that was probably a blessing, as his tetch game was terrible.

"That's because mages cheat!" one of the other players yelled out. That was the real reason for the rule, because most people didn't trust mages to play fair. They didn't trust mages at all.

"Shut it!" Delmin shouted back.

"Ease off!" Tosler said. "No, look, we're making a squad because the University is hosting the Grand Tournament this summer."

Veranix nodded. The Grand Tournament of the High Colleges of Druthal was coming to Maradaine, and most of the athletically minded students could talk of nothing else. "I know that, but I still can't serve on a squad, especially for the Grand."

"Not as a player," Tosler said. "But maybe as a coach or something? Give us some tips. Nobody hits a triple-jack like you."

"That's because mages cheat!" the other player yelled again.

"Get off it!" one of the girls snapped. Veranix didn't know her, but her scarf was red and gray. He briefly wondered how many magic students there were up at the women's school.

Veranix considered Tosler's idea. There were no rules against him doing that. If he wasn't dead by summer, it might be fun. "I'll think about it, Toss. We've got to go."

"Sure, sure," Tosler said, and he ran back over to the game.

"Grand Tournament this summer," Delmin said as they went back toward the campus gate. "Everyone's making such a thing."

"Still a lifetime away," Veranix said quietly.

A high stone archway marked the south gate of the

campus. The path toward it was flanked with flagpoles and life-size statues of founders. Five flags stood on each side, one for each Archduchy of Druthal. Centered in front of the arch was one more statue—a twelve-foot colossus of bronze—and flagpole, larger and higher than the others. The statue was of King Maradaine XI, who had united the ten archduchies in 1009. Flying above him, the flag of Druthal, dark blue with two crossed pikes over a golden circle, the circle in ten colored segments.

Two cadets in gray army uniforms stood at the arch, sabers hanging sheathed at their hips. Veranix didn't know either of them, but they were both students in the University's Army Officer Program. Campus guard duty was part of their training. Fortunately for Veranix, most of them did not take it too seriously. They usually only nodded in approval as students left or entered campus.

On the other side of the arch was Lilac Street, and the busy madness that was Aventil Neighborhood. Opposite the campus wall was a line of shops, buildings made of rough stone and chipped plaster. Every shop had some of its wares displayed on wooden tables out in the street, and other carts with more merchandise were squeezed into any inch of spare space, making it nearly impossible to determine where one shop ended and the next began. Horse carriages, pedalcarts, and handtrucks filled the street, as people darted between them to cross from one side to the other. Newsboys stood in the middle of walkways, hawking their prints and promising lurid stories.

"Scandal on the Parliament floor!" one shouted. "Two ticks for the *South Maradaine Gazette*!"

"City alderman mistress tells all!" another shouted back. "Just one tick for the *Free Aventil Press*! The News you really want!"

As soon as Veranix and Delmin emerged from the arch, a young man came right up to them, clearly lying in wait for students to come out. He was roughly dressed, his pants, waistcoat, and jacket each from different suits, worn and threadbare. On top of his head was a gray hat, with a wide, round brim and flat top.

"Gentlemen, gentlemen, gentlemen," he fired off with manic glee. He stood with his arms wide, as if threatening to embrace them. "What would you fine young men be seeking tonight? Pleasure or sport of any kind?" Veranix kept his eyes on the boy's hands, knowing all too well how quickly they could find purses and pockets.

"We'll find it ourselves, thanks," Veranix said, moving to walk around him as widely as he could manage. The boy bolted backward to stay ahead of them.

"Now, now, gentlemen, that's no way to get along. No way to get along at all. You boys should know well enough that the neighborhood boys are always on hand to help out lads like yourself." He smiled at them.

"We know that just fine," Delmin said, not making eye contact with him.

"Right you are," the boy said. "So what will it be? I have it on good authority that in Golman's Club, just over there, awaits the finest dark beer in Aventil—"

Veranix couldn't help but let out a laugh at that. The boy continued, scowling at Veranix.

"Also there will be at least five bouts of bare-knuckle boxing. Fine sport just to watch, my friends."

"In Golman's Club?" Veranix asked. "That's six blocks over, on Violet."

"Just so, just so," said the boy, "And if you don't want to walk that, I've got my cousin right over there with his pedalcab. He can run you by in a whistle." He pointed down the street, where another young man in a flat-top hat sat with a three-wheeled carriage, ready to pedal off at a moment's notice. Given that these two weren't in their territory, that at least was smart.

"Right," Veranix said. "For how much?"

"Tell you what, tell you what," said the boy, "Since you are two smart University boys, I'm not going to try and pull any fleece here. Four ticks each for the ride."

"Four ticks?" asked Delmin, stammering a little. "That's . . . that's not unreasonable."

"That's the spirit, lad." He slapped Delmin on the shoulder. Delmin winced. Veranix stepped in between, getting in the boy's face.

"We're heading up Rose Street, chap," Veranix said.

"Rose Street," the boy said with a nod. "So it's full stomachs and willing laps you seek."

"Just the meal," Veranix said. He walked away, pulling Delmin with him.

"Oh, come now," the boy said, catching up with them. "Young men like you are always looking for a clean doxy for a roll. Over on Violet we've got more than a few."

"I'm sure you do," Veranix said. He looked the boy up and down, taking in every bit of his look. "You're pretty keen on bringing us over to Violet. Most students don't go farther into the neighborhood than Rose or Orchid."

"I'm just trying—"

"To pull some University coin to your streets," Veranix said.

"Hey now," the boy said, drawing himself up, trying to make himself look taller than Veranix. "Most you Uni kids don't know what they can find over by Violet."

"I'm sure," Veranix said. "But the real question is, do the Rose Street Princes or Hallaran's Boys know you are trying to push into their territory?"

"What you know about it?" the boy said. He scowled and gripped Veranix on the shoulder, pushing hard.

Veranix instinctively slapped the boy's hand away. "Just what I see and hear. I go into Aventil enough to recognize the usual faces who do hassles and shakes. And they never push to Violet. I don't know what gang you and your cousin are in—"

"Knights of Saint Julian," said the boy proudly. His hands went into his coat pockets as he glowered at the two of them. "We'll be running the Uni gates in due course, so you all better learn some respect."

Veranix presumed the boy was getting ready to pull out a knife. It would be a stupid thing for the kid to do, but street gang kids always did stupid things.

"Veranix," Delmin said nervously, "Why don't we just . . ." He trailed off, and looked around them. Everyone on the street was minding their own business.

"We're going over to Rose Street now," Veranix said, pointing down the block. "If you want to follow us, maybe into the Turnabout, you can tell everyone how they need to respect the Knights of Saint Justin."

"Saint Julian, mate," the boy said, his eyes narrowing in anger.

"Right," Veranix said. "Shout that over on Rose Street." Veranix grabbed Delmin by the coat and pulled him around the corner.

"Sweet blasted saints of every town!" Delmin swore. Veranix noticed his friend was pale and covered with sweat. "What the blazes were you doing, trying to get us stabbed by a ganger?"

"Please," Veranix said, looking back behind them to see the kid wasn't following them. "That kid was already off his block. He wasn't going to stab a student in the middle of the street in broad daylight. The RSP and Hallaran's Boys would hit back in Saint Julian territory hard."

"How . . . how do you know this sort of thing?" Delmin stared at him. "I grew up in Maradaine, and I don't know what which gang would do to who and why."

"You grew up on the north side," Veranix said, walking down Rose Street. "Stately houses and tree-lined walks around the Parliament house."

"It's not all like that," Delmin said. "And you grew up on a merchant caravan, even farther away."

"Right," Veranix said quickly, remembering what Delmin believed about his past. He unconsciously glanced over to the window of the apartment over the postal depot; the apartment his parents lived in for only a week. Absently, he wondered who lived in there now. He shook off the thought, turning back to Delmin. "But we live right off of Aventil, and I pay attention to what's going on in the neighborhood."

"Is it just me, or is the neighborhood getting more dangerous?" Delmin asked.

"It's you," Veranix said. He looked down Rose Street, filled with clubs and taverns. The street was narrow, a handful of carriages crammed in single file heading east toward Waterpath. All the shops and houses here were brick, stone, and plaster, nothing higher than three stories. Sunlight reached the street in this neighborhood, unlike Dentonhill, and that warmth and brightness extended to the residents. Along the walkways were several makeshift stands with brick stoves, where locals grilled meat and dished out soup for a few ticks, all of them greeting passersby with a wave and a smile.

Aventil was a decent neighborhood. The Aventil street gangs weren't organized, beyond agreeing that Fenmere's crew shouldn't cross into the neighborhood, nor were they particularly dangerous. They would pick pockets, hustle, and burgle. Sometimes they would aggressively support the neighborhood, pushing people into giving their business to specific vendors, and then shake their favored vendors for a share of the profits. Despite that, they mostly stayed away from flat out bullying and extortion. They would muscle in on brewers to control the sale of beer or cider, but they didn't touch dangerous drugs like *hassper* or *effitte*, stuff that shredded people or ruined lives. Only bosses like Fenmere trafficked in trash like that.

Aventil was a neighborhood where people lived, and the gangs treated it like their home. They gave their neighbors a measure of respect. That included the University. It was well accepted that a student who had had a little too much beer could stumble back to campus without worrying about getting his head cracked open.

"So, are we going to the Turnabout then?" Delmin asked.

"Pff," Veranix said. "We'd be neck deep in Rose Street Princes there."

"They don't care for Uni boys going in there, right?" Delmin said.

"Please don't try and speak in their lingo, Del," Veranix said. "It really sounds pathetic coming from you."

"Don't be a jerk, Vee," Delmin said, snickering. The color had returned to his face, and he was looking relaxed again.

"Besides, unless you want strikers and beer, there's no point going to the Turnabout."

"Right," Delmin said. He grinned. "So it's the R&B you have in mind."

"Absolutely."

The Rose & Bush was a tavern, aptly named for being at the corner of Rose Street and Bush Lane. Like most buildings in this part of town, it was made of rough-cut limestone and dark painted wood.

The people in the Rose & Bush were a mix of students and neighborhood locals. It was a crowded mash of wooden tables and bodies. Shouts and laughter filled the air. Oil lamps hung from every post and the fireplace blazed, filling the place with warm light and warmer air.

Delmin pointed over to the fireplace, where there were still a few open tables. Veranix nodded and went over, while Delmin headed over to the barman. On his way to the table, Veranix dodged around a game of darts, almost disrupted a card game, and accidentally knocked a buxom neighborhood girl into the lap of a fellow student. He took a seat at the table. Instinctively he checked his pockets to make sure no fast fingers had found their way in there. That was all too common at the Rose & Bush.

Delmin came over with two mugs of cider. "Lamb stew and sausages all right?"

"Perfect. Great," Veranix said. He took a long drink of cider.

"I'm telling you, Vee, you have to be more careful," Delmin said. "You're lucky that Alimen likes you."

"Embarrassing me like that means he likes me?" Veranix asked.

"Yes," Delmin said. "Anyone else would have gotten demerits for falling asleep."

"No, no. You should hear him in any of my practicals. 'If only you had the grasp on theory that Mister Sarren has. If only your sense of *numinic* displacement was as finely tuned as Mister Sarren's.'"

"Trust me, Vee. My practicals are worse. Sensing *numinic* displacement is the only thing I do well."

"Alimen is always on me to do it better."

"Because he likes you. He's grooming you for Lord Preston's Circle."

"I guess they want their money's worth," Veranix joked. He knew it was true, though. Lord Preston's Circle was paying for his education, with the pledge that he would join once he finished his four years of schooling.

"At least you have a Circle lined up," Delmin said sourly. "You've got nothing to worry about along that score." Delmin didn't have any Circle as a patron, and had no prospects for recruitment yet. Veranix was surprised to hear him being bitter about it, though. Veranix had never heard of a magic student not getting a Circle invitation after receiving their Letters.

"And you have no obligations," Veranix said. He

tried to make it light, but it came out as a snap, and Delmin noticed.

"Nothing wrong with obligations, Vee. Or stability."

"I didn't say that—"

"You do know how lucky you are, right? For Professor Alimen to find you . . ."

Veranix stopped listening, knowing that Delmin was about to recount what he believed Veranix's history to be, the well-rehearsed lie that Veranix told whenever anyone asked him about his past. Delmin and almost everyone on campus believed his family were Racquin merchant caravaners, that he had lived his life traveling the highways of Druthal before coming to the University of Maradaine. The lie was close enough to the truth that it was easy to maintain. His mother was Racquin, they did travel the highways. Only Professor Alimen and Kaiana knew the truth, and they still didn't know everything.

"Maybe you're right," Veranix said. He glanced over to the corner of the pub and saw one of his obligations watching him.

Delmin drummed his fingers on the table and looked around. "Where is the server? I'm starved. Aren't you?"

"Always," Veranix said. The joke around U of M was that magic students were always hungry and always skinny, but no one personified that more than Delmin. Veranix needed to eat, though, since he had done so much magic in the last day, and he knew he had more ahead of him tonight.

"I'm going to hunt him down," Delmin said. "Another cider?"

"Please," Veranix said. Normally, he would chide

Delmin for being impatient, as he had hardly given the server enough time to deliver their meal, especially in this crowd. This time, however, he was glad Delmin was getting up, because he had noticed Colin on the other side of the room.

Colin, a seedy-looking young man in a threadbare cloak, sat alone at a table in the corner. People at the tables around him looked nervous, only occasionally glancing at him, as if each time they hoped he would be gone. When they did look, their eyes went to the tattoo on his right arm: a rose over a crown. Everyone in the pub knew what that meant: he was a Rose Street Prince. The Rose & Bush was part of the Princes' territory, but they rarely went inside. If anyone in the pub really knew about street tattoos, they would have noticed the crown on his arm had a single star. He was a street captain.

If anyone was really looking at them both, really paying attention, they would notice that Colin and Veranix had the same eyes. Their noses would match, too, if Colin's hadn't been broken two or three times. Their fathers had been twins, so it was only natural that, as cousins, they would have some resemblance.

Colin kept his eyes down, paying no one in the place any mind. If anyone in the bar looked at him, they would have thought he was muttering into his beer.

Anyone but Veranix. Veranix was looking right at his lips.

You hit the fish cannery, didn't you?

Even just reading his lips, Veranix could tell that his cousin was annoyed.

Veranix let a slow, soft breath escape his lips, then

lightly shaped the breath with magic. No professor at U of M taught him this. The hard part wasn't shaping the breath, it was making the magic so quiet that no one else would notice it. The only other mage Veranix knew in the Rose & Bush was Delmin, but there could be others. Even if only Delmin noticed, he would ask why Veranix was doing magic in the bar. Delmin was very good at sensing *numina* shifts, so doing magic behind his back was especially challenging.

The breath took shape and flew across the bar to his cousin's ears.

"You knew I was going to, Colin. Did it draw any heat?"

Of course it did. Colin mouthed the words so hard he spat in his beer, but he didn't look up.

"How did it even come back to Aventil?"

Didn't just come to Aventil, I hear. Went all around. Word is Fenmere is on fire with rage.

"Over a cannery back office? I only took a few papers. Most of it is meaningless."

I think it's the insult that anyone dared touch his stuff.

"His problem. I'm glad he's angry."

He might not care who is responsible, you know, and just lash out.

"Well, I'm hitting him on the Inemar side tonight, so he won't look this way."

Tonight? In Inemar?

"He's got a—" was all Veranix had a chance to respond with when Delmin sat back down, dropping a plate of sausages and bread in front of him.

"Stew's coming," Delmin said. "You all right? You look like you're dozing off again." Veranix snapped his attention to Delmin.

"Right, yeah," Veranix said. "Just need food, I guess."

"I'm sure," Delmin said as he dug in. He leaned in and whispered, "Blazes, I can tell you're tired. You're causing *numina* swirls. Eat up and focus."

Veranix looked over to the table in the far corner, but Colin was already gone.

Chapter 4

THE NIGHT WAS unseasonably cool as Veranix slinked in the shadow of Almers Hall. The waning white moon was still nearly full, and the blood moon was a little over a quarter lit. The grounds of the campus were bright enough that he didn't want to risk being seen running across the lawn. At this hour, few people would be watching, but the ones who would be were prefects. He didn't need any trouble from them right now. Rellings had done a lights-out check at ten bells, which he had never done before, and then another check at eleven bells. After that, two fourth-years got in his face and told him to cut it out and let them sleep. Veranix had crafted an illusion of himself sleeping in his bed, and hoped it would be enough to pass if Rellings looked in his room.

Shadows and bushes kept him hidden all the way to the carriage house. The door was open a crack. Quietly he slipped inside.

"I can't believe you're going out again," Kaiana said. She was sitting on a bale of hay, reading a book by the weak light of her oil lamp. She didn't even look up at Veranix. "Aren't you exhausted?"

"I caught a couple naps," Veranix said.

Kaiana absentmindedly pushed a bundle toward him with her foot. He picked it up and unwrapped the clothes and gear from it. He stripped off his uniform and got dressed.

"New shirt?" he asked her, taking a moment to examine the maroon pullover before putting it on.

"The other one stank of fish, so I burned it with the refuse. Same with the pants. The rest were salvageable."

"Kaiana!"

"I'm not your washer woman."

"I don't expect you to be. But . . . you were supposed to give that money to the church."

"And I did, most of it. A few crowns went into covering your expenses. That isn't wrong."

Veranix shook his head. That wasn't right. "You shouldn't be doing that. If we need money, I have the living stipend of my scholarship."

"Which isn't that much. There's nothing wrong with spending a little of Fenmere's money to fight him." She sighed. "Is this really worth it tonight?"

"The notes gave me a time tonight, and a specific dock. It has to be an *effitte* delivery."

She looked up from her book, her eyes wide. "You really think so?"

"It would have to be, wouldn't it?" Veranix buttoned up his dark leather vest. "What else would be coming by boat in the middle of the night?"

"How much do you think it'll be?"

"No clue." Boots and gloves on.

Kaiana's dark eyes narrowed. "Burn the whole boat."

"Maybe," Veranix said. "I'll have to see." He hung his quiver and bow over his shoulder.

"Veranix—" she said, her voice rising. When it came to *effitte*, her temper was as hot as Veranix's, and with good reason. Her father lay up on the fifth floor of the Lower Trenn Ward, eyes open with no spark behind them. Veranix's mother was in the same place, but she was blameless, force-fed *effitte* until she was an empty shell. Kai couldn't say that about her dad, his brain burned out from years on the *effitte* hook.

"Kai, you know I want that junk off the streets as bad as you do. But I need to see what's really happening before I—"

"I know," She picked up his belt and staff. "Here."

"Thanks." He strapped the belt on and took the staff from her. "Don't wait up."

"I never do," she said, smiling slightly. "Get out there."

He went back out the door, and with two quick jumps, he was on top of the campus wall. Crouching, he eased some slow and quiet magic into his legs. With that, he was off, bounding toward the river a block at a time.

><><><><

The Pellistar Docks were up north in the Inemar district, near the Little East, along the riverbank between the Great Maradaine Bridge and the Upper Bridge. It was out of Fenmere's territory. He might have an iron grip in Dentonhill, but his influence waned sharply on the other side of Oscana Avenue. That suited Veranix well. Whatever Fenmere was up to at Pellistar Docks, he wouldn't be able to do it in the open, and he couldn't send too many of his goons without the Inemar bosses noticing. Or Constabulary, who took their jobs a little more seriously in that neighborhood.

That also meant Veranix had to cross through ten blocks of Dentonhill. His magical method, bounding from rooftop to rooftop, was fast but unconventional. If anyone happened to be looking up, it would draw notice. A few witnesses, and a few threatening questions from Fenmere's men, and someone might trace him back to the University. Veranix didn't need—no one needed—for Fenmere to muscle in on the campus. Despite that risk, Veranix decided he needed speed more than caution tonight.

A few more jumps and he was in Inemar. He had heard no shouts, cries, or gasps, so he presumed he had gone unseen.

Inemar was the oldest part of the city; a few of the buildings were nearly two thousand years old. The neighborhood was crammed and crowded, mismatched buildings pressed together, tiny alleys leading nowhere. The streets still had plenty of activity, even at this hour. Including the occasional green and red coats of the city Constabulary.

One of the church towers rang a bell. One bell past midnight.

Veranix didn't know this part of the city very well. He had only a rough idea where the Pellistar Docks were, and he didn't have time to search. Making his way to the river, he dropped down to the ground in an alley next to a pub. He hated the risk he was going to have to take, but he didn't think he had much choice. He was going to have to ask directions.

He would have to look different to do it, as much as

he disliked that. Most of the time when he was out on the streets, he'd use just a whisper of magic to hold his hood in place, and keep its shadow over his face in a way that obscured his features from any angle. That was easy magic; he could do it in his sleep. But no one would tell a mysterious hooded figure how to get to the Pellistar Docks, and he couldn't risk having his actual face being seen this close to where he was about to hit.

Using magic to make real changes to one's appearance, even minor ones, took a fair amount of concentration, and that had to be maintained the entire time. It was not unlike holding one's breath. Unconsciously, Veranix did just that as he altered his short brown hair into red, grown out to his shoulders. His eyes went from green to blue, and a beard grew in over his face. His whole face felt like a hundred bees were walking on it.

He couldn't hold it long, and he hoped he hadn't made anything into a color that looked unnatural.

He went around the corner just as two men walked out of the pub.

"Oy, friends!" he said, making his best attempt at a Waish accent. Inemar was filled with foreigners, what with the Little East only a few blocks away, so it wouldn't seem too strange. He hoped it was good enough to fool these two. "Where might the Pellistar Docks be?"

"Pellistar?" one of them slurred. "You looking for a barge this late?"

"That I am," Veranix said. "I've got a berth on one, leaving inland in the morning. I spent the evening exploring yer fair city, and I've gotten myself lost. I just need to find my bed for the night."

"Hmm," the other one said, "It's over there, two blocks, across from the butcher sign."

"Much obliged, Druth friends," Veranix nodded and walked away. His magical facade was melting, he couldn't hold it any longer.

"How far inland, friend?" the first man called from behind him. "Itasiana? Fencal?"

"Just to Delikan for now," Veranix said, not turning around. His heart started racing. He knew his eyes had already changed, his beard pulling back into his face. He couldn't let them see that, but he couldn't run off or ignore them either. "From there, who can say?"

"Ah, for the bird hunting," the man said, patting Veranix on the shoulder, resting his hand on the strap of his bow and quiver.

"That's right," Veranix said. "It's quite the sport there." As a child he had passed through Delikan during the pheasant-hunting season, it was a huge event. That truth should keep the story unremarkable. He kept his attention on maintaining his long red hair, letting the rest go. He had to get away from these two without them thinking anything strange was going on, or the whole night would be skunked. Panic clawed at his stomach, making it all the harder to hold the change.

"Word of advice, Waish friend. Next time, leave your bow on your boat when you come into town."

"Well said. I'll be off now." Veranix took a few more steps away.

"Good hunting, then." Their footsteps went the other way. Veranix hoped neither one looked back, as his hair was short and brown again.

He hurried along the road, keeping his head lowered. Two blocks over, he found the butcher shop, and across from it, the Pellistar Docks.

A low warehouse stood at the foot of a gangway.

Spotting a few crates near the wall, Veranix scurried up to the roof on pure muscle power. He didn't want to waste any magic right now, not when he wasn't sure what he was about to face.

From his vantage point, Dock 12 was easy to spot. Every dock on the wharf was well marked, but there were two lamps hanging on the sign for twelve. A barge was docked, tied up and still. No one was about.

Two bells rang.

Nothing happened for some time.

Veranix kept his position. Waiting was fine. It let him regain his strength. The scent of the river, though, made him glad he lived on the University campus. It was probably worse downstream on the west side of Maradaine, over in Benson Court, where the sewers fed into the river.

Two men in dark cloaks entered the wharf and, looking about nervously, went to the boat docked at twelve. One of them was carrying a satchel.

Veranix sat up, making sure his hood was in place. He drew one arrow, readying it in his bow.

"Oy!" one man called in a hoarse whisper, "You there?"

A skinny man stepped out from the barge. Even from this distance, with little light, Veranix could see he was old and scarred.

"You're late," the old man said.

"There's been . . . difficulties," the man with the satchel said.

"Long as there's no difficulties with the money, then the boss gets his package."

"No, none," the other man said. He stepped into the lamplight. Veranix recognized him as the man who first caught him in the cannery the night before. He was now sporting a large bruise on the side of his face. "We want the package."

"That's the money, then? I don't have to count it, do I?"

"Notes of exchange, from a variety of reputable houses," the man with the satchel said. "Forty thousand crowns."

Veranix resisted the urge to let out a low whistle. Forty thousand crowns was a ridiculous amount of money. This was either a huge shipment of *effitte*, or something else altogether. But something that was worth that much to Fenmere was all the more valuable to keep out of his hands.

"Drop the satchel and open it up," the old man said. They did so. He glanced at the contents and nodded. "Good enough."

"Where's our package?"

"Over there. It's in a sack at the bottom of the river, tied to that rope with the blue cloth."

"The bottom of the river?" the first of Fenmere's thugs said. "Are you crazy? Won't that damage it?"

"Won't do nothing to it." The old man grabbed the satchel. He stepped back on his barge, and began to untie the rope holding it to the pier.

"Where are you going?" the bruised thug asked.

"No business of yours. You boys have some hauling up to do."

Veranix was tempted to make his move now. If he could take out all three, he could get the package and the forty thousand crowns. In the back of his head, he already thought of places he could drop off that money. Saint Julian's Church. Aventil Orphanage. The Lower

Trenn Street Ward. Forty thousand crowns could spread pretty far.

Instinct told him to hold off, let the old man and the money go. Taking on two thugs was risk enough.

The old man pushed off from the pier into the darkness.

"I hate this," the bruised thug said.

"Let's get this thing and get out of here," the other said. The two of them found the rope and began to pull. After a few minutes of straining, a heavy, wet sack emerged. Just as they got it onto the pier, Veranix shot the first arrow at the bruised man. Before even seeing where it struck, he drew a second and shot it at the other one.

The shots weren't as true as Veranix hoped; the bruised man took one in the knee, the other in the arm. Both men cried out, and one dropped to the ground. The other drew out his sword with his good arm. Veranix leaped to the street, another arrow nocked. He snapped out another shot, and struck the man in the left shoulder.

"You're gonna get it for that, whelp!" the man said.

"Why don't you just kick the sack over instead?" Veranix said, drawing another arrow. "You're not getting off the pier this way."

"I'm gonna kick you! Come on, Bell!"

Bell, the bruised man, did his best to stand up again, as the other ran at Veranix. Veranix shot the arrow. It sailed past the charging man, who closed the distance faster than expected. Veranix had to drop the bow and flip backward to avoid the slash of the man's sword.

Last night, Veranix had to run away. Tonight he had no intention of running. Last night, he was in a small room with no space to jump and dodge. Here he was in the open. Last night, he was unarmed. Tonight, he had his staff. It was in his hands when he landed on his feet again.

Two slashes of the sword were easily parried, the cheap weapon barely making a nick on his staff. Veranix kept moving, doing flips and jabs, never giving his opponent a still target.

"Get him, Francis!" Bell shouted.

"I'm trying!" Francis replied, desperately swinging at the empty space Veranix was just in. "He bounces around like a sideshow freak!"

Veranix struck him on the left side. "Don't be insulting, Francis." He blocked another attack, and then kicked at Francis's knee. "I was never in the sideshow." Francis crumpled. The staff greeted him in the chin as he dropped, and he fell backward. Veranix leaned over his unconscious body. "I was always the main attraction."

Bell was up, weight on one leg, his sword out, but he hadn't come closer.

"You again?" he asked.

"I didn't have theater tickets," Veranix said. "This show is much more interesting."

"You can't have the sack," Bell said. "No chance."

"Nasty bruise," Veranix said. "Punishment for losing me last night?" With a magic-assisted jump, he did a double flip and landed on a support post near Bell. It was pure showmanship, intimidation. It worked. Bell's face gave away his fear.

"Exactly." He pointed his sword at Veranix, but still didn't close the distance.

"Must have really flamed Fenmere, then," Veranix said. "I take that sack, he'll be fit to burn."

"Not just him. You have no idea," Bell said.

"I've got forty thousand ideas," Veranix said. "If I give you a matching bruise on the other side of the head, you think he'll forgive you?"

"You'll have to kill me," Bell said. His face was pale and clammy, and he was straining just to keep his sword up.

"Then I'd lose my favorite thug," Veranix said. "Besides, who will tell Fenmere that I took his package?"

"Who are you?" Bell asked.

"Just the constant thorn in Fenmere's side." Veranix said.

He leaped at Bell, knocking the sword out of the way with the staff while kicking his face. At the same time, he magicked the floor beneath Bell to become slippery. Bell crumpled and crashed, dropping the sword, the breath knocked out of him. Veranix stayed standing on his chest.

"He'll . . . find . . . you . . ." Bell managed to get out. "Destroy you . . . your family."

"He already did," Veranix said, and cracked the staff across Bell's head.

Veranix grabbed the sack. Surprisingly, it was nearly dry, and was much lighter than Veranix expected. With another burst of magic, he leaped to a rooftop and headed west.

Chapter 5

V ERANIX PUT SEVERAL blocks between himself and the docks before he stopped on the roof of a church. He climbed up to the belfry and looked back down to the street. No sign of anyone pursuing him. No sign of anyone looking up. He figured he was safe, at least for the moment.

He laughed quietly to himself. Souring a forty-thousand-crown deal was more than just giving Fenmere a bloody nose. That was some real damage, even if it wasn't specifically hitting the *effitte* trade.

Veranix examined the sack. It was soft and light, like a laundress's bag, no jars or glass vials. Veranix doubted that Fenmere spent forty thousand on washing his suits. It definitely wasn't *effitte*, though, that was certain. He untied the knots holding the sack closed.

Inside the sack were a cloak and a rope.

That was unexpected.

For forty thousand crowns, there had to be more than just a cloak and a rope. Maybe Fenmere was smuggling something fragile, and these were used to protect the real merchandise. That made sense.

He grabbed the cloak and pulled it out of the sack. As soon as he touched it, he had a heady, giddy feeling. Energized, like he had just drunk several cups of tea. Or like he had pulled in *numina* without doing anything with it. He dropped the cloak, and the feeling went away. He touched the cloak again. Again, he felt it, definitely a *numinic* charge flowing up his fingers.

There was more to it, though. Veranix could sense it, though he wasn't sure what he was sensing. His first thought was that the cloak was magical, but he dismissed that idea as ridiculous. Magicked things were incredibly rare, even forty thousand wouldn't buy them. There was something about them, though, that had an aspect of magic. He wished he had Delmin's gift for sensing *numina*.

He put down the cloak and picked up the rope. Again he felt a charge of magical energy crackling through his fingers, a connection between him and the rope. As easy as thinking about it, the rope came out of the sack, sliding into his lap. He could feel the rope, as if it were a part of his body, an extension of his arm.

There was a commotion on the street below. Someone was pounding on a door. "Open up!"

Veranix was startled, and the rope reacted. In an instant, it shot up, wrapping around one leg, an arm, a wooden crossbeam, the other leg. Before he realized it, Veranix was tied tight to the beam.

"Open!" yelled the man below. Were they knocking on the church door? Was it Fenmere's men, looking for him? Would the reverend of this church let them in? Everyone else in Dentonhill was in Fenmere's pocket, why not the clergy? Veranix couldn't move, and every panicked thought just made the rope constrict tighter. He thrashed and pulled, but the rope moved with him, binding him further.

The pounding stopped, and the door opened. "Missed payments, Orly."

"I know," an old man's voice said. "I've got some of it, but . . ."

"No but, Orly." The sound of flesh hitting flesh. The old man cried out.

No one was coming for Veranix. That calmed him down, and the rope relaxed slightly. Not much, but enough that he could move. He twisted his left arm around behind his back, at an angle he could manage thanks only to his grandfather's training. Painful, but he gritted his teeth and ignored it. The maneuver gave him a bit more mobility, and he was able to pull his arm out of the bindings.

Arm free, he grabbed on to the wooden crossbeam and pulled his body forward, sliding it out of the rope.

"No, I—" the old man cried out. "Please . . ."

"Too late for that." More beatings.

That wouldn't stand. Veranix put his hand on the rope, and focused, like he would to use any magic. He didn't need to pull in any *numina* for this, the *numina* was almost falling into him. The challenge was to hold it back, tame it, shape it, force it to do what he wanted instead of overwhelming him.

The rope unwound, dropping him from the crossbeam. Veranix landed on his feet.

"This is what happens when you don't pay!" The beater's words were accentuated with punches. Veranix stood up and looked down to the street. The shop door stood open, the commotion inside clearly heard. Veranix spotted a house a few doors over, where someone looked out his window and then shut it.

What was wrong with the people in this neighborhood?

He couldn't see the beater, not from up here. No way to get a clear shot with his bow. If he wanted to stop this, he'd have to go down there. If he did that, he could be spotted. After stealing forty thousand crowns' worth of . . . whatever he stole, he didn't need to risk pursuit or capture.

"Please, I can get it!" Hit. Hit. "Please!" Hit.

"Too late for that."

Veranix had to go down there.

Veranix looked across the street and spotted a drying post on the roof of the building. He flirted with the idea of getting the rope looped around it so he could swing down to the ground. As the thought formed, the rope shot forth, wrapping tight around the post. Amazed, Veranix jumped out of the belfry, swinging on the rope toward the shop door. With the rope and his own magic, he slowed his descent to a gentle landing, the rope coiling back to his side as his feet touched the ground.

A muscle-bound goon held Orly, the old shopkeeper, up against the wall as he pummeled his face. The old man didn't look like he could take much more, blood gushing from his mouth and nose.

"Enough of that," Veranix said. The rope responded to his urges, flying into the shop and wrapping around the goon.

"Who?" the goon said as he looked at Veranix.

"Let's take it outside." Veranix yanked on the rope,

half with the strength of his arm, half with magic. The goon was pulled off his feet, rocketing to the door. Veranix jumped out of the way at the last moment, and the goon shot out to land on the dusty cobblestone street. Veranix willed the rope to coil around his own body like a bandolier.

"You're going to pay!" the goon said.

"I don't have any coins." Veranix drew his staff. "Will this do?"

The goon was not ready for someone who would give him a real fight. Veranix leaped in, staff spinning. He cracked the goon across the head, then flipped away. Dazed, the goon punched empty air.

"I'll—"

"You'll leave old shopkeepers alone," Veranix said as he landed. He took hold of the rope again and magicked it to wrap around the goon. It flung out stronger and harder than Veranix intended, choking around the goon's neck. The goon clawed at it, desperate to breathe. Veranix tried to pull back, but the *numina* was flowing hard, a raging river. Veranix felt himself getting lost in the wash of energy pounding his senses. He had to get control, anchor himself.

Veranix felt the rope constricting around the goon's neck. Veranix forced the *numina* thundering through his body to submit, to be shaped by him rather than let it shape him. The rope was an extension of his arm, and he would have control over his arm.

He pulled the rope off, coiled it back. The goon dropped to the ground, unconscious but still breathing.

Veranix glanced back at the shop. The old man had gotten to the door. He looked terrible, face bruised and bloody, but he gave a nervous nod to Veranix. Then he shut and latched the door. Veranix hurled the rope up to the church belfry and pulled himself back up there.

He coiled the rope and picked up the cloak. Whatever they were, Fenmere was willing to spend a lot to get ahold of them. Their value was obvious to Veranix, but why would someone like Fenmere, whose business was mostly girls and drugs, be interested in them?

Veranix decided he needed a rested head to answer that question. He stuffed the cloak and the rope back in the sack, and headed for home.

Chapter 6

WILLEM FENMERE NEVER slept much, and he was usually awake before dawn. This morning, as soon as he woke, his butler told him Bell and Francis were back and there was trouble. Fenmere hated being woken for bad news.

He threw a robe on over his sleeping gown and went down the back stairs to the kitchen. Men like Bell and Francis did not come into the front rooms, especially if there was trouble. If there was trouble, then there damn well better be blood. He didn't need them bleeding all over his rugs.

Blood there was. Francis was laid out on a counter, covered in it. Gerrick patched him up as best he could. Gerrick was no doctor, but he was good enough at stitching the boys. Gerrick had been around for as long as Fenmere could remember, his most trusted captain. Fenmere nodded at Gerrick in approval. No need wasting good money on a surgeon.

Bell was a mess as well, his face had even more bruises than he left with, great deep purple stains. His leg was tied off above the knee, pants soaked with blood. He sat at the small table in the back corner. Fen-mere sat down with him. Thomias, his butler, silently put a cup of dark tea on the table. Fenmere took a few sips. Bell, for his part, was wise enough to keep his head down and not speak until he was spoken to.

"So where is it?" Fenmere asked eventually.

"Gone, boss." Bell barely looked up, his head bead-ing with sweat.

"How many were there? Five men? Six?"

"Just the one, boss."

"One?" Fenmere roared. "One guy did this to the two of you?"

"It was the same guy from the night before, boss!"

"The same guy? You saw him? You saw his face?"

Bell shook his head. "Not his face. He wears a hood over it. But the same guy for sure. He remembered me."

"He talked to you?" Fenmere said. "Who is he?"

"He's a kid. I'm telling you, a scrawny kid. Seven-teen, eighteen tops. But he's all fast and flips around."

"You got beat by a scrawny kid?" Fenmere got up from the table and paced around the kitchen, fuming. "Listen, Bell, there is one reason you are staying alive, and that's because you have a sense of what this kid looks like."

"There's something else, boss. I think he might be a mage."

Biting his lip, Fenmere sat back down. He had to get a grip on himself. "Maybe that's it, then. That's why he went for the stuff. Maybe he's one of the Blue Hand Circle, they took it from you so they don't have to pay me for it."

"I don't know, boss," Bell said.

"What don't you know?"

Bell screwed his face in thought. "I don't think he knew what the stuff was. He just wanted to hit you."

"Where are you getting that?"

"This kid, it's personal with him. He said you killed his family. He said he's going to be a constant thorn in your side."

"I've killed a lot of families," Fenmere growled. "I've had more than a few thorns in my side before. And I always pull them out. We're going to find this thorn, Bell." He waved over to Thomias to bring him some more tea. "Tell me about him. Maybe a mage, you think?"

"I've never seen anyone jump like this one, boss. Plus he must have done some tricks to escape us the other night."

"What else about him?"

"He fights with a bow. And a staff."

"Bow and a staff?" Fenmere asked. There was something odd about that. Something familiar, he couldn't put his finger on it.

"Wasn't there something with some street sellers getting hit by an archer?" Gerrick asked. "For the past few months, I think."

Fenmere nodded. That was probably what he was thinking of. "Nobody fixed that?" Street captains and dealer bosses should have found out who was hitting their boys and buried him in the ground.

"Nobody found out much. Figured it was the usual trash trying to score some *effitte* buzz. Not a player."

"Well, this 'thorn' is a player now. Wouldn't you say, Bell?"

"Aye, boss."

"All right." Fenmere took another drink from his

cup. "Get yourself cleaned up, then get word to Kalas over in the Blue Hand that we need to talk to him."

"You want me to go over to the Blue Hand?" Bell asked. He looked more afraid than ever.

"Yes." Fenmere spat the word out. "Go over there. Someone has to tell Kalas what happened. It's either you or Francis. You want Francis's job?"

"What's Francis's job?" Bell's expression was fluctuating between fear and confusion.

"Francis is busy bleeding to death. Unless you want him to go over to the Blue Hand for you, Bell?"

"No, boss," Bell said. He got up and nodded to Gerrick and Thomias, gave another reverent nod to Fenmere, and left out the back door.

Fenmere finished his tea. "Good. Now where is my breakfast?"

Bell knew this whole trash was his fault. That kid, he had busted into the cannery, and Bell had let him slip away. Then he hit the drop, and Bell had let that all go to blazes. Stupid kid, ruining everything.

Bell couldn't walk to the Blue Hand Circle's chapterhouse, not with his leg still a mess. He had been lucky to make it back to Fenmere's place. Bell laughed dryly to himself. Honestly, he'd been really lucky to walk out of there.

Bell waved to a horsecab. The driver slowed down, fear in his face as he saw Bell. Bell didn't recognize him, but he knew people in these streets knew him, knew what he did, knew he had a post close to the man himself. That meant the cabs blazing well stopped for him.

"Where to, boss?" the driver asked, his voice shaking.

"Price Street, just past Lowe."

"Right away, sir," the driver said, snapping his whip. North of Lowe probably took the driver out of his regular beat, and for anyone else, he probably wouldn't bother, not without forcing extra coin. That wasn't going to happen right now.

Bell settled back in the seat. The Blue Hand Circle. He knew this whole business was going to be trouble. He should have kept out of it. Bell muttered a few curses. He had wanted the cannery office. He had wanted the placement, the extra prestige. He had wanted to show the man he could be more than muscle and pickup. He had been doing good until this special package for the Blue Hand.

Bell could feel his hands shaking. Had to settle his nerves.

Stupid kid.

He reached into his pocket and pulled out his small *hassper* pipe and his pouch of leaf. Not much left. He'd smoked a lot of it yesterday.

He packed a few leaves into the bowl of the pipe. When did he stop burning last night? Had to have been ten or eleven bells. His head was completely clear when the drop turned left. He had been good. That kid just hit them hard and fast.

He looked about the carriage. There were two lamps hanging, but both were dark.

"Hey." He knocked hard on the front of the cab, startling the driver. "You don't got your lamps burning."

"No, sir, no," the driver said, glancing back. "Sorry,

sir. Got to save on the oil, sir, so I don't light them in the daytime."

Bell grunted in disapproval.

"I could stop here at the bakery, sir," the driver said, sweat forming on his brow. "They're sure to have something I can light a taper with, all right?"

"Good," Bell said. He kept a grin off his face. He had no intention of making an incident, and would have been fine with not smoking until after he had arrived at the Blue Hand's chapterhouse. If the driver wanted to be of service, though, Bell would not refuse. The driver reined in the horse and jumped out of the cab.

He decided he would tip the man well at the end of the drive. What had Mister Fenmere said? "Occasional magnanimous acts cement loyalty far more than fear alone."

While the driver ran into the bakery, Bell thought that perhaps, if he was lucky, Mister Fenmere would let him keep his overseer position in the cannery office. That would be magnanimous, wouldn't it?

The driver ran back out of the shop, lit taper in hand. "Here you are, sir, hope that helps you out, sir."

"Thank you," Bell said. The driver spurred the horse forward. Bell lit his pipe, and pulled in the deep, rich smoke. That was better. He snuffed the taper and let the *hassper* ease his cares.

Bell's hands were still shaking, but he didn't care as much anymore. Not until the cab pulled up near the chapterhouse.

From the street, anyone not knowing would think it was just another gray stone row house, no different from any other on the block, or on the next street over. A small wooden sign hung over the door, with the blue handprint in the center. Most of the houses on this block were professionals: barristers or surgeons or secretaries, and all of them had similar wooden signs, so it did not make the house stand out.

The driver, pulling to a stop on Bell's signal, did not take any special notice of the house either. No one would, unless they knew about the men who lived in there.

Bell took out a half-crown and paid the driver. "There'll be that over again if you stay here until I'm out."

The driver looked as if the last thing he wanted to do was wait for Bell, but despite that he said, "As you wish, sir."

Bell took a moment, standing on the stoop and finishing off the last of the *hassper*. It wasn't helping anymore. Nothing would help, save getting the blasted deal over with.

Bell knocked the last bits of ash onto the ground and put the pipe into his pocket. With his heart pounding, he went up the steps to the front door and knocked.

The wait was interminable. He could feel beads of sweat dripping down his face. He had an itch creeping its way up his back. Were the Blue Hand doing that? Just watching him through the upstairs window and messing with him? They certainly could.

That would be petty, even for them.

The door opened slowly, revealing a young man with blond hair and dull eyes. Bell had met this one before, but couldn't remember his name.

"You one of Fenmere's?"

"Yeah, that's right."

"Where's the package?"

That cut straight to it. Bell took a deep breath. "See, something happened—"

The door shut.

Bell stepped back down the stoop. Was that it? He had delivered the message. That should be good enough. He cautiously took two more steps down to the street.

The door opened. "Get in here."

That was not the voice of the young man. Bell swore under his breath. He turned and went up the stairs.

It was Kalas, the neatly groomed gentleman with close-cropped hair and a tiny mustache, and wearing an impeccable midnight blue suit. Bell imagined the Circle brought him out because he at least knew how to talk to people. Kalas gave a quick wave of his fingers, summoning Bell up. Bell worried that Kalas was about to pull him in magically, like he was a hooked fish. Kalas had no such plan, and Bell walked in through the door on his own power.

The door slammed shut when he entered. That was magic.

The place smelled like it always smelled, like dead cats and roasted onions. Bell didn't want to know why. Kalas walked over to a lone chair in the foyer and sat down, brushing bits of dust off his coat.

"So, Mister Bell," he said, glaring at Bell with his piercing dark eyes. "You say that 'something happened.' Please define 'something.'"

"The delivery got hit," Bell blurted out.

"Hit?" Kalas said. "Which means what, exactly?"

"Your items were stolen."

Kalas narrowed his eyes at Bell. "By who?"

"This kid who's been nibbling at Fenmere's gigs. He just happened to hit this one."

"Hmm." Kalas drummed his fingers. He said nothing more for some time. Bell wasn't sure what he should do.

Kalas sprang to his feet, surprising Bell and making him stumble back against the door. Kalas called out through the house, "Lord Sirath!"

"Eating!" came a hoarse reply from down the hallway. Bell shivered. He had seen that man eat before. He didn't want to take a single step in the direction of that voice.

"The items were stolen, Lord," Kalas called back.

"Intolerable!" shouted Sirath from the back. The house shuddered with a wave of power.

"I agree," Kalas said. "Steps are being taken, I'm sure, yes?"

"Yes, Mister Kalas," Bell said, nodding more vigorously than he wished he had. He knew it made him look foolish.

Kalas stepped forward and opened the door, indicating Bell should step out. "I am glad to hear that at least. I trust it will be dealt with expediently." Kalas smiled at Bell, a smile that looked like it was something he practiced in the mirror.

"That is our plan, sir." Bell stumbled backward out the door, not wanting to take his eyes off Kalas until he was outside. Kalas stepped outside with him.

"Excellent," Kalas said, walking past Bell. "You've brought me a cab. I have some business at the University. This will save me considerable time." Before Bell could say anything, Kalas stepped up into the cab and whispered something to the driver. The whip cracked and the horses moved with a sudden burst of determination.

"Blazes," Bell muttered. He should go back to Fenmere's, or to the cannery. Probably the cannery. Grinding his teeth, he decided first he needed to visit the *hassper* den over on Price. He needed another smoke.

Colin hadn't slept well. He knew Veranix had gone out and done something to Fenmere, out in Inemar, and if it was Inemar, that meant the docks. If Veranix was hitting Fenmere out on the docks then he was hitting a shipment right as it came in. Crowns right from the man's pocket, a serious hit. Colin didn't know anyone who would dare such a thing.

Veranix only dared because he wasn't anyone. Just another Uni kid, another face in the uniform. No one anyone on the streets would take any note of.

Unless someone took a real good look at Veranix's face. Blazes, if any of the basement bosses, the old ones, ever took a good look at him, they'd probably see exactly whose son he was.

The business with the cannery, that had rattled more than a few boots on both sides of Waterpath. Not too much, but people were talking, and Colin couldn't figure out if it was a good thing. Hearing about Fenmere's boys getting rattled, knowing it was his cousin who had done it, Colin couldn't help but take some pride in that. Pride was in short supply in Aventil.

No matter how much pride he felt, though, rattling made noise, and that noise was already looking over Waterpath.

Morning light hadn't even properly broke when Colin pulled himself up from his mattress. His usual flop, in the basement under Kessing's shop, where he and his crew of Princes would crash most nights, was damp and gray, and smelled of a rancid earthiness. Despite that, he had a certain fondness for the place, a place that was in some small way his own. It belonged to all the Princes, so if a Basement Boss wanted to yank him from it and give it to another captain, that could happen any time. Colin worked the streets, worked his crew, as hard as he could, and made sure any merch the bosses left in his flop stayed untouched. They'd never have the excuse to yank him.

There were only a couple of tiny windows along the ceiling, at street level, and the dull glow of dawn provided just enough light to find his boots and vest and get to the door.

His fingers went reflexively to his belt, to the knife he kept there, as he came out of the flop and hit the street. Not that anyone would come up on him, not here, not this deep in Prince territory. No one would dare.

The air was cool and brisk, but he rolled up his sleeves, letting anyone out there see his arm. He didn't need to show his color, show his stars; anyone who mattered knew who he was. No cool morning would make him hide the one thing he had that was his, that he earned with sweat and muscle and bone.

A sharp whistle flew across the street. Two young Princes, the ink on their arms still fresh and raw, were working the corner next to the Len House. The Lens were brewers, made some of the better beer in Aventil in their basement, which the Princes guarded nightly. The Toothless Dogs and Hallaran's Boys kept trying to make runs to steal a few casks.

Colin crossed over to them. "Any noise?"

"Nothing much," said one of them, but he nodded up the block. "There's a bloke up over there, though, who's been looking this way for a bit."

"How long?"

"Half an hour, maybe."

"Keep your place," Colin said, patting one of them on the arm. "I'll go give it a look, right?"

"Sure, cap."

The guy didn't give any ground when Colin approached. More to the point, his level of fear didn't change at Colin's approach. The guy looked pretty afraid already.

"If you're the pair of eyes on the brewery, you chose the wrong gig, son," Colin said.

"What?" the guy asked. He shook his head vigorously. "No gig, no. I was told to find a Prince cap."

"You got one," Colin said cautiously. He took a good look at the guy, now that he was close up. An ugly but precise scar crossed from one eye to his ear. A Waterpath Orphan. "What's the noise? Orphans need something?"

"My cap says get a Prince cap, get him to the church."

Colin raised an eyebrow. Orphans wanted a meet at the church? That couldn't be good news. And if it was the Orphans telling the news that meant it was coming from across in Dentonhill.

Damn.

"Fine," Colin said, "But I've got to head to the backhouse first."

The Orphan stammered nervously, looking up the street toward Waterpath. "I'm supposed to make sure you—whoever I find, you know—goes to the church."

"Yeah, and I got to piss, so either wait here or roll off."

The Orphan stood his ground. Colin shrugged and went back over to the barbershop. Before he went into the alley behind it, he pounded on the door of the basement flop. After a moment, Jutie cracked the door open.

"You out and about already, cap?"

"Boot up and come out, Jutie," Colin said. "Orphans calling a meet at the church. Can't be great news at this hour."

Jutie sighed. "You want me, cap? For a meet?"

"You're up," Colin said. "Hurry up, meet me at the backhouse."

Jutie was a good kid, newest in Colin's crew. He was eager, and he was good at scraping and scrounging, but he still had a way to go in learning who was who and what was what in the neighborhood.

Colin trudged through the alley to the backhouse. The worn dirt path was damp and soggy. Colin wondered if it had rained, or if people hadn't even bothered going all the way to the backhouse. He thought it was a damn shame that even a captain didn't rank a flop with its own water closet, but those were rare in Aventil. He had heard that the city aldermen kept promising they were going to finish the water system out into Aventil and beyond, but that's all it ever was.

He finished his business and came back out, finding Jutie waiting for him, carrying a blade almost too big to be called a knife.

"Jutie, it's a church meet," he said, taking the knife away. "You at least have to be subtle."

"I like that knife," Jutie said.

"Can you hide it well, get it out fast?"

"You know I can, cap," Jutie said.

Colin handed him the knife back. "Probably won't need it, but . . . you never know. Orphan looks shaky. Could be real bad news."

"What kind?"

"Only one kind comes across Waterpath."

Saint Julian's Church sat at the corner of Tulip and Vine, a low and unimposing building of gray brick, with squat bell towers. Colin and Jutie found a few others milling about at the top of the steps: green capped Hallaran's Boys, scarred Waterpath Orphans, Knights of Saint Julian with vests and tall hats, and Red Rabbits with their fur-lined coats. All of them, each man and bird, looked displeased with being here before the sun was fully up.

"Here are a couple Princes," one of the Rabbits said.

"This a full meet?" Colin asked as he approached. "Where are the Kickers or the Toothless Dogs?"

"You just got here," the Orphan captain said. Colin had met her once or twice before. Yessa? She'd be a real pretty bird if she didn't have two Orphan scars slashed across her face. "Let's get in." She nodded to the Orphan who had fetched Colin. "Thesh, stay at the door, send anyone else in."

Colin filed in with the lot of them. No one made a point of arguing about place or entry order, which Colin had seen happen plenty of times before. Perhaps they were all too bleary-eyed to bother. There were a few others in the church, mostly old women kneeling at the statue of Saint Julian, a few others scattered about the small altars. Colin wondered what it was about getting old that made women wake up and come to church first thing.

One woman stood out to him, heading out of the church as they all came in. She wasn't old, but quite young, and dark skinned. Napa girl, she probably was. She stopped at the door, and glanced back at Colin. He saw her eyes dart to his arm, noting his ink, and back up to his face. For just a moment, their eyes locked, and she gave a small smile, then went out the door.

"Oy, Prince!" The Rabbit captain was yelling at him. Colin didn't know this one. Didn't know any Rabbits, really. Weak bunch who barely held onto their corners. "We meeting or staring at Naps?"

"Meeting," Colin said, giving the Rabbit a hard glare.

They went out to the main theater of the church, lit with candles all along the walls, the first bits of sun shining through the blue glass behind the large altar. All the gangs took places in separate pews, Jutie sitting behind Colin. Colin could feel Jutie's leg shaking.

"Ease up, Jutie," he whispered. "Friendly meet, that's all."

"Friendly meet, sure," Jutie hissed. He was glaring over at one of the Knights of Saint Julian. "That guy was giving me grief by the gates the other day."

"Uni gates?" Colin asked. Blasted Knights. They're pushing Prince territory again. "Can't have that."

"Oy!" the Hallaran's Boys' captain—Hannik— snapped. "We gonna do this, or what?"

"Ask the Orphan," the Knight captain said. He bared his teeth at her. Colin remembered he was called "Four-Toe," or something like that.

Yessa looked about. "I was hoping the Dogs and Kickers would make it."

Colin shrugged. "You scramble a meet at dawn, you get what you get."

Suddenly the Knight Jutie had been staring at got on his feet, pulling a knucklestuffer out of his pocket. "You think you can throw, Prince?"

Jutie was up and over the top of the pew before Colin knew what was happening, drawing his large knife out. "Take some of this!"

Colin grabbed Jutie by the ankle and yanked him down to the ground. Jutie hit the floor face first, and tried to scramble away to get at the young Knight. Four-Toe grabbed his man, and everyone else was on their feet, shouting and accusing.

"Peace! Peace, please!" A fair-haired young priest came charging up the aisle, putting himself in the middle of the fracas. He didn't sound like he was from around here. "What in the name of God are you doing?"

"These two got a little excited, Reverend," Colin said, pulling Jutie up onto his feet. "You going to apologize to the priest, Jutes?"

"Sorry, Reverend," Jutie mumbled out, his eyes on the ground. Colin glared at Four-Toe. He gave his own man a shake.

"I apologize, Reverend, if my actions disturbed the sanctity of the Church of Saint Julian."

"Show-off," Jutie muttered.

"Church meet is supposed to be peaceful," Colin told the priest. He hadn't seen this priest before, not that he spent much time in the church. "Sometimes people forget."

"Church meet?" The priest looked over the group of them. "I see. Very well, good gentles. You want to meet, then let's meet. What are we discussing?" He looked around to the blank stares from the different gangs. "Come on, now."

"Look to the Orphans," Colin said. "They called this."

"Ah." He looked at the different groups, following the eyes and pointed fingers until his gaze settled on the Waterpath Orphans. "Please, begin."

Yessa looked about uncomfortably. "You know, Reverend—"

"If you are here to discuss plans to break the law, young lady, I will not allow such things under this blessed roof."

"No, that ain't it, Rev," Yessa said. "But, you know, you might not want to know about things that go on out there in the streets."

"Those are my streets as well, child. I want to know everything that I can. Anything you feel you can't say in front of me should not be said in here at all." Colin kept himself from laughing. This priest was not from Aventil. He probably wasn't from anywhere in Maradaine.

"All right." She took a seat again. "We know that there's been someone nibbling at dealers across the 'path, and we ain't been paying that no mind. Last night, that changed."

"What happened?" Hannik asked.

"The guy stepped up and hit a shipment drop, is what we hear."

"How big?" Colin asked. He wasn't sure he wanted to hear the answer.

"No one is talking numbers, from what we hear

across the street. But the word is Fenmere is going to start cracking skulls to find this 'thorn in his side.'"

"So he's going after this 'thorn,' then?"

"And from what I hear, if he thinks the thorn is on this side of Waterpath, no truce is going to keep him from coming over to get him."

Everyone groaned.

"I got to ask," the Rabbit captain asked. "Anyone claiming this? Anyone know anyone who knows anyone?"

Colin put on his best dice game face. Nobody in Aventil needed trouble from Fenmere, and the last thing Colin needed was for any one of these folks to think he had any clue what might have happened. Or who it might have been. But he had a damned good idea indeed.

"No one?" The Rabbit captain shrugged. "Didn't figure."

Hannik scoffed at the Rabbit captain. "You're only asking so you can turn your teeth once Fenmere's boys ask you."

"We ain't never—"

"Rabbits always turn their teeth!"

"Rabbits gonna show you—"

"Enough!" the Reverend shouted. Everyone became silent. He said, much calmer, "Now, so we are clear, none of you claim this 'Thorn' is with any of you."

Four-Toe shook his head. "If he was one of ours, he'd blazing well know not to bring heat like that."

"This is going to be trouble for everyone," Yessa said. "Don't be surprised if you see some rattling out there the next few days."

The Hallaran's Boys stood up, chests out. Hannik

said, "They cross Waterpath to rattle us, they'll get what for."

Yessa shook her head. "Easy for you. Fenmere's goons cross, it's Orphans and Rabbits who bear most of their rattle."

"Princes feel it," Jutie added. Colin glared at him, but that did nothing to hold back his swagger. "And if we find out who this 'thorn' is, we'll leave him in a bloody heap in the middle of Waterpath."

"More loyal to your enemy than a potential ally?" It was the priest who spoke. All eyes went to him. "A thief is no better for stealing from a thief, but is he not doing what you all wish to do yourselves?"

"Fenmere runs his neighborhood, leaves us alone," Yessa said. "That's how it's been for years."

"We've got our own to worry about," added the Rabbit captain.

"You've been quiet," the priest said to Colin.

"I ain't got nothing to say," Colin said. "Fenmere got hit, and he's all steamed. Good to know. We'll watch ours." He got up and went down the aisle. Jutie scrambled after him. He called out behind him. "I've heard everything I need to hear."

Colin couldn't keep his anger off his face, so he was glad he had his back to the rest of the gangs. This was a very bad start to the day.

He was going to have to have a long talk with his cousin.

Chapter 7

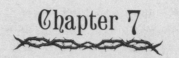

VERANIX WOKE UP when someone pounded on the door.

"Bed check!" came a shout from outside the door. "It's dawn!" Veranix could barely move from his bed. Fortunately, Delmin got up and answered the door.

"Is this really necessary, Rellings?" he asked as he opened it.

"Periodic checks are part of the routine, Sarren," Rellings said. He pushed his way into the room.

"Well, we're both here," Delmin said. "Satisfied?"

"Morning, Calbert," Rellings said, sitting down on the bed next to him. He tapped his finger on Veranix's temple. "Are you with us today?"

"Rutting well am, Rellings," Veranix mumbled. "You must have better things to do."

"Walk to breakfast is in ten, Calbert. I'm going to make a point of taking headcount this morning. And every morning from now on. Morning discipline has been sloppy of late."

"Lovely," Veranix said. "What do you study again, Rellings?"

"Law."

"I need to switch to Law. Clearly, it's frightfully simple."

"Ten minutes, kish," Rellings said sternly, and he stomped out of the room.

"What did you do?" Delmin asked.

Veranix got out of the bed and searched around for his pants. "Do? Me? What do you mean?" Veranix realized he sounded too defensive.

"Because Rellings is on a tear!" Delmin looked angry, despite laughing. "You did something to him, didn't you?"

"To him? Nothing." Veranix pulled his clothes on. "Believe me, I barely think about the guy."

"Somebody chapped him," Delmin said.

"Wasn't me." Parsons, a dark-haired young man, came into the doorway. Eittle, his taller blond roommate, appeared behind him.

"Somebody pissed in his tea, I'll tell you," Eittle said with a clipped, nasal accent.

"And we all get to drink it," Veranix said. "I see we're all having a good morning."

"I was up already," Eittle said from the back. "If Rellings wants his little walk to breakfast, let's line up. I'm starved."

"Same here," Delmin said.

"You two are always hungry," Parsons said.

"I'm a mage," Delmin said. "I don't know what Eittle's excuse is."

"They're stingy in the dining hall, that's what," Eittle said. "I tell you—"

"Bet a crown he says 'back on the farm' next," Veranix said. Eittle was a farmboy from up in Patyma somewhere. Veranix constantly had to remind himself behind that backcountry accent and doughy face, there was a mind of absurd levels of genius, matched by his humble nature.

"No bet," Parsons said.

Eittle's face fell. "Calbert, I thought country boys needed to stick together against these city folks." Delmin and Parsons laughed. Both of them were Maradaine north-siders. Parsons came from money, possibly even minor nobility, but he never talked about it. He did mention his older brothers who all went to the Royal College of Maradaine, though.

Veranix smiled good-naturedly. "I've told you again and again, Eittle. Racquin caravaners aren't country folk. We're road people." Among his friends in Almers, Veranix didn't bother hiding his heritage. His name made it all too clear, and there were only so many lies he could keep up with.

"Disreputable road people," Delmin said.

"Maybe that's why Rellings hates you," Parsons said. "He thinks you'll steal his sister and throw her in the back of your wagon."

"Does Rellings have a sister?" Eittle asked.

"Does Calbert have a wagon?" Delmin countered.

"Don't all Racquin have wagons?" Parsons asked, his tone too dry to tell if he was joking or not.

"I'm going to show all of you the back of a wagon," Veranix said, knocking Delmin in the arm. A loud bell rang out in the hallway.

"Every blasted kish better line up!" Rellings called.

"Come on," Veranix said. "I'm starving too."

Rellings counted through the line of students twice. There was a fair amount of grumbling from the crowd, but Veranix kept his own mouth shut. Whatever was bothering Rellings, he didn't want to draw any more heat than was necessary. He had enough to worry about.

Breakfast was a plateful of eggs and potatoes, with dark bread and tea, which Veranix ate greedily. He really wondered what kind of meals Eittle ate at the farm, because even with his appetite, this was a lot of food.

Delmin stared at a forkful of potatoes, his brow furrowed.

"Problem with your breakfast, Delmin?" Veranix asked.

"Thinking about something I read last night. Theory about the war with the Poasians."

"And it's about potatoes?" Eittle asked.

"Actually, it is," Delmin said. "Potatoes were brought over to Druthal from the colonies in the Napolic Islands."

"Like Vee's stable girl?" Parsons laughed.

"I don't know what you're talking about, Parsons." Veranix wondered how widespread the rumors about him and Kaiana had become. He didn't encourage them, even though it was better people believed that instead of knowing the truth. The rumors alone could create trouble.

"Of course you don't," Parson said.

"Anyway," Delmin said, "the theory is that Poasians invaded our colonies there because they wanted to cultivate potatoes themselves."

Parsons shook his head. "Fifty years of war over potatoes?"

"Ain't what my grandfather tells me," Eittle said. "He said it was just—"

"Was this something we were supposed to read for history?" Veranix asked Delmin, cutting off Eittle before he started on another long-winded war story about his grandfather. After three years together in Almers, Veranix had heard every story three times.

"No, I found it in the library."

Parsons shook his head at Delmin. "Only you would go to the library for extra reading." He turned to Veranix. "What's your plan for today, Vee?"

"Morning practicals with Alimen," he said. "You?"

"Our own practicals," Eittle said, "What's that stuff we're working with?"

"Quicksilver," Parsons said, "We're on metals all semester."

"Cleaner than last semester," Eittle said, shoveling in more eggs. "I'd rather not cut open any more live animals to see how their organs work."

"And yet, you keep eating as you say that," Delmin said.

Parsons shuddered. "Quicksilver is creepy. I prefer vivisection."

"I need to take some Natural Philosophy courses soon," Veranix said. "I need at least two before I get my Letters. What should I take?"

"You've been stalling on them," Delmin said.

"And you've been stalling on practicals," Veranix said.

"I'm better with theory."

Veranix nodded. "By the way, I need to go over that stuff from yesterday's lecture."

"The stuff you slept through?" Delmin smirked at him.

"Shut it," Veranix said, laughing. He looked at Parsons. "What should it be?"

"Yanno's plant life course is good," he said. "Or Hester's astronomy class. You're always up late anyway."

"Right," Veranix said. Tower bells rang nine times. Veranix took a few last bites and gulped down the last of his tea. "Off to practicals."

"History lectures after lunch?" Delmin asked. "You have done the reading?"

Veranix hadn't read yet, though the chapter to read was on Shalcer, the Idiot King. That sounded at least somewhat entertaining. "I'll read during lunch. See you there." He brought his plate over to the steward and left the hall.

><><><><

"Hey, Jutie! Hey, Jutie! Where you been?"

Jutie came up to the corner of Rose and Vine, where Hetzer and Tooser were both leaning against the building, keeping an eye on the street. "There was a church meet this morning, me and Colin went down to it."

"Really?" Hetzer sounded a bit offended. Hetzer was an older Prince, and usually at Colin's right hand for anything. "He took you?"

"I was awake," Jutie said with a shrug.

"We woke up and you were gone," Tooser said.

"So where's Colin now?" Hetzer asked. He had stepped in closer to Jutie, his head cocked to one side.

"Don't know," Jutie said. Colin had said something about getting a bite, and next thing he knew, Colin was gone.

"Slipped out from you?"

"He does that," Tooser said. "He does that real good."

"And, blazes, there was this one Knight, you know, he was giving me the eye, and I almost cut him right there."

"In the church?" Tooser asked.

"Yeah, if Colin hadn't held me back. Knight deserved it, too. They've been trouble."

Hetzer nodded, laughing nervously. "So what's the deal, what's the big meet for?"

"Some comer nipped Fenmere last night."

"Serious?" Hetzer gave a low whistle. "Had to have been a good bit, you know? To make them all go for a church meet first thing?"

"Right on the docks, apparently," Jutie said.

"Blazes!" Hetzer said. He was grinning wide, pacing back and forth on the corner. "That's what I'm talking about, you know? That's what somebody needs to be doing." He punched at empty air. "Giving Fenmere his own right back, you know?"

"Like I said—" Jutie started. For once he had a piece over these two, and it felt good. Then he heard a voice he hadn't heard in months, and that all came crashing down.

"Juteron?"

Jutie turned to see exactly who he didn't want to see. His older brother Wylon, dressed in a heavy leather smock and smelling like the sewers. He sat on a skinny three-wheeled pedalcart, stopped in the middle of the street.

"Juteron, what are you doing?"

Hetzer stepped up to Jutie's shoulder. "Who's this, Jutie?"

"My brother," Jutie muttered. Why the blazes was he even on this block?

"Brother?"

Wylon got off the pedalcart and stepped forward, giving a nervous glance over to Hetzer. "This is where you've been?"

"What's that supposed to mean, Wylon?"

Hetzer leaned in. "Yeah, *Wylon*, what's that supposed to mean?"

"We've been worried sick about you, Juteron," Wylon said. "We didn't know where you had gone. I had no idea you would be hanging around with . . . trash." He said the last word cautiously, as if he had to work up the nerve to say it.

Hetzer started laughing. "This bloke calls us trash, you hear that?"

"The man knows his trash," Tooser said. He came over real close to Wylon, getting his nose in. "Based on how he smells."

"But he's got such a nice pedalcart here, Tooser," Hetzer said, running a finger along the metal frame.

"Get your filthy hands off my ride," Wylon said.

"Your hands filthy, Hetz?" Tooser asked.

"I'm sure," Wylon said

"Course they are," Hetzer said, getting close to Wylon. "I've got them covered with your mother's—"

"Hetz!" Jutie snapped. That was too damn far.

"Sorry, Jutes," Hetzer said. "Forgot my manners. It happens around sewage like this rat."

"Least I have a real job," Wylon said. He brushed Hetzer away and turned back to Jutie. "You still could, too, you know."

Jutie sneered back at his brother. He didn't need to hear this again. "What's this, at the tannery? Or the slaughterhouse?"

"Either one is honest work."

A hand clapped on Wylon's shoulder. "Honest work, really?" Colin came up from behind, one arm wrapped congenially around Wylon. "That's a funny thing to say, you know. Honest how?"

"It's not breaking the law," Wylon said.

"Who is breaking the law?" Colin said, giving Wylon a smile like a fox. "What laws are we breaking?"

"Four pieces of trash, standing on the corner, all of you armed . . ."

"As is our legal right," Colin said. "We provide little services around the neighborhood, and people pay us as they see fit."

"Swindle and scare people—"

"Protect the people, friend."

"You're just common crooks!"

"Better than a common tanner!" Hetzer shouted, and the others laughed.

Wylon ignored them and moved closer to Jutie, his eyes imploring. "It's not safe out here, Juteron."

"Not safe?" Jutie asked. He was boiling with rage, but all that came out of his mouth was laughter. "Wylon, how many accidents you see on the kill floor, eh?" Wylon's gaze dropped to the ground, he said nothing. "At least out here, I've got a fighting chance, hmm? I've got people at my back." He held up his tattooed arm into Wylon's face.

"Jutie's got plenty of brothers, friend," Hetzer said.

Wylon stepped back from the corner, still not looking up from the ground. With a nod, he finally said, "The family would still love to see you, Juteron. Anytime."

"Maybe we'll all drop by for supper sometime," Colin said.

Wylon glanced up at Colin, and turned away. He quickly mounted his pedalcart and rode off down the street.

"Honest work," Colin muttered.

"I'll give him honest work," Hetzer said. He took a few steps into the street yelling after Wylon. "Spend a couple days on Rose Street, you'll see some honest work!"

"Settle down, Hetzer," Colin said.

Hetzer laughed, jumping in the street, and came back over to Colin. "Hear someone gave it to Fenmere real good last night."

"Somebody hit him on the docks, that's what we hear. Big shipment." Colin growled out the words. Jutie didn't get why Colin seemed so displeased with the whole thing.

"Blazes!" shouted Hetzer. A shop owner sweeping off his stoop glared over at them, and then turned back into his shop. "That's brilliant, Colin. That's what people should be doing. Hitting that bastard where it hurts him!"

"Is that why you're crowing?" Jutie looked across the street to see who called out to them. It was a group of Knights of Saint Julian, including the trash who was giving him trouble before. These guys looked like they had already been through the thrasher once: bloody heads, black eyes, torn clothes.

"Damned right," Hetzer yelled back. "You Knights got a problem with that? You do, you shouldn't be on our corner!"

"Well, our corner just had a pack of Fenmere's goons looking for his merch!" The Knight captain led them, stepping off the walkway into the street.

"This becoming a thing in the middle of the day?" Tooser asked.

"Blasted well looks that way," Colin said. "You Knights better get back on your block, you hear?"

"Our block has Fenmere, Princes. So now *your* block has Knights."

Hetzer was now halfway across the street, closest to the group of Knights. "Hey, Jutie," he called out. "Which one of these was giving you the eye before?"

Jutie pointed over. "The one with the dark vest to match his eye."

Hetzer drew out a knife, pointed it casually at that Knight. "He's claiming you, friend. Unless you head on home."

Tooser and Colin stepped off the corner, and Jutie followed them. Out of the corner of his eye, he saw a few more Princes coming out of the flop over the Turnabout. The Knights were going to be badly outnumbered if they pushed.

"Maybe we should—" one of the Knights said.

"Don't think Fenmere's just gonna hit us, Prince," the Knight captain said. "If he's on our block, he'll be on every block."

With that, the Knights backed off down Vine.

Hetzer snickered and turned back to the corner. "Blazes of a day, ain't it, cap?"

Jutie looked over to Colin, who shoved his knife back in his coat and stalked off.

Crossing his way over the lawn to Alimen's office, Veranix glanced at the south wall of the campus. The wall was low here, made of crumbling stones. One could easily see over it, where there was a line of trees, and Lilac Street on the other side.

One of the trees had two cloths tied around a low branch, a red one and a white one. Most people, passing in a hurry across campus, wouldn't notice them. Even if anyone did notice them, they wouldn't think anything of them.

Veranix knew exactly what they meant. The white cloth was a signal from Colin, letting Veranix know that they had to talk.

The red cloth meant Colin was angry.

Colin was going to have to wait until lunchtime, though. After dozing off in lecture yesterday, Veranix couldn't miss a practical. Professor Alimen wouldn't stand for that, no matter how much he liked Veranix.

Alimen's office was at the top of Bolingwood Tower, as were his personal apartments. It was the traditional place for the University's Egracian Chair, the position Alimen held as the head of the Magic department at U of M. It held quite a bit of prestige, even if the department only had two other faculty, and at most twenty students at any given time. Bolingwood was the tallest building on campus, which meant that Veranix had to race up seven flights of steep stone stairs to reach the office.

"Only five minutes late, Mister Calbert," Professor Alimen said. "For you, that's something impressive." Alimen was not alone when Veranix entered. Two other men were in whispered conference with him. Despite being here for his appointed time, Veranix had the distinct impression he was interrupting something.

"My punctuality would improve if we held lessons

on the ground floor, Professor." Veranix gave his best winning smile.

Alimen chuckled warmly. "The stairs help keep my students in top condition. You're the only one who comes in here not winded, Mister Calbert."

"I must be living right, sir," Veranix said. The two men were looking at Veranix with dark, disturbing eyes. Veranix didn't like them at all. "If you're indisposed, Professor, I could return later."

"Nonsense. These gentlemen are here to observe the lesson. This is Wells Harleydale, from the Circle of Light and Stone and on my right is Fenrich Kalas, from the Blue Hand Circle." The two men couldn't be more different. Harleydale, despite his age, wore little more on top than a garish yellow vest, so the lighthouse tattoo on his chest was plainly visible. His hair was a wild mop of gray curls. He would have fit right in with the clowns from the circus. Kalas, though, was dressed in a deep blue gentleman's suit—an expensive one, with silver clasps on the jacket and waistcoat—including matching gloves and coach hat. His dark hair was cropped short, and he sported a disturbingly tiny mustache. Veranix found both of them disturbing.

Veranix buried those feelings and straightened his posture, reaching out to shake hands with the two men. "Veranix Calbert," he said. "It's an honor to meet you both." Harleydale returned Veranix's handshake with warm vigor, but Kalas acted as if the physical contact was an imposition he had to endure. A memory sparked, and he turned to Harleydale. "Light and Stone. You were involved in—"

"The Circle Feuds a few years ago," Harleydale finished for him. "A most regrettable incident."

"Series of incidents," Professor Alimen said under his breath. That was still selling it softly. In 1212, five different Mage Circles, all over the city, fought in the streets. Viciously. Savagely. Mages weren't the only casualties, as plenty of bystanders were also killed.

Veranix bit his lip to keep from saying anything. It was almost laughable. No brawl between the Rose Street Princes and the other Aventil gangs had ever had that much collateral damage. From what Veranix could gather, not even in 1194, when Fenmere rolled the whole neighborhood and Aventil fractured—not even then did innocent people get badly hurt. Yet Colin and his Princes were hounded, and Mister Harleydale and other Circle members walked about unmolested.

"Really, Alimen," Kalas said, his voice full of open contempt, shaking Veranix out of his reverie. "This is your top student? I don't see anything about his aura that impresses me that much." Veranix's eyebrows went up at hearing that.

"Top student in practical exercises," Alimen said. "Quite remarkable when it comes to practical application. His study of theory . . . still requires attention."

"Hmph," Kalas said. "As does his punctuality. Perhaps I should have just gone to the Royal College of Maradaine, instead."

"If you wish, Kalas," Alimen said. "I was simply giving you the courtesy of meeting Mister Calbert."

"Your courtesy overwhelms," Kalas said. "I thought you had a gifted bloodhound in your stable as well."

"I have a student who has exceptional talent in sensing *numina*," Professor Alimen said. Veranix could hear him gritting his teeth as he said it. "But he is explicitly bonded to another Circle already."

"Pity."

Veranix thought the professor must have been talking about Delmin, but he wasn't promised to any Circle yet. Was he just flat-out lying to keep Kalas away from Delmin? Veranix could hardly blame Alimen for that.

"Where do his strengths lie?" Harleydale asked. He was walking around Veranix, looking him up and down as if inspecting a horse he would buy.

"Practical innovation." Veranix held up his chin high. If these mages wanted to check him out, he'd give them his best.

"True," Alimen said. "Mister Calbert has been quite clever in how he shapes magic."

"He has good tone," Harleydale said, groping Veranix's shoulder.

"Thank you, sir." Veranix thought this disturbing. He didn't know he was going to get pawed over by anyone today.

"Yes, well," Alimen said. "Perhaps we should begin, yes? I thought we would do the Vase Exercise." Veranix was confused. Alimen appeared to be showing him off to these two, but the Vase Exercise was one of his worst.

"If you say so, sir," Veranix said.

"I really don't need to see that," Kalas said. He went to the door.

"I guess I'm not being recruited by him, then," Veranix let slip.

"The Blue Hand Circle does not recruit," Kalas said from the door. "We invite. Exclusively."

"Must be very exclusive. I've never heard of you."

"Veranix!" Professor Alimen said sternly.

"We do not need to shout our name," Kalas said. "A whisper will do. Good day, Alimen." He left the office.

Alimen let out a deep exhale. "What a horse's ass."

"I wasn't going to say it," Harleydale said. "I've never liked him."

"I was about to say it," Veranix said.

"You shouldn't, Mister Calbert," Alimen said. "Blue Hand is a very small Circle, but they are powerful."

"Couldn't prove it by me," Veranix said.

"Your professor means they have a lot of money, young man," Harleydale said. "Money makes the University pay attention to them."

"I was just being polite," Alimen said. "I was surprised as anyone he came out here."

"I'm just glad he's gone," Harleydale said. "If you ask me, the Blue Hand are especially odious. A little boys club, if you get my drift, and they all nearly worship their leader. Disturbing man. I only met him once and it was two times too many."

"Wells, let's not be petty."

Harleydale sighed dramatically. "As you wish. Are you ready, Mister Calbert?"

"Of course, Mister Harleydale. I'm more than happy to demonstrate my skills to you, but—and correct me if I'm wrong, Professor—I'm pledged to Lord Preston's Circle." And he was more than happy to keep things that way. He didn't understand much of anything about Circle law or politics, or how that allowed Harleydale's Circle of Light and Stone to not face any charges after the Circle Feuds. That was the whole point of Lord Preston's. They were strictly academic, and stayed neutral in any sort of Circle politics.

"Not exactly pledged. Nothing is official until induction."

"Which can't occur in any Circle until after I get my

Letters of Mastery," Veranix said, ignoring the implications of what Professor Alimen said. He didn't even want to think about what might or might not happen after receiving his Letters. "That is still over a year away."

"At least, if not more," Alimen said pointedly.

"Then, forgive my impertinence, but . . . why are you here, Mister Harleydale?"

"Light and Stone want to know who to have their eye on early. Like the Blue Hand Circle, we are small, and we are not in a position to place potential students in the Universities with a pledge for later induction. We are not a moneyed Circle like Lord Preston's." He gave a knowing smile to Alimen.

"We invest in the future, old friend," Alimen said, smiling back.

"Would that we could as well, Gollic," Harleydale said. That was the first time Veranix had heard anyone use Professor Alimen's given name. "Please, continue with your lesson as if I were not here."

"As you wish," Veranix said. "Vase Exercise then, sir? That is one of my weak points."

"I'm well aware of that, Mister Calbert, so we'll start there," Alimen said. "But you do need to work even more on sharpening your *numinic* senses. I wasn't kidding about that."

"Isn't that why you've paired me up with Delmin?"

"Indeed." Alimen went over to a shelf of glassware and took down a crystal vase, placing it on a stone pedestal in the center of the room. "I mentioned Mister Sarren to you, didn't I, Wells? Very gifted with his *numinic* senses."

"I don't need trackers, Gollic."

So Alimen was specifically keeping Delmin away from the Blue Hand.

"As you wish. Get in place, Mister Calbert."

"All right," Veranix said. He stood next to the pedestal. The exercise was simple in concept. Alimen would try and destroy the vase. Veranix had to keep it safe. How he did that was up to him.

"We'll begin now," Alimen said. Veranix pulled *numina* into himself, ready to react when Alimen struck.

The vase shattered next to him.

"I forgot to mention, Mister Calbert. You'll need to protect it from Mister Harleydale as well as me. Now repair the vase."

The midday sun was painfully bright as Veranix made his way to the Rose & Bush. The past two nights, followed by the relentless pounding from Alimen and Harleydale, had left him feeling dazed. He was so out of sorts he was completely taken by surprise when two hands pulled him off the road and into an alley. Veranix was about to react with a hard blast of magic when he recognized Colin.

"I'm rustling a Uni boy for a few coins," Colin hissed. "Play along. What did you do?"

"Please, no," Veranix said out loud. He then whispered to Colin, "I hit Fenmere's exchange at the docks. Why aren't we meeting at the Rose & Bush?"

"Because whatever you did was huge, and I needed to actually talk to you. Was it *effitte*?"

"No," Veranix said. Despite his success last night, he

remained disappointed that he didn't hurt Fenmere's *effitte* trade. "Something else. Big. Forty thousand crowns big."

"What?" Colin almost shouted. He quickly covered with, "Uni boy only has a few ticks on him?"

"This is risky," Veranix whispered. "I didn't think street captains did their own rustling."

"I know," Colin said. He pushed Veranix against the brick wall roughly. "I told my boys I needed some practice. Fenmere has had goons shaking people down all over. Mostly Inemar, but he's not respecting anyone's territory right now. For forty thousand I see why."

"Don't hurt me," Veranix said, faking tears as he fumbled in his pockets. He whispered under his sobs, "It wasn't a normal deal. He was buying a cloak and a rope."

"For forty thousand? That's ridiculous."

"I know. I can't figure it out."

"Take a few nights to figure it out. Maybe a month. Long enough for Fenmere to forget about the 'thorn' he's asking about."

"What's he asking?"

"Someone with a bow, with a staff. Maybe a mage. Maybe an acrobat. And definitely interested in *effitte* sales."

"So he's asking the right questions, then."

"Questions that might lead him to put pieces together."

"He won't figure out who I am."

"But he may figure out where you're tied to, cousin. He didn't forget your father for twenty years. He won't forget now."

"I don't want him to forget."

Colin answered by punching him in the face, a little too hard for it to be just for show. Veranix grabbed Colin's vest, about to strike back.

"Don't, cousin," Colin whispered. "Fenmere has loyal eyes here."

Veranix let himself drop down to his knees, burying his instinct to knock Colin on his back. "And the Lower Trenn Ward, you keep telling me."

"Especially there." Colin glanced out to the street, and then pulled Veranix up by the front of his coat. "I made a promise to your father I'd keep you safe. Even from yourself."

"I didn't ask—" Veranix said, getting another punch from Colin in response. This one he did hold back on.

"Don't even say that. Your father made a choice, so you could be in there, on the green side of that wall, hear? You respect that. So lay low."

"Fine," Veranix said. "A few nights." He threw a handful of copper coins on the ground. Colin scooped them up.

"That's real smart, Uni boy," Colin said as he slinked into the shadows. "You just stay smart."

Chapter 8

"HE'S RIGHT, you know," Kaiana said. She dabbed a foul-smelling paste on the bruise on Veranix's face. They were in a dark corner of the carriage house, out of sight if anyone came in. "You gave Fenmere a deep, solid cut already. Let it lie."

"Let it lie?" Veranix asked. "So he can lick his wounds?"

"So he's not expecting you!" Kaiana said. Her dark, angular eyes were intent on him. "Surprise is your best weapon against him."

"But it's not enough!" Veranix said. "It's only for Colin's sake that I don't kick Fenmere's front door down."

Kaiana laughed, but stopped when Veranix glared at her. "You'd just get yourself killed doing that. Better to strike at the *effitte* and his dealers. That hurts him plenty."

"It hurts his purse, but that means he'll probably sell more *effitte* to make it up!" Veranix was sure Kaiana, of all people, would see that.

"You've hurt him, and he wants to hurt you back, it sounds."

"Let him try," Veranix said. "There's no one else he can hurt."

"Really?" Kaiana said coldly. She picked up her mortar and pestle and got up.

Veranix had stepped in it. The last thing he wanted was for Kaiana to think he didn't care about what happened to her. "Kaiana, I didn't mean that, I meant . . ."

"I know what you meant," she said. "I have work to get to, or Jolen will sack me. You have just enough time to make it to the dining hall before lunch ends."

"Right." He went to the door of the carriage house, and stopped. He didn't want to leave her on such a poor note. Feebly he said, "Thanks. For the bruise."

"Right." She put her things away in a cabinet, not looking back at him. "Please, Veranix, just . . . be careful, all right?"

"All right. A few nights of studying and decent sleep will do me some good."

Lunch was still going on, though the crowd had thinned to a handful of stragglers, none of whom Veranix recognized. The food remaining was equally meager—only dark bread and beet stew. Veranix was hungry enough to not care; he filled a bowl and went to the closest table, near a group with blue and white scarves. Philosophy students, deep in argument.

One of them tapped hard on a newssheet. "Pointless vote! Parliament doesn't have the authority to enforce it, regardless of the outcome."

"That's not the point," another said. "The point isn't about whether they can make the king remarry."

"The whole thing is a head count! It's testing the waters of where members of Parliament stand." The first one picked up the newssheet and shook it violently before throwing it down on the table, where it slid near Veranix.

Veranix rarely read the sheets—newsboys would scream out the headlines, so he heard enough of what he wanted to know—but one thing caught his eye. Two priests found dead in Saint Polmeta's church. Wasn't that the church he had stopped at last night? He couldn't remember.

"Hey, mage kish!"

He kept his attention on the sheet. Saint Polmeta's was in Dentonhill. Two priests had been murdered, in a gruesome manner. The article spent far too much time on the sanguine details.

"Mage kish!" the philosophy student said. "Get your own blazing newssheet!"

"Sorry," Veranix said, sliding it back down to them. "Did you see that about the priests?"

"Dentonhill murders?" The other one shook his head. "There's always at least one in any sheet."

"Two priests is a slow night over there," the first said.

"Right," Veranix said. He turned back to his stew, tuning out the rest of their conversation about the impotency of the Druth throne in the modern age.

Each bite gnawed at his gut. The more he thought about it, the more certain he was that Saint Polmeta's was the church he'd stopped at, and he couldn't convince himself that was a coincidence.

By sunset, Veranix was lighting oil lamps in his room, determined to focus on reading *Benton's Theories on Magic and Numina* for a few hours before falling asleep. Two pages into the chapter on the mystical properties of various gemstones, and his head was already swimming.

"Finally cracking that open?" Delmin asked as he came into the room.

"Funny," Veranix said. "I don't know why I even need to know this stuff. I mean, I don't need it to actually do magic."

"You do to understand what you're doing."

"I understand it fine," Veranix said. "Blazes, Alimen is telling people I'm the best practical student he has."

"Is he?" Delmin asked. His voice cracked slightly.

"He's talking about you as well," Veranix said quickly. "Right in front of me, he told another mage you were the most gifted he had for using your *numinic* senses."

"But he called you his best practical student?"

"Don't worry, he knows my theory is awful. I mean, right here. *Numinic* conductivity of gemstones. How am I supposed to remember which stones are the most conductive, and why does it matter?"

"Robins sing daily to every open person," Delmin said in complete seriousness. There was no indication on his face that he thought the string of nonsense he just said was anything but a rational response to Veranix's question.

"Are you drunk or something?" Veranix asked.

"No, that's how you remember the list of the most conductive, in order," Delmin said. "Rubies, sapphires, diamonds, topazes, emeralds, opals, pearls."

"Right, I'm not going to remember either one." Veranix had an idea. "What about cloth?"

"What about it?" Delmin asked.

"Well, is there any kind of cloth that has a high conductivity of *numina*?"

Delmin sat on his bed and thought it over. "Not that I can think of. I mean, maybe individual strains of cotton or flax might grow that have some affinity for *numina*, but I can't imagine you would be able to cultivate enough to make anything that would be worth the trouble. Some woods, yes, but most of those trees are slow-growing ones that—"

"Fine, fine," Veranix said. He searched for his place on the page. "Forget I asked."

"Besides, you really should be studying mystical metals. Dalmatium, napranium, everything else you slept through yesterday."

"I didn't sleep through dalmatium," Veranix said. "I remember that all too well."

"Well, napranium was actually more interesting—" Delmin started. He was interrupted by a pounding, desperate knock on the door. Veranix opened it. Eittle was standing there, looking wild-eyed and pale.

"Something's wrong with Parsons," he said urgently. "You've got to help me." Veranix was already in the hallway, running to the room Eittle shared with Parsons.

Parsons was on the floor, his body in convulsions. White foam formed around his mouth. His eyes were wide open, bloodshot, and staring blankly.

"Get a prefect!" Veranix screamed to no one. He got on top of Parsons, pinning his arms down on the floor. Delmin came in and stopped dead, stunned by what was happening.

"He sick or something?" Delmin asked. "Call for a Yellowshield!" Parsons's legs thrashed out violently.

"No time! Hold his feet down before he brains me!" Veranix yelled. Delmin dropped and held Parsons down.

"What the blazes happened?" someone asked from the door. A small crowd had gathered, with Rellings in the front. He looked around at everyone, his eyes blaming. Eittle was almost cowering to the side.

"He was talking to me, and then he started acting silly."

"Silly?" Veranix asked, still struggling to hold Parsons. "How do you mean silly?"

"Like, he was talking, and then he started giggling. I mean, like a little girl, he was giggling. Then laughing like crazy."

"Laughing so hard he couldn't breathe?" Veranix asked. "And then the fit started?"

"That's right."

"Blast," Veranix swore. Not here. Not on campus. Not on his own floor. He bent over Parsons's face and smelled his breath. There it was—a bitter scent with a hint of lavender. No doubt. He smashed his fist futilely on the floor.

"What?" Rellings demanded, looming over them. "What is it, Calbert?"

"Hold him down, Eittle," Veranix said, getting up as Eittle came down. He went over to Parsons's desk, looking through the drawers. "I'll tell you what, Rellings. Something you should be far more concerned with than bed checks and bullying. *Effitte.*"

"*Effitte?*" Delmin asked, shocked.

"He didn't take *effitte*," Rellings scoffed.

Veranix dug through Parsons's drawers and found a small vial, buried under several pairs of pants. He held it up to the lamplight. Sure enough, there was the residue of a thick, purple liquid.

"Right here, Rellings."

"That—that's crazy." Rellings said. "He'll be expelled."

"If he's lucky, he'll even be aware of that," Veranix said.

"What's *effitte*?" Eittle asked.

"Nasty stuff," Delmin said. "Makes you happy and energetic, but too much makes you crazy, destroys your brain."

"Only street trash take *effitte*," Rellings protested. "Where did he get it?"

"I don't know," Eittle said. "Just before dinner, I saw him over at the east gate, talking to some . . . I don't know. He looked unsavory, but Parsons said he was an old friend."

"East gate, by Waterpath?" Veranix asked. His blood boiled. "The Dentonhill side?" Fenmere's sellers were coming onto the campus. They were poisoning his friends. That wouldn't stand.

"All trash in Dentonhill," Rellings muttered. "Parsons wasn't like—sweet saints, Calbert!"

The vial shattered in Veranix's hand. He realized he'd channeled loose magic into his hand, hot, angry, messy. He threw the shards on the ground, shaking off the pain. Realizing there might be drops of *effitte* on his hand, he focused that magic, burning it all away before it could seep into his skin. The last thing he ever wanted was to come in contact with the stuff.

"That was evidence, Calbert!"

"You've got all the evidence you need right there!" Veranix shot back, pointing at Parsons. Parsons stopped convulsing, and lay still, his breath shallow.

Rellings ground his teeth, glancing at the assembled crowd outside the door. "Right, then. Moment has passed, everyone. I'll send word to the deans in the morning."

"He needs a doctor," Veranix said. "Delmin and I will go fetch one."

"You'll do what, Calbert?" Rellings asked. He raised his back up, clearly trying to intimidate Veranix.

Veranix wasn't even fazed. "We'll get help. Step aside."

"You forget who is the kish and who is the prefect, Calbert."

"Not at all," Veranix said. Rellings wasn't going to get in his way. Not tonight. Not after this. "It's the prefect who should stay and try to keep things calm here." He pushed past Rellings and went straight to the stairwell, Delmin running close behind him.

"Is your hand all right?" Delmin asked.

"It's fine," Veranix said as they went down the stairs. "Just pain. It'll pass."

As soon as they were outside Almers, Veranix stopped in the middle of the lawn.

"All right, Del, go for the doctor. I'll be back late. Cover for me."

"Cover for— Veranix! What the blazes are you going to do?"

"Just . . . just say we went looking for different doctors or got separated or something. I have to take care of this." He headed toward the carriage house.

"Take care of what?" Delmin asked.

"That!" Veranix pointed up toward the building, up where Parsons had probably already lost any chance of speaking an intelligible sentence, let alone finishing school. "Not another drop on campus."

"Veranix," Delmin called. "It hasn't been the dark girl every night, has it?"

"Better you don't know," Veranix said.

"Parsons is already ruined, Vee," Delmin said. "Don't you throw away your future as well. Whatever you're going to do—"

"Just trust me," Veranix said. "I've got to go to work." He dashed off before Delmin could say anything else.

He slipped into the carriage house, and was down in the Spinner Run in a matter of seconds. He changed clothes and put on his gear. Tonight wasn't going to be about sneaking or stealing. No bloody noses or banter. He was going to find *effitte* and break anyone selling it.

He was about to dash off when he remembered the rope and the cloak. Whatever they were, whatever Fenmere had intended them for, they were his now. He could take them, master their power, and use that against Fenmere's men. That would be fitting. That would be just. He put the cloak on and hung the rope at his belt. Again he felt that charge of *numinic* energy flooding into him. He was prepared for it this time, not losing himself in the rush.

He scrambled back out of the Spinner Run. As he went out the door, he heard a scrape behind him. Kaiana had opened the door of her bedchamber. She said nothing, only shook her head and closed the door again.

He knew he could tell her what just happened to

Parsons, and she'd be behind him, pushing him over the wall herself. He was about to go to her door and do just that, but stopped himself. He was too angry to bother explaining himself, even to her. For Parsons, for his mother . . . for every mind ruined by *effitte* . . . he wasn't going to play games with Fenmere's boys anymore.

He left the carriage house and went to the wall. Tonight he would hit them as hard as he could.

A light rain was falling as Veranix perched himself across the street from the Dogs' Teeth Pub, a shabby place where light crept out of the holes between mismatched wooden slats. The whole place looked like it was shoved into the empty space between the tight angles of the brick row houses along the two streets of Cole and Helter.

The people at the Dogs' Teeth were as ugly as it was, and smelled worse. It was the kind of place where the poxy whores were so sick, they would vomit after each client, and the men who used them wouldn't care. Most of them were hooked on *effitte* as well.

The rain fell on Veranix, but he couldn't feel it. The water just rolled off his cloak. After a few moments of watching the door of the Dogs' Teeth, he realized the cloak wasn't getting wet. He looked down at it. In the rain and dim moonlight, it shimmered. The thought passed through his mind that it might make him easily seen from the street below.

With that thought, the cloak vanished. No, not vanished. It suddenly blended into the background, looking just like the roof he was sitting on. He moved his leg under the cloak, and the blended image moved with it, nearly imperceptible. Veranix almost laughed out loud with giddiness.

Was it possible the cloak was actually enchanted with its own magic? He wracked his brain, trying to remember Alimen's lectures on the subject. It was a lost art, no one in Druthal knew how to do it. There had been solitary mages, centuries ago, who did it, but their secrets had long since been lost. It was possible that in other parts of the world there were mages who knew how to make such things.

He decided to try something else. He let the thought cross his mind that the cloak should be red. As soon as he did, the cloak changed, to exactly the shade of red he imagined.

This time, he could feel it. The magic came from him, but the cloak did the work of pulling in the *numina*. It, as well as the rope, accepted the magic, made it effortless. What were these things? He had never heard of anything like these items. Forty thousand was selling them short. These items were priceless.

He changed the cloak again to blending into the background, concentrating on extending the field of it to surround his entire body. He stood up tall. Anyone who looked up would have seen only a shadow in the rain.

Someone was coming out of the Dogs' Teeth. Veranix needed to get down to the street quickly to catch them. Odds were strong anyone coming out that place knew someone who sold *effitte*, and anyone who sold it would be tied, eventually, to Fenmere. He just needed to work his way up the chain, and break every man he found along the way.

The man who walked out of the pub was a dirty mess of tangled hair and beard, wearing a torn-up, mud-covered cloak. He stumbled as he exited, his boots slipping on the wet road, and he took a moment to right himself and get his bearings. The man whistled a drinking song as he went off down Cole Street.

Veranix leaped off the roof. In the seconds it took to drop down to street level, a strange instinct took hold of him. The rope at his belt quivered, and his hand went to it. As soon as he touched it, the rope became like an extension of his arm. He threw the coil, and it shot out like an arrow. It found its mark, a stone gutter protruding from the roof of one of the row houses, and wrapped itself around it tight and strong. Holding on to the rope, Veranix swung up and flew forward. The moment Veranix wanted it to, the rope unwound itself from the gutter, returning to his hand as he hurtled through the air toward the man. His feet crashed into the man's back, flattening him. Veranix rolled with the blow and landed a few yards away, crouched and ready.

"What . . . what . . ." was all the man was able to stammer out.

"*Effitte!*" Veranix roared, his own voice surprising him.

"I . . . I don't have any," the man said, trying to stand up.

"Who sells it? Where?"

"I know a bunch of guys!" the man said. He looked around him. "Where are you?"

"Right here!" Veranix grabbed the man by his dirty shirt and pushed him against a brick wall. The man screamed in terror. Veranix realized why. With the cloak masking him, he looked like the rain itself had become man-shaped.

"What guys?" Veranix said. "Where?"

"B-back at the Dogs' Teeth. There's Lemt and Jendle."

"Is that it?"

"That's all I know!" the man cried. He was a blubbering mess. "Please don't kill me!"

"Not today," Veranix said. He threw the man to the ground. "Go home and sleep it off."

"Yes! Yes!" The man scrambled away, running before he even got on his feet.

Veranix coiled the rope back at his belt. As he walked back to the Dogs' Teeth, he grinned savagely. The more he used the rope and cloak, the more natural they felt. With these items, this power, he could really damage Fenmere and his *effitte* operation.

Veranix decided to be bold. Lemt and Jendle were in a pub full of people, and more than a few of them probably worked for Fenmere in some capacity. He could hardly sit around and wait for them to come to him. Even with the cloak and the rope, with magic and his staff, he couldn't fight every man in the place.

Not without using a little of that old circus showmanship.

He went up to the door of the Dogs' Teeth, and drew *numina* into himself. With the cloak, it was as easy as breathing. He released a focused burst and blew the door off the hinges. With a thought, the cloak appeared to be engulfed in black flames, obscuring his features.

"I'm here for Lemt and Jendle!" he shouted, his voice magically augmented to a shattering boom. "All others can save themselves!"

Lemt and Jendle were not card players, nor were they gifted liars or tricksters. When he called them out their faces gave them away in an instant. The room was filled with panic and screams, but the two men near the back of the pub froze with fear.

Veranix jumped up to a crossbeam, making way for the screaming crowd racing out the door. Not taking his eyes off Lemt and Jendle, he swung over and landed on the bar. A few people stood their ground; lackeys for the sellers, or addicts whose taste for *effitte* bought their loyalty. Still, there were fewer than a dozen people left in the pub.

Veranix grabbed the rope and threw it out at one of the two, the older man with a pointed gray beard. The rope wrapped tightly around him, and Veranix yanked him from his seat. He knocked over the table and three of the men standing in the way, like so many bowlpins. Veranix was surprised at how effortless it was. If he had tried that with an ordinary rope, he probably would have passed out from the strain.

"What? What?" the man shouted. He struggled to get free of the rope. In Veranix's hand, the rope was now hard as steel, but light as air.

"Are you selling *effitte*?" Veranix growled. "Are you just a seller, or a source?"

"Seller! I just sell it, me and Jendle, we just sell it!"

"Shut it, Lemt!" Jendle said. He turned to the men still standing, "Will one of you get this guy?"

"I'm asking the questions!" Veranix said, and with a flick of his wrist he swung Lemt into the table in front of Jendle, and then yanked him back. Jendle smashed into the back wall, covered in the splintered remains of the table.

The rest of the lackeys didn't move an inch, standing agape in frozen horror.

"Are any of you crossing Waterpath?"

"If we go into Aventil—" Lemt began.

"On campus!" Veranix shouted. "Who is selling at the University?"

"I don't know! It wasn't me!" Lemt blubbered.

"You spineless toad," Jendle muttered, getting to his feet. Veranix swung Lemt over to Jendle again, this time making the rope bind Jendle with him. They both squirmed and struggled in the constricting rope.

"Where's your stash?" Veranix asked. "Where are your vials?"

"Can't . . . breathe . . ." Lemt wheezed.

"Tell me!"

The rope tightened. One of the lackeys pulled a bag out from under the broken table.

"Here! Here! This is their stuff!" He threw the bag to the floor below Veranix. Veranix snapped his fingers, and the bag was engulfed in blue flames. In moments, it destroyed all the *effitte*.

"You . . . idiot!" Jendle managed to get out. "That was over fifty crowns' worth—"

"Only fifty?" Veranix sneered. "A drop in the bucket when I'm done. Who is your source? Where is he?"

"Don't tell him anything!" Jendle shouted. Veranix flexed the rope tighter around them. There were several sickening crunches, ribs cracking. Both men screamed.

"Name and street!"

"He'll kill us," Lemt whimpered. "Fenmere will kill us."

"Source!" The rope coiled tighter still.

"Nevin!" Jendle shouted. "Third floor apartments above the dressmaker on Lolly!"

"Thank you, gentlemen," Veranix said, bowing with a flourish. "You all should consider a new trade." He bowled Lemt and Jendle into the group as he released them. He leaped out the door, and hurled the rope up. It coiled around another gutter outcropping, and holding tight, he pulled himself up to the roof of the row house.

Once there, he collapsed, barely able to catch his breath. Even with whatever *numina*-drawing abilities the rope and the cloak had, that took a lot out of him. They also gave him a heady, giddy feeling, like being drunk. He was lucky that he was able to get out of the pub when he did, without having to fight any of them, because he knew he wouldn't have been able to maintain the illusion any longer.

He ran his hands over the cloak and rope, feeling the distinctive charge of *numina* running into his body from them. *These are good tools,* he thought, *but they are no substitute for skill. I can't let them make me careless or lazy.*

Bells rang midnight. There wouldn't be much time before Lemt or Jendle or someone else warned Nevin. He caught his breath, pulled himself back to his feet, and headed north to Lolly.

Chapter 9

CHARL NEVIN HAD spent most of his fifty years in street trade, and survived it by knowing when to push and when to keep his head down. His body was lean and hard; he knew how to scrap. He had spent three years serving in the war, and more than twice that living in alleys and gutters. He could sell, he could hide from the constabulary, and he could run a crew. He had done well with it, giving him a good piece of Boss Fenmere's *effitte* trade. He had a good flop with a solid bunk. Simple comforts.

Nevin pulled himself out of his bunk, leaving the blonde doxy dozing there. She was one of those *effitte*-hooked sacks who was always good for a roll in exchange for a dose. She hadn't fallen apart much yet, so she was still worth taking to his bunk. He'd let her doze for a bit before tossing her out. In an hour or so, she'd be in a low, woozy state, with the *effitte* wearing off, and it would be easier then.

Any roll with a doxy always left Nevin with a powerful thirst, and tonight was no exception. He lit a candle and went to his kitchen. His larder was not very well stocked, but he had a half-empty jug of cider sitting on the table. He poured himself a cup and gulped it down. He winced as it hit his throat. The cider was turning. Still drinkable, but not very good.

He was still thirsty. He considered going to the pump out behind the shop to get some water. It was raining and cold out there. He'd have to put his boots and trousers on. It didn't quite seem worth the trouble. He decided to wake the girl up and make her go get him water. That would be good.

He didn't get the chance to do it, as someone crashed through his window.

Whoever it was came in with intention, flying feet first at Nevin's head. Nevin's reflexes were sharp, and he jumped out of the way as the intruder smashed into the chair and table.

Nevin was never far from a weapon in his own flop. At this point, he pretty much expected that people would try to kill him where he lived. Two knives on a belt hung on a peg right by him. Nevin grabbed them and charged at the intruder.

The intruder was already on him, swinging his staff. He was fast, not having lost a moment regaining his footing. Nevin pulled back, barely getting out of the way. He darted around, moving inside to get a good swipe with one knife. The intruder was fast enough to block him. Nevin needed to parry with both knives to hold him off.

Nevin had been in plenty of scraps, and he knew how to size up a fighter. This guy was quick, but he wasn't very strong, at least not as strong as Nevin. He was a scrawny tosser, as much bone as muscle. Nevin pushed the staff away hard, and took a quick swipe. He only grazed the guy. The intruder grunted in pain.

"That's for my chair, tosser!" Nevin said.

"Sorry about that," the intruder returned. "Furniture always ends up a casualty." He took several quick thrusts, pushing Nevin back, keeping him from using his knives.

Nevin knew this tosser wouldn't have the space to use his weapon well, not in a cramped flop. Nevin charged in to tackle him. The guy tried to knock him down, but he wasn't able to get a strong swing in. Nevin got cracked across the shoulder, but he'd been hit worse plenty of times. He was close enough to drive his knives in deep.

The intruder dropped the staff and got his arms up, taking the cuts there instead of his body. He grunted, and pushed out. The guy must have been stronger than he looked, because Nevin felt like he had been hit by a horsecart. It surprised him enough to make him lose grip of the knives, but not lose his close ground. They were both unarmed now, making this an honest knuckle scrap.

Nevin always liked an honest knuckle scrap.

He took a hit in the jaw, and returned it with two jabs to the tosser's stomach. That winded the guy, giving him the opening to throw a good solid hook. Nevin had pushed him back toward the wall. The tosser tried to kick him, but he was too dazed to land it. Nevin was able to get a hand around the guy's neck and slam him up to the wall.

"Got a lot of nerve, pal, coming at me in my flop." Nevin tried to get a good look at his face, but the shadow of his hood was impossibly dark. Damnedest thing.

"Next . . . time . . . I'll invite you . . . out . . ." the tosser squeaked out. The guy was trying to pull off Nevin's grip with one hand, and reach out toward the window with the other. Nevin thought that was odd, but he didn't really care. This was going to be over now.

"No next time," Nevin said. He drew back his arm to smash the guy's face.

Shouldn't have let go of the rope, Veranix thought. *Stupid mistake.* He had gotten too excited, thought he could crash through the window and take out Nevin in a moment. Whatever control he could exert over the rope, it didn't work well when he wasn't touching it. Taking a few punches made it that much harder to focus his own energy on calling it over to him.

Nevin had him half choked, lifted off the floor, and was about to hit him again. Veranix braced himself against the wall with one foot, and kicked Nevin in the side. He couldn't kick very hard, but he could do it fast. He got in four shots before Nevin's punch landed. Veranix's head smashed into the wall, the cheap wood cracking from the force of the blow. Pain shot through his skull, firing down through his gut. Despite being dazed and nauseous, Veranix didn't let up with his fast kicks. He clawed at Nevin's grip around his neck. It took all he had to keep himself from being choked tighter, from blacking out. He couldn't draw any *numina*, even with the cloak.

Nevin pulled back to deliver a finishing punch. Veranix used that space to bring up his knees, forcing Nevin to take all his weight with just the one hand. It was more than Nevin could take, and his arm buckled, dropping Veranix. He had already committed to the punch, smashing his hand against the plaster. From his crouched position, Veranix sprang up and punched Nevin in the jaw, augmenting the blow with as much magic as he could draw in.

"Twisty tosser, you are," Nevin coughed, blood oozing from of his mouth. "You're full of surprises."

"You have no idea," Veranix said. He threw several fast punches, sweetening them with hints of magic, but Nevin was too quick, too ready to block. Nothing got through. His own blows were fast and strong, a practiced brawler. Veranix dodged, but knew he couldn't last much longer pinned in the corner.

He focused magic hard and fast, putting it all into his next punch. Nevin blocked it, but he couldn't have been prepared for the raw power Veranix had channeled into his fist. The punch landed square in Nevin's chest, knocking him back. Veranix used the space to roll away from the wall, springing over to the window, desperate to catch his breath.

Nevin grabbed one of the knives from off the floor and hurled it at Veranix, piercing deep into his shoulder.

Veranix cried out. He forced himself to stay on his feet, forced his arm to move despite every muscle screaming at him. He had to focus through it, get control. He could feel the rope, right outside, a few feet away. The cloak gave him just enough of an edge, enough extra push on *numina*, he could try once more to bring the rope to him. Letting it go when he swung in was just sloppy.

Nevin had the other knife in his hand, and dove in to deliver a killing blow. Veranix reached out the window, pulling with as much magic as he could gather, and grabbed hold of the rope.

In an instant, the rope came rocketing into the room, and wrapped itself around Nevin, midair in his jump. Almost without thinking, Veranix flung the man out the window. A moment later, as the rope coiled back in his hand, he heard the dull thud of a body hitting the cobblestones.

Veranix slumped down to the floor. After taking a moment to compose himself, he got up again, stumbling over to the wrecked table. He picked up a shirt of Nevin's, discarded on the floor, and tore off a strip of it. Then he pulled the knife out of his shoulder. Blood started flowing out of the wound. With a little hint of magic, Veranix willed the strip of cloth to wrap around the wound, binding tighter than he could have managed with one hand.

He looked around the apartment for the first time in earnest. The place was a mess, mostly due to the fight. Up against one wall was a dresser that hadn't been damaged. Veranix opened the drawers. He searched through each one, finding only clothes and other personal items. In annoyance, he slammed the last drawer shut, hearing a distinctly metal thud. He pulled the drawer out again, taking it completely out of the dresser. Nestled in the empty space was a metal box.

Veranix took the box out. It was locked shut, but a touch of his finger and a crackling whisper of magic took care of that. Inside the box were quite a few silver coins, and even more exchange notes. Veranix didn't count it, but he figured it was a few hundred crowns in all. There was also a small leather-bound notebook.

"Blast," Veranix muttered. This was a good find, but it wasn't enough. "Where's the *effitte*?"

"He never keeps it here."

Veranix spun around. A woman—really barely more than a girl, even though her face had the cracked and weathered look of age—was lying in the bed, naked save for the blanket, which didn't cover anything. Veranix was surprised he didn't notice her before.

"It's not here?" Veranix asked cautiously.

"Never more than a taste." She stumbled to her feet. She looked dazed and disoriented, too unaware of herself for any modesty. "In case someone tries to rob him. Heh."

"Right," Veranix closed the box. He couldn't decide where to look, finally settling on watching her feet, so he could see if she attacked him. The girl took a few steps before dropping down to her knees and retching. Whatever vile thing she had eaten earlier smelled like death coming back up.

"Right bastard he is," she said, trying in vain to wipe her face clean. "Need more than the little bit he gave me."

"You don't need any," Veranix said. He went over to her, trying to help her stand.

"You have any?" she asked him. "Building your own stash?"

"Not a chance," Veranix said.

She threw up again. Veranix jumped up on the bed to avoid any landing on him.

"Come on, brother," she said, reaching out to him. "Help me out, I can give you a taste as well."

Veranix grabbed the shirt he had torn and cleaned her face with it. "I'll get you some help. Come on."

"You know someone who's got some?" she asked. Her eyes half closed, she slumped on top of him. She was cold and sweaty. If he didn't do anything soon, the fits would start. He didn't want to see that again, not twice in one night.

"What's your name?" Veranix asked. Without letting her drop down again, he pulled the blanket off the bed and wrapped it around her.

"Maxianne," she muttered, almost asleep.

"All right, Maxianne," he said. He touched the rope, and one end of it started to coil around her body. It held her in a gentle cradle, and she became as light as a feather.

"Oy! Constable!" yelled a voice from the street below. "Some tosser tried to kill me in my flop!" A shrill whistle followed.

"There's irony," Veranix muttered. He grabbed the box and his staff, and brought Maxianne to the window.

"Cold," she murmured. Her body was shivering.

"There's the one!" Nevin yelled from below Veranix. He was cradling one arm and limping. He had likely broken several bones in the fall. Two constables, in their crisp green and red coats, ran over from the corner.

"Never one when I call," Veranix muttered. He willed the cloak to shroud him and the girl.

"I just saw him!" Nevin yelled. "He was right there!"

Veranix sent the free end of the rope up to the top of

the building, and then pulled himself and Maxianne up to the roof. As bruised, broken and bleeding as he was, he still felt strong magically. He couldn't waste any more time. Maxianne was shuddering, and he was sure it wasn't just the night air. Pulling in as much *numina* as he could muster, he took a running leap off the roof, and soared southward.

The Lower Trenn Street Ward was a large stone monstrosity sitting on the southernmost point of Aventil neighborhood, a remnant of a fortress from over a thousand years before, when the city itself ended where Waterpath now ran. Over the centuries, it had served as a garrison. It had been the home for generations of dukes of Maradaine. It had been a prison, had held the royal treasury, and had even been a great library. It had then been abandoned, a hiding place for the city's most wretched, a place of crumbling decay in every sense.

Only for the past fifteen years had it been the Ward, a hospital and asylum for those same wretched. It was as good a place as it could be, given that the duke and the Council of Aldermen gave it barely enough crowns to keep operating.

Veranix pounded on the great wooden door, having laid Maxianne's unconscious body down on the stone steps at the entrance. After a few minutes, a young doctor came to the door, carrying just a candle for light. He was at best only a few years older than Veranix, wearing a leather smock over his shabby clothes. He looked down at Maxianne, then back up. Veranix stayed in the shadows, only letting himself be seen enough so the doctor would know he was there.

"What happened to her?" he asked.

"*Effitte*," Veranix said, "Probably been doing it for years." The doctor crouched down, opening her eyes and holding the candle close to her face.

"Still get too many of those. Was she talking at all?"

"Some," Veranix said. "Her name is Maxianne."

"You bothered to learn her name before you rolled with her," the doctor said derisively. "And you brought her here afterward. You should put your name in for a saint."

"Not like that," Veranix said. "A dealer had used her and left her. I just found her."

The doctor looked up at him and gave a begrudging grunt of approval. "You should have called a Yellow-shield."

"Didn't think there was time."

"I meant for you, friend." The doctor pointed to his shoulder.

"It only looks bad."

"I know what bad is—"

"Tend to her!"

The doctor pressed his hand to her head. "Not much fever. She has a chance. But if her head isn't gone, she'll just go get another taste once she's on her feet." He picked up her limp body and draped it over his shoulder.

"Maybe so," Veranix said. "But she deserves to get on her feet."

"Why should this buzzed doxy deserve that, friend?"

"They all deserve it, doctor," Veranix said. He opened the metal box and took out the journal. He closed the box and tossed it over to the doctor. "That's a bit of what the Ward deserves. Use it well."

The doctor opened the box, his eyes going wide

when he saw the money inside. "Hold on, friend!" he called, but Veranix was already gone.

Veranix knew he was hurt, that he shouldn't waste any time, but he was already at the Lower Trenn Ward. He couldn't help but climb up to the fifth floor and look. With a few painful leaps, blood oozing from his shoulder, he was outside the iron-barred window.

There were too many beds, cramped next to each other in the large hall. Even with candles burning throughout, he couldn't see all the way to the other end of the room. It seemed the beds went on forever, full of oblivious, insensible people.

Many of them lay with their eyes open. Some were sitting up, or even moving around. None of them spoke.

His eyes went to his mother's bed. She was sitting up, staring vacantly at the other side of the room. Her hair had recently been cut down to nothing. Veranix forced himself not to be angry about that. She had always kept her hair long, in the Racquin tradition, braided down her back. Wigmakers bought hair from the Ward, especially from these patients, and it helped keep the place running. He still hated seeing it.

What he hated most was seeing her so still. She used to have such grace, her every muscle used to move in such fine-tuned perfection. If any part of her mind was still in there, trapped without voice or words, it must be screaming over the soft lump of nothing her body had become.

He wanted to be able to go inside. To hold his mother's hand and tell her he was there. It didn't matter that she wouldn't be able to speak or even squeeze his hand. She would know he was there, he was certain she would know.

He didn't dare. Colin had made it clear—painfully clear—that Fenmere had eyes on her. Anyone visited her, Fenmere would know. Fenmere had kept her alive almost three years in this state as bait, just to see if there was anyone out there to catch.

For all that time, Veranix had been waiting. He couldn't stand waiting much longer.

Veranix bit his lip to keep from crying. He turned away, not being able to bear seeing her for another moment. Tears pouring down his face, he climbed up to the top of the Ward, and launched himself toward home.

It took the last of his strength to get back to campus. His makeshift bandages had soaked through with blood, and his thoughts were hazy. He was barely able to stand when he reached the back window of the carriage house. He rapped lightly on the window, not for the sake of staying quiet, but because it was all he could manage. The window opened, Kaiana's face full of anger as she hissed at him.

"I can't believe you actually—oh blessed saints!" All her rage melted away as soon as she saw him. Veranix nearly fell over, but she grabbed him, her powerful arms pulling him into her room.

"You should see the other guy," Veranix managed to say. Then everything went dark.

Chapter 10

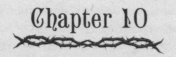

THREE MORNINGS IN a row now, Fenmere had woken up to bad news. This morning it was waiting in his front parlor. He was going to have to dress properly to greet this problem. He rubbed his eyes and pulled himself out of the bed, pointedly ignoring the outstretched hand of his manservant.

"Set the main table and offer breakfast to our guests, Thomias," he told the servant. He went over to the chamber basin and relieved himself. "Have Gerrick and Corman join us at the table as well."

"Very good, sir," said Thomias, who had moved over to the wardrobe.

"Be about that, then," Fenmere said. "I'll dress myself."

"As you say, sir," Thomias said. He gave a small bow and took the basin as he went to the door.

"And Thomias," Fenmere called after him, "serve the Imach coffee instead of tea."

"Of course, sir," Thomias said. He left, shutting the door behind him.

Fenmere growled to himself as he took out a red silk

shirt from the wardrobe. These people needed to be re-
minded who he was, what he could do. Napolic coffee
and Turjin silk would drive it home. He laced up the
shirt, and took out the matching vest, his fingers fum-
bling with frustration as he clasped its gold buttons. He
had to force himself to calm down before he went over
to the mirror to comb any tangles out of his beard. His
hands still shook with rage as he picked up the comb—
pure walrus ivory from Bardinæ—and he could barely
manage to use it.

"Get a hold of yourself," he muttered to his reflec-
tion. "You are Willem Fenmere, and no one messes
with you."

He stared into his own eyes and said it again. He
kept saying it until he believed it.

⌲⌲⌲

Fenmere came down the stairs to his dining room,
where his guests had already begun breakfast. Only
four seats at the end of the long table were being used.
On one side were old Gerrick and Corman. Corman
was a brains and numbers man, but he was also big
and broad shouldered. Fenmere never used Corman as
muscle, but he looked the part.

On the other side were the mages from the Blue
Hand Circle, Fenrich Kalas and Lord Sirath. Kalas
dressed the part of a gentleman, with his dark hair
and mustache groomed a little too neatly. Kalas always gave Fenmere the impression that he was playing a role, deliberately putting on a mask of how he
was expected to behave around "normal" people.
Lord Sirath was an impossibly thin man. Fenmere had
known more than a few wizards, and they were al-

ways skinny, but not like Lord Sirath. His skin looked pale and stretched, almost colorless, and his dark eyes were deep sunken into his head. He didn't look so much like a man as a walking skeleton, save for the bright shock of red hair, which he kept long and unkempt. Unlike Kalas, Lord Sirath never bothered putting on airs of any sort.

Both the mages were eating voraciously, though Kalas was doing it with a sense of manners. Lord Sirath was like a wolf feasting on the deer he had just felled. Gerrick and Corman watched them eat in transfixed horror. Gerrick had pushed his own plate away.

Fenmere steeled his nerves and approached the table.

"Lord Sirath," he said brightly as he approached. "I'm so pleased you could join us this morning."

"Mmm," Sirath grunted. He grabbed the loaf of bread sitting on the table and tore off a hunk with his bare hands. "You fix it?"

"Fix it?" Fenmere asked, sitting at the head of the table. He waved a finger to one of the butlers, who came and poured a hot, steaming cup of the Imach coffee. "By 'it' you mean . . ."

Kalas pointed his fork at Fenmere. "What Lord Sirath means is, have you recovered the items he has paid so handsomely for? And the answer is, no, you have not." Fenmere bottled up his stewing anger. He did not like Kalas's tone. He did not like people pointing anything at him, even forks.

"No, we have not," Fenmere said. He sipped the coffee with deliberate slowness to control his feelings. "Unless there's been developments in the night that I've yet to be informed of, Mister Gerrick?"

"No, sir," Gerrick said. "Not in terms of recovering the stolen goods." Fenmere caught a glance from Gerrick that told him other things did happen last night, and they were not good.

"We have had very good dealings with you in the past, Fenmere," Kalas said. "Thus we counted on you to be able to handle these items with the level of delicacy which they require."

Fenmere smiled pleasantly at his guests. "A snag. A minor one, to be sure."

"A pest!" Lord Sirath rasped. "A thief!"

"That he is, Lord Sirath," Fenmere said. A butler came and brought over his plate. "But we do have certain assurances with this pest, and this merchandise."

"It is not merchandise!" Kalas snapped.

"No, of course not," Fenmere said.

"But our thief will not realize that," Corman said. "Given the unique nature of your . . . goods, he can't possibly understand what he actually has. In all likelihood, he will try and sell the things he stole, and any fence who tries to move the items will inevitably lead back to us."

Kalas scowled. "Presuming he is local to this neighborhood."

"We do have influence outside of Dentonhill," Corman said. "We are pushing our contacts. Everyone knows that no common thief will get away with stealing from Willem Fenmere."

"Common, hmm," Sirath said. He stabbed a fork into the sausage on Gerrick's plate and shoved it into his mouth.

"We will take care of him," Gerrick said cautiously. "We have our own talent for this sort of thing."

"Talent, indeed," Sirath said, while chewing on the sausage.

"Yes," Fenmere said. "Believe me, Lord Sirath, we will look in every bramble for this particular thorn."

Kalas had finished his own meal, and was using a spoon to scrape all possible remnants off the plate. "We are anxious to see the results of your search. We did try searching ourselves, tracking the items by our own means. Unfortuntately, the trail became . . . muddled."

Corman leaned in to Fenmere. "The incident at Saint Polmeta's."

"I'm aware." Fenmere said. "We have taken care of the mess there." Kalas's boys had torn two priests to ribbons, and Fenmere had convinced one of his men at Constabulary to pin it on Francis, who was already too dead to complain.

"Thank you for that," Kalas said. "After everything you have done, we'd hate to decide you were of no use to us."

Fenmere wanted to slap Kalas in his smug, hollow-cheeked face, but that wouldn't do. "I would remind you, Mister Kalas, you came to us for this delivery because you had failed in your own attempts to smuggle it into Maradaine. Multiple attempts. Let alone everything else we do for you."

"Speaking of," Corman said, "our books do show you have been delinquent in payment for our latest delivery of, the . . ." He faltered, as Sirath was staring hard at him, baring his teeth.

"Livestock," Kalas supplied. "Yes, we have been. Which is why we are being so forgiving now, giving you an opportunity to rectify your error. We need them by the evening of the thirteenth."

"What is today, Corman?" Fenmere asked.

"The tenth, sir."

"Three days, then." Fenmere put on his best smile. "I'm sure my people will come through in that time—"

"Find my items!" Sirath hissed. He stood up from the table, grabbing the other half of the bread loaf he had mangled earlier.

"So commands Lord Sirath." Kalas nodded as he stood up.

Gerrick coughed loudly. "I was wondering, Lord Sirath. Where is your estate?"

"What?" Sirath spat out, turning back to Gerrick.

"I was curious," Gerrick said. Sirath fumed, his eyes piercing, but Gerrick held his ground. This was why Fenmere loved Gerrick so much: no one scared him. "As you are a lord, there must be an estate to go with the title. What are your parentage and holdings?"

"Bah! I need no parentage or holdings!" Sirath spat, and the plate sitting in front of Gerrick shattered. Despite being struck by eggs and porcelain, Gerrick did not flinch.

"As you say," Gerrick said. Sirath stalked out toward the main door.

"Three days, Mister Fenmere," Kalas said. "The Circle of the Blue Hand cannot spare any more. Good day to you." He nodded and followed Sirath out.

As soon as the door closed, Fenmere let out the breath he wasn't even aware he was holding. "That went poorly," Fenmere said. "What else is there?"

"The Thorn struck again last night," Corman said. "Mister Nevin is waiting in the back courtyard."

"Nevin?" Fenmere asked. He jogged his memory. "Dealer boss?"

"Yes, sir. Shall we?" Corman got up from the table, leading the way.

Gerrick followed behind, wiping off his coat. "Ridiculous!" he muttered as they went into the kitchen. "You can't just decide on a whim to call yourself 'Lord this' just because you feel like it!"

"That's the part you're angry about?" Corman said.

"I'm angry about a lot of things," Gerrick said, "but that just finishes it. It's pretentious and presumptuous. Why the blazes does he think he's better than us, and why should we take it?"

"The Circle makes a useful ally, Gerrick," Fenmere said. "We'll put up with that. At least until we rectify matters on our end."

"Great wizard or no, if he keeps up that attitude, I'll put a knife in his belly."

"Not today, Gerrick," Fenmere said, hard as stone. He led the way out through the kitchen to the back courtyard, where Nevin waited. Nevin's face was a mess of bruises, one arm in a sling. He managed to look contrite and angry at the same time, holding his cap in his good hand, while his eyes burned.

"Mister Fenmere, sir," he said. "Sorry to say, I let you down."

"You had a run-in with the Thorn," Fenmere said.

"He came to my flop. My boys, it seems, gave me away. I'll attend to that."

"I'm sure you will, Nevin. You get a good look at him?"

"Afraid not, sir," Nevin said. "Gave him a right good scrap, though. Weren't for his fancy rope, I'd have had him."

"Rope?" Fenmere asked. His blood began to boil again. "He was using a rope?"

"Oy, yes. Threw me out the window with it."

"He's using it?" Fenmere said half to himself. "That confirms it. The Thorn is a blasted mage!"

"He is?" Nevin asked. "That explains what my boys said."

"I've underestimated him, then," Fenmere said. He clapped Nevin on his good arm. "You gave him a good fight, though?"

"Best I had, sir," Nevin said. "Wasn't good enough."

"All right," Fenmere said. Nevin was the right sort. Fenmere knew better than to punish him further for just getting beat. "You take care of the squealers you've got, you hear?"

"Trust me. They'll be wishing they were in the river by noon."

"Good man."

"He threw my flat, though, sir. Found my lockbox."

"You lost money?" Fenmere said.

"A few hundred, sir, but that's my problem. I'll round that back up." Fenmere nodded. Nevin cleaned up his own messes, and took responsibility. He wished he had more men like Nevin. "But my book was in there as well."

"The book's in code, though, right?" Gerrick said. "Shouldn't matter."

Fenmere thought it through, stroking his beard. "The Thorn is clever, and we've been underestimating him. He might break the code."

"He does, he'll know when the next *effitte* drop-off is," said Nevin. "That seems to be what he cares about."

"You're sure about that?"

"That's what my boys told me. He was on a tear about keeping *effitte* from crossing Waterpath."

Fenmere paced around the courtyard. "When is the next drop-off for Nevin, Gerrick?"

"Two days from now. Midnight in the park. I can move things around with—"

"No, no. Keep that drop as planned. In fact, put some whispers in the street that it's got to be a big one to make up for the losses. And make sure those reach the Aventil gangs. If the Thorn isn't an Aventil, or at least friendly with them, I'd eat my hat."

"You're thinking bait," Corman said. "How many boys should I round up to jump him?"

"None. That might reach the Aventil gangs as well. No, quiet, and out of our house."

"We're not going to look for him?" Corman asked.

"Of course we are," Fenmere said. "Tear up every blazing rock and house in both neighborhoods. But if we don't find him that way, we need another plan in place. Gerrick, how much do the Three Dogs cost?"

"A thousand crowns," Gerrick said. "Each."

"Send them word," Fenmere said. "We'll need them two nights from now. And tell them there's another thousand bonus for whichever of them kills the Thorn. I want him plucked out."

Veranix gradually awoke, sunlight pushing its way through his closed eyelids. Hushed voices whispered near him. Cautiously, he opened his eyes, unsure of where he might be or how he got there.

The first thing he saw was the red and green uniform of a city constable.

He wasn't exactly sure where he was. It wasn't his room, or anywhere in Almers, but it was definitely somewhere on campus. He was in a bed, in a bright, sunlit room, the walls whitewashed and clean. He was in quite a lot of pain, but his wounds were dressed. The constable was quietly questioning Delmin, who, for his part, looked as nervous as Veranix had ever seen him. Professor Alimen was there as well, and the rough-looking gray-haired man that Veranix knew was Master Jolen, the head groundskeeper. Rellings was in the room as well, pacing back and forth, fuming silently.

"Where . . . what?" Veranix tried to say. His throat was dry, making it almost impossible to speak.

"Mister Calbert," Professor Alimen said warmly. All eyes turned to Veranix. "Glad to see you are back with us."

"Professor, I— " Veranix wasn't sure what to say, or how to read the situation.

"It's all right, Vee," Delmin said quickly. "You're safe now, in the University's hospital ward."

"How did I—"

"I'm Lieutenant Benvin, from the Aventil station-house," the constable said. He had the dripping honey accent of eastern Druthal. Monim, probably. Veranix never cared for the people out east. Or Constabulary, for that matter. "It seems the Napa girl found you on the lawn. Beaten, stabbed, and almost stark naked."

"Naked?" Veranix said.

"I had told them, Vee, about how we went for a doctor in Aventil, and we got separated. And I didn't see you after that."

"He should be expelled!" Rellings shouted from the back of the room.

"Mister Rellings, your opinion has been heard," Professor Alimen said. "We do not expel students for being attacked when off the grounds."

"But he was out of—"

"We have been forced to expel one student, Mister Rellings. I would think that would satisfy your morbid desire for discipline."

"Now," Lieutenant Benvin said, "you do confirm that it was not the Napa girl who attacked you."

Master Jolen growled out, "That girl's a right pain, but she's no thief or rustler."

Lieutenant Benvin frowned at Jolen. "So you say."

"No, no," Veranix said. He gestured to a jug sitting on a nearby table. Delmin ran over and poured a cup of water for him. Veranix drank it down deeply. "She didn't hurt me. Never."

"Very well, then, Mister Calbert," Lieutenant Benvin said. "If you can give me some details of what happened, Mister Calbert. For instance, where were you?"

Veranix was about to tell him Dentonhill. Throwing a bit of additional heat in the neighborhood from the constabs appealed to him. Then he realized that the last thing he needed was any word going around Fenmere's boys that could lead back to him.

"Aventil," he said. "Down by Drum Street."

"See?" Delmin said, "I told you, we got split up in Aventil."

"Thank you, Mister Sarren," Professor Alimen said dismissively.

"Drum and where?" the constable asked.

"Not sure," Veranix said. "Maybe Bear?"

Lieutenant Benvin nodded. "Drum and Bear. Did you get a look at who attacked you?"

"It was a group that jumped me."

"It would have to be a whole group to get the jump on you, Mister Calbert." Professor Alimen grinned amiably.

"All looked the same. Green caps." Veranix added.

"Green caps, eh?" Lieutenant Benvin's face brightend. "That's something." Veranix knew exactly what. Hallaran's Boys wore green caps. The gang was a rival to Colin's Rose Street Princes. Giving them a hard time might even shift the balance of power in Aventil a bit in the Princes' favor.

"Think so," Veranix said. "It's all a blur."

"Seems they were more into beating you than money," Benvin added. "They kept you all night."

"I did put up a bit of a fight," Veranix said.

"And did you get away, or did they let you go?"

"Got away," Veranix said.

"Now, you were a good ten blocks from the campus. Why did you work your way back up here? Why not use a whistlebox and call Constabulary or Yellowshields?"

Veranix was starting to wonder about this constab lieutenant. Most of the whistleboxes in Aventil had been torn up: no door, no whistle. Even if you found a decent one and put out a call, almost no sticks or shields would come.

"I didn't want to draw notice," Veranix said. "Blow the whistle, and I might just bring the green caps back."

"All right." Benvin patted Veranix on his good shoulder. "The saints were watching over you. You are a lucky young man."

"Thank you, sir," Veranix said. The constable nodded to all, put on his cap, and left the ward. Wordlessly, Mister Jolen went out with him.

"Now, Mister Calbert," said Professor Alimen, sitting down on the edge of the cot. "Given that you are expected to make a full recovery, I see no reason to not see you at the next lecture. You missed today's. And you should be fully rested, so there should also be no reason for dozing off."

"As you say, Professor," Veranix said.

"Good," said Professor Alimen. "Very good, indeed. I think we will take it easy on you in the practicals, however."

Rellings was still fuming in the back of the room. "This is unacceptable, Professor! An incident like this should be investigated, and Calbert should have to face an inquiry."

Professor Alimen stood up and turned to Rellings, his face dark and scowling. "Mister Rellings, if anything should be investigated, it should be your own standing as a prefect. Perhaps we should look into why one of your charges was bringing drugs in to your floor of your building, and how you didn't see any problems with him until it was too late to help him! Perhaps if you were more concerned with treating the students under you as peers that you can mentor and guide—the role that a prefect is supposed to fulfill—and less concerned with trying to puff yourself up with the petty degree of authority you have been granted, incidents like this would not occur!" His voice was only a fraction louder at the end, but he spoke with such force that it seemed to knock all the air out of Rellings.

"Yes, Professor," Rellings said, staring at his feet.

"Very well," Professor Alimen said. "Let's leave Mister Calbert to rest, and you will join me in addressing the rest of the students in Almers."

"May I remain with Veranix, sir?" Delmin asked.

"If that's acceptable to Mister Calbert, of course. But do not tax him too much."

"It's fine, sir," Veranix said. "Thank you for your help, sir."

"Of course, Mister Calbert. I will see you tomorrow." He gave Veranix another jovial pat and left the ward room, Rellings in tow. Delmin sat down on the edge of the bed. He said nothing; he just shook his head.

"So," Veranix said after a moment, "are we going the route of awkward silence, then?"

"I just want to know what the blazes you were thinking, Vee," Delmin said.

"I was thinking that I didn't want another drop of that junk coming onto campus!" Veranix said.

"And that's the real reason you've been going out all the time?" Delmin asked.

"Well . . . wait." Veranix sat up. His head started swimming from changing positions. "How much do you know?"

"I know you've been lying to me for years, Vee," Delmin said. He stared hard, his jaw clenched. It suddenly occurred to Veranix this was the most upset he had ever seen Delmin. He was so used to seeing a goofy smile cracked across his face, it was like a different person was in the room with him. "I thought we were friends."

"We are," Veranix said. Not until he said it did he realize how much he meant it.

Delmin shook his head. "How many times have I covered for you, lied for you? I thought you were just having a lark with that girl, and . . . now I don't even know what."

"You've helped me a lot, Del," Veranix said. "I appreciate that, I do . . . but—"

"But what? Give me one good reason why I shouldn't go and tell Professor Alimen what you've been up to. Why shouldn't I let you get expelled? Why have you been lying to me?"

Delmin was fuming, his eyes red.

"Because this was my fight, Del," Veranix said quietly. "I couldn't—I couldn't afford having anyone know the whole truth about me. Who I really am. Where I came from. I . . . I didn't know who I could trust with that."

"Three years, Vee! Three years we've lived in the same room, and for three years I've not once—"

"You're right, Del," Veranix said. "You're absolutely right."

"You're damn right I'm right," Delmin said. "So you're going to tell me the truth now?"

"I am," Veranix said. He managed a weak smile. It felt good just to say that to Delmin. "What exactly happened to bring me here? I remember getting here last night, but I wasn't naked."

"Well, you were when I first saw you," Delmin said.

"So . . . did you see Kaiana? Or talk to her?"

"Kaiana being the dark girl in the carriage house? I saw her, but I've never talked to her," Delmin said. "The groundskeeper sent her away as soon as possible. So, does she know what you do?"

Veranix nodded. "She and I have something in common." With a heavy groan, he pulled himself up and got out of the bed. "You have some clothes for me?"

"You shouldn't be getting up, Vee," Delmin said.

"That's what every muscle is telling me. But I need to go talk to Kai. And I may as well bring you along.

You know enough about what I'm doing, and I need your opinion about something."

Delmin handed Veranix a bundle of clothes. "Here's an opinion. Stop it. You almost got killed last night!"

"I got hurt, Delmin. There's a big difference." He slowly pulled his shirt on and laced up the front.

"Hurt bad," Delmin said.

"It was quite the fight," Veranix said, grinning despite himself. He finished putting on pants and shoes. "No coat?"

"Frankly, when I got your clothes, I wasn't sure if you'd still have the privilege to wear it. If I had told the truth—"

"I know, I know," Veranix said. "I really do appreciate it, Del."

"Right," Delmin said. He shook his head disapprovingly, but smiled for the first time.

"So, I guess Parsons is expelled, then," Veranix said.

"On paper, but it hardly matters. He woke up, but he's . . . he's not there."

"*Effitte*-trance," Veranix said. He felt his blood boil, and gritted his teeth to keep his temper from overtaking him. "An overdose, or a bad dose, destroys the mind. They're taking him to the fifth floor of the Lower Trenn Street Ward, right?"

"That's what Professor Alimen said. You know all about it, I guess."

Veranix took a moment, gathering the strength to walk as well as tell Delmin. "My mother and Kaiana's father are in the same place."

"The same place?" Delmin asked. "I thought your parents were dead."

"My mother isn't dead. She's been up on the fifth floor for almost three years."

"For three . . . sweet blasted saints, Vee! Why didn't you—"

"Come on," Veranix cut him off. He limped out the door. "I'll tell you the rest while we go talk to Kaiana. I've got something I need to show you."

The bright sun was a bit too much for Veranix's eyes as they left the ward building. He held his hands over his face as they started across the lawn. Delmin kept looking at him expectantly as they went on. Veranix finally relented and started talking.

"All right, to start with, I wasn't raised in merchant caravans like I've always said."

"You know, I always thought something wasn't right about that story."

"Really?" asked Veranix. "I thought I had worked it out pretty well."

"That was just it," Delmin said. "Anyone ever asked you a question about your past, you always had an immediate, intricate answer, and it was often repeated word for word. Like you were reciting a script."

"Huh," Veranix said. He didn't realize that. He'd have to work on making his answers more natural.

"So, you grew up on the streets in Aventil."

"No," Veranix said, shaking his head. "I never came to Maradaine until I was fourteen, when I started school here. My father, however, was from the Aventil streets."

"Was? He is dead, right?"

"I'm getting to that," Veranix snapped. "Back then, the Aventil gangs were all united under one family, the Tysons. My father's family."

"All right," Delmin said, nodding. "So what happened?"

They crossed under the shadow of the High University Tower, past the clock bells, and made their way toward the south lawn.

"He made enemies, and started a street war. So he ran out of town, changed his name, and joined a traveling circus. He worked as a trick shot archer, and then met my mother. She and my grandfather were contortionists, acrobats, and tightrope walkers. She . . . you never saw anything like her aerial baton show."

"So you grew up in a carnival?"

"Circus," Veranix said. "Going from town to town, archduchy to archduchy. That's why I came up with the merchant caravan story; it was close enough to the truth. Anyhow, I grew up, learning both archery and acrobatics. And I was using magic, but I didn't really realize it at the time. Not until Professor Alimen saw our show. He convinced me to come here to study, and my parents agreed. I didn't know at the time that my father still had enemies in Maradaine."

"So you came here, and they found him."

"They found him, and tortured him, and killed him." Veranix said, feeling the fire in his blood rising up. "They also captured my mother, and forced *effitte* down her throat until her brain was burned out. The only thing they didn't know was why he had come back to town."

"You," Delmin said. "They don't know you exist?"

"Not as a son of Cal Tyson," Veranix said. "Veranix Calbert is a magic student who grew up in a merchant caravan. No connection at all to the Tyson family or the

Aventil gangs. No one his enemies would notice or care about."

"So then . . ." Delmin stopped, standing in the middle of the lawn. "What are you doing?"

"The one who did this is Willem Fenmere," Veranix said. "He's the crime boss of Dentonhill."

"I've heard the name," Delmin said cautiously. "Big businessman, importer."

"He imports *effitte*," Veranix said. "That's the real core of his enterprise. So I go out there and shut it down. Shut him down."

"How, exactly?" Delmin said.

"How do you think, Del?" Veranix said, getting up close. "I told you, my father taught me archery. My mother and grandfather, acrobatics and the staff. And here I'm learning magic. I'm putting all those skills to good use." He turned away and looked across the lawn. "I think I see Kaiana over there." He started walking again. Delmin caught up.

"How is she involved, exactly?"

"She helps me because she believes in what I'm doing," Veranix said. "Her father was a soldier in the war. When he came back, he got hooked on the *effitte* until he burned out. She only has a job on campus because an old friend of her father's felt sorry for her. We . . . found in each other a mutual hate of Fenmere and *effitte*."

Kaiana was pruning trees along the southern edge of campus when they found her. The rains of the night before had made the day hot and muggy and her straw hat and linen shirt were wet with perspiration. As Veranix and Delmin approached, she dropped down to the grass below, her face angry.

"So you lived," she said.

"Thanks to you, Kai," Veranix said.

"Shut it," she said. She eyed Delmin up and down. "So he's brought you along for protection."

"You want to smack him, I'll hold his arms," Delmin said.

"I'm so glad you two can be friends," Veranix said. "Delmin Sarren, this is Kaiana Nell. Kai, Delmin."

"It's a pleasure to finally be introduced," Delmin said.

"She's been here the entire time you've been a student, Del," Veranix said.

"Well, I know. But students never really talk to grounds staff, except for you, and we all figured you were just, well . . ." He stammered and gestured at Kaiana, his ears turning red.

"Just what?" Kaiana asked. She looked back and forth at the two of them, her eyes narrowing angrily.

Veranix held up his hands defensively. "Honestly, I did deny it. Vehemently."

"Which really only made us believe it more, Vee."

"Are you saying you've thought he's been out at night because he was rolling me?" Kaiana said.

Delmin shrugged sheepishly and looked at the ground as if trying to avoid her hard stare. After a moment, he just said, "Sun's awfully hot right now. Can we find some shade?"

"This is nothing," Kaiana said, squinting up at the sky. "You boys spend too much time in the lecture halls."

"Kai," Veranix said, "I need to know where my things are. Especially that rope and cloak."

"It's always about your things, isn't it?" she asked

him. She stormed over to the carriage house. "I should have damn well brought you over to the ward with everything on you! Let you try and explain it!" She made it halfway to the carriage house before Veranix and Delmin started moving.

"Kaiana!" Veranix jogged after her. He reached her just as she entered the carriage house. As he went in after her, she grabbed him by his shirtfront and pushed him against the wall.

"Tell me you did something," she said. "Tell me you did some damage out there."

"I did," he said. "I burned up a bag, and took a few hundred crowns of drug money."

"Where did that go?"

"The Lower Trenn," he said.

Delmin caught up, his eyes wide. "How many hundred crowns?"

"Quiet!" Kaiana said. She let go of Veranix's shirt. "Did you—"

"I didn't go in," he said. "I was in bad shape at that point."

"Right," she said. She went over to the stables, to the trapdoor to the Spinner Run.

"A few hundred crowns, Vee?" Delmin asked in a quieter voice. "How, what . . . do I even want to know this?"

"When I'm out, if I take money from the sellers, I give it somewhere else. I don't keep it."

"You gave away a few hundred crowns?" Delmin said, his eyes half popping out. "How could you even . . ."

"That money is covered in blood," Veranix said.

"Blood and misery. I give it to the Ward, or the church, or somewhere else where it can do some good."

"Well, then . . ." Delmin stammered. He went over and sat on a small wooden bench, rubbing his head. "I changed my mind, Vee. Go back to lying to me. This is all a bit too much for me."

"Just wait," Veranix said. "Don't break your brain yet."

"Too late." Delmin looked around. "Where did she go?"

"Down into the Spinner Run," Veranix said.

"The what?" Delmin asked.

"It's an abandoned tunnel that runs from the carriage house to Holtman. Near as I can tell, no one's used it for years."

"Abandoned tunnel. Of course, I should have guessed."

Kaiana reemerged from the stall, carrying a bundle of cloth. "I left the weapons down there."

"That's fine," Veranix said. "I really just want Delmin to see the cloak and the rope." She handed the bundle to him. He unwrapped it and took out the cloak.

"What is that?" Delmin asked.

"That's what I was hoping you could figure out," Veranix said. "It seems magical, but I thought that things couldn't be enchanted with their own magic."

"Well, no, that's not entirely true," Delmin said. "It's just the understanding of how to do it is limited, and the risk a mage takes doing it is far greater than any value to making the thing. We don't understand enough about the theory of how it's done—"

"Then what is this?" Veranix asked. He held up the cloak and wrapped it around his arm. With a thought, he made his arm vanish from sight.

"Wow," Delmin said. He looked at Veranix, and the blank spot where his arm should be. "Well, that's not the cloak. That's you."

"Me? Are you sure?"

"I may be worse at practical magic than you, but I'm pretty good with sensing *numina* flow. That came from you. It's just the cloak is more . . . wait a minute." Delmin stared into the space around Veranix for a moment. "The *numina* flow around you is intense. Are you drawing any in right now?"

"No," Veranix said.

"You've both lost me," Kaiana said. She picked up the leather notebook from the bundle and started thumbing through it.

"Well, it's like . . . but that's impossible."

"Like what?"

"Napranium."

"You've mentioned that before, from the lecture the other day."

"Where you fell asleep. Anyway, napranium is supposed to act like this, drawing *numina* to it, and being very receptive to magic affecting it. But it's a metal. And it's really rare."

"Maybe someone can make a cloth, or create a fiber that acts like napranium," Veranix suggested.

"Maybe," Delmin said. He took the rope and looked closely at it. "Or, perhaps . . . Napranium is a very soft metal, too soft to make weapons or armor. However, if someone could hammer it as thin as thread . . ."

"And use it make the cloak and the rope?"

"Theoretically, yes." Delmin frowned. "It would be practically impossible, though. The amount you'd need, and the skill to do it. I don't think it exists in Druthal. The only ones who could possibly do it, who have the mystical knowledge, are the Tsouljans. Or—"

"Poasians," Kaiana said harshly. "Right?"

"Right," Delmin said, looking very confused. Kaiana looked over at Veranix, and everything clicked in his head.

"Of course," he said, looking at the cloak. "Fenmere already had the smuggling operation to bring in *effitte*. If someone wanted to smuggle something else Poasian here, he's the man to use!"

"Now you've lost me," Delmin said. "Can you explain all that? Where exactly did you get these things?"

Veranix sighed and sat down on the bench next to Delmin. "I stole them from the gang boss of Dentonhill. It was a delivery that I thought was going to be *effitte*."

"No, really, where did you get them?"

"Really!"

"He really did," Kaiana said, still looking through the notebook.

"This is the craziest conversation I've ever had," Delmin said, burying his thin face in his hands. "Go back to the Poasian thing."

Kaiana looked up from the notebook. "*Effitte* is made from a plant resin. The plant only grows on a few Napolic islands. Paktphon is one of them."

"This part I know," Delmin said. "Paktphon is a Poasian-controlled Napolic island, which used to be Druth until the end of the war."

"It used to be called Bintral," Kaiana said. "It's where I was born."

"Oh," Delmin said. "I'm sorry. I mean . . ."

"It doesn't matter," Kaiana said. "The point is, the process of making the plant resin into *effitte* is a Poasian one. It's done only on Paktphon."

Veranix nodded and added, "Fenmere, the Denton-hill boss, smuggles it into the city. Has for years. He has his whole network in place to get it from Paktphon to Maradaine."

"Fenmere, right," Delmin said. "That would be the crime boss who you stole these from." His voice jumped up almost to a squeal. He was up from the bench, pacing wildly around the hay-strewn floor.

"I know it's a lot to take in," Veranix said meekly.

"Fine," Delmin said, calming down a little. "You know what, Vee? I'm just going to willfully pretend I don't know about all the elements of this that I don't want to think about. Crime bosses, smuggling, and you being, apparently, the master thief of the University."

"I'm not—" Veranix objected.

"Hush!" Delmin said, holding up a trembling finger. With gritted teeth, he forced each word out with careful deliberateness. "I don't care about that! Instead, I'm just going to focus on this rope and cloak, which I'm only theorizing might be made with napranium, and for the purposes of this discussion, any hypothetical origins of them are only speculation for the purpose of pure scholarly conjecture."

"All right," Veranix said, trying not to crack a smile. "So, theoretically, a Poasian craftsman could get enough napranium, and spin it into thread, and weave that thread into a rope and a cloak."

"Theoretically, I would think so."

"So, these things can draw *numina* to them?"

"Yes, that's what napranium does. But it draws it in a way that magnifies its flow. And the napranium itself is more susceptible to magical influence. Unlike dalmatium, which draws *numina* in and absorbs it."

"That's why I can control the rope," Veranix said. He picked it up, and with a thought, formed it into a rising coil that wrapped around one of the upper beams of the carriage house.

"Right." Delmin's eyes went wide as the rope continued to slide around the beam like a great snake. "You could do that with a regular rope as well, I bet, just it would take a lot more effort on your part. Same with anything you do with the cloak."

"Is that why these things do nothing for me?" Kaiana said, taking the cloak. She held it up, and creased her brow in concentration.

"Right," Delmin said. "You'd have to be a mage to actually use either of these things. To anyone else, they'd just seem to be ordinary things."

"Even a mage wouldn't necessarily see anything," Veranix said, letting the rope come down. "I couldn't see the way the *numina* flows stronger."

"You could feel it, I'm sure," Delmin said. "And if you worked on training your magical senses a bit more . . ."

"Yes, you're very good at that," Veranix said. Delmin took the rope. The moment he touched it, it started to fly wildly around the room, lashing and whipping about. Kaiana dropped to the floor. Veranix dove out of the way of the hurling rope, and then with a blind grab, snatched the wild end. He took control over it immediately. It coiled itself and wound back to him. Delmin let go of his end with a startled cry.

"That . . . you . . ." Delmin stammered. He looked shocked and confused.

"Are you all right?" Veranix asked.

"Yeah, I think." Delmin rubbed his hand. "That was like trying to hold on to a wild animal."

"But it came from you, right?" Kaiana asked, slowly pulling herself up.

"It did," he said, "It was like . . . the change in *numina* flow was too much for me, and it just burst out. If you hadn't . . . I don't think I would have gotten control over it." He looked hard at Veranix. "You really can handle that?"

"Wait a minute," Kaiana said. "So these things, only mages can use them, but just some mages?"

"So it would seem," Veranix said, taking the cloak from her and rolling it and the rope back into a bundle.

"What the blazes is a drugs-and-doxies dog like Fenmere doing with this?" she asked. "Even in a city this big, how many people are there who could actually use these things? How many in all of Druthal?"

"In the whole city, maybe a hundred," Delmin said. "And I would bet my Letters every one of them, save Veranix, is a fully trained member of some mystical Circle."

"Right," Veranix said. "So, that means what? That a Circle is working with Fenmere, hired him to bring these into Maradaine?"

"The question is who are they, and why did they want it?" Delmin said. He creased his brow in thought. "And why a rope and a cloak?"

"That's not the question," Kaiana said. "The question is, since Veranix stole their things, what are they going to do next?"

Wordlessly, Veranix gathered the bundle and went down the hatch into the Spinner Run. He found the niche in the wall where his other gear was hidden and put the things in there. He went back up and closed and covered the door to the Spinner Run. Kaiana and Delmin watched him silently, bewildered.

"All right, Del," Veranix said. "Can you sense any unusual *numina* flow with the things down there?"

Delmin looked around, his eyes staring into an empty middle distance. "No, I don't think so."

"What about in here?" Veranix asked. "I know we studied something about residual *numina* signatures leaving traces . . ."

"Right," Delmin said. "I'm not exactly a bloodhound with this sort of thing, you know."

"Residual what?" Kaiana asked, her face again full of anger. "Veranix, this is where I sleep! If you've—"

"I'm not sure," Delmin said, interrupting her. "There's traces from me, like I did magic in here, but nothing about it seems unusual. In fact . . ." He trailed off, looking around some more.

"In fact what?" Kaiana said. "I need to know if I'm in any danger if someone comes hunting through here."

"I can barely sense any trace from you at all, Veranix. It's like, when you use them, it masks your *numina* signature. Oh, stop that stupid grin." Veranix forced his face to take a more serious expression.

"Wonderful," Kaiana said. "Now both of you get out, I have work to do." She handed the small notebook to Veranix.

"What's that?" Delmin asked.

"Oh, I took this from the strongbox of an *effitte*

dealer," Veranix said. He thumbed through its pages. It was full of notes and tables, but none of it made any sense.

"I didn't want to know that," Delmin said, shaking his head. "All right, Vee, for the purpose of pure intellectual research, I'm going to read up on the different Circles that operate in Maradaine, and see if I can figure out why, hypothetically, one would want a *numina*-enhancing cloak and rope."

"And you should rest," Kaiana said. "I don't want to see you sneaking your gear on tonight."

"Yes, ma'am," Veranix said. He held up the notebook. "I'll just try and figure this out."

"That?" Kaiana said offhandedly. "It's written in one of the old Army codes. My father used to use them all the time. Now go before Master Jolen comes hunting for me."

Veranix smiled as he went to the door, Delmin right behind him. "You're a beautiful person, Kai."

"Oh, shut it. Scat."

Chapter 11

I T WAS WELL into midday when Colin woke in the flop he'd crashed at the night before. The Rose Street Princes had four main flops, and most of the boys and their birds would sleep at whichever one they were close to when they got tired. Colin had spent the night rolling dice with a few loaded marks he had met at the Turnabout, and when he was done, he was far too tired to head back to his usual pad in the basement under Kessing's shop. The flop above Hechie's barber was right next to the Turnabout, and served just fine, even though Colin always found it a bit too crowded for his taste. The Princes were all family, but he never liked trying to sleep right next to one of his mates rolling with his bird. There were always at least a dozen people at the flop over Hechie's, if not more than a score, and about any surface flat enough to lay out on had someone dozing there.

Colin had slept far later than he should have. He grabbed his boots and quietly went over to the door. He was more than a little disgusted at the number of people still sleeping on the floor as he went out to the half-broken wooden staircase in the alley. These boys really should be out doing something useful, pulling in a little scratch. He at least had a pocket full of silver from last night's dice.

He sat down on the top of the stairs and pulled his boots on. The sun had burned off all the rain from the night before, and the day was already bright and oddly warm for this early in the spring. He didn't have a cap with him. All his caps were over at Kessing. He frowned up at the sun as he went down to the street.

Rose Street was quiet for midday. Usually there would be plenty of his boys out there, working the crowd, arranging cart rides, doing what they could to scrape together a few crowns. The few Princes he saw were standing about in front of the Turnabout, doing their best to look inconspicuous. Colin was about to get angry, until he noticed the constabs. At least five of them, in uniform, strolling along Rose Street. Colin had never seen five constabs at once on Rose Street in his life, not even during the Cassada Rumble.

Colin went up to the boys. "Blazes is going on?" he asked.

"Geh," Hetzer said. "Some Uni boy got seriously grabbed and thrashed by somebody. Word is it was Hallaran's Boys, but they say no. So the sticks are out putting on a real good show."

"Oy," Colin said. He fished a coin out of his pocket and gave it to Jutie. "Go get me a striker, would you?" Jutie took the coin and went into the Turnabout. Colin rubbed the stubble on his face as he looked over the rest of the crew. "So, the colors are out, we keep it clean today. No knocking, keep the cart rides honest. Blazes, someone really thrashed a Uni boy?"

"Thrashed hard, I heard," Hetzer said.

"Even still, one Uni boy getting thrashed wouldn't really bring them out like this."

"That ain't all," said Tooser, a tall, skinny bloke whose head was covered in scars. He grinned like a dog expecting a mutton chop. "I heard there was all kinds of noise over in Denton."

"Noise in Denton ain't our noise," Colin said. "Unless it was an Aventil gang that made it."

"Don't know," said Tooser. "Word is, it's the Thorn." He said this with awed reverence.

"The Thorn?" Colin asked. His teeth started to itch. "What do you mean?"

"That's what they're calling that wolf who's been smacking on Fenmere. Thorn in his side."

"I know that, Tooser. So what did he do last night?" Colin asked. He already knew he wasn't going to like this.

"Tore up the Dogs' Teeth, is what he did!" Tooser said, his eyes wide with excitement. "Gave those Denton *effitte* tossers a real smack in the face!"

"Yeah!" Hetzer said. "That's doing it!"

"Ain't right," Colin said.

"Ain't right?" Hetzer got up close to Colin. "The Thorn is driving the nails into Fenmere, which we should be doin'!"

"We can't drive nails into Fenmere, boys," Colin said, pushing Hetzer away. "He's got all the hammers."

"He might have the hammers, but we've got the Thorn!" Hetzer said.

"Thorn told them to keep their junk on their side of Waterpath," Tooser said with a nod.

"He . . . what?" Colin couldn't believe his ears.

"Look, boys, I know this sounds like a real good dustup. It ain't. This is bad news for the Princes, and bad for Aventil. Fenmere gets the idea the Thorn is one of us, he's gonna roll any truce and pound across Waterpath. We'll be the ones under the hammer."

"Why would he do that?" Hetzer asked.

"The Thorn has hit him this hard, he'll do what it takes to dig it out. We've all heard the stories about '94."

"Stories from scared old men," Hetzer said. "What we gonna do, give Fenmere the Thorn?"

Colin swatted Hetzer across the head. Hetzer got his back up, his hand to his knife. Colin hissed at him. "Don't be stupid, Hetz. We can't give him the Thorn. He ain't a Prince, unless one of you ain't telling me something." All the boys shook their heads. "Right, we can't give what we ain't got."

Jutie came out of the Turnabout with the striker. Colin took it from him greedily. Famished, he bit into the crispy bread. The thin sliced lamb and potatoes inside it were hotter than he expected, and he exhaled sharply to keep from burning his tongue.

"All right," he said between bites, "We ain't going to worry about what happens in Dentonhill, unless Fenmere's goons come and give us trouble. It's not a thing until it's a thing, you know?"

"Old Casey and the others won't like that," Tooser said.

"Then Old Casey can talk to me. I've got boots on the stones right now."

"So what's the plan, Col?" Hetzer asked. He sneered at Colin, challenging him. Colin knew Hetzer was itching to make street captain. Hetz had the spirit, but not the head, for it. Colin took another bite and wiped the sauce from the corner of his mouth with his sleeve.

"You want a plan? First, forget about this Thorn business."

"But, cap . . ."

"Another thing," Colin said. "We've given up too much ground at the south gate. Other boys are catching the Uni traffic, getting business should be ours."

"I heard Old Casey said—" Jutie started.

"I don't give a blazes about Old Casey!" Colin snapped. All the boys stepped back a bit. Even one of the constables across the street perked up, glancing over at them. "I'm saying, pass the word to other street caps. Tell them we're taking it back. I wanna know when Uni boys are coming in the neighborhood."

"Rustle them?" Tooser asked.

"When the Uni and the sticks got their eye over here?" Colin asked. "You crazy?"

"We take good care of them, right?" Hetzer said. With a bit of a bitter sneer, he continued, "Nice and friendly, like we always used to. Show them a good time, the right and proper way. And they'll slip scraps of silver for our hospitality."

Colin nodded. "That's the way. Go get about, then," he said. The boys headed off in different ways. He finished the last bites of the striker and went into the Turnabout. He needed a drink now.

"Oh, cousin," he muttered to himself, "why you have to be that stupid?"

Excused from classes, Veranix spent part of the afternoon alternating between trying to decipher the journal's code and reading up on war history to find out more information on those codes. It was little use to him. He had figured out the concept behind the code, but cracking the key of it involved math that was beyond him.

Parsons had been good at math, he could have figured it out. Not anymore.

Veranix grabbed the journal and shoved it into the pocket of his jacket. He jogged across the lawn, making no attempt to hide the fact he was heading to the carriage house. It was only three bells after noon, the sun was still high, and if anyone asked, he was thanking the person who saved his life.

Kaiana was not around when he came into the carriage house. He decided to wait until she came back. After a few minutes of pacing around, he got restless. He stripped off his jacket, shirt, and boots and cleared away a space on the wooden floor. His whole body still ached, and he needed to attend to it.

Gingerly he began going through the series of stretches his grandfather and mother had taught him since before he could walk. He worked his way through the whole cycle and, despite the pain of doing it, it helped with the aches and stiffness. The last step of the series was a handstand, to test the strength of his shoulder. The knife wound had been bad, but he could bear the pain, at least for a minute. He got back on his feet, flexing his arm back and forth.

Taking one of Kaiana's gardening tools as a makeshift staff, he then moved on to the balance exercises, climbing on top of the stable wall. He was up there on one foot, leaning back as far as he could without falling when Kaiana came in, a heavy-looking sack over her shoulder.

She dropped the sack on the ground with a resounding thud. "You know, it doesn't help my reputation to have a shirtless student hanging around in here."

"Maybe I want to ruin your reputation," Veranix joked. He jumped and flipped backward, tossing the hoe in the air as he went. He landed on a handstand, catching the hoe with his feet. His shoulder screamed out, muscles on fire, but he held up. He would not let his arm buckle, no matter how much it hurt.

"Right," Kaiana said, taking off her straw hat and hanging it by the doorway. She started pulling off her gloves and boots, putting them on top of the sack. "You lose me, and I don't know what you'll do."

"I'd figure out something," Veranix said, struggling to hold his position despite the pain in his shoulder. "Maybe someone from the girls' college would like the danger of being my helper." As soon as he said that, he got Kaiana's glove thrown in his face. He toppled over into one of the stalls.

"Helper?" Kaiana asked calmly. "Is that really what you want to call me?"

"Confidante?" Veranix tried, sitting up. He managed to avoid hurting himself further in the fall.

"Better," she said. She grabbed a bucket and went over to the water pump in the corner. "So why are you here? You better not be thinking of hitting the streets tonight."

"No, not at all," Veranix said. He came over to her as she filled up her bucket. "I thought I'd come over here, and devote some time to stretching and practice, you know, so I stay sharp and don't get hurt when I do go out next."

"Right." Kaiana didn't sound convinced.

"And I wanted to spend time with my good friend, who I rarely see outside of running off to the streets, or when she's patching me up from my fights, or . . ."

"Oh, blessed saints, Vee," she said, glancing back at him. "Just say, 'Kaiana, I can't decode the journal. Please help me.'"

"Am I that obvious?" he asked.

"Yes." She took a cloth and soaked it in the bucket. Wiping the dirt off her face and arms she added, "The journal is sitting on top of your jacket over there."

"Can you do it?"

"Maybe." She wiped her hands off on her skirt and picked up the book.

"You're the best," he said. She was already sitting on the ground, nose-deep in the journal. "You know . . ."

"Back up there," she said, pointing to the stable wall. "Practice."

Memory sparked, and Veranix found himself talking with a Racquin accent. "Practice, yes. Always practice. Or fall and die."

She burst out laughing. "What was that?"

"What my grandfather would say." He slipped into the accent again. "Practice and train. Muscle and bone."

"Where was he from?" she asked.

"Kellirac," Veranix said, trying another handstand on the bad arm. It hurt too much. "Though he was a baby when his parents fled from the *yashta*."

"What was the *yashta*?"

"Some kind of civil war in Kellirac." There was more to it, of course, but Grandfather—and every other old Racquin in the circus—was always tight-lipped on the subject. Whatever the *yashta* was, it was too terrible to speak of, even though it was the main reason the Racquin were in Druthal. Veranix had given up asking by the time he was ten.

Kaiana must have sensed that he wasn't going to talk about it, either. "Fine. Practice. Quietly."

Veranix spent the next hour running through his old routines, making a point of doing them without magical aid. Kaiana worked in silence, getting up to light lamps and fetch ink and paper.

"You're putting all your weight on your left arm," she said after a while.

"I took a knife in my right shoulder, Kai." Veranix jumped down to the floor. The wound was throbbing, but he kept himself from showing any signs of pain. Back in the circus days, he had done shows with broken bones. He could hold up through this.

"Still, be aware," she said.

"Thanks for the tip."

"I don't want you getting killed out there," she said. "Practice more." She kept working, scratching figures with focused concentration.

Veranix went down to the Spinner Run, grabbed the cloak, and came back up.

"The blazes are you doing?" she asked when he emerged.

"You said to practice," Veranix said, putting on the cloak. Again he felt the sudden rush of *numina* course through his body. "Let's face it, I've been mostly using this thing on instinct."

Kaiana scowled. "Fair enough."

Veranix focused *numina* back through the cloak, willing himself to disappear. "Can you see me, Kai?"

She looked up at him, her narrow eyes squinting. "Sort of. You're the same color as the wall behind you, so if I didn't know you were there, I might not notice you. But looking for you, knowing you're there, I can make out your shape."

Veranix didn't like that. He kept the image through the cloak, and quickly bounded across the room, doing his best to make each landing as soft and quiet as possible. He ended ten feet away from Kaiana, and right when he hit the ground, he whispered a bit more *numina* into his voice.

"Now?" he asked, the sound of his voice coming from the other side of her.

"Now," she looked up again, in the wrong direction. "Now I can't . . . where did you go?"

"Here," he said, touching her shoulder.

Kaiana grabbed his hand and yanked, pulling his body into her as she brought her knee up. She knocked the breath out of him, and he dropped to the ground, his illusion of camouflage vanishing.

"Sorry about that," she said, though she didn't sound apologetic.

"Blazes, you're strong. You . . . you should come out there with me," he said between gasps.

"No, thank you," she said. "Are you all right?"

"Only my pride is seriously hurt."

"That was a good trick, though."

"Thanks." He thought of something else he might be able to do. As he had the other night in Inemar, he focused the *numina* on changing his appearance. He kept the changes subtle, making his face a little thicker and older, his hair darker. This was a different experience. He had to keep his focus on it, as always, but with the cloak it was more like holding his arm in a pose, instead of holding his breath.

"How do I look?"

"Ordinary," Kaiana said. "Is that what you were going for?"

"Not specifically," he said. "But maybe that's what I was thinking about. Looking like a guy you wouldn't look at twice." With another tweak of the *numina*, he changed the appearance of his clothes from the University uniform to the street clothes of a typical Aventil artisan. Plain and uninteresting. He went to the door.

"What are you doing?"

"I was thinking I might go get some dinner," he said. "It is almost six bells."

"You promised me you weren't going to go out there tonight!"

"I'm not!"

"Veranix, you go out there with that cloak on—"

"Just the cloak, Kai." Veranix put his hands up defensively. "Promise you. No weapons, no rope. No trouble. I just want to find out what's going on out there. All right?"

"Don't start anything."

"Of course not."

"Stay in Aventil."

"Absolutely."

"I mean *nothing*, Veranix Calbert." Her eyes were hot and fierce.

He put one hand over his heart, mimicking the form of the school pledge. "Even if someone tries to sell a whole carafe of *effitte* in front of me."

She cracked a smile. "Blazes, no, if that happens take him down."

"Fair enough," he said. "But it will take that much."

Chapter 12

V ERANIX REALIZED he had never actually been inside the Turnabout before. He had walked past, glanced through the swinging wooden doors, but hadn't dared to step foot in there. It wasn't that University students were forbidden, or even ill-treated if they went in. It was understood, though, that the place belonged to the Princes.

The Turnabout had a certain run-down air to it. Not actually shabby or broken, like the Dogs' Teeth, but a worn, aged feel. Veranix mused that the place might be much the same as it had been when his father had been part of the neighborhood.

The faded wooden menu, hanging up on the wall, with its cracked paint and layer of dust and grease, looked like it had been there since those days as well.

"Eh, brother, you staring or you gonna buy?"

Veranix startled as he was nudged from behind. A couple of guys stood there. Veranix glanced at the tattoos on their arms— these were a couple of Princes.

"Right, yes," he said, backing away. He went up to the barman and ordered a beer and striker. He glanced back at the two Princes. They had taken no further notice of him. A few moments later he had his meal, and was given a look that he should step away from the counter.

Veranix chose a seat in the far corner, kept his head down. He was amazed how easy keeping his magical disguise remained. He made a point of not relaxing, though. He couldn't afford to do that, if for no other reason than so he wouldn't have every eye in the room on him when he suddenly changed appearance.

The place was quite busy, though there was a hushed, subdued feeling to the room. Plenty of Princes kept their eyes on the door, always glancing as if expecting something to happen, someone to walk in at any moment, and prepared to do whatever needed to be done in that moment. From the tattoos, Veranix spotted two captains, but Colin was not there.

Veranix ate quietly, softly coaxing magic to bring snippets of conversation to his ears.

"... went down over to Lilac, it's totally clear, we could make a move ..."

"It's clear because the sticks are cracking on Hallaran's Boys. That ain't gonna last more than a couple days, just to show them not to move on Uni kids ..."

"... heard Fenmere is cracking every skull he can reach, trying to find the Thorn ..."

"... big score like never seen ..."

"... Fenmere had his boys cracking the Red Rabbits ..."

"... he's crossing Waterpath?"

"The Thorn did that ..."

"'Bout time someone did ..."

Suddenly all the talking stopped, all eyes went to the door. An older man walked in, hair thin and white, but he walked with vigor and vitality, his arms strong and muscular. The Prince tattoo he wore showed stars and diamonds. This was one of the basement bosses.

The two street captains approached immediately, deferential. The boss brushed them off and went to a table. As he sat, the dull murmur of conversation started up again.

Veranix kept his attention on the boss, but other than the barman bringing him a plate of strikers and pie, no one came up and spoke to him. The boss ate silently and, while the rest of the room kept their eyes on him, everyone in the room slowly returned to their old business.

After he had eaten, the boss glanced around, and waved over one of the younger Princes. Veranix was ready to pull the sound to his ears when the boss whispered, "Where's Colin? Go find him, bring him here for this." The young Prince ran out the door without question or comment.

Veranix's curiosity over what "this" was didn't wait long to be sated. A few moments later, two more men walked in the door. This time, every sound stopped dead. These two men had no tattoos on their arms. Instead they wore dark green vests and caps.

Hallaran's Boys.

Once Kaiana had cracked the code, the information in the dealer's journal came easily and clearly. It was a detailed look at the daily operations of the *effitte* trade, and she was sickened and fascinated by every bit she read. The raw numbers, the sheer amount of money that went in and out, and into Fenmere's pocket, boggled her.

The crowns Veranix stole from the dealer, that was nothing. Fenmere probably made that ten times over today.

She closed the journal in disgust.

There was a knock on the door of the carriage house.

That wasn't Vee, he never knocked, on the door at least. Master Jolen never knocked either. No one knocked on her door.

"Who's there?"

"It's Delmin Sarren," came the response. She opened the door to find Veranix's skinny, string-haired, grinning friend. He was carrying several books. "Remember, we met earlier today."

"I remember," she said. "What do you want?"

"Is . . . is he here? He wasn't at dinner, and he wasn't in the room, and he wasn't at the library. He's never at the library, of course, but that's where I was and I didn't see him." The boy was fidgeting and looking at the floor.

"He's not," she said. "Get in here before anyone sees you."

He cautiously stepped inside, as if not sure that he was really allowed to come in. She shut the door behind him.

"He went into the neighborhood," she said.

"He's not . . . he's not . . ." Delmin let the question hang there, and he waved his hands around as if to pantomime fighting.

"He better not be," she said. "He didn't take his gear, just the cloak."

"Oh." Delmin looked disappointed, and sat down on one of the benches. "Did he leave the rope?"

"He did," she said. She remembered the incident in the morning. "You don't want to touch it again, do you?"

"No, no," Delmin said quickly. "I just want to see it. Maybe you can tell me, for instance, how much it weighs?"

Kaiana sighed. Magic students. "One click," she said, and went down into the Spinner Run, coming up with the rope. "I'd say it was five pounds."

"Five? And how long is it?"

She uncurled it and laid it straight on the floor. "Huh. Ten feet, give or take. It seems like it would be more."

His eyes went wide. He put the books down and crouched on the ground. He moved over the rope, inches away from it, clearly not daring to actually touch it. "It's really . . . it's fascinating to see the *numinic* flow through and around it."

"You can really see it?" Veranix never talked about this sort of thing, and she was curious to know more.

"In a way," Delmin said. "The theory is that the ability to sense the flow of *numina* is based in the part of the brain connected to the eyes . . ."

"So you interpret that sense visually?"

Delmin's smile grew wider. "Yes, exactly! I don't actually see it, I just think I do." He turned his attention back to the rope, still taking care not to make direct contact. "As far as I can tell, the weave is laced with *napranium*, spun like thread. Fascinating. How much did Veranix say they were paying for this?"

"Forty thousand crowns."

"A bargain," he said. He walked back to his books and thumbed through it. "I've been doing research—or trying, at any rate—all afternoon. Information is . . . rare on the subject."

"Because *napranium* is rare?"

"Yes!" He laughed nervously as soon as he said that. "You know, I try to drill this stuff into Veranix's head, and he never gets it."

"He has a good, thick skull," she said. "Good for getting hit, bad for learning."

"No, he's—he's actually very smart. He just doesn't really get academic discipline. Of course, if he grew up in a traveling circus, that all makes sense. He probably had no formal schooling before coming here."

"That's not a bad thing," Kaiana said icily.

"No, of course not," Delmin said. He shook his head as if dismissing a thought. "I forgot my point. *Napranium!* Very rare. Even just a few ounces laced into a five-pound rope would be . . . incredibly expensive. At least in Druthal."

"But maybe in Poasia it's more common? Or in the Napolic Islands?"

"Which may explain why the Poasians invaded them back in the war. Not potatoes." Delmin picked up a notebook and wrote something with his graphite stylus. "Worthy research topic."

"Did you lose your point again?"

"Yes, I did," he said. He picked up another book. "Information on *napranium* is rare, mostly reference to studies done by Tsouljans, Poasians, occasionally Kierans. Druth mystical studies are quite lacking."

"Do you have a point, Delmin?"

"Yes, I do!" he said. "Or, maybe not. I mean . . . what

I'm trying to say, between the rope and the cloak, that's a lot of *napranium*. Add in the skill and delicate work necessary to take the raw metal and make it into the rope and the cloak . . . it's kind of boggling."

"What's boggling, exactly?" She realized Delmin was far too excited about many different things to be able to hold coherent conversation, and she needed to help him focus.

"Why?" he responded.

"Why what?"

"Why a rope and a cloak? Why not, say, rings, or bracelets, or a crown? What does it give . . . whoever actually wanted these things in the first place . . . what advantages do those forms of *napranium* give them?"

"I don't know," Kaiana said. She hadn't thought about that, and she was certain Veranix hadn't either. He just thought they were useful to him. "Surely not for the same reasons Veranix finds them useful."

Delmin considered that. "Probably not. But for whoever it is, those specific forms were specifically needed, else why go through the trouble?"

Kaiana didn't know, but if it involved people who were wrapped up with Fenmere and his business, it couldn't be good.

"When do you think he'll be back? Curfew bells are in a couple hours."

"He'll probably be back before that," she said. "He promised he'd stay out of trouble."

The Turnabout was looking like it was going to become trouble. Two of Hallaran's Boys, probably captains by the look of them, were in the doorway, and every Rose

Street Prince in the place was on their feet, each with a hand reaching for a weapon. Veranix himself instinctively built up a well of *numina* deep in his gut, ready to burst out if he needed to defend himself.

"Evening, Casey," one of the Boys said. The boss in the back gave a whistle, and most of the rest of the Princes stood down. The two Prince captains stepped up to the Hallaran's Boys, arms wide. The Boys returned the gesture, then slowly reached inside their vests. They both pulled out a few blades and placed them on a table.

The Boss—Veranix figured this must be Old Casey—waved them over. They approached slow and easy. Veranix was still filled up with *numina*; it was starting to buzz at the back of his skull. He knew well enough not to hold onto it in his body too long.

He bled some of it into holding his disguise, some of it into pulling the conversation over to his ears. It took a painful amount of attention, forcing him to bow his head over the table. If anyone had looked over at him, it must have seemed like he was drunk. He barely registered the exchange of posturing pleasantries between Casey and the Boys. He hadn't noticed Colin coming up to the table until his cousin had spoken.

"Beck, Rile, always a pleasure," Colin said as he sat down with the two Boys and Old Casey.

"Good old Colin Tyson," one of them said. "How's your feet?"

"Still running," Colin said. "So what's the noise you're making?"

"We wanna ask you all. You losing the gates or something?"

"Feh," Colin said. "Knights of Saint Julian were trying to make a play, I think. We'll show them to stay on Violet."

"We didn't beat up the Uni kid, but we've got all the crack from the sticks."

"Sticks cracking you ain't our problem, Beck," Casey said.

"Says you," Beck said. "They decide to crack us, then it's all over the neighborhood."

"Sticks did do a real show of force out there today, boss," Colin said. "It'll pass in a day or two. You know that."

"The Uni kid pointed the sticks at us," Rile said. "That's what they say, anyway."

"Probably a setup," Colin said. "You didn't come over here just to mewl like kittens, did you?"

"Shut your face, Tyson."

"Saying this ain't nothing but mewling."

"You want to throw?" Rile was out of his chair.

"I don't throw with kittens."

Old Casey barked out, "Colin! Shut it!"

"Sorry, boss."

"Colin's right, though. You Boys got a point or something? You wanted the parlay."

Rile sat back down. "We can handle the blasted sticks. It's Fenmere's action bleeding across the 'path, that's the real problem."

"That's happening?" Casey looked to Colin.

"Not business or rustle," Colin said. "They're shaking for answers, nothing more."

"Shaking answers?" Casey asked, his voice rising. Veranix winced, his magicking of the conversation made it blast his ears. "That's how any bleed starts."

"They aren't doing a bleed," Colin said.

"You know that?"

"They want a guy," Beck said.

"The guy whose been giving them trouble, what are they calling him?" Casey asked.

"The Thorn," the two Boys said in unison.

"Right," Casey said. He turned to Colin. "So who is this guy?"

"Nobody knows," Colin said. Veranix noticed the twitch in his cousin's eye when he said that.

"Nobody knows," Beck echoed, his voice dripping with hostility. "Nobody knows about a guy called 'the Thorn,' especially on Rose Street."

"He ain't ours!" Colin snapped.

"You sound pretty sure," Rile said.

"He one of yours, Rile? Maybe he's living down on Drum."

Rile chuckled dryly. "Maybe he thrashed the Uni kid."

Colin did not look amused. "Are we going anywhere with all this, or what?"

"We've got trouble," Beck said. He was looking at the door, where a few more green-capped boys were coming in, looking nervous.

Veranix didn't think this looked like a brawl about to explode, at least not from the Hallaran's Boys. The Princes, to the man, were getting on their feet.

"Oy, oy!" one of the Boys said, holding up open hands. "All peace, all peace."

"We should have done this at the church," Colin muttered.

Old Casey shook his head. "New priest in charge over there. Doesn't want to get involved."

Beck was on his feet. "What's the noise?"

"Sticks cracking across the neighborhood." Veranix noticed one of the Boys had a gash across his skull.

"How bad?" Colin asked. More Princes had come to the door. Despite the uneasy looks between all the Princes and Boys, no one moved against the other.

"They're in groups of four, with wagons," said a Prince. "They've been grabbing anyone on the street they see."

"Anyone with a green cap, you mean," said a Boy.

"Not from what I saw."

Voices were rising, Princes and Boys were getting nose to nose, pointing fingers at each other. Beck and Rile were racing over to pull their guys away from the Princes.

Colin swore and looked around the room. Veranix hadn't realized how intently he must have been paying attention to his cousin until Colin was staring hard back at him. "What's your problem, stranger?"

Veranix flushed with panic. His disguise rippled and fell. Colin's eyes went wide and he jumped from his chair. Before anyone else reacted, Veranix focused his magic to disappearing. Colin was on his feet, charging over to Veranix's table.

Veranix ducked and rolled away to a far corner, long gone by the time Colin reached the table.

"Colin, what—" Old Casey snapped.

"There was—there . . ." Colin looked around. "I thought I saw something."

Old Casey walked over to Colin, cuffing him across the head. "What is wrong with you?"

"Nothing, boss," Colin said.

"Get this mess cleaned up." Casey pointed over to

the door. "Next the sticks will come cracking in here, and that's something we don't need."

"Right," Colin said. He went over to the crowd at the door. "Hey, hey! Rile! Beck!"

Colin started bullying the Hallaran's Boys, and Veranix slowly crept across the room, doing his best not to make a sound. He figured he could sneak out to the block's backhouses. The Turnabout, like most of Aventil, hadn't built water closets yet, and from that lot he should be able to cut through a flop or scramble over a wall to the next street over.

Chapter 13

COLIN HAD NO IDEA what Veranix was playing at. Hitting Fenmere in such a loud and public way was stupid enough. Colin knew damn well this story of the jumped Uni boy was Veranix trying to cover his tracks. Blaming Hallaran's Boys for it, that was creative.

And stupid.

Then sneaking into the Turnabout, spying on him. What was he trying to do? Was he trying to prove something? Veranix was getting too clever, too over-confident, too damn magical for his own good.

Saints, what a mess Veranix had made. That was clear just from the fact that Casey was here, in the Turn-about, handling things personally. Colin almost never saw him anywhere but his basement office. He would have only taken such direct action if he had gotten word from Vessrin himself. And, blazes, Vessrin, the "King" of Rose Street, was almost more legend than man at this point. Colin hadn't laid eyes on him since he was a kid.

Colin swore under his breath. Rile and Beck had their Boys under control for the moment, and the Princes, while they all had their backs up, weren't about to move without a nod from Old Casey or one of the captains. Colin knew he wasn't about to give that nod.

"You all best get back to your own flops," Colin told Beck. "Before this burns up."

"Already full of embers," Beck replied. "If I have boys who've been cracked and wagonned, then someone is going to pay for it."

"Who are you going to make pay?" Tooser had stepped up, facing down the Boys. "You gonna crack the sticks back? Or the Uni?"

"Might as well crack Fenmere!" said another Prince.

"Only the Thorn doin' that!" one of the Boys said. Colin couldn't tell if the guy was proud or angry about it.

"What's this about a Thorn?"

A constab lieutenant stood in the doorway, a pack of sticks backing him up.

"What's it to you, stick?" Beck asked.

"Anything you barrel of rats do is my business," the lieutenant said, eyeing the whole room. He wasn't from this neighborhood. Didn't even sound like he was from Maradaine. If Colin had to guess, he was from an eastern archduchy.

"You the new left in the neighborhood?" Colin didn't know this particular stick, but he had seen the type before, who looked at everyone on the street as the same. Rose Street Princes or Hallaran's Boys, Toothless Dogs or Red Rabbits, Waterpath Orphans or any other Aventil gang, this guy couldn't care less. Street cleaner. Every few months a new one of them came to the neighborhood, usually from the north side of the city, thinking they were going to be the one to change things.

They never lasted that long. This lieutenant would be no different.

"That's right," the lieutenant said, tapping his brass badge. "Lieutenant Benvin."

"Hear you all are rounding up the wagon, left," Colin told him.

"Been some trouble down here, boy," the lieutenant said. "We need to make sure you all aren't causing any more."

"Who's causing trouble?" Colin asked. "We're all having a few beers, enjoying our evening. That a crime, left?"

"Depends on how you enjoy." Lieutenant Benvin walked over to Colin and grabbed him by the lapels of his coat. He opened up the coat and pulled out one of Colin's knives. "What's this?"

"That there is my right, left. Ain't I a free Druth Man?"

"Right now you are. You think that lets you carry this?"

Colin grinned, baring his teeth. "It is the right of every free Druth Man to have arms and carry them on his person to protect himself from those who would impose false authority on his honest life." Colin may not be a Uni boy, but he knew that part of the Rights of Man like the ink on his arms.

"And this is your honest life?" the lieutenant asked with a scoff.

"I think maybe you and your sticks should be on your way," Colin said.

"Don't think you can tell me what I should do, boy."

"Make a push, then, left, see how long that lasts you."

Rile and Beck stood at his shoulder. The other Princes and Boys took their places as well. The two gangs would as soon tear each others throats out as look at each other, but against the sticks they would let that all drop.

The sticks behind Lieutenant Benvin all moved away from the door. The lieutenant didn't flinch.

"You got a charge on any of us?" Beck asked.

The lieutenant pointed to Beck and the rest of the Hallaran's Boys. "Why don't you take yours and go back to your own flops now?"

"We were just about to do that, left." Beck whistled to his Boys, and they all filed out of the Turnabout. The sticks all scrambled out of their way.

"We still have a problem?" Colin asked.

"We'll see," the lieutenant said. "It'll be nine bells soon. Let's make sure all yours are off the streets before curfew."

"What are we, Uni brats? There's no curfew in the streets."

"Let's pretend there is," the lieutenant said.

"This won't roll, left," Colin said.

"We'll see, cap." The lieutenant gave quick salute to Colin, cocksure and mocking, and walked out of the club.

"Back to it all, boys," Old Casey told the various Princes. Everyone slowly went back to their tables. Casey waved Colin over.

"The blazes was that all about?" he asked when Colin sat down.

"New left in Aventil, using this Uni brat thing as an excuse to try and crack us all."

Old Casey shook his head and took a long pull off his beer. "Uni brat brings in the sticks, the Thorn brings in Fenmere, and we're squeezed in the middle."

"That's life on Rose Street, ain't it?" Colin forced himself to laugh, to show Old Casey it was nothing to worry about. Of course Casey was worried, he was here, in the Turnabout, dealing with this, instead of farming it out to one of the minor bosses like Hotchins. As far as street level Princes were concerned, Casey was as high up as things got.

"What's the word over at Waterpath?"

"Ain't no word, not that I hear," Colin said. "The Rabbits and the Orphans are getting pressed, and they're taking it."

"Do we have to make Waterpath our problem?"

"I really don't think this is a bleed, boss."

"And why do you think that?" Old Casey asked. His eyes narrowed. "You, of all the young ones on Rose Street, should know what happens when we don't pay mind to the signs. You've got a name to earn, Colin. It was your father—"

"Don't you get into it with my father, Casey!" Colin knew damn well what Casey was trying to do, trying to put his back up. It would work, if Colin let him.

Colin knew damn well that Aventil shattered and Fenmere got them all under his boot because of his father. He knew his own captaincy was earned despite his Tyson name, not because of it.

Every basement boss in the Princes knew they could rattle his hat by mentioning his father. His father the failure, who had done one thing right: protect his brother by sending him out of town when things were going bad. Everyone loved Colin's uncle. Even folks from Hallaran's Boys or the Waterpath Orphans would bow their head at the mention of Cal Tyson.

He was tempted to tell Old Casey everything—who the Thorn was, what he was doing, and let the bosses of Aventil do what they would with that. Blazes, if they knew he was Cal Tyson's son, they'd throw him on their shoulders and parade him around town.

He bit his tongue. Veranix was screwing everything up, but that didn't change the promises he'd made. He had promised his father that he would be there for Uncle Cal if he ever returned. He had promised his uncle that he would keep Veranix safe. He had sworn those things in blood, sworn them to Rose Street.

"What do we got to do?"

"We need to cool the air, that's what we got to do. You were playing the streets legit today, right? Keeping the sticks from finding fault?"

"Damn right," Colin said.

"Smart. We've got to do something to blow the heat from Fenmere, then."

"That heat will blow over on its own, boss."

"You really think so?"

Colin thought for a moment. Casey wasn't going to let it drop easy, and he couldn't look like he was sticking up too much for the Thorn.

"Yeah," Colin said. "Let's ride this heat a little longer, and if it gets any hotter, we'll do something to blow it off."

"Like what?"

"I don't know yet, boss!" Colin got up from the table. "That'll depend on the heat."

"Colin—"

"Trust me, boss. I've got it."

Casey's beer was empty, and he signaled over to Kint the barman for another. "You say you got, you got it. But if I hear of more noise, I want to know you've done something, all right?"

Colin sighed and nodded. "If we need to do something, boss, I'll make sure it's taken care of."

"Good man."

"I better go check on the boys out in the streets. What with the sticks cracking down and all."

Old Casey waved Colin off. Experience had showed Colin not to bother staying in Casey's sight once the wave was given.

Hetzer was waiting outside. "Some mess out here tonight, huh, cap?"

"Some mess, all right," Colin said. "Where's Jutie and Tooser?"

"Hustling outside of the R&B. Should we go round them up?"

"Sticks are looking for an excuse right now," Colin said. "Best not give them one."

"At least let them use their excuses on the green caps, huh?"

"Sure," Colin said, and led Hetzer down Rose Street.

✖✖✖✖✖✖✖

Veranix scrambled out of the backhouse alley into the street, focusing his magic on blending into the surroundings. He didn't think anyone noticed him.

He could hear a lot of commotion around the corner, in front of the Turnabout. The Hallaran's Boys were clearing out one way, constables heading off the other. Looked like no blood was spilled, everything cooled down. Veranix was curious to find out exactly what happened, but he knew at this point, trying to satisfy that curiosity would only get him in deeper with Colin.

Colin was definitely mad at him.

Veranix scoffed. Colin would just have to get over it.

Someone walking past him looked around, confused. Veranix realized he was still shrouded, and his scoff must have sounded like it came out of nowhere. He slunk into the shadows and willed his appearance back to the ordinary looking man he was using earlier.

It was getting late, the curfew bells on campus would be ringing soon. The last thing he needed was for Rellings to have another excuse to dig into him.

He had only taken a few steps toward the University gate when he heard a scream. It had come from a few blocks up Rose Street. Possibly as far as Waterpath.

"Stop it! Stop it! Help!"

He turned and ran up Rose Street.

It was a woman's voice, a shout of terror. Veranix had gone charging toward her, and was past Bush and nearly to Waterpath before he realized he was unarmed.

He stopped his run, his heart pounding. He wasn't unarmed, of course, not really. Not ever. Especially not with the cloak on.

That would put him at risk. He'd definitely draw notice using magic. He shouldn't be drawing notice. He promised Kaiana he wouldn't get into trouble.

"Get your hands off of me!"

That was all he needed to hear.

There was already a crowd gathering at the intersection of Rose and Waterpath. Several gentlemen, well dressed for the neighborhood, were outside the general store on the corner, blocking the entrance. A woman, heavy-set with streaks of gray and a simple dress, was at the forefront of the crowd, trying to get into the store. Veranix wasn't sure, but he thought she was the wife of the proprietor.

She made another attempt for the door, only to have the men push her back at the crowd. The people caught her gently, but none of them made any further attempt to help her.

"Just stay over there, missus," said one of the thuggish gentlemen.

"Get off my door!" she shouted.

"We're just having a word with your husband," he said, crossing his powerful arms in front of him. "Won't take a click."

"Where do you think you're hassling?" The shout pierced through the crowd. The people split open, allowing two Princes to come forward. One of them took the woman gently by the shoulders while the other moved up to the gentlemen at the door.

"Step off, boys," he told the man in front.

Princes getting involved. Good. Everything should be sorted without him having to step up. No getting noticed.

"You all step off, Prince." The gentleman scowled and leaned in aggressively. "There's only two of you."

"This is Rose Street, friend," the Prince said. "There's never just two of us."

"And that's Waterpath," said the gentleman, pointing across the street. "Want to guess what's right over there?" These were Fenmere's men, then.

"You really want to do this?" The Prince's voice rose to a shout. "You're gonna cross to hassle a shopman?"

"We've just got some questions."

"You got questions, you ask us."

The gentleman stepped forward, poking the Prince in the chest with a single finger. "When we've got questions for you, we'll ask them."

The Prince snarled and grabbed the finger, twisting it hard. The gentleman winced but didn't give any further ground. His hand shot out to the Prince's throat. The Prince pulled a blade and sliced the man's arm.

The whole crowd went up like kindling, screaming and crying out, as the two Princes leaped at the gentlemen with knives and fists.

Veranix was about to jump in when Colin and another Prince came charging up.

"Rose Street!" Colin's companion called out, and they dove into the fray.

More men came out of the building from the other side of Waterpath. This was turning into a full-on rumble, and Colin and his Princes were about to be outnumbered.

To blazes with getting noticed.

Veranix drew in as much *numina* as he could, and used it to jump over the crowd and place himself between the rumble and the new group of Fenmere's men, at the same time changing his appearance into his usual outfit for going into the streets, including a hood over his face.

Fenmere's gang all stopped in their tracks. "That's him!"

"This is all for me?" Veranix asked. "I'm so flattered!"

Despite being in the midst of grappling with each other, the Princes and Fenmere's men in front of the shop all stopped fighting and stared at him.

"It's the Thorn!"

"It's really him!"

"Get him, then!" one of Fenmere's men shouted.

The group in front of Veranix all charged at him. He channeled more magic into his feet, jumping over them, sending another blast at their backs. Not strong enough to hurt them, just knock them to the ground.

"Yeah!" shouted a Prince, who took advantage of his sparring partner's attention being on Veranix. His knife found its mark in the man's back.

Veranix grabbed one of the men lying on the street and gave him a magic-enhanced toss back into the building he came from. Even with the cloak, that took more out of him than he expected. He was still getting used to just how much the cloak augmented his own abilities.

"Waterpath is your line!" Veranix shouted at the Fenmere's men. "You don't cross it. Not tonight, not ever!"

A cheer came up from the crowd.

Colin couldn't believe it. They were cheering for him.

This was too damn much. Colin needed to end this mess right now.

His boys had made short work of the thugs outside the store. Fenmere's goons were far too reliant on fear in their neighborhood. When it came to a real scrap, they rarely held their own.

Colin grabbed one of them, senseless from his beatings, and threw him down on the street with the others Veranix had knocked down.

"Get out of here," he shouted. He pointed at Veranix, standing far too confidently over the group of Fenmere's thugs. "You want him, there he is!"

Despite the hood over his face, Colin could tell Veranix was surprised. It was only a moment, but it was clear.

Veranix quickly recovered, though, giving a quick laugh. "Of course, they have to catch me!" He saluted the Missus Gemmen, who had gotten into the door of her shop. Fenmere's thugs had cleared out of there, and her husband was at the door, bruised but well. Then Veranix jumped up, far higher than any man could naturally jump, and was shortly on the roof of the tenement on the other side of Waterpath. "Have a good night!"

Then Veranix—"the Thorn"—was gone.

Bells clanged from down Rose Street. Of course the sticks would show up now.

"Scatter!" Colin snapped at his boys. They took off in every direction, and he did the same, running down an alley that would take him over to the Uni gates.

He scrambled up a backstair in the alley, climbing up over the top of a window frame and pulling himself up over to the top of the roof. This wasn't his scene, he had never been much of a roofman or eave runner, but he could do it when he needed to. From up there, he was able to look back at Rose Street. People had scattered good, Princes and Fenmere's goons alike, as well as the neighborhood folks. The sticks had no one to hassle besides the Gemmens, who wisely argued with the sticks from inside their own doors. He could see the new constab lieutenant looking around the intersection, clearly annoyed at not getting anyone to throw in the wagon. His own problem.

Colin turned around and went along the top of the building until he was at the Lily Street side, facing the Uni.

A vague shape came flying out of the night, landing with a soft thump a few feet from him. Colin had his knife out and was going at it, before it cleared into the form of Veranix in his school uniform. Colin was already swinging, and only had the chance to drop the knife and pull the punch slightly, knocking his cousin in the chest.

It felt good to do that.

"I deserved that, I suppose," Veranix said.

"You think so?" Colin hissed.

"Yes, I do," Veranix said. "I didn't mean to get involved in anything tonight. Things just . . . happened."

"You didn't mean to?" Colin asked. He couldn't believe it. "You are involved, cousin. That mess down there, every bit of mess in Aventil tonight, that is all about you. The trouble you are starting."

"I didn't start it!"

"No?" Colin slapped Veranix across the face, who did nothing to stop him. "Hitting Fenmere's dock shipments? Going after his dealers and bosses? What did you think would happen?"

"I thought I'd be hurting him!"

"You hurt him, he makes trouble here. You get it? And I bet you were the Uni kid who got beat up last night by, what, Hallaran's Boys?"

"I—I needed to tell the constable something! I woke up in the ward with him already hovering over me!"

"And that was just brilliant!" Colin was boiling now, unable to hold it in. "Because when it comes to protecting Uni brats, the sticks really know to only hassle one gang over here. Like they really care which of us did it. Of course, none of us did it, so the Boys are fuming over someone setting them up!"

"I know, I know," Veranix said.

"Right, because now you're sneaking in the Turnabout, I saw. Are you that stupid?"

"I was just—"

"Just what? What was that, some magic trick? Make yourself look different? That's not a place for you!"

"It's a free city."

Colin pulled up his sleeve. "That is a place for people who know what's on their arm. People who know what they stand for. People who know who has their back. People who give their own." He grabbed Veranix's arm, pulling up the sleeve. "What's on your arm, cousin? What do you stand for?"

"You know I can't—"

"I know nothing about you," Colin said. He shook his head. Time to lay it all out. "Do you really understand what happened here, with our fathers? My father started trouble, and when the heat of it came, he told his little brother to run. So your father ran, to keep Fenmere from going after him. People here *loved* your father."

"So did I." Veranix said.

"So did I! And so did my father. Long after the mess, my father was a broken man, and he made me swear, swear to Rose Street that I would do anything for yours if he came back. And just about every Prince out there would do the same."

"I know that!" Veranix's voice cracked. He was still such a boy.

"Then you should know the one thing your father wanted was that *you* stayed safe, out of this mess. You aren't part of this." He drove his fingers into Veranix's chest. "Get out of Aventil, Uni brat."

Up until this point, Veranix had maintained a hint of a smirk on his face, a sign that underneath their fighting, everything was actually fine, he would apologize, and things would be as they had been.

That smirk melted away, and Veranix's gaze dropped to his feet. He said nothing, didn't move, for what felt like an impossibly long time. Colin wasn't about to give any ground, give Veranix another word. He just wanted him to go.

The silence was broken by the peals from Saint Julian's. It was nine bells.

Veranix glanced back in the direction of the church, a flash of fear and concern washing over his face. He gave a last look at Colin and leaped off the roof, changing again into a vague shadow, a hazy outline of a man gliding down across the street and over the Uni wall.

Colin's legs buckled from under him, and he dropped down, almost slipping off the edge of the roof. He sat, stewing in rage and grief. His street. His own cousin had brought Fenmere's heat right to his street.

He had known for years, from the moment Veranix first told him he would go after Fenmere, that the heat would burn him back. He should have put a stop to things before they started.

This was the end. If Veranix wanted to cause more trouble, he would take the heat on his own.

Colin had half a mind to let Fenmere know exactly who the Thorn really was. Not just pointing him at the student on the Uni campus, but letting him know exactly who that boy was: the son of Cal Tyson.

Colin stopped himself, barely aware that he had already gotten to his feet to take action. He couldn't go that far. Writing off Veranix was one thing, but he couldn't actively betray him.

If he did that, he wouldn't be worthy of the ink on his arm.

Colin shimmied down a drainpipe to the alley floor.

The streets had gone quiet; word of the sticks' informal curfew had gotten out. Colin didn't like it, but he figured it wouldn't last for more than a few nights. Things like that never did. Sticks and their heat really were the least of his worries.

He decided it would be best to play the night cautious, though, and pulled down his jacket sleeves. Shoulders up, head down, he went out into the street, walking at a brisk pace to the flop under the barbershop. Hopefully the rest of his boys made it back there safely.

Chapter 14

V ERANIX LANDED ON the soft grass, just a short
space from the carriage house. His magical shrouding, even in the red glow of the nearly full blood moon,
left him unnoticed. At least, he didn't hear a cry from
any of the cadets, and he had to presume that the sight
of some unknown thing soaring over the walls into
campus would have gathered some attention.

He had gone too far, and had lost Colin. Had it been
helping against Fenmere's goons, or sneaking into the
Turnabout? Or setting the constabulary on the neighborhood?

Or had it been simply that Colin had only been in-
dulging him as long as he didn't cause real trouble? He
had never wanted Veranix to really go after Fenmere,
really break the man. Colin was comfortable with how
things were, and he had wanted Veranix to be comfortable with it too.

That wasn't going to happen, not as long as Fenmere
was alive.

Veranix slipped into the carriage house. Kaiana was

reading under a dim oil lamp, Nevin's journal lying casually at her feet. She looked up at his entrance, eyes darting nervously.

He realized he was still shrouded, and dropped the disguise. Kai startled, and then relaxed.

"You missed curfew bells."

"I know," he said. "I'm going to hold on to the cloak to get back into the dorms."

"Fine by me," she said. "Delmin came in, wanting to see the rope."

"You let him?" Veranix wasn't sure how he felt about that. He trusted Delmin, but he remembered his friend losing control the moment he had touched the rope.

"I didn't let him touch it!" Kai laughed. "He just looked at it. He did ask an interesting question, though."

"What's that?"

"Why a rope and a cloak?"

"What do you mean?"

"Delmin seemed to think they were crafted with a very specific purpose in mind."

Veranix hadn't thought of that. "Did he have any idea what?"

Kai shook her head. "You've got to get out of here, you know."

"Yeah, I know. Any luck with the decoding?"

She held up a scrap of paper for him to see. "This is the code key. You'll be able to work out the rest of the journal with it."

"You didn't decode it?" he asked.

She scowled at him. "I figured out the key, Veranix. That was a lot of work."

"I know," he said defensively. "I appreciate it."

"Good," she said. "Anyway, you now have the tools to figure it out, but it's up to you to do it. I am tired. Unlike you, I need my sleep."

"I need mine, too," Veranix said.

"Then go and get it," she said. She started going around the carriage house, blowing out lamps. Veranix tucked the paper in the journal.

"Kaiana, really. Thanks for . . . for everything you do," he said falteringly. He was about to tell her about what happened out in the neighborhood, what happened with Colin.

"Are you going to cry or something?" she asked mockingly. She blew out another lamp.

"Oh, shut it," he said. The moment was broken, he didn't want to get into it now. "A bloke tries to say how he feels."

"And he feels like crying," she said, laughing. "Get gone, already."

"Aye, miss," he said, shrouding himself again. "I'd hate to further hurt your virtuous reputation." He slipped out the door before she said anything back and dashed across the lawn.

Colin reached the flop without incident. Jutie, Hetzer, and Tooser were already waiting, sitting on the floor playing cards around a few lamps. They all got on their feet when Colin came in.

"Cap, we thought you got pinched," Jutie said.

Hetzer snorted. "I never thought that."

Tooser came up and closed and latched the door. "Crazy night, huh, boss?"

"Complete mess, is what it was." He dropped down on the floor. "We got anything to eat in here?"

"There's some ham and cheese in the larder," Jutie said.

"Go get it." He pulled off his boots and tossed them over by the door. "Sticks causing trouble, Hallaran's Boys and the other gangs. And Fenmere had his goons hassling in Gemmen's store!"

"That ain't right," said Hetzer.

"Damn blazes that ain't right."

"Good thing the Thorn straightened them out."

Colin got on his stocking feet and smacked Hetzer. "Is that what you think happened out there?"

"Blazes, yes!" Hetzer's eyes flashed with anger. "We would have gotten creamed if he hadn't have shown!"

"They only were there because they wanted him!" Colin shouted. "We're only getting heat from Fenmere because of him!"

"At least he's out there doing something to Fenmere!"

Colin threw up his arms in frustration. Hetzer was a good bloke, but he could never see the bigger picture. That was why a guy like him would never make captain.

"You think it's trouble?" Tooser asked.

"I think Old Casey told me to keep an eye on this Thorn business," Colin said. "We got a real problem with what happened out there."

"What's that?" Jutie asked. He brought over a plate with the cheese and some ham. Colin cut off a slab of the meat and gnawed into it before continuing.

"Let's think, boys. Just for a moment, actually think things through to their logical ends."

"We ain't stupid, cap!" Hetzer snapped.

"I know, boys. So, Fenmere's thugs come across Waterpath, and shake some shopkeepers about the Thorn. A few Rose Street Princes come and defend their turf. They scuffle, and who shows up and takes sides with the Princes?"

"The Thorn."

"When news of that hits Fenmere, what conclusion do you think he's going to draw, Hetz? What would you think?"

"That the Thorn is working with us," Hetzer said.

"Or he's one of us," Jutie added.

"Exactly," Colin said. He had a few more bites of cheese. It was getting hard and sour. "Anything to drink in here?"

"Jug of cider I bought this morning," Tooser said.

"Bring it here," Colin said. Tooser poured out a cup, and Colin washed out the taste of the cheese from his mouth. "If Fenmere's men are already crossing and hassling just because they want to ask some questions, you can bet your arm that they'll bring a hard boot down on us if they think we have the Thorn."

"Bring the hard boot," Hetzer said. "We've been living like we ought to be afraid of it too damn long."

"That what you want, Hetz? You want to tell Old Casey and the other men in the basements that? You remember the last guy who said, 'Bring the hard boot'? What was his name?"

Hetzer met Colin's eyes, blazing with anger and fierce pride. "Den Tyson, captain. And he was right!"

Colin looked away from Hetzer's intense gaze. "My

father broke the neighborhood standing up to Fenmere. I'm not going to be the guy who breaks it again. And I'm not going to let the Thorn do it either."

Jutie stepped up, putting himself between Hetzer and Colin. "All right, cap. What do you want to do about it?"

"Jutie, drum up some paperboys. Hetz, Tooser, you go down to Harkie the printer and put some squeeze on him. Do it decent, though, tell him it's a legit job with silver for him."

"You're gonna throw down silver on this?" Hetzer asked.

"Tonight the line at Waterpath was cracked. We want to keep the line held, it's worth the silver," Colin growled. "Rest of you, roust up anybody who can be wallpainters."

"We're gonna paper and paint?" Tooser asked. "What we gonna say?"

"Something that says that Rose Street rejects the Thorn. He ain't one of ours, and we don't want him."

"Bit much, you think?" Tooser said.

"You can do it," Colin said. Tooser wasn't that smart, but he was clever when it came to a paper and paint job. He could always come up with a picture that sent the message. "Spread word to the other gangs in Aventil, they'd be wise to do the same."

"That's what you want," Hetzer said crossly, "pass some silver." Colin handed him a few coins.

"Get out there and do it. I need some sleep."

Delmin had dug through every book with references to napranium that he had been allowed to carry out of the library, starting with the dry *Compendium of Mystical Materials* to the obscure *Tsouljan Secrets of Magic* to the bizarre *Brenium's Northern Travels*. That last one made Delmin swear to himself that he would never go to Waisholm or Bardinæ. He had been so engrossed that he hadn't noticed the curfew bells had rung and Veranix had yet to arrive.

He didn't realize that until Rellings threw open the door. "Curfew has passed. Where is Calbert?"

"I—I'm not sure," Delmin stammered out. "I haven't, er, that is, I don't know . . ."

"What don't you know?" Rellings casually looked around the room, moving the blanket on Veranix's bed, gently pushing a paper or two aside on Veranix's desk.

"I haven't seen him."

"Since when?"

"Since this morning!"

"This morning? In the hospital ward?"

"Maybe he went back there," Delmin offered. "Blazes, if I had gotten hurt like that I wouldn't have left."

Rellings raised an eyebrow. "You think I didn't consider that, Sarren? You think I didn't have someone run over to the ward and check if one of the students under my charge was lying up in there?" He crossed over to Delmin's desk. Delmin was shorter and skinnier than Rellings, and sitting down he was dwarfed by the prefect.

Delmin gulped loudly. "And he isn't there?"

"No, he isn't there."

Delmin sprang to his feet, in no small part to get out from under the prefect's towering gaze. "Maybe, then, he's succumbed to his injuries somewhere!"

"What?"

"Yes!" Delmin said, he realized with a bit too much enthusiasm. "Hurt like that, surely his strength would have given out on him. He might have been unable to get all the way up to the third floor, Rellings. Did you think of that?"

"No," Rellings said. He puzzled on that for a moment. "I really hadn't."

"That's very insensitive of you," Delmin said, moving out of the room into the common area. He kept talking, his mouth acting almost of its own accord. "I mean, someone in Veranix's condition is in serious need of assistance, and are you looking to help him? It doesn't seem that way."

"That's not fair, Sarren." Rellings stalked after him. "It's exactly because of what happened to him last night that I'm—"

"What, Rellings?" Delmin asked. "Looking for a chance to bust him down?" He could feel beads of sweat forming on his brow. He didn't even know what he was saying to Rellings, he just kept talking, hoping vainly that Veranix would show up any moment and end the whole ridiculous thing.

"I'm responsible for—"

"I know what you're responsible for, Rellings. You are responsible for all of us in here. Like Parsons."

The veins on Rellings's forehead bulged, and he ground his teeth, making his next words almost unintelligible. "What happened to Parsons—"

Delmin quickly threw up his hands defensively. "Might have been inevitable. But because of that, Veranix went out looking for a doctor, and because of that, he ended up in the hospital ward, and maybe now because of that, he might be lying somewhere in need of help!"

Delmin was amazed at how convincing he made that speech sound, since he could see Veranix just outside the window of their room.

Chapter 15

V ERANIX WAS ABOUT to magically pop the iron
  grate off the window of his dorm room when he noticed the door was open, and he could see into the hallway. And people in the hallway could see into the room.

Fortunately, the only person apparently looking into
his room was Delmin. Unfortunately, Delmin was
talking to Rellings.

Very briefly, his eyes locked with Delmin's. It wasn't
much, but it was enough to let him know that he could
be in a lot of trouble.

He swung around on the thin ledge, getting out of the
line of sight, and shrouded himself again, in case anyone
on the ground was looking up. The only people who
would be were prefects or cadets, and neither one would
be good for him right now.

He had never tried magicking sound to his ears
through glass. He imagined it was going to be harder.
He slowly reached over to the window and touched this
glass gently with a couple fingers. He pulled in a trace
of *numina*, and eased it through those fingers into the
room.

The glass cracked.

Blazes.

He pulled his hand away, and prayed to whichever saint might listen that the sound of the glass hadn't been loud enough to get Rellings's attention.

One thing was clear to Veranix. He couldn't possibly sneak into his own room and act as if he had been there since before curfew bells rang.

Focusing on maintaining the shroud, he moved along the ledge, slowly and carefully. What were his choices at this point? The water closet had a window, that could work. So did the water closets on the second and fourth floors. Then he wouldn't have as much risk running into a prefect who was eager to bust him down.

He climbed up the wall, finding the little fingerholds in the brick. Simple enough, even with his shoulder screaming in pain. He reached the ledge of the next story and pulled himself up onto it.

Now he had to find the water closet.

The safest presumption was that it was directly above the one on his floor. He had a vague memory of Parsons or Eittle or some other Sciences student saying something about pipes needing to be aligned together or something like that. That made sense, didn't it?

The window he presumed was the water closet had a few lamps burning in it, and peering in, he confirmed it was the water closet. It also had two first-year students washing up and talking about whatever stupid thing first-years talk about when they were washing up. Veranix sighed. Maybe he should have gone to the second-floor.

They were still talking.

He decided to save a little time and magicked the metal grate off. Those two kishes wouldn't notice anything outside the window.

Veranix stopped himself. He had actually just thought of them as "kishes". This night was really getting to him. He didn't need any further aggravation.

Their conversation died down, and Veranix heard the sound of the door open and close. Without wasting any more time, he magicked the lock on the window and threw it open and dove into the room.

There was still one first-year in the room.

Veranix had kept his shrouding on, so for all the poor kid knew, the window just flew open of its own accord and a vague, shimmering shape leaped at him. Any sensible person would scream or faint.

The boy had the good sense to scream and faint.

Several pounding footsteps came charging to the door.

This was not going well at all.

Before the door opened, Veranix threw another blast of soft magic around the room, blowing out all the lamps. When half the fourth floor came charging into the water closet, it was completely dark.

"The blazes is happening in here?"

"Did Cackly just scream?"

"Scream like a little girl."

"Get a damn lamp in here!"

A few lamps came in from the hallway, and the collected boys of the fourth floor found young Cackley sprawled out on the ground, wet with his own mess.

Veranix had magicked his appearance to an average, ordinary looking student, wearing his bedclothes. No one that anyone else would really look twice at.

"I don't need to see anything else," he said to the group, who didn't make any note of him other than to let him slip out through them into the hallway.

"What's going on?"

Veranix found himself face to face with the fourth-floor prefect.

"Cackly screamed and passed out, sir," Veranix said. "Don't know why."

"The window's open!" someone called from the water closet.

"Great, another thing." The prefect didn't really look at Veranix, or anyone else for that matter. "Listen, chaps, apparently someone is missing from the third floor."

"Third floor is all trouble!" shouted someone.

"Right, and rather than presume that one of them has—again—snuck out into the night, Rellings has the idea that something might actually be wrong. So he wants to search the building."

"Looking for volunteers?" Veranix asked. This was a complete mess, but if he was clever enough he could at least take control over something. It was his only chance to get in bed and get one night of decent sleep.

"Yes, thanks, um . . . Henson." The prefect looked confused but waved Veranix on. "Go on down to third and ask what you can do."

Veranix's mind raced while he went to the stairwell. They were already searching for him, and he needed to find out why they were searching for him. They thought something was wrong. What might that be? He needed to know, and decided it was wiser to maintain his disguise rather than just stroll in and act normal. With some luck he could find a place to hide on the third floor, and act like he'd been there all along.

He came out of the stairwell on the third floor, and the common room had several people milling about in their bedclothes, annoyed looks on their faces. It was nearly ten bells at this point, most of them were probably wanting to be in bed by now. Delmin and Rellings stood at the center of the group.

"Now, we know for certain that Calbert isn't on the third floor," Rellings was saying. That eliminated trying to hide somewhere here.

Delmin added to that, talking just a bit louder than he probably needed to. "Remember, though, wherever he is, it's very possible that he is hurt and unable to respond. This will take more than just calling out for him."

Delmin couldn't know that Veranix was in the room, but it was possible he was trying to get a message out there. Delmin had seen him outside the window, Veranix was pretty certain. Perhaps this whole search was a desperate ploy on Delmin's part to buy time.

Veranix was finding that he might owe Delmin several times over before too long.

"You come from the fourth floor?" Rellings was talking to Veranix.

"Yes," Veranix said, lowering his voice a little. "He's not there."

"Then we search downward. All the way to the basements."

Basements. Perfect.

"We should get on it, then," Delmin said.

Veranix went back into the stairwell before anyone

else could get out there. He quickly shrouded his appearance and leaped down the stairs as fast as he could.

Right before he hit the landing, he drew in another burst of magic to mute the sound of his feet on the stone. He did it again: leap, draw, mute. Twice more and he was on the ground floor.

He could hear the search party coming into the stairwell above him. They were moving slowly, methodically. Calling out his name. That gave him both time to get in position and noise to cover it. Muting his footsteps had taken more out of him than he expected.

This particular staircase went down to the basement, where hardly anyone ever went, especially after curfew. There wasn't even a door to the outside in this stairwell, so hardly anyone on the ground floor ever used it.

That would work just fine for his purposes.

The search party above him was going onto the second floor, and probably waking people up calling out for him. Of course, there would be no legitimate reason for him to be hiding on the second floor, but if Delmin was buying him time by organizing an Almers-wide game of Find the Cat, he was more than happy to play along.

He scrambled down the stairs, dropping all magical disguises. He then realized that wasn't going to work very well, since then he would be wearing the cloak, and surely someone might ask a question or two about it.

A breath of magic later, he appeared to be just wearing his uniform, though said uniform was dirty and wrinkled. For an additional hint of showmanship he gave himself a bruise on the side of his head. He briefly considered blood, and then decided that would be that step too far. That would require maintaining illusional blood for an indefinite period of time.

He blew out the lamps at the bottom of the stairs, giving him a fair cover of darkness, and then lay on the landing, twisting his body into an uncomfortable angle, head pressed to the ground.

Now just to wait for discovery.

Several minutes passed. Veranix considered several times the merits of emerging from his position, crafting a story of barely being able to pull his injured body up the stairs. Each time he considered the only advantage of this method was allowing him the comfort of getting out of the basement stairwell. The disadvantages involved in not being discovered by the search party were too great. There was nothing to do but wait it out.

His stomach growled.

Those guys better find him soon.

There were footsteps above him, voices calling out his name. They were pretty close. Close enough to give them some help.

Veranix let out a low moan.

"You hear that?"

"I didn't hear anything."

Veranix stifled the urge to shout at them. Another moan.

"That was definitely something."

"If you say so."

Veranix didn't know whose voice that was, but he was going to make sure that whoever it was would have some kind of magical unpleasantness happen to him in the near future.

"Hello?" Veranix croaked out. His throat was drier than he thought it would be, which meant he didn't have to force much performance. If this went on much longer, he wasn't going to be faking being weak and woozy. He might even pass out.

"That was something," said the first voice.

"Is anyone there?" the second voice called out.

"Help!" Veranix returned. It wasn't very loud, but it didn't need to be. The two students came down the stairwell, one of them carrying a lamp.

"Blazes, it's Calbert!"

"What happened to him?"

Veranix allowed himself to be picked up, faking being too weak to stand on his own. "I was . . . I slipped at the top of the stairs . . ." He took a good look at his two rescuers. He recognized them, at least in the sense that he knew they lived on the third floor, but he couldn't remember their names.

"Blazes, he fell down all those?"

"Lucky he didn't break his neck."

"Come on, Calbert," said the first one, pulling Veranix's arm around his shoulder. "Let's get you upstairs."

The other one took Veranix's other side. "Everyone's looking for you. How long were you down here?"

"What—what time is it?"

"Bit past ten bells, I think."

"Ten bells!" Veranix exclaimed, followed by a feigned dry cough. "It was . . . it wasn't even eight bells when I was coming up the stairs."

"You're lucky, Calbert," the first one said. "If Rellings hadn't turned out the doors to find you, you could have been there all night."

"Should we take him up, or to the hospital ward?"

"I—I don't think I'm—let's try and get to the third floor, all right, mates?"

"If that's what you want." His hand patted Veranix's back. "Something wrong with your coat?" He was probably feeling the cloak through the illusion. Thank every saint these two weren't magic students. Of course, of the hundred or so magic students on campus, only a handful lived in Almers. Odds were in his favor.

"Hey, we found him!" They shouted up the stairs, and several people came out in the staircase, including Delmin and Rellings.

"Blazes, Veranix," Delmin said. "What happened?"

"I fell down those stairs," Veranix said, laboring his breathing as much as he felt he could without it sounding false. "I was coming up and I guess I was pushing myself too hard."

"You probably were," Delmin said, his eyes narrowing. "You did wake up in the hospital ward this morning."

"I guess I wasn't as healed as I thought."

"I would think so," Delmin said.

"All right, all right," Rellings said. "You don't need to henpeck him like you were his mother, Sarren."

"That's Rellings's job!" someone called from up the stairs.

"Enough!" Rellings snapped. He came over to Veranix, looking at the bruise Veranix had magicked across his forehead. "Cracked yourself good there, Calbert."

"Probably looks worse than it is," Veranix said.

Rellings eyebrow went up, and he glanced at the two who found Veranix. "You found him at the bottom of the stairs?"

"We were lucky we found him," the first guy said.

"They told me I have you to thank for the search party, Rellings," Veranix said.

"Well, now that's all over. You good to get up there, Calbert, or do you need to go to the hospital ward?"

"Let's try and get upstairs," Veranix said. "I don't think there's anything wrong with me that won't be cured with a decent night's sleep."

Rellings took over supporting Veranix from the other two, leading him up the stairs. "Show's over, everyone. Man found, everything's fine. Lights out by the end of the hour."

Allowing Rellings to help him, but doing his best to keep the cloak situated in a way that Rellings wouldn't touch it, Veranix got to his room. Delmin came right behind them. After a last bit of questioning, which Veranix felt lay somewhere between well-meaning concern and interrogation, Rellings left them both to go to bed.

Delmin waited a few seconds after the door closed to drop his facade.

"What the blazes happened to you tonight?"

"Lost track of time," Veranix shrugged, hoping that would satisfy Delmin. The look on his friend's face confirmed that wasn't about to happen. "I went out into Aventil. Not to cause trouble, just to get a sense of what was happening in the city. And to get a better sense on how to use this." Veranix dropped all magical pretenses, the cloak appearing, his uniform cleaning, and his bruises vanishing. Delmin's eyes went wide.

"You . . . you were able to maintain that degree of magical illusion with the cloak on?"

"Pretty amazing, huh?"

"That's . . . that's beyond amazing, Vee."

"It's powerful, I admit," Veranix said, taking off the cloak. "I was able to—"

This was all he said before he dropped the cloak on

the bed, and the second he let go of it, he felt all of his strength leave his body. He collapsed to the ground, and would have cracked his head open for real if Delmin hadn't been there to catch him.

"Blazes, Vee, what was that?"

Veranix gasped for breath. He wasn't expecting anything like that. He could barely keep his eyes open, keep himself from drifting off into a gray haze. Delmin put him on the floor and went over to his desk.

"I thought something like this might happen," Delmin muttered as he went into the bottom drawer. "Good thing I'm ready for an emergency." He came back over to Veranix with an apple and dried lamb.

"I—I—" was all Veranix could say. Delmin forced the food into Veranix's mouth.

"Keep eating, I'll be right back," Delmin said. He grabbed a pitcher from the bed table and left the room.

Slowly, Veranix chewed and swallowed. Small bits of strength returned to him, and with that he moved his hand back toward the cloak. If he could get his hand back on it, he might be able to—

Delmin returned, and as soon as he saw what Veranix was doing, he rushed over and swatted his hand away. "No, Vee, don't do that. Not yet." He offered Veranix some water from the pitcher.

"What . . . what is happening?"

"Something I thought might happen," Delmin said. "You've got to be careful when you use that thing, Vee."

"Careful how?" Veranix was able to sit up again.

"As in, when you're wearing that, you have no sense of how you're really using your own *numina*. It all feels like a rush, doesn't it?"

"Yeah, but I'm able to control the rush," Veranix said. "It's not like . . . it's not like *effitte* or something, if that's what you're driving at."

"No, not like that!" Delmin said. He laughed a little. "You just have to learn how to be aware of how you are drawing *numina* out of your own body when you have that thing on. You had depleted your own strength, and had no idea because of that thing feeding you *numina*."

"So what you're saying is, just because I have that on, I shouldn't push myself much further than I would without it."

"Else when you take it off, you fall on your face."

Veranix pulled himself up onto his bed. With a quick swipe of his hand, he knocked the cloak onto the floor, and then kicked it under the bed. Even that brief contact gave him a surge of *numina*, which then faded as quickly.

"I'm making a mess out of everything, aren't I?"

"Probably," Delmin said. "At least your marks are still decent, though I don't know how you manage that without studying."

"That's really what I should be doing, isn't it?" Veranix asked. Saying that opened a floodgate, a rush of anger and remorse that he was too exhausted to hold back. His voice broke with sobs as he went on. "I mean, my father had a safe, happy life in the circus, and because I needed to come here—begged to come here, Delmin—he came back to the one blazing place in Druthal that wasn't safe for him. The least I could do is make sure I learn something."

Three days. That was all they were going to stay in Maradaine. Get Veranix delivered to the college, do two shows out on the east side, far away from these neighborhoods, and leave. Despite that, Fenmere still found his father and killed him. Then destroyed his mother for good measure.

Delmin watched Veranix quietly. "So what did you learn tonight?"

"Trouble is brewing out in the streets," Veranix said. "And it might be my fault."

"Might be?"

"All right, it is my fault. At least, between hitting on Fenmere's dealers and sending the constables onto the Aventil gangs . . . not everyone out there is happy with me."

"But do they know that you are . . . you?"

"That depends on just how angry Colin is."

"Who is Colin?"

"Colin is my cousin, and he's one of the Rose Street Princes."

"You . . . you have a cousin in the street gangs?"

"Do you want to know all about that as well?"

Delmin sighed. "No, I don't. I want to get some sleep." He pointed a stern finger at Veranix. "I want you to as well."

"Excellent idea." Veranix could get on his feet again. He still felt weak as a kitten, but he was able to strip off his school uniform. "Kai told me you went to see her."

"She did?" Delmin's voice cracked. "She mentioned me?"

"You're wondering why a rope and a cloak?"

"It does seem, you know, specific."

Veranix shrugged. "Perhaps so. Perhaps they're just the simplest things to do with the *napranium*."

"What do you mean?"

"Well, you mentioned before that it's soft. Too soft for weapons or armor, right?"

"Right."

"So, maybe it's as simple as that. You can't make armor from *napranium*, but you can make a cloak. You can't make a sword, but you can make a rope."

Delmin scratched at the fuzz on his chin. "Might be just that. Can't shake the feeling there's something I'm missing."

Veranix shrugged. "Let's sleep on it, and maybe we'll think of something else."

Chapter 16

SUNRISE CAME TO Fenmere's home without incident. He rose from his bed and threw on his robe, cautiously waiting for the first bit of bad news to come rushing at him. Thomias wasn't already knocking, so there wasn't any major news.

Fenmere sighed. He had actually hoped there would be some good news. That, perhaps, they wouldn't bother waking him for. He went down to the dining room.

Tea and bread were already laid out on the table, as well as morning presses. As Fenmere sat down, Gerrick came in from the back and joined him.

"Morning, Willem," he said with a nod of his head. "Sleep well?"

"Somewhat," Fenmere said after a sip of tea. "Any news this morning?"

"Relatively quiet night," Gerrick said, pouring his own cup.

"No action from the Thorn?"

"Didn't say that," Gerrick said. "Though it was . . . different."

Fenmere was intrigued. Gerrick wasn't usually one for drawing out something for drama.

"Not a hit on the dealers or dens?"

"Not at all," Gerrick said. "Some of our men had gotten a little . . . overzealous in their questioning of some shop owners on Waterpath."

"On the Aventil side?" Fenmere asked.

"That was an aspect of their zeal, yes."

Fenmere nodded. It was best that his men didn't kick up any dust in Aventil, but it was good to remind the gangs over there that they didn't scare him.

"Did they draw any heat?"

"A scuffle with some Rose Street Princes."

"So what about the Thorn?"

"The Thorn, apparently, showed up in the scuffle and sided with the Princes."

Fenmere scratched at his beard. "Where was this scuffle? Waterpath and Rose?" Gerrick nodded. "So you think the Thorn is a Prince?"

"Possibly," Gerrick said. "From the reports our men gave, the Princes were just as surprised by his appearance. Then constabulary broke it up."

"Really?" Fenmere asked. Thomias came in with a plate of eggs and fruit and put it front of Fenmere. "I'm surprised they even bothered."

"There's a new lieutenant in charge of the neighborhood, and it appears that the Hallaran's Boys are getting more aggressive with University—"

"Yes, yes," Fenmere said, taking a bit of eggs. "We don't need to worry about that, other than it keeps the Aventil gangs distracted and divided."

Gerrick pulled a few papers out of his coat. "The Princes, and the rest of Aventil gangs, are united on one thing. They all worked through the night to disavow the Thorn." He placed the papers in front of Fenmere. All of them slips from paperjobs, all variations on the same theme.

"These are all over Aventil?"

"Mostly on Waterpath," Gerrick said slyly. "For what it's worth, they're practically falling over themselves to let you know that they do not ally themselves with him."

Fenmere liked that, a smile pulling at his mouth. "They're afraid of what I'll do to them. Good."

"Of course, sir, we aren't any closer to retrieving the two items that the Blue Hand ordered."

Fenmere shrugged. "That's important, of course. We don't want to be seen as men who don't fulfill their bargains."

"But?" Gerrick asked.

"But if they don't get their merchandise in time to do whatever magical, mystical thing they want to do, frankly, I couldn't care less."

Gerrick frowned. "It took a lot of work to form the bond we have with the Blue Hand Circle. I'm not happy with them, but what they can give us still exceeds the usual mage for hire."

Fenmere scowled. Gerrick was right. "Especially if this Thorn is a mage. Are we set for the Three Dogs at the drop tonight?"

"Everything is arranged, sir," Gerrick said. "That is, of course, presuming he'll show."

"He'll show. I've got a hunch that, when you boil everything down, what he's about is coming after me and the *effitte* trade. He's not with an Aventil gang, I can tell you that."

"You're sure, sir?"

Fenmere nodded. "Look at what he's doing, Gerrick. He's drawing heat to Aventil, and he clearly doesn't care what that does. Aventil gangs are a pain in the neck, but if there's one thing they have in common, they're all fiercely loyal to protecting the little patches of nothing they all have. This Thorn, he's a different sort than them."

"If you say so, sir," Gerrick said.

"I'm well rested today, Gerrick. A good night's sleep clears the mind wonderfully."

Veranix had slept fitfully, plagued with dreams of Colin telling him to get out of Aventil, his mother lying immobile on the ground, Nevin smashing his head against the wall. In the morning Delmin told him that if he had bothered studying, he'd know that intense nightmares tended to accompany the exhaustion of overdraining *numina*.

Morning breakfast was filled with gossip and drama, as people talked about Veranix being found in the basement, and how some kid on the fourth floor swore he saw an *ashaya* in the water closet. Many people came up to Veranix and Delmin and asked them if *ashayas* were real or just old Waish legends. Delmin fell back on his usual answer of "There's no proof, but there's plenty of anecdotal evidence." Veranix thought that was a polite way of saying it was a stupid old legend.

Veranix couldn't skip any of his classes today. He had been given more than enough latitude the day before, and he couldn't push any further without causing trouble to his academics. That didn't stop him from taking the journal with him to his classes to break its secrets.

The process of decoding the journal was painstaking and time-consuming, converting strings of numbers into letters. Veranix felt it was worth it; the intelligence he was getting about Fenmere's *effitte* operation was priceless. He learned about drop points, names of runners and sellers. Even if Nevin got his throat slit for failing, the basics of the operation wouldn't change, not that much.

Morning Magic Theory class gave him very little opportunity to work on decoding. Professor Alimen was on a tear about the *numinic* conductivity of gemstones and other minerals. Veranix tried to take a few notes, while focusing properly on the journal, figuring Delmin's memory trick about singing robins could get him through any exam. But then Alimen started writing numbers on the slateboard and doing mathematics. Not just sums and differences, but real, intense mathematics. With symbols Veranix didn't even recognize. Everyone else was copying notes and asking questions—Delmin was fearfully engaged—and a deep panic set in Veranix's stomach. This was going to be on end of term exams, and he didn't understand it in the slightest. Veranix shoved the journal into his coat pocket and started copying everything on the slateboard into his own notebook.

"Did you understand that?" he asked Delmin as they left the lecture hall.

"For the most part," Delmin said. "Though there were some equations I'm going to have to practice with."

"Equations?" Veranix asked. "Am I going to have to memorize those or something?"

"Probably," Delmin said. He must have seen the panic on Veranix's face, as he patted him on the shoulder. "Hey, you'll pass the exams. I'll get you through it."

"Thanks," Veranix said. Though between taking that exam and another brawl with Nevin, Veranix would rather take the fight. There he'd have a chance. If he learned more from Nevin's journal, he might get the chance. "I'm going to skip lunch."

"Not even," Delmin said, grabbing Veranix by the lapel of his coat. "I don't think you understand the kind of damage you've been doing to yourself. You can't skip any meals."

"But—"

"No!" Delmin pulled Veranix toward Holtman. Lowering his voice, he added, "I swear, if you worked on studying half as much as you've put into that journal, you'd have full honors."

Veranix ate as fast as he could, and despite Delmin's disapproving looks, went back to working on the journal. He reached a portion regarding the *effitte* delivery drops. Dates, times, and places. This he had to get decoded.

"You're not skipping history," Delmin said.

"I'll come," Veranix said. "But I may need to borrow your notes afterward."

Delmin all but pulled Veranix to the afternoon history lecture, where he pretended to take notes on the reign of Cedidore II, a king mostly known for his utter insanity, while decoding the journal. Professor Besker droned on about Quarantine and the Druthal Wall. Veranix remembered the circus performed next to the Druthal Wall, as going along the Sauriyal Canal was part of their usual travel circuit. The wall was nothing, a decayed pile of stone.

He realized he was transcribing notes about a drop that was going to happen. He looked back at what he had written out to confirm. The drop was tonight at one bell after midnight, for one thousand crowns' worth of *effitte*.

"One thousand?" he whispered in surprise.

"One thousand what?" asked the student next to him. He looked down at his own notes in panic, as if he had missed a key point.

"Nothing," Veranix said. "I just . . . nothing. Never mind."

"Shh," Delmin whispered. He gestured to Professor Besker, who had paused briefly to note the disturbance Veranix had caused. Veranix smiled and gave a show of attention.

"Opiska was freed, though mostly out of convenience," Professor Besker went on. "The final piece finally broken off the shattered kingdom. Cedidore II willfully completed the work that Shalcer began out of incompetence."

Veranix scowled. It was a huge drop. He couldn't figure out how much *effitte* that would actually mean, and then back to the street value of it. Hundreds upon hundreds of doses. Hundreds of people who wouldn't get their brains melted. Hundreds of lives saved.

Nevin was still alive, though, and he must know Veranix had the journal. He'd cancel the drop, for sure. Or be ready for Veranix. It'd be a huge risk.

But if he didn't cancel the drop, and Veranix stopped it, it'd be one thousand crowns out of Fenmere's pocket.

That was reason enough to risk going out there.

He just needed to know where "out there" was, exactly. Last part to decode.

Veranix went through, checking each letter carefully. O-s-c-a-n-a-p-a-r-k. Oscana Park. Made sense. North side of Dentonhill, relatively close to the docks, and far from any prying eyes that mattered. On the off chance Constabulary did catch someone, it was public property. Nothing to tie to Fenmere.

Oscana Park was a big place, though. More letters. S-t-a-t-u-e-o-f. Statue of someone. The park was full of statues. N-i-y-o-l-c-d-w-s. Niyolcdws? That didn't make any sense. Veranix checked through the last letters again. N-i-y-o-l-c-a-r-m.

"Niyol Carm." Veranix said upon completion.

"What did you say, Mister Calbert?" Professor Besker's full attention was on Veranix. As was the rest of the class. Besker tapped his walking stick impatiently while glaring up at Veranix.

Veranix's mind went completely blank. No suitable lie came to him. So he just told the truth. "I . . . uh, I said Niyol Carm."

"Niyol Carm?" Besker's eyebrow went up. "Is there a reason you are a full seven and a half centuries behind the rest of us?"

"It was . . . just something that crossed my mind."

"Yes, well join us in the part of history that we are studying today. The year we are on is 765. What is the era we are discussing, Mister Calbert?"

"The, um, Centuries of Darkness and Light?"

"An answer I find far too poetic for my taste, Mister Calbert. It would be correct if you were taking a Literature course, but sadly, you are not. We are in the Shattered Kingdom, Mister Calbert, specifically the Possession Wars. And in 765, who is the king of Druthal?"

Veranix had been paying enough attention to answer that. "That would be Cedidore II."

The whole class gasped. "Is he right?" Besker asked, looking around, hobbling over to some other student in the front row.

The student's lip quivered as he answered, "No, Professor."

"No, he isn't," Besker said, slamming his walking stick on the poor student's desk. "Cedidore II is the king of Druthalia Proper. And there is no kingdom of Druthal in 765, nor a king of Druthal. That's why the era is called the Shattered Kingdom, Mister Calbert. Name the various countries that stood in place of the Kingdom of Druthal."

All eyes were on Veranix again. He dug through his brain to find something geographic. The only thing that came to mind was the full circuit of the circus, starting from the south of Druthal. "Scaloi, Yinara, Linjar, Kesta, Monim, Oblune . . ." The look on Professor Besker's face was encouraging. "Acora, Patyma, Maradaine, Sauriya."

Professor Besker shook his head. "Congratulations, Mister Calbert. You have just named the current archduchies. Mister Sarren, perhaps you might have better luck."

Delmin gave an apologetic glance at Veranix. "Druthalia Proper, Free Opsika, Scaloi, Yinara, Linjar, Kesta, Monim, Oblune, Patyma, Acoria, Brellin, and the city-state of Monitel."

Professor Besker gave an impressed nod to Delmin.

"Including Monitel was a nice touch. I'll make a merit mark in your record. To balance out the demerit mark in Mister Calbert's. To continue, Cedidore II put his five brothers in charge of the military in the different regions of Druthalia Proper, and these brothers all become key figures in untangling the royal lineages that follow for the next century."

Veranix closed up the journal and gave his full attention to the lecture. He didn't need to figure any more out, not now. His leg bouncing, fingers tapping, he did his best to learn about King Cedidore II, the Shattered Kingdom, and whatever else he needed to know to pass exams. He didn't need his marks dropping any further.

Veranix did not sprint across the lawn to the south gate, as much as he wanted to. He had to know what else was going on tonight. He knew Colin wouldn't want him to go out, but that was too bad. This was too sweet a cherry not to eat.

He passed the gate and immediately found a street rat in his face.

"What's your pleasure, Uni?" he asked. "What can we do for you?"

"Not in—" Veranix started, about to brush the guy aside. Then he saw, this rat had his shirtsleeves rolled up, his Rose Street tattoo in full display. The Princes were at the gate. That was a good sign. Perhaps things had cooled since last night, and the Princes could push back and reclaim this block. Veranix coughed and began again. "Not anything much. I was thinking Rose & Bush."

"Fine choice, my friend," the Prince said, all oil and charm. "Let's make sure you get there proper, right?"

"Proper?" Veranix asked.

"Oy, there's been trouble," the Prince said with a nod, waving at Veranix to walk with him. They headed over to Rose Street. The action on the street was subdued, hardly anyone hawking from the curb. The Prince smiled and waved at one shopkeeper, who waved back tentatively. "That's how it goes, you know. You probably heard one of yours was knocked and hassled out here."

"I think I heard something about it," Veranix said.

"That ain't good for no one. We like the Uni boys, they do good business. Isn't that right, Mister Ressitor?" He shouted this question out to a man sweeping at the doorway to bakery.

"Very much so," Mister Ressitor said. "You need a cake, Hetzer? You got a sweetheart who wants a cake?"

"Girl I want don't want a cake from me," Hetzer said. "Uni boy, you need a cake?"

"Not today I don't," Veranix said. He couldn't help but smile. "When I do, though . . ."

"I will make you the best cake."

"He sure will," Hetzer said. "I'll see you later, Mister Ressitor."

"Yes, of course," Ressitor said. They walked on. As they approached the intersection of Rose Street, Veranix noticed many loose papers on the ground, strewn about and stamped on, all around the neighborhood.

"He's a good man," Hetzer said. "Good cakes, really."

"Someone do a paper job?" Veranix asked. He bit his tongue as soon as the words came out.

"That's good, Uni," Hetzer said, cackling. "That's right."

"I've heard it said." He picked up one of the pages.

"You got good ears on you, I'll give you that," Hetzer snapped the paper out of Veranix's hand before he could look at it. "Ain't nothing. Nothing you need worry 'bout, you know."

"Right," Veranix said. He gave an exaggerated nod. "Street business."

"That's the deal." Hetzer's tone turned oddly hard. "We like you Uni boys, I said, but ain't your worry."

"Fair enough," Veranix said. He was about to ask Hetzer another question when Colin rushed over to them, grabbing Hetzer by the shirt.

"Blazes you doin', Hetz?" he asked. Confusion raced over Hetzer's face.

"Doin' a safe walk with a Uni boy. I was working the gate like we said."

"Right, right," Colin said, pushing Hetzer away. He didn't look at Veranix, not even a glance. "Where you takin' him?"

"Rose & Bush," Veranix offered.

"Well, it's just over there," Colin said, still talking to Hetzer. "He can see it, you get back to the gate and earn your place."

"I earn it, damn it!" Hetzer said. "If you weren't screaming and spooking—"

"I'll spook who I spook!" Colin sputtered. Eyes never flashing at Veranix he said, "He walked you, you gonna give him his due?"

"Of course," Veranix said. He dug out a half-crown, which was more than Hetzer would normally expect.

He handed it to Hetzer, and looked pointedly at Colin. "Is that good?"

"Ain't no matter to me what you do, Uni boy," Colin said. He stalked off, pushing through Veranix, heading away from the Rose & Bush.

"Aye, right," Hetzer said. He straightened up, jutting his chin proudly. He pointed down the street. "Rose & Bush, Uni. You be safe, right?"

"Right," Veranix said. Hetzer walked away. Veranix stood still for a few moments and then picked up another of the pages lying on the street.

The paper was just a small square, barely bigger than his hand, with a picture printed in red ink. The picture was a caricature of a street rat, specifically a Rose Street Prince, since he was sticking his arm out to show his tattoo. The arm was freakishly large in the picture, and the rose tattoo was shown in as intricate detail as a woodcut print could manage. Veranix had to admit that the work was impressive. Next to the street rat's head were the words in block letters, "NO THORNS HERE."

Veranix looked back and saw Colin stalking into the Turnabout. He considered chasing after, but realized it was pointless. The message was clear enough. Colin had nothing more to say.

Veranix's stomach growled at him, so he continued over to the Rose & Bush.

The place was quiet, no customers save two old men playing cards in the corner. Both of them looked wiry and lean, dressed in clothes that were well-patched enough to look decent. Veranix sat at a table close enough to keep an eye and an ear on them.

The server came out of the kitchen and headed straight to Veranix. "Cider or beer?"

"Cider," Veranix said. "What's in the kitchen today?"

"There's a Rancher's Pot, and hot sausages—"

"Lamb?" Veranix asked.

"Pork," the server said, shaking his head. He sneered. "You don't want it."

"Fair enough."

"There's Chicken Thalin," the server suggested.

"Really?"

"That's what the cook called it."

"Then that's what it'll be."

"Three ticks for the lot."

Veranix dug out the coins from his pocket and slapped them on the table. The server slid them into his apron and went behind the bar.

Chicken Thalin was quite the surprise. Veranix hadn't had that in several years. The circus traveled all over Druthal, but the closest place it had to call home was the Thalin region in the Archduchy of Sauriya. It was definitely the strongest influence on his mother's cooking.

The server came back over to the table with Veranix's cider.

"You see all that paper outside?" the server asked Veranix.

"I saw it," Veranix said, quickly adding. "I never understand those."

"You see something like that, this part of town, you know there's going to be a rumble soon." The server looked over to the window. "Hope it's not here."

"Princes and other rats trying to avoid a hammer," one of the old men coughed out. He pulled out a coin from his pile of winnings and tossed it to the server. "Another beer, boy."

"What's the hammer?" Veranix asked as innocently as he could manage. No need to appear as anything other than a naively curious Uni kid.

"Trouble from the big boss across 'path."

"Don't follow, friend," Veranix said.

"Shut it and play," the other old man said. He threw down two cards from his hand on the table. "Double treat, beat it."

"Moon doubled, with three of the Grand," said the first, showing his cards. He pulled the pot over. Glancing at Veranix he continued, "Ain't nothing, kid. Street trash doin' street trash things. Some troublemaker cuts into the big man's business, and the rats over here all want him to know the troublemaker isn't one of theirs."

"Big man losing money," said the second man. "He's got to work double to make it back, and find someone to blame. So he's gonna look across 'path."

"Why would he do that?" Veranix asked.

"Who else would make a play on his coin?" said the second old man. He threw some more coins into the middle of the table and dealt out more cards to himself. "Blazes, long as I remember Aventil and Dentonhill been scrapping at each other."

"How it is," said the first.

Veranix leaned closer to the two old men. "So, he's going to want to sell hard on the streets, too."

The first old man turned and really looked at Veranix for the first time. "College boy?"

"That's right," Veranix said.

"You hooch yourself up with anything?" the old man accused.

"No, sir," Veranix said fiercely. The old man nodded in approval.

"Be smart, college boy. You finish up, you move to the other side of the river. Get your nose out of the mess of this neighborhood."

The server came over with Veranix's dish. As soon as the scent hit his nostrils, Veranix was a little boy again. Before any show night, his mother would be at the wagon stove, cooking butter, onions, and peppercorns in the clay pot. He would watch her from his bunk while she added wine and mustard and other spices, then finally the chicken, and thin slices of potato. Then it would sit on the stove, slowly simmering while they performed the show. At the end of the night, they'd go back to the wagon and the whole place would smell glorious.

That was the scent.

Veranix took a bite. It was good. Not perfect—too much mustard, not enough pepper—but it was quite good. Almost how his mother would make it.

Almost, but not quite right at all.

Quietly, he kept eating, every bite delicious. Every bite wrong. Every bite driving home the inevitable point that had never crossed his mind before.

He would never eat his mother's Chicken Thalin again.

He didn't care what Colin thought about what it would do on the streets. He didn't care about his marks in history, or what Rellings would do if he was caught out of house after curfew. He didn't care if Kaiana would be angry.

The man who had broken Veranix's mother was making his lush living on the poison he was selling; the poison he had used on her until she couldn't stand on her own, let alone leap and fly like she once did. And that man needed to sell, now more than ever.

Veranix knew where and when. He'd spoil the drop. He'd spoil every drop, and when Fenmere was as broken as Verona Calbert was, when he was begging to die, only then would Veranix finish him.

Tonight he would hit him again.

Chapter 17

THE CURFEW BELLS had long since rung when Veranix crept into the carriage house. He had made a good show of being seen in the common area before going to bed, magicking off the window grate and slipping out. Delmin had given him a brief look of disapproval, but said nothing.

A few oil lamps hung over the Spinner Run stable. Kaiana sat on a small wooden crate, calmly munching on an apple. She looked up at Veranix as he approached, her face unreadable.

"Big drop of it tonight, right?" she asked. She took another bite of the apple.

"Right," Veranix said cautiously. "You already knew."

"I knew yesterday," she said glibly. "Shirt off, come on."

"Wait, what?" Veranix said.

"Shirt. Off." she said. When he still didn't react, she continued. "You took a knife in your shoulder the other night, remember?"

"Yeah, I remember," Veranix said. He took off his coat and started unlacing the shirt.

"So let me check the wound and dress it again," she said. "If you're going to go start something tonight, you'll need that."

"You aren't going to try and stop me?" He pulled the shirt over his head.

"You've already shown I can't do that," she said, unwrapping the dressing. The wound was oozing slightly, but the stitches were still holding strong. She poked at them gingerly. "Those won't tear when you shoot?"

"Don't think so," he said, flexing the arm.

"Still, I should probably do them fresh when you get back," she said. She started bandaging it back up.

"Not so tight."

"You need it tight," she said. "Try to avoid scrapping this time. You can sour the milk without kicking the bull."

"I plan to," he said. "I went in angry the other night. I wanted to scrap. I wanted to hurt them."

"And tonight?" she asked. She finished with the dressing and squatted down in front of him.

"Still angry. But not stupid. In quiet, wreck the drop, slip out," he said. "Stay low, nothing fancy."

"Stay out of fish bins as well," she said, the slightest smile pulling at the corners of her mouth. She pulled the crate over. "Get dressed and go. I'll leave the window unlatched. Wake me up when you get back." Veranix stayed still as she headed over to her quarters. "What is it?"

"I'm still waiting for the yelling."

"Veranix," she said, "I know you're going out no matter what I say. So I can either boot you from here, or I can do what I can to make sure you always come back." She bit her lip and looked to the ground, avoiding his gaze. "You're out there fighting my fight, too. Just fight it smart."

"As you wish, Kai," he said, not hiding his smile. She didn't look back up. She gave a quick nod and went into her quarters. Veranix put his gear on, blew out the lamps, and slipped out into the night.

Oscana Park at night was one of those places that had gotten so dangerous it had become safe again. Ten years prior, anyone crossing through there in the dark was sure to get roughed, robbed, and killed. This was known, this was accepted, so no one who had anything worth being killed over went through there. Nowadays, the only people to be found there were those who had nothing, whose lives were worth almost nothing, even to themselves. The most pathetic, desperate, and destitute congregated in the park, forming tiny communities among the half-dead, dried out trees and weed-choked scrub.

That Oscana Park had at one time been a beautiful place was almost a legend in Maradaine. It was something people often said, but it had been over a century since it had been true; no living memory of its former glory existed. Only the statues remained.

There were several statues throughout the park, marble masterpieces carved centuries ago, commemorating Druth heroes from the Rebellion. Most were thoroughly vandalized: faces broken, missing limbs, or even shattered. The statue of Niyol Carm—Veranix couldn't remember what he did in the Rebellion—was oddly intact. It was hidden away in a small enclave under a rock wall, with a fair amount of trees around it.

In the dark of night, it was nearly impossible to see it, even though Veranix knew he was right near it.

Perfect place for an illegal exchange, he thought. He crept toward the statue with meticulous care. The ground was littered with fallen branches and twigs, which would snap and crunch at the slightest provocation. Veranix could hear someone breathing by the statue. At least one of his targets was here. The last thing he wanted was to make his presence known.

There was a crunch a few yards behind him.

Every muscle in Veranix's body tensed. Slowly, he pulled out his bow and drew an arrow.

Another crunch.

The person at the statue stopped breathing. Veranix could make out a shadow, now holding very still next to the statue. Another shadow came through the trees, approaching cautiously, but not making any effort to conceal himself. This person was carrying something large.

"Pen?" the figure by the statue whispered. In the still of the dark night, every little sound was a ringing bell to Veranix.

"Here," said the approaching man. He moved closer, emerging from the thicket of trees. He was an immensely large man. Possibly the tallest, most muscle-bound man Veranix had ever seen—and that included Lomo the Lifter from the circus.

"You got the stuff?" the other one said.

"Right here," Pen said, holding up the thing he was carrying.

That was all Veranix needed to hear. He fired the arrow at Pen, and as soon as it was loosed, he grabbed the rope at his belt. He heard the arrow strike, and a grunt of pain from the man. He willed the rope to leap out and wrap around the thing in Pen's hand. In a moment, he could sense that it had a solid grip; he yanked the rope to bring it to him.

It didn't move.

That was surprising.

The large figure grabbed the rope from his end, and pulled. It happened too fast for Veranix to realize what was happening, too fast to react. He was torn from the ground and flew across the air, hurtling at the statue. The man over there jumped up. Veranix heard the grinding swipe of metal blades being pulled out of their sheathes.

He had only a moment to act, more out of instinct than thought. He drew in a surge of magic, and transformed it into a blast of pure light. The man at the statue cried out and turned his head away. Veranix flipped himself around so his foot connected with the man's head.

The man held his ground despite the blow. He swiped up with a blade, but Veranix was already past him, still out of control from being thrown. He crashed into the rock wall.

Pen was charging in. Veranix was still holding on to the rope, and he sent it wrapping around Pen's legs. He got tangled up, tripping over the rope. The momentum of his charge kept him going, right at Veranix. His massive fist came swinging forward. Veranix barely dodged out of the way.

Veranix jumped up as hard as he could, landing on Pen's shoulder for a second before bounding away from the statue. The other man was on top of him before he was able to get another step away. He had knives in both his hands, slashing furiously at Veranix. Veranix ignored the pain from the cuts, and rolled with the man's tackle. He kept his grip on the rope and willed it around the man's body, constricting like a snake. The knives dropped.

Pen was turned back around. Veranix flung the other man at him and ran. Pen caught the other man, his enormous arms almost gentle in how he handled him.

"Cole? You all right?" he asked. Veranix was already crashing through the trees, the rope coiling back up in his hands as he ran.

"Get him!" Cole shouted. Pen put Cole down and ran after Veranix. He pounded through the brush like a mad bull.

Fear forced bile up from Veranix's stomach. He was running as fast as he could, too panicked to focus on anything but getting away. He cleared the patch of trees, racing into open field, out in the scarlet moonlight. Pen was right behind him.

"Stupid, stupid, stupid," he caught himself muttering. He couldn't run fast enough, out in the open, to get away. Those huge hands were going to grab him, and when they did, they would tear him to pieces. He had to get out of their reach.

The magic flowed through him, triggered by survival instinct. Desperate to get away, he channeled the magic out beneath him, and launched straight up into the air.

Fear left him as he rocketed up, as if it shot out of his body with the magic of the jump. As his ascent slowed, he looked back down to the ground. He could understand what he was up against, assess it with a clear head. Pen stood in the clearing, staring up at Veranix.

He really was a ridiculously large man. Cole came out of the copse of trees, a tiny ball of hair next to Pen, knives in his hands, more knives sheathed in the belts that crossed his chest.

"The Thorn's a bird now," Cole said.

"He'll come down," Pen said.

Veranix realized Pen was right. He reached the peak of his jump, and he could feel he was about to drop, and land right in their midst.

He still had his bow in one hand, and the rope in the other. The rope had coiled itself when he ran. He clipped it onto his belt and drew out an arrow. Just as his upward momentum ended, he pulled back the arrow and fired it at Pen. He shot another as he started to fall.

Cole threw his knives, knocking the arrows off course. Veranix was astounded by his accuracy.

"Sam! Get him!" Cole yelled.

Veranix plummeted. He looked up, and saw a third man on top of the rock outcropping above the statue. He was lankier than the other two, and he was carrying a large crossbow. He fired.

With controlled magic, Veranix slowed his descent, falling like a feather instead of a stone. The man with the crossbow hadn't anticipated the sudden shift in acceleration; he missed. Veranix shot at Pen and Cole. Cole blocked the arrows again, and followed that with two more knives at Veranix.

Veranix realized his slow descent now made him an easy target. He willed the cloak to change around him, becoming a blur in the dark, starry sky.

Another arrow whizzed past him, far closer than he would have liked.

"Don't see him," Cole said.

"He's still there," Pen said. "Keep throwing." Cole drew out another knife.

Veranix had to get out of the air. He slung the bow over his shoulder and took his staff in one hand. He grabbed the rope, and as fast as he could, lashed it out toward the top of the rock wall, where he spotted a birch tree.

"There!" Pen shouted. Cole threw the knife.

Like lightning, the rope coiled around the birch tree. Veranix reeled himself in, the knife hurling through the space where he had just been. Veranix flew toward Sam—the man with the crossbow—and swung with his staff as hard as he could with one arm. Sam rolled away at the last moment, and Veranix only managed a glancing blow.

Veranix didn't even properly get his feet on the ground. Sam had spun around to plant a heavy kick in Veranix's chest. Veranix was knocked back, his hands reflexively opening with the blow.

He let go of the rope and the staff.

Veranix tried to grab the rope again, but Sam was already up in front of him, leveling his crossbow square at Veranix's heart. Before he could fire, Veranix flipped over backward. He kicked the crossbow out of Sam's hands, sending the bolt wildly up toward the sky.

Veranix didn't land right, closer to the edge than he realized. His hands slipped on the loose rubble at the top of the rock wall, and he fell over the brink. He reacted only quickly enough to push away and avoid cracking his skull on the edge. He flipped over again and righted himself, landing on his feet just behind the statue. His knees and ankles screamed when he landed, but he bit back any sound from his throat.

"He's dropped back down!" Sam called. "You see him?"

Veranix scrambled up against the rock wall, willing the cloak to surround him in an image of the stone. He made a silent prayer to every saint he could think of to keep him unseen.

Cole was coming back through the bramble and trees. "Nothing," he muttered.

"He can't have gone far," said Sam. Veranix tried to look up, but he couldn't see anything over the lip of the rock. "He lost his special rope."

"Haw!" Cole laughed coarsely. "Fenmere said something about a rope, right?"

"He said if the Thorn had a rope, we needed to bring it to him," Pen said. Now that Veranix could really hear him speak, Pen's voice came off as surprisingly eloquent, an accent representing a highborn education.

"Pendall," Sam said, "Come up here and get the rope off the tree. Coleman and I will keep cover."

"Cover?" Coleman asked. "I don't see him at all. Maybe he's gone."

Sam chuckled coldly. "He's there in the dark somewhere. I can hear him breathing."

Veranix held his breath. Coleman had emerged from the thicket of trees, what little moonlight was available glinting off the knives in his hands.

"He's quiet now," Coleman said.

"For now," Sam said. "He's got only one way out, and I've got it covered. Take your time."

Veranix knew he wasn't invisible, he was only camouflaged into the rock. Even in the darkness, Coleman might see him. Coleman was slowly searching around the rock face, using every sense, stalking him like a cat.

Veranix knew he had gotten lucky before, he had the rope before. He thought about trying to summon the rope to him, but from where it was, it would take all his concentration. He'd lose his cover. Coleman was very good with those knives. Veranix didn't have a chance if Coleman found him before he was ready.

Moving as slowly as he could manage, focusing his energy on maintaining his blended cover, he reached behind and unhooked his bow. He took care not to make a single movement too fast, or to make any sound. Coleman was less than twenty feet away, searching in the dark shadows.

"This rope is like steel!" Pendall called from above. "Even I can't uncoil it from the tree."

"It's got some magic trick to it," Sam said quietly. He called down toward the statue. "Our boy Thorn knows some magic, doesn't he?"

"Magic ain't nothing," muttered Coleman. He touched one knife to the rock, and scraped it along, making sparks and an evil noise.

"You hear that, Thorn?" Sam said. "We're not worried about magic. We've killed more than a few magic men."

There was a great smashing sound from above. Coleman looked up, and Veranix used the moment to get the bow in front of him.

"What the blazes?" Coleman called up.

"I can't get the rope off the tree," Pendall said. "So I'll get the tree off the rope." Another great smash, with the crack of wood splintering. Veranix had a hand on an arrow, half pulled from its quiver. Coleman snorted and focused back on the hunt. He was less than fifteen feet away.

"An axe would be faster," Sam said dryly.

"Do you have one?" Pendall said. Another pounding, splintering blow was heard. Veranix had the arrow out of the quiver. Coleman was close to the wall, sniffing. He had one knife pointing right at Veranix. He was no more than ten feet away from Veranix.

"No," said Sam. "You have an axe, Thorn? So we can cut this tree down and get your fancy rope?"

"Shh," hissed Coleman. Veranix had the arrow nocked. Coleman moved closer, along the rock, one blade leading his path. He was only five feet away.

No time left. Veranix pulled back the bow, the strain on the string quite audible.

"What?" Coleman turned, his knife hand already striking out.

Veranix released the arrow, square in Coleman's shoulder. Coleman staggered back. The arrow had barely left the bow, had yet to reach its killing speed, but it gave Veranix the moment he needed. He jumped up, half aided with magic, to the top of the statue and then to the top of the wall. Sam was at the edge, his crossbow still aimed at the thicket. He had only just started to react to the sound when Veranix was already there.

Veranix cracked his bow against Sam's head, a solid blow. Sam, surprised, slipped over the edge. Veranix's bow was ruined, almost snapped in half. He discarded it and turned toward Pendall and the tree. Pendall had hit the tree again. It was split and cracked, almost to the point of falling over. The rope was at his feet, part of it still coiled around the broken tree. Veranix's staff lay between the two of them.

Pendall turned back to Veranix. "I can see you, little Thorn," he said. "Just barely."

"So charge, big man," Veranix said. "Give me a nice, big run, like before."

"Samael? Coleman?" Pendall called.

"Just you and me, now," Veranix said.

"That's fine," said Pendall, chuckling. "Come fight me. I'm the strongest man in Druthal!"

"Was there a contest and no one told me?" Veranix jeered.

"Keep talking, Thorn," said Pendall. "It will help me find you."

Veranix breathed a whisper of magic, to make his voice sound like he was moving one way, while he crept the other way to his staff. "I'm serious, Pendall. How can you claim being the strongest man in Druthal when you haven't really tested that? I think that's very presumptuous of you—"

Pendall gave a charging smash to the spot Veranix's voice was coming from, which was ten feet away from where Veranix was. Veranix sprung forward when Pendall charged, grabbing his staff and rolling to where his rope was.

Pendall swung at empty air and turned around to face Veranix, just as Veranix picked up one end of the rope.

"Nice trick," Pendall said. "You think you can hold me with that rope?"

"Not gonna try," Veranix said. He pulled on the rope, which was still wrapped around the tree. Pendall had nearly cracked the trunk of the tree clear through, and Veranix broke it the rest of the way.

Veranix smashed the tree into Pendall.

"Good night, gentlemen," Veranix called out. "Sleep well." He coiled the rope back at his belt, and took two steps to make a magic-fueled leap back toward home.

Just as he jumped, his leg exploded with pain.

Careening through the air, he turned back to see Samael clinging to the top of the rock face with one hand while holding his crossbow in the other hand. Even in the darkness, Veranix could see a hint of a smile on Samael's face.

Veranix landed a quarter of a mile away, almost crashing on his face. He couldn't stand on his right leg. A crossbow bolt had sliced his thigh. Fortunately, it had only clipped him, but it was still a nasty wound, bleeding significantly. He couldn't make another jump until he dealt with it, and it wouldn't take the three assassins more than a few minutes to catch up to him. *Samael isn't dead*, he thought, *and given my luck this evening, Pendall and Coleman are still on the hunt as well.*

A tiny creek, barely more than a trickle of water, ran through this part of the park. There was a small wooden bridge crossing it only a few yards away from where Veranix landed. Using his staff as a crutch, he hobbled his way to the bridge and crawled into the tiny space underneath it. He braced himself in place with his good leg and held his staff up, ready to drive it at anything that appeared. He held his breath and listened.

The night was quiet, save for the light flow of the creek, and the drips of blood from his leg.

The pain was sharp and strong, screaming for his attention. He didn't hear anything outside, but at least one of those three had to be a good tracker, a quiet hunter. He didn't dare lower his guard, not when one of them might come under the bridge at any moment.

He looked at his leg. It was soaked in blood, but the cut wasn't too deep. He was feeling weak and cloudy from the blood loss. He had to deal with this injury now.

He breathed a whisper of magic into the rope, and it snaked from the loop on his belt to the wound. Veranix made the rope wrap around his leg tightly, covering the wound. He pushed more *numina* into the rope, willing it to become searing hot, just for a moment, at the wound. Skin and cloth smoldered, acrid and sweet smoke combined. Veranix let out a sharp cry, and prayed to Saint Hespin that the assassins would not hear it.

He uncoiled the rope. The wound had stopped bleeding. The pain was still incredible, but he felt he'd at least be able to walk on it. Gingerly he put his weight onto the injured leg, sliding out from his hiding place under the bridge. He took a few steps out, keeping his staff at the ready to strike at anyone he saw.

After only five steps, his head spun and he stumbled. He fell into the tiny creek, just as he heard a high-pitched voice saying, "There he is!"

Chapter 18

HANDS GRABBED AT VERANIX. Four hands. Small hands. Kids.

Two of them, not more than eight or nine years old. They were grabbing at him as he pulled himself back up.

"That's enough!" he said, shoving them off.

"Whoa!" one of the boys said, falling back. The other boy let go of Veranix's wrist, holding his hands up over his head.

"It's all right, Thorn!" he said. "We need to get you out!"

"Get me out?" Veranix rasped. He had the one boy clutched by the front of his ratty coat. "Get me out of where?"

"Out of the creek, out of sight," the boy he was holding stammered.

Out of sight was good. He needed a moment to collect himself. "Where to?"

"To our moms," the other boy said.

"Your moms?" Veranix asked. He got his feet under him, not releasing his grip on the one boy. "They know you're loose in the park at this hour?"

"We live here," the first said. "In the southside thicket. Right over there." He pointed to the patch of trees. Veranix could see a few moving shadows, a flicker of campfire.

"You've got some muscle after you, Thorn," the other kid said. He looked clever, almost cocky. His friend at least had the good sense to look scared. "We saw them when they first came into the park."

"All the more reason for you kids to get out of here." The last thing he needed to do was bring trouble on people who had enough already.

"You're in no shape to run or fight, Thorn," the scared kid said.

"I'll be . . . why are you two calling me Thorn?"

"You are the Thorn, right?" the clever kid said. "The one who's been giving Old Fenmere what for?"

"Something like that," Veranix said. His grip on the scared kid relaxed, more out of his own faintness than of conscious choice.

"In the thicket, then," the clever kid said, "before that muscle finds you."

The kids led him into the thicket.

There was a small clearing in the thicket, and a fire burning in an old copper drum. A few kids slept in huddles around it, and a few women were standing around. Worn women, with hard lines on their faces. Their tops were torn and loose fitting, and their threadbare skirts were shorter than polite fashion allowed. Veranix knew at once this was a doxy camp.

"What're you bringing someone in here, boys?" one of the doxies snapped as soon as the three emerged from the trees.

"He's hurt!" the scared boy said.

"That's not our problem."

"He's the Thorn!" the clever boy said. "He's been fighting Fenmere's men!"

"Right," another woman said, laughing. "He's the Thorn, and I'm the Duchess of Maradaine." Veranix dropped down, taking the moment to rest.

"Wait." Someone walked over to the light, and crouched down in front of Veranix. She looked him hard in the face. "I think that is him." Veranix focused his weary eyes on her.

"Maxianne, right?" he asked. "You look better."

"That's him," she said. She stood up and looked to the others. "That's the Thorn."

The women all stopped what they were doing. They came closer, all looking at him carefully. One of them rummaged through a bag and pulled out a small hunk of bread. She brought it over to him.

"You're the real thing, aren't you?" she said, handing him the bread. Almost instinctively, he took it and began eating.

"I'm not sure what you mean by that," Veranix said.

"I mean . . ." she started. She paused, thinking for a moment. "You could have left Maxi up in that flop. You could have rolled her, left her to die from *effitte* sweats."

"No, ma'am," Veranix said. "I couldn't have done that."

"That's what I mean," she said. "That's how you're the real thing."

"You ain't meaning to muscle in on Fenmere, make yourself boss," Maxianne said. "You're doing what the constabs won't."

"And you looked after one of ours, which Fenmere never does," the first doxy said. "He just gets us hooked on the smoke or the *'fitte*. Makes us his. Muscles on us. Vanishes our kids."

"Vanishes?" Veranix asked. "What do you mean?"

"Doxy kids and other park rats," the clever kid said. "They've been vanishing."

"Nobody walks alone no more," the other kid said.

"I don't know anything about that," Veranix said. "You think Fenmere is behind it?"

Maxianne nodded. "Nothing happens in Dentonhill that Fenmere ain't behind. Nothing 'cept you."

Veranix was uncomfortable with how they were all looking at him. Expectation. Hope.

"Look," he said, pulling himself onto his feet. The leg still hurt, but he could walk on it. No other injuries, but he was still a bit lightheaded. He wasn't sure if that was blood loss or just pushing himself magically, but he didn't have time to figure that out. "I don't know . . . I really don't know much of anything. I'm mostly just trying to get through this night without dying."

"That's all any of us are doing," the old woman said.

"Right," he said. He limped his way over to the edge of the clearing. "I think I can get out of here now. It's probably safest for you all if you have nothing to do with me."

"Too late for that, Thorn." Veranix turned and saw Pendall, standing on the other side of the clearing. He was amazed a man that big could approach without being heard.

"Pendall, old boy," Veranix said. "I already hit you with a tree. That was a hint to leave."

"I remember, Thorn," Pendall said. With surprising speed, he lashed out and grabbed one of the girls who was dozing close by. He held her with one hand, gripping the top of her head. She winced and cried.

"Put her down, Pendall!" Veranix said. His hand went to the rope.

"Try it, Thorn," Pendall said. "Go for your special rope, and I crush her skull."

Veranix held his hands up away from his belt.

"All right, Pendall. No skull crush."

Pendall laughed. "Blasted saints, is it that easy?" he said. "Threaten to kill one girl, and you go soft?"

"Put her down, man," Veranix said. "You want to throw with me, throw with me."

"We're paid to bring your head, Thorn," Pendall said.

"Fenmere, right?" Veranix said. "How much is he paying you?"

"A thousand crowns each," Pendall said. He looked far too pleased with himself.

"Is that it?" Veranix asked. "Well, now I'm just insulted. And you should be, too."

"Shut it, Thorn!" Pendall barked. He squeezed slightly, and the girl cried out.

"Hey, I'm just saying, he was paying forty thousand for this rope and cloak. I would think he'd put at least half that much to get me."

"Forty?" Pendall asked.

"I mean, I'm worth it," Veranix said. "Aren't you?"

"Shut up! You throw down that rope and cloak on the ground. No tricks or she dies."

"Right," Veranix said. "Nice and slow." He unhooked the rope and tossed it in front of him, and then threw the cloak down. A wave of fatigue hit him when he dropped them, but he forced himself to ignore it.

Numina still pooled around them, he could feel it at his feet, even at this distance.

"Good," Pendall said. "Weapons, too."

Veranix dropped his arrows—useless as they were now—and his staff to the ground. "All right, Pendall. I'm unarmed. Let the girl go." He held his hands above his head.

"Stupid," Pendall tossed the girl to the side negligently. She landed in a heap, but she was alive, breathing. Veranix gave Pendall a crooked grin.

"I'm stupid?" he asked. "Pen, what did you forget?"

"That you're an acrobat?" Pendall said, moving closer to Veranix. "I think I can still catch you and pummel you to death."

"No, Pen," Veranix said. "You forgot that I'm a goddamned mage."

Veranix poured as much *numina* as he could channel through his body into a blast of pure force, and slammed it into Pendall's chest.

Pendall went flying backward, far out of sight. Veranix dropped to his knees, spent, barely able to breathe.

"Wow!" yelled one of the boys. "You knocked him to the river, I'd bet!"

"Let's hope," Veranix rasped. "Cloak "

"What?" Maxianne asked "What is it?"

"The cloak," he said, clawing weakly at the open air. "Give it to me."

The girl that Pendall had been holding hostage scrambled over to him, picking up the cloak and putting it into his hand. Touching it brought *numina* rushing into his body, which he drank up like cold water.

"Thanks," he said. He got to his feet, putting the cloak on. "I've got to stop having nights like this."

"That was loud," the old woman said. "If he has friends, they won't be far off."

"No, they won't," Veranix said, strapping his arrows on. "You may want to find a new camp. I'm sorry—"

"Don't," Maxianne said. "Don't apologize. Just get out of here."

Veranix didn't need to be told twice. He grabbed the rest of his gear and pushed his way through the trees. Every step hurt, but he gritted his teeth and ignored it, pushed it out of his head. He didn't have time to let something like pain get him killed.

He came out at the edge of the park, right at the corner of Justin and Paller. He had three blocks to Necker Square, and then three more to Waterpath. As battered and beat as he was, he felt he could do that. He took three more steps before he heard the hooves pounding toward him. His hand went to his staff. Two horse riders were approaching.

"Stand down in the name of the law!" one of the approaching horsemen called. He was holding up a lantern, so Veranix could see both of them were in green and red uniforms. City Constabulary. The other one was holding a crossbow.

"Stood down," Veranix called out, slinging his staff on his back and holding up his hands. "I am standing down, sirs."

The two horses stopped a few yards away from Veranix. The man with the crossbow slid off his horse, keeping his aim trained on Veranix the whole time. "Think you can cause trouble in the park, rat?"

"Cause trouble, sir?" Veranix asked. "No, sir, no such thing."

"Right," the one with the lamp said. "Those huge crashes and screams just happened."

"No, there were three men, officer, they . . ."

"Of course there were three men, and we've got one of them now," the armed officer said.

"No, not me, officer. I'm a student at the University of Maradaine and . . ."

"And, what?" the one with the lamp said. "You were out for a moonlit stroll in the park, with a quarterstaff and a rope?"

"Well," Veranix started. He heard a crack from the dark trees. Someone was out there. "You know what, officers? It is, indeed, very strange and unexplainable. Clearly you must arrest me."

"He smell drunk, Ollie?" the one with the lamp asked.

"Not a drop, Hal," the one with the crossbow said.

"Right," Hal said, "So we have a sober, armed boy, asking to be arrested."

"I think he's covering something up in the park," Ollie said, looking over to the woods. "Some job or scheme he doesn't want us finding."

Hal smiled wryly at Veranix. "Sorry, pal. Afraid you found the two constabs who aren't in Fenmere's pocket, so whatever you're up to, we aren't going to . . ."

"Oh, thank the saints," Veranix said. "Because Fenmere has three killers in the park trying to . . ."

That was as far as he got before the knives came whistling out of the trees. Both constabs were hit square in the chest. They dropped down to the ground. Coleman stepped out of the woods, two more knives in his hand. His shirt was soaked in blood, left arm in a makeshift sling. He was pale and breathing hard, but he looked determined.

"Hate to kill honest men just doing their jobs, but I couldn't have them interfering."

Veranix didn't bother replying or bantering. He pulled out his staff and charged in, willing his cloak around him to blend his image away. Coleman threw, deadly accurate at Veranix's heart. Veranix twisted to the side and batted it away with the staff. He swung it back around, grazing Coleman. Nothing resembling a solid hit.

Coleman struck back with his knife, almost too fast for Veranix to block. He had to fight defensively, as Coleman's constant barrage of attacks left him no opportunity. Even one-handed, Coleman was outmatching him.

"Yes!" Coleman shouted joyfully. "This is a fight!" His eyes glinted with delight.

Veranix realized Coleman was only toying with him. Having fun before taking the killing shot, or possibly keeping him occupied while Samael got in position to shoot.

Veranix wasn't going to let that happen. This was not going to be another fight like the one with Nevin. He wasn't boxed in here.

He swung up with the staff, sweeping the knife out of his way, and flipped backward. His feet connected with Coleman's chin as he went over—not as strong or as hard as he wanted, but enough to daze the knife fighter for a moment. Staying camouflaged, he pulled back, getting to the other side of the street, keeping most of his weight on his good leg. He was pushing himself, willpower alone keeping his body going. He didn't know how much longer he could keep it up.

"Close quarters or distance, no difference to me," Coleman jeered, despite looking like he would drop any minute. He threw the knife in Veranix's direction, and dove at the body of one of the constabs, yanking his knife out of the dead man's chest.

Veranix jumped up to avoid the knives, grabbing the metal awning of a barbershop. His palms were sweating, he barely could keep a grip. Veranix flipped over to the top of the awning. Knife after knife flew past him, each one only a hair away from him. Breath short, heart hammering, every muscle ready to give out, he couldn't keep dodging. As another knife raced at him, he jumped off the awning. Wildly, he cast out the rope, wrapping it around a high tree branch jutting out over the park side of the street. Coleman kept his eyes to the sky, knives at the ready.

Veranix swung himself over the tree branch, looping high as he could before diving back down. He reeled himself down with the rope, catapulting at the ground.

Coleman was alert and threw two knives, and then two more, aiming wide; Veranix's camouflage and velocity made it impossible to aim accurately. One of the knives grazed Veranix's arm. It didn't matter to him as he plummeted hard and fast directly at Coleman, rope in one hand and staff in the other. Right before contact, he swung his staff, imagining Coleman's head was a tetchball and he was going for a triple-jack.

He hit Coleman's face, cracking the staff in half.

Veranix stumbled his landing, barely staying on his feet. Coleman was down, either knocked out or, more likely, dead. Veranix didn't feel like sticking around to check. Samael couldn't be far away, and given his skill with a crossbow, he didn't need to be very close, either.

Veranix dropped the broken half of his staff. It was nothing he couldn't replace, just a polished stick of heavy wood, but he had a twinge of regret. His grandfather had given him that staff years ago.

He didn't have any fight left in him, he couldn't waste any more time. He mounted one of the Constabulary horses. It was a risk if the law caught him, but it was the fastest way to put some distance between him and the park. He gave it a sharp kick, and it started to canter down the street. Veranix steered it down Paller.

He wanted nothing more than to lie down on the horse's back and rest, only giving it the minimal leading it needed to reach Waterpath. Instinct told him not to let his guard down. He glanced back toward the park. Up on a roof, framed in the ruddy glow of the nearly full blood moon, he saw a figure running at full tilt, chasing him.

Veranix drove his heels into the horse, pushing it to a gallop.

The running man was beating the horse's pace, never losing pace to jump to the next roof or clear an iron grate. Veranix stole another glance and spotted the crossbow in the man's hand. It was undoubtedly Samael.

One block away from Necker Square, Samael overtook Veranix with a bold jump from a four-story row house to the one-story shop across the street, using the cloth banner over the shop to slow his descent. He charged forward, never looking at his feet, secure that every step was sure. Veranix was more than a little impressed.

Samael bounded off a railing, onto the awning of a tailor, down to a wooden cart. As he stepped off the

cart, he twisted his body around, raising up the crossbow. He was going to block the way through into
Necker Square, and Veranix knew the moment his feet
touched solid ground he would shoot the crossbow.
Crashing forward on the horse, Veranix had no way to
turn or dodge or retreat. He couldn't cloak himself and
the horse.

His hand went to the rope, and he lashed it out at
Samael. Like lightning, it whipped forward and
wrapped around the crossbow. Just as Samael landed
on the ground, the crossbow was wrenched out of his
hand.

Veranix barreled the horse forward, pounding toward Samael and knocking him on the cobblestones.
Not losing another second, he turned down Necker
and galloped at full pace toward the campus.

Samael got up from the road, disgusted with himself.
He had underestimated the Thorn, and he should have
known better. Cornered cats are always the most dangerous. He should have taken a clean kill shot back on
the ridge, but he'd wanted to make sure the Thorn had
the merchandise Fenmere wanted first.

He gingerly pressed his chest. He had probably broken a couple ribs. The gash across his skull was bleeding badly as well. Coleman was dead, in all likelihood,
and he wasn't sure exactly what had happened to Pendall. He hoped he was still alive.

Lying on the ground in front of a smoke shop was
the smashed remains of his crossbow. That angered Samael more than anything else. Pen and Cole were good
friends, but the crossbow was a true treasure. He could

rebuild it, of course, but that would take time and money. He bent down to look at the mess and see what could be salvaged.

He grinned. The scope was intact. That was an amazing bit of luck. He was certain the lenses would have shattered. He put it up to his eye. It worked fine. A small blessing on this poor night; the scope was the most expensive component of his crossbow.

Samael walked over to Necker, where the Thorn had raced away, and looked down the road through the scope. Sure enough, he saw the Thorn at the end of the road, getting off the horse. He gave the beast a few slaps until it ran off. Samael watched as the Thorn glanced carefully around, and apparently satisfied that he wasn't being seen, climbed over the University wall, and dropped down into the campus.

Now the night wasn't a total loss. He didn't get the Thorn, but he knew where he went. That should be worth a hundred crowns at least.

Chapter 19

V ERANIX PUSHED himself on pure will to the carriage house. Kaiana had fallen asleep sitting on a
bale of hay, her head lolled over to one side lying
against the wall. Her book lay discarded at her side,
and her lamp was burning low, almost out of oil.

Veranix stumbled over to her. He was already feeling terrible, but he knew it was about to get worse. Best
to do this close to her.

First he dropped the rope next to her. Letting it go
made his whole body shudder for a moment. He took
a moment to catch his breath.

Next the cloak. Taking that off and putting it on the
hay bale was like a hammer to the chest. Suddenly every muscle hurt. He didn't even bother trying to hold
himself together, and slumped down on the ground,
nudging Kaiana awake.

"Hey," he said. "You said to wake you up."

Kaiana opened her eyes blearily, and looked down
at him. "Oh, sweet saints, Veranix. Another one of
those nights?"

"Ambush tonight," he said. "I should have expected it. Stupid."

"You made it out." She got up, stretching her arms and neck. "How bad was it?"

"Three real pros," Veranix said. "An arrow almost missed my leg."

"You were hit?" She bent down to examine him.

"I stopped the bleeding on it. A few small slices here and there. I got lucky, really."

"Lucky is good," she said. She looked him over. "Those pants will have to be burned, you know." She crossed the carriage house, leaving him on the ground, and then came back with a cup of water and some dried meat.

"You think so?" Veranix asked. He took what she offered without question.

"I have no intention of washing or sewing them, all right?"

"Fair enough," he said. "Where are my regular clothes?"

"Under the hay, back in the corner there," she said, pointing into the empty stable. "Where are your bow and staff?"

"Casualties of the evening," Veranix said. Summoning as much strength as he could muster, he pulled himself back to his feet. He frowned as he went into the empty stable and began stripping off his bloody clothes.

"If you plan on going out again in the near future, you can't go unarmed," she said, turning her back to him. "Even with that fancy rope and cloak. Look how bad it is when you can fight back."

"I need to have more nights where I don't fight anyone," he said.

"That's a good choice too. Can you replace the weapons?"

"Staff is easy," he said. He glanced around the carriage house, spotting several gardening tools. "I can see a few replacements right here."

Kaiana snorted with laughter. "Master Jolen would love that. What about the bow?"

"It would cost a few crowns, but . . ." He trailed off, lost in idle thoughts, his mind too tired to stay focused. Everything in his body ached, but he might have just enough strength to get back to his dormitory.

"What is it?" She glanced back at him, and quickly turned away again. "Can you get your pants on?"

"Right," he said. He grabbed the clean pants and pulled them on. The wound on his leg still hurt like blazes, but it wasn't in any danger of opening up, probably wouldn't get infected. He made a note that he would have to stretch it more than usual to keep it from healing tight. "I just remembered I have my father's old bow in the trunk in my room."

"Sounds like you're all set," she said.

"Even still, God and the saints willing, I won't be going out for a bit." He tossed the cloak and the rope over to her. "They wanted that stuff, and Fenmere clearly has his mad on for it. So let's hide it and lay very low for a few weeks."

She picked up the things and smiled. "Consider it hidden. Glad you've come to your senses on this."

"I just need the rest," he said. "Tomorrow is Saint Senea Day. Break from classes, and I'm just going to sleep all morning. I hear they're going to be doing *Three Men and Two Wives* over in Cantarell Square in the afternoon. You want to go see it?"

"Break day for you," she said. "I still have work to do."

"Right," he said. "Sorry."

"It's not a big deal," she said. "*Three Men and Two Wives*? Raunchy junk."

"It's hysterical!"

"Hardly," she said. "Now, if it were one of Whit's history plays, like *Queen Mara*, I'd make it work."

"*Queen Mara*? Really?"

Kaiana picked up a spade and held it up like a Druth pikeman. "This crown, this throne, this *kingdom* is mine by birthright. You tell every last traitor that I will hold it, alone if I must, even if the borders of Druthal be no greater than the walls of this room. I will keep the crown on my head for as long as I have breath in my body and strength in my arm!"

She was good. Veranix had no idea she had that in her, and had to respond with applause. "You know that speech?"

She snapped back to looking at him. "I know the whole play."

"Wow," Veranix said. "We should find someone to do *Maradaine XVI*. You could do a blazing good job playing—"

"If you say Queen Majara, I will hit you with this shovel."

"Any role you wanted," Veranix finished. He wasn't sure if she was joking or not. But even if she was interested in the stage, playing the half-Napolic former queen of Druthal was clearly not something that appealed to her.

"That play isn't even Whit, it's Kelter mimicking his style," she muttered. She put down the spade and looked at the slices on Veranix's arm. "I think you'll live. Get back to your room before the sun starts coming up. I'll take care of this stuff."

"Thanks, Kai," he said, smiling. "One last favor?"

"You mean one last for tonight?"

"Yeah. Just . . . keep your eye on me until I'm in Almers. Make sure I get in there."

"Right, right," she said, playfully shoving him to the door. "Now move."

Veranix slipped back out into the dark night. He was exhausted, sore down to his bones, but he also had a sense of rejuvenation. As he crept over to the side of Almers Hall, he began to feel almost giddy. He realized the damage he had done to Fenmere. The kind of anger, the kind of wrath that Fenmere had sent down on him didn't come from petty swats, or even a bloody nose.

Veranix climbed up an ironwork trellis on the side of Almers, pushing through the pain, ache, and fatigue. Just a few feet more. To stay focused, he started to think up a plan. He would lie low for the rest of the month. In Joram, he would start knocking dealers and pushers around the park, and the north end of Dentonhill.

As he reached the third floor, he thought about Maxianne and the other doxies. The kids with them. That gave him pause. Could they wait until Joram? Were things going to be even worse for them, with what he'd started? Would they think he had given up on them, left them to fend for themselves against Fenmere? They were going to have to. He couldn't help them if he were exhausted or dead, which he would be if he kept up at this pace. Blazes, he was already exhausted. When he reached the window to the third-floor water closet, he could barely muster the minute amounts of *numina* needed to pop the iron grate covering it.

He slipped in the window and magicked the grate back into place. It took every ounce of strength and willpower not to collapse right on the floor. He pulled himself over to the water basin and filled it. He bent down and sipped some, and then splashed the rest on his face. A glance at the mirror showed he had gotten most of the blood and dirt off himself, enough to not draw stares from anyone who saw him. Tomorrow he would go to the baths. That would be good.

He slipped off his boots and hid them in the bottom of the linen cabinet, behind a pile of sheets. The dormitory stewards didn't work on holidays, even on a minor Saint Day, so they would be safe through tomorrow. He left the water closet and trudged down the hallway. A few lamps still burned low in the third-floor common room. As Veranix slipped through, he saw Rellings sleeping in one of the chairs. He had a few books around him, so he might have been studying, but knowing Rellings, Veranix figured he was sitting watch.

Veranix noticed a sheet of paper lying in Rellings's lap. Despite the low light of the lamps, he could read it. Rellings had been writing a letter to Parsons's parents. They had already been informed by the University, Veranix was sure. He looked closer, and saw that the letter was far more personal, Rellings telling them of how sorry he was for Parsons's accident, taking blame for it, and good things about Parsons's life at the University.

Veranix never thought Rellings had it in him.

"Rellings," he said, nudging the prefect. "Wake up."

Rellings startled, opening his eyes and groping around at the arms of the chair. "What, who?" He looked up, focusing his eyes. "Calbert. What time is it? Why are you out of bed?"

"Water closet," Veranix answered. "I'm not sure about the time. Maybe around four bells."

"Mmm," said Rellings. He glanced around, obviously still a bit disoriented. "Fell asleep in the chair."

"Keeping an eye on us all, eh?" Veranix asked, but without the usual bite he would give to Rellings.

Rellings squinted at him, clearly waking up a bit more. "You should be in bed, Calbert."

"You too, Rellings," Veranix said. "You'll hurt your neck sleeping that way."

"Right," said Rellings. He stood up. "All right, go, Calbert."

"Yes sir," Veranix said, giving Rellings a bit of a wink. He walked over to his own door. "Holiday tomorrow, Rellings."

"Right," said Rellings, nodding as he picked up his books and papers. "No wake-up or walk to Holtman."

"Thank the saints for that," Veranix said. "Good night, Rellings." He went into his room. Delmin was fast asleep, sprawled out facedown on the bed. Veranix peeled off his shirt and pants and dropped onto his own bed. He was asleep almost the moment he landed.

Fenmere hadn't slept the whole night. This had not been his choice. Lord Sirath and Kalas had invited themselves into his parlor at eleven bells, this time bringing two of their own heavies with them. They had spent the entire evening waiting for their merch to return, demanding food and wine from his staff.

In twenty years, Fenmere had never been muscled on like this. It was humiliating. The only saving grace to the whole business was the fact that Sirath and his Blue

Hand boys didn't move in his normal circles. This wouldn't get tracked back to him, wouldn't carve into his action.

It was still degrading.

Fenmere had spent much time out of the parlor. Sirath, at least for the duration of the evening, had the grace not to follow him around the house. He spent much of the night waiting on the balcony outside his office, which from three stories up overlooked Inemar and the river. The night had been bright and clear, and he could see quite far to the north side of the city, making out the rough shape of high towers against the horizon.

Hainara had come at two bells. He had almost forgotten that he had arranged for her. He had presumed that the whole business would be done by one bell; the merch would be delivered, and the Thorn's head would literally be on a platter. She was to be his celebration. She wasn't one of those common street doxies; she was an artist, the real pride of his stable. Keeping her for himself tonight cost him another hundred crowns, at least, but she would have been worth it. With Sirath and his Circle still there, with no news from the Three Dogs, there was nothing to celebrate. Even Hainara's gifted hands couldn't lift Fenmere's dark mood.

The sky was lightening. A few blocks away, the bells over Saint Polmeta's would ring soon. Fenmere picked up his pipe, a small treasure of gold and ivory, and packed a pinch of *hemas* leaf into it. He lit a taper off one of the candles on the balcony, and lit the pipe. He took a deep pull of the smoke. It did little to calm him.

Thomias knocked on the glass door. "Sir? They . . . they're asking for you."

"Are they?" said Fenmere, not turning to look at his

servant. "Very well. How have they . . . comported themselves?"

"One of them left to go to the bakery. They have asked for the cook to prepare some breakfast."

"Of course they have," said Fenmere. He took another pull off the pipe. He put on a large smile as he turned around. "Whatever they need, Thomias. They're our guests." He patted Thomias on the shoulder genially. Thomias scuttled off down the back stairs, toward the kitchen, as Fenmere headed to the parlor.

The room was normally a testament to Fenmere's success: walls and doors of dark mahogany, shipped up from the southern archduchy of Scaloi; plush chairs from the Kieran Empire, in the High Age style of the eleventh century; Imach carpets, intricately woven masterpieces; five paintings commissioned from Len Hovath and a sculpture by Corrin Essel. The room was a display case, showing his guests how much he had accumulated over the years of enterprise. Now it was sullied by Lord Sirath and his companions.

Sirath sat in one of the chairs in the corner of the room, lounging with an infuriating air of disdain and disregard. He was lying back, with a platter resting on his stomach that contained nothing but chicken bones. Sirath was sucking on the bones, taking in every possible bit of edible flesh. Kalas was in the middle of the room with another member of the Blue Hand, a young man who looked as hateful and haggard as Kalas. Fenmere had heard his name was Forden, but he didn't care to know too much about the man. The two of them were playing Doubleback Dice with Fenmere's board, the board that was a gift from Baron Hemlier, the board that had been another item on display. No one had ever played a game on that board before. Both of them had glasses of Fuergan whiskey sitting half empty next to the board, sweating moisture on the wooden table.

"Nearly five bells," Kalas said without looking up. "We should have had news by now."

"We should have," Fenmere said, nodding. "We knew the Thorn was a tough customer. Clearly he gave the Three Dogs quite a challenge."

"Failure," muttered Sirath.

"What's that?" Fenmere asked. Sirath snorted and focused his attention back on the chicken bones.

"He gave them failure," Kalas said. "These were supposed to be professionals, I thought. Some of the best assassins in the city."

"They are," Fenmere said. He picked up the bottle of Fuergan whiskey, glancing at the label. As he feared, it was the fifty-year-old Astev bottle. He brought it over to the sideboard and poured out a glass for himself. He gave a silent prayer to a few saints that Sirath and the rest hadn't thought to raid his cellar, where the truly rare and valuable liquors were.

"We should have sent Kent or me," Forden said. "At least to observe."

"There's no need for that," Fenmere said. He sipped the whiskey. "More people would have just got in the way of the Dogs."

"So you say," Kalas said. He gave the dice a roll and moved his pieces across the board, claiming two pieces.

"Blast," the young man said. He looked over at Fenmere. "We don't know if your Dogs even found the Thorn today. Or if they did, that they would return with the items."

"Of course they will," Fenmere said. "They were

told we needed to recover the stolen goods. Perhaps that is what the delay is."

"What do you mean?" Kalas asked.

"Killing him would be quick," Fenmere said. "But if they had to get him to tell where the goods are, that might take some time. Then they would have to go recover the goods."

"So you're suggesting that they have captured him and tortured him," said Kalas, nodding. He rubbed his chin, thinking the idea over. "That makes sense, but wouldn't they have sent word?"

"Men like these aren't ones to send status reports," Fenmere said. "They come when the job is done."

"Or lost," Sirath said. He discarded the plate of bones on the floor, having sucked out every useful morsel he could.

"These men don't declare a commission lost as long as he still breathes," Fenmere said. "Out of honor, they would pursue him for as long as it takes."

"We do not have 'as long as it takes,' Fenmere," Kalas snapped, his face reddening. The veins on his forehead bulged. "Tonight the circumstances are ripe."

"Yes, I know, Kalas," Fenmere said, glaring hard at the mage. "You have said so several times."

"And yet you fail us," Sirath snarled.

Two men came into the parlor. The first was presumably Kent, the other mage from the Blue Hand, who walked in like it was his own home. He carried a paper bag full of bread, still steaming fresh, casually eating a handful of it, leaving crumbs on the floor. The other man limped in, clutching his side, bruises along his face.

"Found this one out in the street," Kent said. "He's got nothing, but he smells of the stuff."

Forden dashed over to the injured man, moving his face in close, seeming to sniff at him. Lord Sirath went for the bread, tearing the bag out of his associate's hands.

"Yes," he said. "He's been in contact with our things."

The injured man responded by clocking Forden with the back of his fist. "Get off, freak."

Forden raised a hand at the injured man, but Kalas whistled at him, and he backed down.

"You're one of the Dogs, then?" Fenmere asked.

"Right. Name's Samael. You're the man with the contract, then?"

"That's right," Fenmere said.

"I told this one," he said pointing to the mage who arrived with him, "I only would talk to you."

"Talk now," said Sirath.

"The Thorn showed up, just like you said."

"Is he dead?" Fenmere asked.

"Of course he isn't dead," Kalas said. "If he were, this one would have brought back our things with his head."

"Unless he's pulling a trick," Forden said.

"I just love being called 'this one,' " Samael said. "It's such a sign of respect." He walked over to the young mage. "What do they call you, eh, bloke? I ain't met a mage who can survive a knife in the chest, or an arrow. So you want to go for a run, mage?"

"You think you could 'run' me, then?"

"I think you've never been in a real scrap, life on the line, teeth and hands against another man." Samael grinned. He turned to Fenmere, giving no heed to the mages. "That's the thing about the Thorn. He knows how to hold his own, push himself. He knows what do when his life is on the line."

"Tough one, he is?" Fenmere asked. "He must be if he got away from the three of you."

"That's right. Took out Pendall, killed Coleman, and ran me over with a horse."

"Where did he get a horse?" Fenmere asked.

"Stole it from a dead constable."

"He killed a stick?" Fenmere whistled low. "I didn't think he had that in him."

"Nah, that was Cole. But the Thorn has the stones to do what he has to."

"This is all fascinating," Kalas said. "But the point is that the Thorn got away, and our goods are still lost."

"Failure!" Sirath said. "Kill him."

"Wait, wait, wait," Samael said, holding up his hands. "No need to be doing that sort of thing."

"I agree," Fenmere said. "I'm never one to kill something I can use again." He crossed over to Samael, looking him in the eye. "You are of use, aren't you?"

"Like blazes I am, boss." Samael held out a finger at Sirath and the other Blue Hand mages, as if just by pointing he could hold their magic at bay. "I know where he goes. I know where he runs to."

"And why didn't you follow him?" Kalas asked.

"Could barely walk, mate, let alone run the seven blocks to catch him."

"So, where does he go?" Fenmere asked. "Where does he run to?"

"What's it worth?" Samael asked.

Fenmere liked that. Cocksure, even in the face of death, willing to push just a little harder to get something out of it. "How about a chance to redeem yourself, and a little more work? That would be worth your while, no?"

"Where?" Sirath snarled.

"To the campus, University of Maradaine," Samael stammered out, suddenly spooked and backing away from Sirath. "I saw him go over the wall."

"So, possibly a student, or someone on the staff," Kent said.

"Or even a professor," Kalas said.

"Rose Street Princes and the other Aventil gangs are bending over backward to disavow him," Fenmere said. "Makes sense if he's on campus."

"So we need to go get him and our things," Kalas said.

"Right," Fenmere said. He put down the glass and paced the room. "Crossing the wall, it's not easy, but I've got some boys who can do it. They'll put on a good hunt. Samael, you're going to take them, and search hard and dirty. Shake it up and make some noise. At this point we need to show everyone—not just the Thorn—that you don't make noise in my part of town without getting it visited back on you. That includes the blasted campus." He was getting hot, blood boiling. "Too long we've respected that wall, but it's time to put an end to that. The Thorn isn't going to hide on the other side, and he sure isn't going to run me out of my neighborhood or anywhere else!"

Fenmere glanced about. The only people in the room were Samael and the Blue Hands. None of his own men. No one who cared, no one who was invested in his business. Just four poor allies and one hired killer. He felt Kalas's hand on his shoulder.

"Actually, Willem," Kalas said with a familiarity that Fenmere found infuriating, "I think we have a better way to achieve our goal here, one which will make less noise. At least, the kind of noise that would turn undue attention this way."

"What would that be?" Fenmere asked.

"The Circle has academic contacts, favors to be called in. Nothing you have to worry about."

"We'll find him," Sirath muttered. "Breakfast first." He left the parlor, heading toward the kitchen. The two young Blue Hands followed, with Kalas taking the bread. He stopped and turned back to Fenmere.

"We will still need our arrangements for tonight, though," he said. "Come on, now, Willem. You must be famished. I know I am."

Fenmere stayed in the parlor for another minute before he realized Samael was still there. He took another moment before addressing the assassin.

"Stick around today, Samael," he said. "Despite their confidence, it might be best to have additional plans."

"That'll cost you, sir."

"I know that," Fenmere snapped. "It'll be worth your while, though. And you'll get another crack at the Thorn."

"Does that mean I'm invited to breakfast, Mister Fenmere?"

"If you want." He sighed as he headed to the door. "I'll warn you, though, watching these mages eat can really ruin your appetite."

Hetzer was woken up by someone pounding on the door. He had crashed out in the basement pad under Kessing's general store. He liked sleeping there because it was usually quiet. Hardly any Princes ever stayed there, besides Colin's crew. No one ever pounded on the door this early.

Blearily, he opened the door a crack. Jutie was there, looking sweaty and nervous. He had a bird with him. She stood out like a fire in a dark alley. Dark brown skin, wide nose, narrow eyes. Napa girl, if ever he saw one. Honestly, he hadn't seen many, not in Aventil. Mixed-blood and foreign-borns didn't really live in the neighborhood, staying to the Little East in Inemar and the dregs out in the western neighborhoods. She was dressed in working clothes, linen shirt and rough canvas pants and heavy boots, and she was carrying a satchel. She was a pretty one, though. The way Jutie was shaking, Hetzer thought the kid was looking for a private place for his first roll.

"What's up?" Hetzer asked.

"Colin here? This bird has a drop for him."

That was a surprise. "Bird with a drop? You check her for weapons?"

"W-weapons?" Jutie stammered.

"Yeah, weapons." Hetzer was amazed that the kid didn't think of that.

"Let me see the cap," she said.

"Right, let a strange girl just walk in his pad." Hetzer sneered at Jutie, who cowered at his look. "Jutes, you know better than that. She could work for the sticks."

"She don't work for the sticks, I think."

"Right. Or she could be with the Waterpath Orphans, or the Kickers, or . . ." Hetzer gritted his teeth. Jutie just brought a strange girl to the cap's pad. He shook his head.

Lamely, Jutie said, "She's got a drop for him, is all."

"Stupid," Hetzer said. "Get in here." He opened the door a bit more and grabbed the bird by the wrist. He pulled her inside, and slammed the door shut again just as Jutie squeezed through. The bird was rubbing her wrist, glaring at him as he latched the door.

"All right, what's the drop?" Hetzer asked.

"It's in the satchel, for your cap, if he's the right one," she said.

"If he's the right one?"

"I need to see him to know," she said.

"That's convenient," Hetzer said. "Jutie, did you check her out at all?"

"Well . . ." Jutie said.

"Stupid," Hetzer said. He went over to the bird, who was giving him a hard glare. "You think you can just walk in and see the cap, eh?"

"Thought I might," she said. She didn't flinch as he got closer, her eyes locked on him. He reached over and tried to take the satchel from her. Just as his fingers touched the handle, her fist swung out, cracking him across the jaw. "This isn't for you, Prince."

"You got iron and spit, Napa," he said, rubbing his jaw. "No doubt about that."

"Most Napa girls do," she said. "We're soldiers' daughters."

"Question is, you got a knife hidden on you? You got ink on your skin?"

"What's that got to do with anything?"

"You want to see the cap, everything. Put the satchel on the ground."

"You don't touch it."

"Course not, bird," he said. "Just put it down and open it up." She did so. It looked like it just had cloth in it. "You looking to be a laundry girl or something?"

"Maybe," she said. "But not for you."

"Fine," Hetzer said. "Now take off the boots."

She glared at him, but didn't give him any lip about it. She pulled off one boot and held it upside down, showing nothing was hidden in it, and dropped it on the ground. Then she did the same with the other. She sneered at him. "You want anything else? You need to check me completely?"

"Yeah, I think so," he said. She was a pretty one, with a strong body. He certainly wanted to see more of it.

"Fine," she hissed. She started unlacing her blouse.

"That's enough," said Colin, coming out from the back.

"Cap, we were just—" Hetzer said.

"I know what," Colin said. "You looking for me, girl?"

The Napa girl crossed over and looked Colin over, examining his face closely. "Yeah, I'm looking for you."

"I know you, girl?"

"Not me," she said. She went back over to the satchel and closed it up. "We have a mutual friend."

"Who would that be?" Colin asked. Hetzer noticed the two of them both glanced at him and Jutie nervously.

"I think you know," she said. She tossed the satchel over to Colin. "You need to keep that safe for him."

"I don't need to do anything for him," Colin said, his voice rising.

"Say that if you like," she said. "Doesn't make it true."

"Why the blazes should I do it?" Colin said, looking at the satchel in his arms.

"Because he needs it to be hidden," she said. She gave another glance at Jutie and Hetzer. Hetzer had no idea what this was all about, but Colin obviously did.

"Is this as much heat as I think it is?"

"I think so," she said. "But you keep it quiet, and the heat won't need to come here."

Colin frowned at her. "He told you to give it to me?"

"He told me to hide it," she said. "I knew you'd be the safest place."

Colin shook his head. "Fine. But he's got to stay low from now on."

"I'll keep him safe," she said.

"Get your boots on and scat." He returned to the back room, still holding on to the satchel.

"You heard him, bird," Hetzer said. He didn't get any of what just happened, but the girl made her drop. She was already putting her boots on. "Unless you want to stay for something else."

"Not a chance, Prince," she said. "Unlatch the blasted door."

Hetzer gave a nod over to Jutie, who scrambled over to open it. As soon as he did, the bird was out and gone.

"What the blazes was all that?" Hetzer asked.

"I'm not sure," Jutie said.

"Yeah, well, next time don't let a pretty face make you stupid, Jutes."

"I . . . I don't think I—"

"It's all right," Colin said, coming back out. He still was holding on to the satchel. "Let's go get some breakfast, all right?" He didn't look at either one of them as he went to the door.

"Sure thing, cap," Jutie said.

"And this whole business didn't happen. Clear? Not to the other boys, not the other caps, not the bosses, not no one."

"Sure thing," Hetzer said.

"Swear on the street, Hetz," Colin said. That took Hetzer by surprise. Colin rarely invoked that, but that meant this was serious business. That was the most sacred thing Colin could tell him.

"I swear it on Rose Street," Hetzer said. "Quiet as a knife."

"All right," Colin said, going up and out to the street. Hetzer followed after him. The whole morning felt wrong to Hetzer. Starting the day like this made his guts churn. Today was not going to be a good day.

Chapter 20

THE NEXT DAY WAS Saint Senea Day. Saint Days meant no classes. On the minor Saint Days, Veranix and Delmin would go to the morning services in the campus chapel, followed by joining fellow students for cider and cards, or going to a house social at the women's college. Major holidays, like Fenstide earlier in the month, or Terrentin or Quiet Night, the University would organize a more formal event.

Saint Senea Day was minor, and surely the faculty resented having another holiday so close to Fenstide. Veranix knew from experience the chapel services would be nearly empty. Very few people honored the Saint of Righteous Outlaws.

But as far as Veranix was concerned, Senea was *his* saint.

For Saint Senea Day, to start, Veranix had decided to sleep, at least late through the morning. He felt this was a fine plan, one that honored Saint Senea, rest well earned doing righteous works of outlawry. Come sunset, he would perform appropriate acts of gratitude at the chapel.

It wasn't even nine bells when his plan was ruined. Delmin charged into their dormitory, slamming the door behind him.

"Get up!" Delmin shouted. Veranix recognized the tone of panic, and was immediately awake and alert. Delmin was pale and sweaty, his breathing labored.

"What, what is it?" Veranix asked.

"There's . . . there's . . ." Delmin gasped. He was too winded to get the words out.

"All right, calm down," Veranix said, getting to his feet. "What happened? Fire? Or worse?"

"Worse," Delmin said. He caught his breath. "Campus is about to be locked down on emergency curfew."

"Emergency curfew? In the middle of the morning on a Saint Day?" Veranix was shocked. Emergency curfew was one of those things students talked about in hushed whispers, one of those things everyone feared, but it never actually happened. It was a protocol in case something or someone dangerous was believed to be on campus. All students were restricted to dorms. Campus gates were shut. Cadets and prefects patrolled walkways and lawns.

Delmin nodded. "I think it's for you."

"Me? Why do you—"

Bells clanged in rapid succession from every direction. That was the sign. Veranix scrambled to the window. Outside, cadets were running across the lawn, ushering people into buildings.

"What happened, Del?" Veranix asked. He grabbed a shirt and put it on.

"Well, I went to Alimen's office. I wanted to ask him about properties of napranium, you know, learn more about the stuff and . . ."

"Right, and then?"

"When I got there, there were four men in his office with him. All mages, and I mean I could see the *numina* flow just bristling about them. These guys are major players. They were telling him that they knew their goods were somewhere on campus, and that there was a thief who had brought the stuff here."

"Their goods?" Veranix asked. "You mean . . ."

"The rope and the cloak, I'm sure," Delmin said. "They didn't say so explicitly, but they didn't need to. Professor Alimen was arguing with them, but . . ."

"Wait, first. All mages, right? No thugs or muscle?"

"I don't see how that matters, Vee!" Delmin said.

"It matters in that these are not Fenmere's men. They're his buyers. The ones who were supposed to get these things in the first place."

"So?"

"So, none of them have seen me as the Thorn. They don't know . . ."

"Maybe, maybe not," Delmin said. "Anyway, they insisted that Alimen lock down the campus so they could search for the thief."

"And he agreed?"

"Not readily," Delmin said, "but they told him he didn't want to make an enemy of the Blue Hand Circle, and . . ."

"Blue Hand?" Veranix asked. "I met one of those guys before, in Alimen's office. He was a jerk."

"Well, now there are four of them, and none of them are guys you would want to trifle with. Are the things here, though? I have a plan."

"No, they—what plan?"

Delmin smiled a bit. Veranix recognized the look on

Delmin's face. It was the one he had whenever he thought he was being especially clever.

"The way I see it, those Blue Hand men are gifted enough to track *numina* flow to the things."

"You said you couldn't see anything strange when I used them."

"I couldn't, but by themselves, they stand out. Even if you hid them underground, I would think one of them is good enough to spot the irregularities of them."

"Kaiana," Veranix whispered. He went out into the hall.

"I haven't even told you the plan." Delmin ran after him.

"So, what is it?" Veranix asked as they both went down the stairs. Delmin pulled something out of his pocket and put it in Veranix's hand. It was a lump of cold metal, and Veranix immediately felt dizzy and winded. He stopped walking, taking a moment to regain his equilibrium.

"Dalmatium?" Veranix asked.

"Put that with the goods, and they cancel each other out. No strange *numina* flow to track."

"Del," Veranix said, his eyes widening, "That's brilliant. How did you . . ."

"It was on Alimen's practice table," Delmin said. "I swiped it when he was arguing with the Blue Hand mages."

Veranix laughed. "We'll make a thief of you yet."

"No, thanks," Delmin said. "But you have to get to the things before they do. How are you going to do that with the curfew on?"

"Remind me, Delmin. We're restricted to where?"

"Dormitories and dining halls, during meal times."

"Right," Veranix said. He headed down to the main door. As he predicted, there was a prefect at the door. It wasn't Rellings, at least. Veranix went to the door, walking like he had no intention of stopping.

"Hey," said the prefect. "Curfew lockdown, kish."

"Breakfast, prefect," Veranix said. "We still get to eat."

The prefect raised an eyebrow. "A bit late on that. Breakfast ends at nine bells."

"Not nine bells yet," Delmin said.

"Maybe two minutes from," the prefect said.

"Come on," Veranix said, pointing to Delmin's scarf. "We're magic students. You know we can't miss a meal."

"Should have gone earlier."

"I slept in," Veranix said

"Your problem."

Delmin leaned in to the prefect. "Listen, what would you rather have, two annoyed, hungry mages, or two mages who owe you a favor?" The prefect thought about this for a minute, and then opened the door. He pulled out a whistle from his coat pocket and gave it two sharp blows.

"Two coming over," he called out to another prefect standing outside Holtman.

"Two coming, aye!" the other prefect called back.

"I will collect on that favor, kish," he told them. They nodded and dashed across the walkway between Almers and Holtman. As they reached the wooden double doors, held open by the prefect guarding it, Delmin turned to look back at Almers.

"Blessed Saint Justinia," he muttered. "They're coming."

Veranix turned his head and saw the group approaching Almers from the other side. Professor Alimen walked in front of them, the scowl he wore marking his obvious annoyance. Mister Kalas was with them, looking far too pleased with himself. Seeing Kalas made everything clear. He and his Blue Hand Circle were Fenmere's buyers, the ones the cloak and rope were for. Whatever the Blue Hand Circle wanted, whatever they were doing that required the items, it couldn't be good.

The two men behind Kalas were younger men, but clearly mages, wearing blue robes over their woolen suits. Veranix wasn't as skilled as Delmin at seeing *numina* flow, but these two were gushing wells of it. As strong as they were, they were nothing compared to the man walking in the back of the group. He gave the impression of being an old man, despite his bright red hair, walking slowly as if his withered body was too frail to move any faster. Veranix realized right away that was not the case. This man was the most powerful mage he had ever seen, pulling so much *numina* into his body the grass wilted under his feet.

Veranix stopped in the doorway, transfixed until Delmin pulled him in the building. Once inside, Veranix found himself gasping for breath, his heart racing. His skin was covered in a layer of sweat.

"Who . . . who was that?" he asked, his voice cracking.

"I don't know," Delmin said, pulling Veranix by the arm. "I don't want to find out."

"But you saw, didn't you?" Veranix said. He stumbled down the hallway. "You saw the kind of power he had, didn't you?"

"You have no idea," Delmin said. He stopped and

leaned against the wall. Veranix could see that his friend was at least as scared as he was.

"Del, you realize what a man like that, if he got the cloak and rope, what he could do? The kind of power—"

"He could crack the city in half," Delmin said plainly. "And if he's the sort of man who does business with crime lords . . ."

"There's no way we can let him get the items," Veranix said. "Come on!" He dashed down the hallway.

"How are we going to . . ." Delmin started, chasing after him.

"The other end of the Spinner Run," Veranix said, "comes out at this storeroom over here. We can get to the . . ." He grabbed the doorknob and turned it. It didn't move. The door was locked. Instinctively, he magicked the door open, but nothing happened.

"Why isn't it—"

"The dalmatium," Delmin said. "You can't do any magic with it. Give it to me and . . ."

Veranix had already kicked the door open. The dry wood around the lock splintered easily, and the door burst open.

"Vee!" Delmin gasped. "How . . . how can you . . ."

"Fix it," Veranix said, going into the room. He went right to the trapdoor hidden behind the far shelf.

"Fix it? How do I fix it?" Delmin asked.

Veranix opened the door and got halfway into it. "You're a mage, Mister Sarren," he said with a wink. "Figure something out." He dropped to the dusty floor below, pulling the door shut with him.

The Spinner Run was completely dark. With the chunk of dalmatium in his hand, Veranix couldn't make any light. He ran down the hall on memory and sense of direction, brushing against the stone walls several times before he reached the other end. He felt around at the ground, searching for the hidden niche where he had stashed his gear. After several frantic minutes, he found it.

Empty.

He checked it three times. Nothing was there at all.

Blindly, he scrambled for the ladder at the end of the run, and raced up it. He knocked open the trapdoor and leaped out into the carriage house.

"Kai!" he shouted. "Kaiana!" He looked around frantically, not even seeing her.

"Shut your screaming mouth," Kaiana hissed at him. She came around from one of the other stables. "You think you can get caught in here? They rang the bells for . . ."

"I know! That's why I'm here. The lockdown is so they can search for the cloak and—"

"For you," she said. "Wonderful."

"They don't know it's me, Kai," Veranix said. He was in a panic, not able to think clearly. He came over to her, grabbing her shoulders. "But if they find it, it'll—"

"They're not going to find it here, though," she said.

"It's gone," he told her, "The things are gone!"

"I know that, Veranix," she said calmly. "I've already moved them."

"To where? Kaiana, where are—" Veranix was interrupted by several voices outside. Someone was opening the door.

"Blasted saints," Kaiana muttered. With surprising

strength, she grabbed Veranix by the shirt and pulled him into her quarters.

"Kai, what . . ." Veranix whispered. She shushed him, and as the main door to the carriage house opened, she shut her own door.

"I'm quite certain of it," a voice outside said. "The *numina* trails are quite clear."

"I'm surprised you didn't notice them yourself, Professor," another voice said.

"I noticed nothing unusual." That was Professor Alimen. "Nothing inconsistent with daily activity in a place where mages live."

"Mages live in the carriage house now?" a sneering voice said. Veranix recognized it was Kalas.

"No, of course not, Fenrich."

"Search it all!" a raspy voice hissed. Sounds of men searching the stables began. Footsteps came close to Kaiana's door.

"Stupid," Kaiana muttered. Veranix wasn't sure what she meant, but before he could ask, she was already moving. She came up to him, tore open his shirt and pushed him onto her bed. A moment later, she had thrown off her own clothes and jumped on top of him, kissing him passionately.

Veranix reeled, unsure how to react, unable to think of anything other than the sweet wetness of her mouth. Before he could do or say anything else, the door flew open. Veranix's heart was slamming against his chest, his thoughts racing. For a moment, he had forgotten about napranium or the Blue Hand Circle. He couldn't even remember why he had come to the carriage house. All he knew was he hated whoever had opened the door.

"Well, well." The young man at the door—the blond with Kalas's group—leered at the two of them.

"What?" said the rasping voice. As the rest of the mages crowded into the small room, Kaiana was already on her feet, pulling her blanket around her.

"How dare you!" she said with indignation. "Barging into a girl's room like this!"

"Quiet, harlot!" Kalas said. He held up one hand, and Kaiana was pushed, falling back down on the bed. That brought Veranix back to his senses, and he sat up, ready to tackle Kalas.

"Don't you dare—" he started, putting himself between Kalas and Kaiana.

"Mister Calbert!" Professor Alimen said, moving to the front of the group. He looked around for a moment. "You are aware that the campus is on emergency curfew, aren't you?"

Veranix's mind raced, quickly putting ideas together, catching up with the events occurring around him. "No, sir," he said. "I didn't hear any bells. But I wasn't paying attention, really."

The mage who opened the door snorted with laughter. "I shouldn't wonder."

"Enough, Mister Kent," Alimen said to him. "Mister Calbert, ignoring official bells is a serious matter. Regardless of the . . . distractions at hand."

"I understand, sir," Veranix said, bowing his head. "Perhaps we should remove ourselves from the young lady's quarters to discuss the consequences?"

"I agree," Professor Alimen said, "for the sake of propriety. Gentlemen, if we can continue this elsewhere . . ."

"We are searching here!" rasped the frightening, red-haired mage.

"Sirath," Alimen said to him, "I don't think—"

"Lord Sirath!" barked the other young mage.

Alimen regarded this with barely hidden disdain. "Mind your manners, Mister Forden. The point is you traced unusual *numina* signatures to the carriage house. Mister Calbert has clearly been spending his spare time in here—"

"For obvious reasons," Kalas said, still leering at Kaiana as she wrapped her blanket around her body. Veranix's blood boiled, seeing Kaiana embarrassed and ogled like this. Despite her Napolic heritage, he had always known her to be demure and conservative. Having all these strangers see her so exposed, it must have been awful for her. She looked miserable. That wasn't performance on her part. The extent of what she did hit him deep in his stomach.

"That's enough," Veranix said, grabbing Kalas by the shoulder. Kalas reacted immediately, swatting Veranix across the face with the back of his hand. Veranix's hot blood ran across his tongue and lips.

That cracked it.

The full measure of Veranix's anger came rushing through his skull. Rage for his parents. Rage for Kaiana. Rage for Fenmere. Rage for the dead and dying on the streets of Maradaine, poisoned by *effitte*. Rage for these presumptuous mages who call themselves Lord or Master with no cause other than their own hubris.

He would not stand it anymore.

Fueled by that rage he pulled in *numina* and blasted it out his hand at Kalas.

The blast did nothing. It was as if he had thrown a bucket of water on Kalas, harmlessly splashing off him.

"Mister Calbert!" Professor Alimen shouted, shocked.

Kalas was neither shocked nor angry. He chuckled, amused. "This is your prize pupil, is it not, Alimen? This is the best that the University of Maradaine has, and he is nothing."

Veranix remained shocked at what happened. Was Kalas strong enough to resist his magic?

"This is all quite enough, all of you!" Professor Alimen barked. "Fenrich, out of courtesy, I have put up with your accusations and your intrusions, but these further violations and insults will not stand!"

"Will not stand?" Sirath said, his tone mocking. "Who are you to say what will not stand?"

"I am a chair and professor here, Sirath," Professor Alimen said, shooting a look at the two young mages, as if daring them to challenge him. "My authority stands on this campus."

At the outside door, someone was making a commotion. Master Jolen, the head of the grounds, came in with three cadets following after him.

"Don't you boys tell me where I can't go!" Jolen's face blazed red with anger. He came marching up to the group of mages. "What the blazes is the big idea, Professor?"

"These . . . these men were searching for something," Professor Alimen said to Jolen. "But it's not here, and they shall be going."

"Searching for what?" Jolen said, looking around. "Nothing here but horses and that useless . . ." His eyes found Kaiana, still holding the blanket around her body. He then looked at Veranix: shirt open, red-faced, fuming. Professor Alimen had already moved in front of Jolen, holding his hands up.

"Not all is what it seems, Jolen, you—"

"You should keep a tighter leash on your boys, Professor!" Jolen shouted. "And you, you tramp, you were finally caught! I should knock the sin out of you!"

"Enough!" roared Sirath, and the whole carriage house shook with his voice. Veranix felt the raw power coming from the man vibrate through his bones. Everyone stopped and stared at him. He looked around the room slowly, taking time to inspect Veranix thoroughly. Despite the screaming fear Sirath's gaze put in his stomach, Veranix held his ground. He stared right back into Sirath's dark eyes. He wasn't going to cower to any man, and with his own stare he let Sirath know that.

"This boy," Sirath eventually rasped, his eyes still fixed on Veranix, "lacks the basic ability to account for the *numina* traces we tracked here. He is barely anything."

Veranix suddenly realized what happened. The piece of dalmatium was still there in his pocket. It had been there all this while. The fact that he had been able to blast anything was impressive. It also meant that Sirath had no idea what he was really capable of.

"I might surprise you, Sirath," Veranix said.

"Mister Colbert!" Alimen said.

"I doubt that, boy," Sirath said. "Are our things here or not, trackers?"

"No, Lord Sirath," Forden said, looking around. "And now the *numina* traces are a bit of a muddle, but give us some time and . . ."

"No," Alimen said, "I've entertained your fancy too long. You have no time."

"Do not cross us, Alimen," Kalas said.

"This is over," Alimen said. He turned to the three cadets standing at the door of the carriage house, who all looked frightened and confused. "Cadets, please escort these gentlemen to the campus gates. Lift the emergency curfew, on my authority, and let your officers know that the members of the Blue Hand Circle are not welcome on campus grounds."

None of the cadets came too close to the mages, but they directed them toward the door. Sirath and the other Blue Hands glared at Alimen, but they left without further words.

"Leave the trollop to me," Jolen said, grabbing a whip off the wall.

"Master Jolen!" Alimen barked. "You will not hurt this girl. Fire her from your employ if you feel you must, but leave her unmolested."

Jolen fumed, red-faced. He looked at the whip with disappointment. Growling, he looked back at Kaiana. "Fine. Sacked, trollop. Be gone by noon bells, or I will make up for the beating you're not getting now."

"Mister Calbert," Professor Alimen said, "compose yourself and come with me to my office. We have much to discuss."

"Yes, sir," Veranix said. He gingerly went back into Kaiana's room, closing up his shirt.

"Kai, I'm . . . I'm sorry that—"

"It's all right," she said, not looking at him. "I'll be fine." She looked over at Alimen and Jolen, who were both still watching them carefully. "I've got friends in the neighborhood who will help me. Just like you do." She looked back at him pointedly.

"You've said enough, boy," Jolen said. "Now go."

Veranix finished closing his shirt and stormed out of the carriage house. Professor Alimen was right behind him. The professor said nothing as they walked across the lawn toward Bolingwood Tower. Trumpets sounded from the walls of the campus, indicating the end of the emergency curfew.

Chapter 21

VERANIX CLIMBED the stairs to Alimen's office, not looking back to see if the professor was with him. He charged over to Alimen's desk and threw himself into the chair in front of it, chest heaving with anger. He sat there for several minutes, stewing in his rage, before he realized that Professor Alimen hadn't arrived yet. He turned back to the door. Alimen was just entering, winded from the walk.

"That's quite the pace you can manage," Alimen said. He held his hand over his chest. "Did it help?"

"How would it help?" Veranix asked. Alimen came over and sat at his desk.

"Did it burn off some of that anger?"

"Those people had no right—" Veranix started.

"No, they didn't," Alimen said. "I'm sorry I granted them the latitude I did. I should have investigated their claims more closely before acting on them."

"Do you think so?" Veranix shouted, springing to his feet. "You call an emergency curfew and give those . . . people free reign over the student body, and you didn't investigate their claims?"

"Watch yourself, Mister Calbert!" Professor Alimen snapped. "I am not to be questioned by you!"

Veranix dropped back down into the chair, scowling. He bit his tongue to keep himself from further shouting.

"Now, I am no fan of the Blue Hand Circle, but they do have a fair degree of influence and importance. Mister Kalas had spoken of them funding a fellowship, which I was in the process of getting a firm commitment on. I'm certain that will now fall apart."

"What kind of fellowship?" Veranix asked.

"For a new faculty member in the Magic department, not that it's any of your business."

"One of them?"

"Which they would pay for."

"You shouldn't take their blood money," Veranix muttered.

"Blood money?" Alimen said with a raised eyebrow. "The Blue Hand Circle, and certainly Sirath, are not the most scrupulous people I've ever met, but I'd say that is a bit much."

"They're—" Veranix started. He bit his lip. He knew the Blue Hand was working with Fenmere, but he couldn't explain that to the professor. Alimen glared at him, waiting for him to say more. "They're disgusting, and you know it."

"They hold to a doctrine that I don't agree with, true, but that's—"

"What doctrine?" Veranix asked. Alimen was silent for a moment. "What do they want?"

"The Blue Hand Circle have ideas of magical superiority. Which, to them, includes excluding women and others from practicing magic." He looked down at the floor, avoiding Veranix's eye, and then mumbled, "I believe they also advocate for what is called a Magocracy."

"Exclusion and rule by mages." Veranix had never been a good history student, but he knew that there had been long centuries of persecution of mages because average people were afraid of exactly that. Only in recent decades had public opinion been accepting enough for magic to be practiced openly, taught at schools. People like the Blue Hand Circle would ruin that. "You would have them be in charge of a teaching position? Aren't you concerned with—"

"That is quite enough," Alimen said. "My primary concerns are your behavior, Mister Calbert. Let alone you dallying with a member of the staff, you lost control of your temper and your magic."

"Kalas hit me!"

"Which is the only reason you are not receiving sterner punishment, Veranix! Even with that, for you to magically attack someone else is inexcusable!"

Veranix dropped his head. Despite his anger, he was ashamed about what happened. "I'm sorry, I lost my head there."

"You saw what happened when you let rage fuel magic, didn't you?" Alimen said. "That was the most ineffective magic I have ever seen you do, Mister Calbert."

"Yes, it was," Veranix said. There was no need to let the professor know what really happened.

"Perhaps it's lucky," Alimen mused. "If you had actually hurt Kalas, who knows what he might have done."

"I guess the Blue Hand will continue to underestimate me," Veranix said, half to himself.

"Don't overestimate yourself, though, Mister Calbert," Alimen said. "Don't think that the walls of this University can or will protect you if you go too far."

"I'm not expecting the University to protect me, sir," Veranix snapped.

"You should!" Alimen said, grinding his teeth. "I don't know if you appreciate the latitude I've given you here, Mister Calbert. Many would say you should get probation, if not expulsion, for attacking another person the way you did Kalas. You can't risk expulsion, Mister Calbert."

"Am I risking it?" He knew he was challenging the professor, pushing too hard, but he didn't stop himself.

"A magic student cannot afford to risk it, Veranix," the professor said, his eyes hard. "We had no control over the natural gift we were born with, but in having it, we must—"

"Be responsible to society and to ourselves," Veranix droned. He had heard that line every semester since his first year.

"Yes," Alimen said. "I'm sorry if that basic truth bores you, Mister Calbert. The other truth is without receiving Letters of Mastery, you would not be inducted into Lord Preston's Circle. Or any other."

"I know that," Veranix said quietly.

"Uncircled." Alimen let the weight of the word hang there.

"I know," Veranix said again, this nearly a whisper. Without Letters, without a Circle, a mage's life became very difficult. It was more than just brotherhood, it meant legal protection. Legitimacy, for a mage, meant respect.

"Without a Circle," Alimen said, as if he were reading Veranix's thoughts, "you might as well have a target on your back."

"I know what that's like," Veranix muttered.

Professor Alimen stood up from his chair and crossed in front of the desk, sitting down right in front of Veranix. He took a moment, clearly struggling with what to say next. "I've always been concerned about you, Veranix. When you first came here, you asked me to not tell anyone of your circus performer origins, and to not ask you why."

"And the second part still holds, sir," Veranix said.

"I have respected your request for three years, Veranix. I will continue to do so. I will always respect your privacy."

"Thank you, sir," Veranix said. "Is that all?"

"Well . . ." Alimen stammered. "It's not . . . what I'm saying is, Veranix, that it's clear you have quite a few things going on. I have noticed the constant sleepiness during lectures. The occasional odd injury. And I would imagine that the other night was probably not your first dangerous encounter on the streets."

Veranix wasn't sure what to say. He chewed his lip and looked up at Professor Alimen. He knew he had stayed silent for too long to make any kind of convincing denial. "Professor, I—"

"Veranix, whatever path you are on will only lead you to further danger. The other day, street gangs, today the Blue Hand Circle, getting your friend fired, and I don't know what for tomorrow."

"I don't have specific plans for tomorrow, sir," Veranix said.

"Well, don't make any," Alimen said. He crossed

away from the desk, walking over to his workbench. Veranix took the moment to slip the dalmatium out of his pocket and onto the desk. Alimen continued, his tone harsher than Veranix had ever heard before. "Starting tomorrow, we will increase your level of work and responsibility, Mister Calbert. That should minimize your opportunity for trouble."

"Professor," Veranix started lamely.

Alimen waved his hand dismissively. "I'm going to respect the Saint Day and not put you to task now. Though I'm sure it's just a day without lecture for you." He spat that last part out with resentment.

Anger sparked again in Veranix's gut, dancing as wild *numina* up his arm. He got a hold of it before it lashed out of him, focusing the energy as a cool, red flame in his palm. Alimen jumped back, defensively pulling in his own *numina* so strongly even Veranix could sense it.

Veranix put all his attention on the flame, shaping it into an icon of a hooded woman. "Give me your blessing, Saint Senea. Put your eye upon me, protect me, as I act in the name of the right. Give me your strength, to fight against the unjust, to stand for the oppressed. If my body is broken, guard my soul and deliver it to stand before judgment, which I will never fear as I act in your name." He released the image.

Alimen's eyes narrowed, and his own energy dispersed. "Do you know where that prayer comes from?"

Veranix knew perfectly well. "From mages in the tenth century. Traditionally before execution for the crime of being mages."

"Glad to see you paid some attention in History of

Magic," Alimen said. "All right, go on. Blessed Saint Senea Day to you. Make good, safe use of it. I have quite a few things to attend to, myself."

"Yes, sir," Veranix said, getting up and going to the door. "Thank you, Professor." Alimen only grunted in reply. Veranix left and went down to the ground floor.

Campus activity was returning to normal, though Veranix could sense energy in the air, a tension in the student body. Veranix went over to the carriage house, but found only a scowling Master Jolen standing outside. He didn't bother approaching any closer, lest the groundskeeper take another opportunity to scream at him.

He couldn't see Kaiana, or do anything for her right now. He couldn't go after Kalas or Fenmere. His leg was throbbing, and the last thing he wanted to do was push through the pain any more. His whole body hurt. He also was still covered in sweat, grime, and blood from the night before. He headed over to the west side of the campus, where the bathhouse was.

The bathhouse was built on top of a natural hot spring, one of the few in the northwest of Druthal. Delmin had once rattled off the whole history of the discovery of the spring millennia ago, when Druthal had been a protectorate of the Kieran Empire, and the city had become a popular retreat for Imperial aristocracy. There had been a lot more to the story, but Veranix had completely forgotten it. What mattered to him was getting clean and refreshed.

A valet approached him as he entered. "Good morning, sir. The baths, or other services?" There was a whole range of services available if one had the crowns to pay for it: barber, laundering, hot rooms, massage.

The University bathhouse was renowned all over the south side of Maradaine, often used by the general public for these services. Students were permitted to use the baths for free, but anything else they wanted cost just the same.

"Just the baths today," Veranix said, heading over to the enclosed courtyard that housed the bathing pools. The room was lined with wooden benches around the outer edge, with several small baths and one large pool in the center. Veranix went to one of the benches and stripped off his clothes, leaving them in a loose heap.

Veranix climbed into one of the small baths, grabbing the wooden bucket with soap and sponge that sat next to it. Patrons were expected to clean off in the small baths, and Veranix got to work scrubbing off the past few days' worth of grime and dried blood. He paid special attention to the wound in his shoulder. It still looked bad, though the stitches were holding. Which was good, since Kaiana wasn't going to be able to fix them any time soon.

He hoped she would be all right. He promised himself that he would use whatever money he could spare, and whatever he took from Fenmere in the future, to help get her set up. He'd make sure she was safe, with a decent flop of her own. He laughed quietly. If he wasn't careful, he'd have to move in with her.

What did she mean, she had friends in the street? As far as he had seen, she hardly ever left campus.

Deciding he was clean enough, he got out of the small bath and into the large pool. This was where the water was hottest. Veranix knew quite a few students who couldn't stand it, but he relished it. Under the water, he stretched out his leg. There was still a nasty

wound there, purple and swollen, but no blood or pus.
The muscles were tight, but he felt sure it would heal
well enough in time, given he let it rest for a while.

The heat of the bath sank deep into his body, and he
succumbed to it, letting it take him into a relaxing doze.

Fenmere's parlor was once again sullied by the presence of the Blue Hand Circle. This was becoming all too
common, and Fenmere was troubled with how comfortable they made themselves in his home. He took
solace in one small fact: their presence meant that they
had failed. He drew every ounce of satisfaction out of
it that was possible.

"So you've come back," he said as he bit into a plum.
He had given his staff explicit instructions not to offer
or deliver food to any of the Blue Hand on this visit. All
four of them eyed the plum in his hands like dogs being kept out in the yard, denied entry to the kitchen.
They sat on one side of the parlor, all on the couch save
Kent, who paced back and forth behind them. Fenmere
had long known how to tame dogs and spot which one
most needed the whip.

At this meeting, the whip was his authority, giving
these mages a show of strength. He sat in his favorite
chair, giving more of his attention to the plum in his
hand than his guests. Gerrick and Corman stood behind
his chair. Nevin and Samael both sat in a far corner by
the fireplace; Nevin sharpened knives while Samael put
together a new crossbow. Bell and a few more heavies
stood by the door.

Fenmere ignored all sense of propriety and let the
juice of the plum drip down his chin.

"We were ejected from the campus before we found the goods," Kalas said.

"And so you come back to me, hat in hand," Fenmere said, wiping the juice with his sleeve. He looked over at the Blue Hand as they stewed in anger and naked hunger. "Why, Fenrich. You're still wearing your hat."

"What's this, Fenmere?" Kalas sneered.

"I said you are coming to me hat in hand, and yet you still wear your hat. You are sitting in my parlor with your hat on." He stared hard at Kalas, taking a savage bite into the plum.

"Fenmere, we have—" was all Kalas got out. Fenmere pelted him in the face with the plum as hard as he could. Kalas might be able to turn him into a potato, but that felt good.

"Do you see anyone else in here with a blasted hat on, Mister Kalas? No, by blazes, because it isn't done! You come into my blazing house, you rutting well better take your blasted hat off and hold it in your blasted hand!"

With slow, simmering deliberateness, Kalas took off his hat and held it in his lap with one hand. With his other, he wiped remnants of plum off his face and licked them from his gloved fingers.

Silently, Lord Sirath reached out with his bony hand and took the half plum that sat on the floor and shoved it in his mouth.

"Now, that's better," Fenmere said. "So you went to campus, tried to find your goods, and you failed."

"We are almost out of time, Fenmere," Kalas said, looking around the room at all the men assembled. "We must have our things by midnight."

"That could be tough," Fenmere said.

"We have invested a considerable amount of money in you, Mister Fenmere." Kalas got up from his seat and crossed over. "You should at least have the decency to show concern in our interests."

"Frankly, Kalas, I don't even understand your interests. You came to me because I could get Poasian-made things into the city. You want to do some crazy magic thing and you need your crazy magic things on the day when the crazy magic is right. Great." Sirath and the others were all fuming now. Fenmere continued, "But your stuff got pinched. I hate it, but it's part of business. The Thorn is going to pay for doing that. Maybe today, maybe next month, maybe in ten years. But I won't let him go, believe you me."

"Doesn't help us," Sirath said.

"Give me something to work with, and maybe I can help," Fenmere said.

Gerrick offered, "All we know is he's somewhere on campus. We can turn Dentonhill upside down in a day, but the University would take more time. You saw yourself, Mister Kalas, it's not that easy to search for something there."

"The girl," Kent said.

"What's that?" Gerrick asked.

"Nothing," Kalas said. "He saw some dark Napa naked and he got far too excited about it." Kalas gave an angry glare at the young mage.

"It distracted me," Kent growled. "Shouldn't have let it, that was stupid."

"It was," Sirath said.

"She had our things. She had touched them." Kent was worked up and red-faced. He shouted, "That dark beast had put her filthy hands on our things! I could smell it all over her, and I didn't realize it because she tempted me with her wickedness!"

"Well," Fenmere said. "That was helpful. And a disturbing look into the mind of your young friend."

"So, she had our goods," Kalas said. "We'll go get her, then."

"Perhaps I should send my men this time." Fenmere pointed to Bell and his boys. "Take the other young mage with you. He seems less excitable, and he'll be able to help you find the girl."

"Right," Bell said. He limped over and tapped Forden on the arm. "Let's go." Forden shrugged and got up from the couch.

"Bring her to the warehouse we've set aside for our friends," Fenmere called out as Bell and the others headed out. "The rest of you should head over there, get everything ready. Tonight is your big night, isn't it, Lord Sirath?"

"Yes," Sirath croaked as he got up from the couch.

"I'll come out there to make sure everything is going well, but first I'll be heading to lunch." He got up and went to the door of the parlor, and with the subtlest of gestures had Gerrick and Corman follow him. He turned back to Sirath and Kalas, who looked ready to eat the furniture. "You all don't have membership at the Ullman Club, do you? Shame. The roast lamb is divine."

Kaiana didn't know how much longer she would be able to stay on campus, and she had no idea where Veranix was. She had tried to get into Almers, but the prefect at the door told her in no uncertain terms that no

women, especially a "common strumpet" such as herself, would be allowed to enter. She asked if she could
leave a note, but the prefect scoffed at her, casting his
doubts on her ability to read and write at all. She left
her handprint on his face before she left, which almost
got the cadets put on her.

She couldn't leave him a message at the carriage
house. She had full faith that Jolen would scour the
place and burn anything he found of hers. She couldn't
get into the Spinner Run, either, not knowing exactly
where the other end of it was.

The simple truth was she didn't have any idea where
else Veranix might be. She cursed herself for not knowing more about where he went on any given day, even
on a Saint Day. Would he go to the campus chapel? She
had no idea.

What had he told her last night? A show at Cantarell
Square. Would he still go there, even with everything
that had happened today? *He might, if he thought I might
be there.*

She could go look for him there, but she knew once
she left campus, she probably wouldn't be able to get
back in. It was the only idea she had.

Kaiana took her bag, an old canvas feedsack that
held her few possessions, and went across the south
lawn to the gate.

"Child!"

Instinctively she turned to the calling voice. Most of
the professors on campus called her "child," despite
the fact she was as old as any of the students, and she
didn't lack in height or muscle. The magic professor,
Alimen, was running over to her. She slowed her pace

to allow him to catch her, but didn't give him further regard.

"I'm glad I caught you," he said as he came up. He was breathing heavily, and bent over double to catch his wind.

"Did you need something, sir? I don't have much time before I catch a whipping." Her words came out harsher than she intended.

"Yes, child, about that—"

"It's Miss Nell or Kaiana, Professor. Preferably the former." She had had enough patronizing for one day.

He looked surprised, and nodded, appearing to accept the chastisement. "Miss Nell, of course. Forgive me. I am deeply sorry for everything that has occurred today. You, unfortunately, got caught in the middle of things that never should have touched you."

"Happens all the time," she said. She started to walk away. Alimen put a hand gently on her shoulder. She shrugged it off, but walked slower, allowing him to keep pace with her.

"Be that as it may, I feel a certain responsibility." He took a small purse out of his pocket and handed it to her. "Not a lot, mind you, but enough for you to pay rent for a few weeks. Enough to get settled."

"If the landlord doesn't mind renting to Napa girls." She immediately regretted saying that. "Thank you, though." She took the purse cautiously.

"It is the least I can do, given my role in your dismissal," Alimen said. They approached the gate. "Normally, I would say it is no business of anyone regarding your relationship with Mister Calbert, but clearly—"

"About Veranix, sir," she said, hopeful. "I need to

get a message to him, but privately. Could I ask you to—"

"Deliver one to him without reading it?" he offered. He gave her a warm smile. "Of course, Miss Nell. An old man like me doesn't need to read the secrets of young romance."

"Thank you, sir," she said. "I have some ink and paper here, it'll just take a moment . . ." She started to rummage through her bag.

"That's odd," Alimen said. "There's usually cadets watching the—"

Kaiana looked back up at Alimen, but he wasn't moving, not in the slightest. His mouth was half open, frozen forming the words. "Professor?"

"That's a handy thing," said a deep voice behind her. Large arms wrapped around her body. Before they could gain full purchase on her, she lifted up one leg and smashed it down on the knee of the person grabbing her. She turned around, landing a hard punch in his chest. He staggered back, but he had three others with him, including one of the men who had come to the carriage house earlier. A mage.

"Got some fight," he said, grinning at her darkly.

"Do it to her, too," the one she punched ordered.

"Can't take a girl?" the mage asked. Before any of them could answer, she hurled her sack at the mage. It fell apart as it struck him, her belongings scattering on the ground.

She wanted to run, but that would mean leaving the professor. He was still standing there, paralyzed and helpless. Her father hadn't left her much, except for soldier's wisdom. "Never leave a man to be taken," was one of his favorite things to tell her.

Even though she was a soldier's daughter, and her arms were as strong as any man's, she had never fought three men at once. These men were determined to take her quick and quiet. Despite her fight, six hands grabbed and held her, covered her mouth. The mage came over, and touched her forehead. With that, she couldn't move at all.

"Quick now," the mage said. "Take them both." She could still hear and see, feel every hand on her body as she was picked up off the ground. Before she knew what was happening, she was in darkness, tossed into the back of a cart, Alimen's inert body next to her. The cart started moving. Kaiana couldn't even force her throat to scream.

Chapter 22

CLEAN, relaxed, and in fresh clothes, Veranix made his way into Aventil. Unable to find Kaiana anywhere on campus, the only place he could think to look for her was in Cantarell Square, on the off chance that she went there looking for him. He didn't want the day to pass without finding her, and starting to put things right for her.

There were no cadets at the south gate, though he spotted two of them walking up the street, strikers and beers in hand. It was odd for both cadets to leave their post during their shift, but he'd seen it happen before.

No local boys were outside the gates either. That was even stranger. It was a Saint Day, though, so it was entirely possible that there were plenty of students out in the neighborhood, keeping the street boys busy. Maybe even the Princes would go to services.

Cantarell Square was bordered by a low brick wall, no higher than Veranix's knee, with two marble statues on ten-foot plinths at opposite corners: Lord and Lady

Cantarell, once Baron and Baroness of Aventil, when there was such a thing. In the center of the square, an ancient white stone fountain—long in disrepair—was one of the few remnants from the sprawling garden that had filled the land where the neighborhood now stood. Delmin had once told Veranix that the square was supposed to stand as a reminder of the generous donation of land the Cantarells had made, so that the city could continue to grow. Of course, the truth was the Cantarells were deeply in debt, and selling the baroness's garden to the city was the only way to pay it off. The Square Players' stage was built over the fountain, a hasty structure of several wooden platforms that could be easily disassembled whenever a city official decided it shouldn't be covering the landmark.

The square was full of activity, as the show was going on, and many Aventil vendors and street boys crowded along the edges to pick up the business that would come from the people watching. Veranix hoped that Kaiana would be easy to spot, even in this crowd.

A huge burst of laughter came from the crowd. Up on the stage, the actors were performing one of Veranix's favorite scenes from the play. *Three Men and Two Wives* was a ridiculous comedy in which a poor baron marries off his two daughters to rich merchants, but through a series of misunderstandings three weddings are promised with only two daughters to fulfill them. Every time the show played in Cantarell, Veranix tried to come out to see it. In the scene, the baron was disguised as a washerwoman, while one of his daughters was disguised as a gentleman, and neither recognized the other. The crowd laughed raucously, but Veranix could barely manage to look at the stage. He kept searching for Kai, and she was nowhere to be found.

"Oh, but these clothes are perfectly clean," the disguised actress said, fending off the ersatz baron, who was trying to take her clothes. "There's no need to wash them today!"

"Washing must be done, clean or no!"

On any other day, Veranix would be unable to breathe, he'd be laughing so hard. Most people in the crowd were in such a state. He moved to the outer fringes of the crowd, searching the faces for a flash of darker skin. He saw nothing but fair Druth complexions, brown and blond hair. Then he saw a familiar face.

Colin stood at one corner of the square, under the statue of Lord Cantarell, giving half his attention to the show, the other half to the crowd around him. More than likely he was keeping watch while some of the Princes stole purses and picked pockets. The square marked the border between Rose Street Prince territory and two of the other Aventil gangs, Waterpath Orphans and Red Rabbits, as far as Veranix remembered.

Veranix approached Colin, but as he moved in Colin spotted him. The two of them locked eyes for a minute, Colin's burning with anger. Colin spit on the ground in Veranix's direction, and then gave a sharp whistle.

In response to the whistle, two other Princes on the outskirts of the crowd pushed each other, knocking over a pie stand. People around the stand screamed and cried, and all attention turned to them. Veranix spotted several other Princes dashing out of the crowd, and when he looked back to Colin, his cousin was gone.

Kaiana didn't know where she was when she saw light again. She was no longer paralyzed, but she was tied to a wooden post, someone else bound at her back. She presumed it was the professor. She was in a large room, a great warehouse by the looks of it, gray brick walls and stone floor. There were no crates or other storage, just people. Some were thugs like the ones who had grabbed her, some were the mages who had come hunting in her carriage house this morning. The others were gentlemen, at least by their clothes.

"What is the meaning of this?" Alimen shouted from behind her. "Kalas, did you really think you could get away with assaulting and kidnapping me, a member of the University and—"

"Actually, no, Gollic, that wasn't part of the plan," the older mage said as he slowly circled the two of them. He leered appreciatively at Kaiana. "Why did you take him, Forden?"

"He was there. He was disrespectful of us earlier."

"He was indeed," Kalas said. "Very foolish, Professor."

"You are the foolish one," Alimen said.

"I can feel you, Gollic," Kalas said. "Don't even think of building up your *numina*. I already have a hand around the girl's heart. You can feel that, yes?"

"Yes," Alimen said, his voice dejected.

"Good," Kalas said. He came around to face Kaiana. "Now, young lady, I believe you have been in possession of something that belongs to me."

"I'm just a poor groundskeeper," Kaiana said. "Blazes, thanks to you lot, I'm not even that now."

"I told the professor I had my hand on your heart, girl," Kalas said, holding his empty hand up to her. "I am quite serious about that." He tensed his fingers slightly, and Kaiana's chest was flooded with pain. Nothing could hold in her screams.

"Stop it, Kalas!" Alimen said. "Let the girl go. If you have a quarrel with me—"

"He really thinks this is about him." Forden giggled.

Kalas leaned in closer, his face barely an inch away from Kaiana's. The pain stopped. "Shall I ask again?"

"No," she gasped, struggling to get her breath. "You don't need to."

"That's very smart," Kalas said.

"You don't need to," she said again, looking up at him defiantly, "because I won't answer."

"Stupid girl," he said, and her chest was again nothing but agony. Only the fact that she was tied to the post kept her from falling over. She screamed, but forced herself to keep her eyes open, to stare at Kalas and every other man in the room, to memorize every face. The gentlemen stood in the back, watching what was happening with vague disinterest.

The young blond mage, the one Alimen had called Kent before, came leaping over, his face red with rage. "Tell us, you dark whore!" he screamed. Kalas hadn't released his grip, her chest was still on fire. Despite this, she spit in Kent's face.

He hit her with the back of his fist in response. "Try that again, filth!"

Suddenly Kent was knocked back by an unseen force. "Leave her!" Professor Alimen cried. He was wheezing out of breath.

"Poor choice, Professor," Kalas said. He squeezed

tighter on Kaiana's heart. She couldn't scream. She couldn't even breathe.

Kent stood back up and grabbed a cudgel from one of the thugs who was just standing and watching. He stalked over to the professor and hit him across the head. Then he hit him again, and again.

"Enough!" said one of the gentlemen. Neither Kalas nor Kent reacted. The gentleman came up and put a hand on Kalas's shoulder. "Enough!" Kalas released her, and two of the goons pulled the blond mage away from the professor. She could feel his body hanging limply behind her, held up only by the post.

"She knows!" The last mage, the impossibly gaunt one, came over and pointed an emaciated finger at her. "She's had it!"

The gentleman shook his head. "It doesn't matter."

"Let us handle this, Fenmere," Kalas said to the gentleman. Kaiana's heart, already pounding uncontrollably, raced even faster. This was Fenmere, the man responsible for so much death and pain, in her own life and so many others. She was surprised how ordinary he looked, especially next to these powerful mages.

"I don't think this is going to give you anything, Kalas."

"But she has had our items," Kalas said. "I can feel it on her!"

"I believe you," Fenmere reached out and lifted up Kaiana's chin, appraising her face. "But I know something about breaking people, making them talk. I've made men tell me secrets they wouldn't tell God." He looked deeply into her eyes. "This girl won't tell you anything."

"So what do you expect us to do?" Kalas asked.

"We do this our way," Fenmere said, walking away. "Very simply. We want the Thorn. We want what he has. We have something of his."

"Arrange a trade?" another gentleman asked. "For tonight?"

"Exactly, Corman," Fenmere said.

"How do we set the deal?" one of the thugs asked. "How do we get word to the Thorn?"

"You lack imagination, Bell," Fenmere said. He turned to the gentlemen, asking a question he clearly knew the answer to already. "How do we get word to the Thorn, Corman?"

"Hire a paper job, along Aventil and the campus."

"Exactly. And just to make a point, Mister Corman, muscle a weaker Aventil gang to do it."

"Muscle or hire?" Corman asked.

"Oh, hire, of course," Fenmere said. He smirked at Kaiana. "Pay them well for the job. Just make it perfectly clear that not taking the job isn't an option for them."

"Red Rabbits would be good for that," Bell offered.

"Red Rabbits it is, then," Fenmere said as he approached Bell. He gently cupped the thug's face. "I trust in your judgment here, Mister Bell. Please don't disappoint me."

"I'll—I'll get on it," Bell stammered out. He whistled to a few other thugs and left the room with them.

"Good," Fenmere said. "That's all settled, then. Does this suit you, gentlemen?" Kalas and the other mages nodded.

"We're going to trade the girl for the goods?" Kalas asked.

"No, we're going to say we are," Fenmere said. "When the Thorn comes, we kill him, and you get your things." He waved dismissively at Kaiana and the professor. "The two of them are your problem, but keep them intact until it's done."

Chapter 23

VERANIX HAD searched up and down throughout Aventil, with no luck in finding Kaiana. He even asked shopkeepers and strangers, but no one had seen anyone who looked like her. One man had offered to get him a young Napa girl for twenty crowns. The man backed off when Veranix threatened to thrash him.

His search brought him to the front steps of Saint Julian's Church. Desperate for any kind of guidance, he went inside.

In the first part of the church, through the large wooden doors, was the life-size statue of Saint Julian, depicted as a shield-bearing pilgrim, to protect the innocent as he was said to have done. Theological history was another subject in which Veranix's studies were less than what they should be. Surrounding the statue, scattered and pinned at the base, were tokens of prayers, small wooden carvings or brass figures, representing whatever it was people were hoping Saint Julian or God would help them with. Most of the tokens were in the shape of a heart or a coin: love and money, the most common of prayers. Two old women were kneeling at the base as well, muttering their prayers.

On the other side of the room was a coin box. Veranix went over to it and dropped a half-crown in.

"I don't have a prayer for Saint Julian," Veranix whispered. "But today is the day of Saint Senea. Look after my friend, Saint Senea. The law is on the side of the man who sacked her, but I don't know a more righteous soul than hers. Please protect her tonight. Intercede on her behalf. Help her to . . . help her, like she has always helped me."

"Don't see many students in here," said a man's voice behind him. Veranix startled, and turned to see the priest. Young enough that his face had few lines, and his fair hair hadn't begun to whiten.

"We mostly go to the Campus Chapel, I suppose," Veranix said.

"Who is the patron saint of that chapel?" the reverend asked.

Veranix had to think for a moment to answer that. "I don't think there is one. It's more vaguely toward all the saints. Students come from all branches of the church."

The reverend shrugged, as if the idea disappointed him. "Did you come seeking something more specific?"

Veranix glanced back at the statue. "I'm not sure the Humble Prince can help me today."

"Why did you come here, son?" the reverend asked.

"Looking for a friend," Veranix said. "I don't know where she is."

"Perhaps she went home."

"She lost her home today."

"So she needs a new one." The reverend nodded

thoughtfully. "You do know we have no sisters' cloister here. You could try Saint Arrianne's in North Colton."

"I don't think she will take holy orders." Veranix laughed. "She's not the type."

"What type is she?" the priest asked.

"Loyal," Veranix said.

"Loyalty is a pillar of virtue," the priest said, pointing to the statue. "Saint Julian was most noted for it. Loyalty is often rewarded."

"Not if you have to be loyal to more than one thing." Veranix started down the steps.

"Are these loyalties in conflict?" the priest asked.

Veranix stopped, his heart suddenly pounding. "I'm—not exactly. But they don't exactly work together that well either."

"A man can serve two masters. Or more," the priest said. "You study several courses at school, yes?"

"Quite a few," Veranix said.

"And each professor you have considers himself your only master. You must serve each of them."

"It does seem that way," Veranix agreed. "But one in particular takes precedence."

"Of course. When the time comes for you to discover what loyalty takes precedence for you, you will know." Six bells rang above them. "The hour is late, son. If my knowledge of University rules is correct, you do need to be back by the sunset, yes?"

"Not exactly," Veranix said. "But I should keep looking for my friend. Thank you."

"Thank you," said the priest. "For the donation."

"The least I can do, Reverend," Veranix said.

"Then the blessings of God and Saint Julian be with

you," the priest said. He retreated deeper into the church, and Veranix returned outside.

The sky was starting to get dark, but there was still plenty of activity in the streets. Shopkeepers were gathering up their goods, bringing them inside for safekeeping. People were heading home, or to the taverns. Young men were racing about, tacking up sheets of paper along any surface they could stick them to.

Another paper job, Veranix thought with wry amusement. He wondered if Colin was going through the trouble of showing him further disapproval. He went to look at one of the pages.

Across the top of the page was a picture of a thorn. He ripped the page off the wall and looked at it closer. It was definitely a message for him. At the bottom of the page was a blue mark, a hand in a circle. The center of the page was a scale, with a bag and a crown on one side, and a figure of a man and a woman on the other.

It clicked in his mind as clearly as if it had been written in plain prose. The Blue Hand Circle, and with them Fenmere, wanted to trade the rope and cloak for someone. Two people, a man and a woman. The rest of the message made it clear that they wanted to meet at the fish cannery at midnight to make the trade.

A man and a woman.

Kaiana.

Deep in his gut, he knew it meant Kaiana. They had figured out his identity, and they knew to take her to get him. Then who was the man? Was it Delmin? Could it even be Colin?

Veranix barely realized he was running, running as

fast as he could, back toward campus. He didn't know what he would do. He didn't even have the cloak and rope. He couldn't make the trade.

He bolted past the south gate, past the two cadets at guard with barely a wave. They waved back but did nothing else. He pounded up the walk toward Almers Hall, bursting through the main doors. He charged up the steps, pushing past several people, ignoring a few startled complaints. He didn't listen or care. He didn't stop until he reached his room, where Delmin sat, quietly reading.

"Delmin!" Veranix shouted, his heart leaping up on seeing his friend. He raced over, grabbing Delmin by the shoulders. He looked him over, searching for any signs that he had been hurt. "You're all right?"

"Yes, I'm fine," Delmin said. "Why wouldn't I be?"

"Well, they . . . I thought . . ." Veranix paused for a moment. His head was still racing, still swimming. "Maybe they don't know, then."

"They don't know what?" Delmin asked.

"They don't know for sure who it is," Veranix said, half to himself.

"Who what is? What are you on about?"

"They grabbed Kaiana. And someone else, I think," Veranix said.

"Someone else? Why?"

Veranix showed him the paper. "Two people, male and female. I had thought it was you, if they knew who Kaiana was." He shook his head. "Then they would know it was me. Who else might they take?"

"Well . . ." Delmin trailed off, looking like he wasn't sure if he wanted to say what he was thinking.

"What is it?"

"I was supposed to meet Professor Alimen at one

bell after noon. He wasn't at his office. I had asked around, and no one had seen him. I didn't think much of it, but—"

Veranix nodded, his gut churning. Alimen gone all day couldn't be a coincidence. "I bet that's it. They took him too. They took them both, and they want the rope and the cloak in exchange for their lives." He wanted to throw up. The two people who had done the most to help him, to protect him . . . they were both in danger now, because of him.

Delmin's eyes went wide, his face lost all color. "Who? That gang boss, what's his name, Fenson?"

"Fenmere. No." Veranix thought for a moment. "At least, not alone. His thugs couldn't take Alimen."

"So, who then?"

"The Blue Hand Circle, and that Lord Sirath."

Delmin swallowed hard. "Lord Sirath? That mage who looks half dead already?"

"Who else could capture the professor?" Veranix asked. Delmin sat down on his bed. He looked like he was going to throw up, Veranix felt the same way. The professor and Kaiana had both put themselves at risk when the Blue Hand was searching for him. He hadn't asked them to, but they both fought to save him.

He had to do the same for them. Whatever it took.

He went to his trunk, opened it up, and pulled out the false bottom. His old gear, including his father's bow, was sitting underneath.

"What are you going to do?"

"I can't leave them," Veranix said, pulling out his burgundy leather vest and soft boots. "I can't let Sirath hurt them, and I can't let him have the cloak and the rope."

"Are you sure, I mean . . ."

"Delmin, you saw him. If his natural ability was amplified by the napranium, what could he do? What *couldn't* he do?"

"He'd be . . ." stammered Delmin, growing paler. "I'd say he'd be unstoppable, but he seems pretty unstoppable now."

Veranix put on the vest and buttoned it up. His father's bow—his bow now—lay wrapped in cloth at the bottom of the chest, with all his father's oils and waxes. He bent down and placed his hand on it. He'd taken care of the bow whenever he had the chance, whenever Delmin wasn't around. It was good that he had, since he didn't have much time to get it ready for action.

"I have to try, though."

Delmin squatted over next to him. "Try with what, Vee? You think you're going to be able to shoot arrows at someone like Lord Sirath?"

Anger burned through Veranix's skull. "What do you think I should do then? Just leave them?"

"No, no . . ." Delmin said. He put his hand on Veranix's shoulder. "I'm just saying . . . I don't even know what I'm saying."

"Right," Veranix said hotly. He strapped on the quiver, and pulled one arrow out. "I just need to take him by surprise. One good shot."

"You miss, and he'll turn you to dust."

"I won't miss!" he ranted. "Even if I do, I'll give him dust!"

Delmin suddenly burst out laughing. "What does that even mean?"

Despite his anger, Veranix couldn't help laughing as well. He laughed so hard he lost his balance and fell over. "I don't know," he said, lying on the floor. "Sweet blessed saints, what a ridiculous thing to even—"

He stopped mid-sentence. He looked at the arrow still in his hand. An idea came to him. It was ridiculous, but it might work.

"That's exactly what I'll do."

"Exactly what you'll do?"

"Dust," Veranix said. "That's . . . how I'll get him."

"Now you really are talking crazy, Vee."

"No, I . . . I have a plan," he said. "Delmin, I'm going to need your help, though. I need to find them before they're ready for me. Do you think you could track their *numina* wakes, or Professor Alimen's, and lead me to where they all are?"

"I . . . I don't know, Vee," Delmin said. He looked nervous again.

"Alimen says you have the sharpest *numinic* senses he's seen." Veranix hoped that would give Delmin the push he needed.

"I think I could, but . . ."

"Just get me there, Del," Veranix said, putting his hand on Delmin's shoulder. "I won't put you in any danger."

"Right," Delmin said. He knit his brow, "Don't worry about it." He swallowed hard. "For the professor, I'll walk into any dark pit you do."

"Good to hear it, mate." Veranix smiled. He bundled up the bow and arrows in his maroon cloak and charged out the door full of purpose. He crashed into Eittle.

"Watch it, Calbert," snapped Eittle. He shook his head and stepped away from Veranix, raising his hands up defensively. "Sorry, I just . . ."

"I understand," Veranix said. He hadn't seen Eittle since Parsons overdosed. "You doing all right?"

"Yeah," Eittle said. He looked at Veranix and Delmin. "You two going to see it? I wasn't going to at first, but it's so rare, I figured I ought not miss it."

"See what?" Delmin asked.

"The Winged Convergence," Eittle said. Veranix and Delmin both gave blank looks. "You know, Namali is full tonight, and at one bell after midnight, it passes in front of Onali, which is at a quarter full waning. So Namali looks like it has white wings."

"Winged Convergence," Veranix said, nodding. It took him a moment to remember that "Namali" and "Onali" were the proper academic, Old Imperial names for the Blood Moon and White Moon. "Right, right. Of course. Alimen wants us to see it from Bolingwood Tower, so, that's where we're going."

"Good place to see it," said Eittle, managing a weak smile. "You all right, Sarren? You look like you're going to throw up." Veranix turned to look at Delmin, who was pale and clammy.

"Yeah," Delmin said, wiping the sweat off his forehead. "Bad fish at dinner. I'll . . . I'll be fine, though. You said this thing is rare. How rare?"

"It happens only every forty-seven years," said Eittle. "At least from Maradaine."

"Right. Come on, Vee. The professor is waiting for us." Delmin grabbed Veranix by the elbow and dragged him over to the stairwell.

"What's wrong?" Veranix asked when they were alone.

"This is bad," Delmin muttered as they went down the stairs. "This is very, very bad."

"Tell me." They reached the bottom of the stairs and went out the door, where the prefect on watch gave them a cursory nod as they exited. Night had fallen.

"All right, this is pure speculation, pure theory, but it adds up." Delmin looked up at the sky. The blood moon—Namali—was full, climbing in the sky, while Onali hung higher, a perfect half-moon. "Reading up on napranium, I pulled out a book called *Brenium's Northern Travels*. Brenium was a Kieran mage, from several hundred years ago, who traveled through the wild lands of northern Waisholm, and then to Bardinæ. Places where mystics practice Physical Focus."

"Physical Focus?" asked Veranix. "I know I've read that somewhere."

"Physical Focus, Veranix. Ancient arts like runecasting, reading entrails, blood rituals, astrology." He said the last one pointedly, glancing up at the sky.

"You've lost me, Delmin," Veranix looked up at the sky. "Are you telling me that this Winged Convergence thing is significant somehow?"

"At one point Brenium met an old mystic who claimed he could crack into *numina* and create a *jaäboushu*, a creature of pure, living *numina*. He needed animal blood, and the ritual could be performed only 'when the red moon flies on its wings.'"

"That . . . that's ludicrous," Veranix said "Old tales of nonsense." He quickened his pace to Bolingwood.

"I don't know," Delmin said. "Some scholars have theorized that phases of the moons could affect *numina* flow, the degree of it has never been properly charted. Who knows what a rare convergence might do?"

Veranix looked up again. "Yes, but . . . Brenium never saw it actually done, right? There was no proof that the whole thing wasn't just the raving of a madman."

"Right, the old mystic didn't perform the ritual, because he didn't have the proper things. 'Clad to establish his power, and bindings to control the beast.' That's what it says."

It hit Veranix like a blow across the head. "In other words, a cloak and a rope. This is very bad. Very, very bad."

Delmin stopped for a moment and smiled. "But you don't have them, he can't get them. So that's all right, then."

"Right," Veranix said. "And how angry is he going to be about that? And what will he do to the professor and Kaiana in retaliation?" He looked up at the tower. "Come on, let's get moving. First we need to go to the professor's office."

"Why do we need to do that?" Delmin asked.

"I told you. I have a plan."

The Turnabout was full of sound and spectacle. Dozens of Rose Street Princes filled the tables that rounded the outer edge of the floor, everyone laughing and drinking. The small wooden stage in the corner housed two musicians, playing a raunchy number on the horn and fiddle about a city girl who got lost out in the country. Some people in the place were singing along. Others paid more attention to the open ring of the floor, where two hopeful recruits brawled fist-to-nose, hoping to earn prestige with the senior members of the gang. The most senior present, Hotchins, paid them no mind, focusing his attention on a game of flip-stone with one of his lieutenants. Hotchins wasn't a street cap, anyway. Basement bosses like him didn't care about their blood.

The only street cap in the place was Colin. He sat by himself in one corner at a table illuminated by a lone candle, his heckie pie barely touched. The gravy had gone cold, congealed and greasy. He tapped the pie tin absently with his fork.

"Oy, you see this?" Hetzer slapped a piece of paper down on the table and sat down next to Colin. "Red Rabbits are running all around papering this. Both sides of Waterpath, and along the campus wall."

"Both sides?" Colin asked. That wasn't good news. The Rabbits were the weakest gang in Aventil. If they were running paper on both sides of Waterpath, they were doing it with Fenmere's blessing, if not for Fenmere. That was the kind of toehold into Aventil Colin didn't want Fenmere having. He frowned and looked at the paper. It was a lot of images, pretty complicated for a paper job, but the one that stood out immediately to Colin was the spiny thorn on the top. "You ask Tooser what he thinks it means?"

"He thinks it's a message to the Thorn," said Hetzer.

"That I got, pike," snapped Colin, scowling. "The rest?"

Hetzer pointed to the image of the scale in the center of the page. "He thinks it's about a trade they want the Thorn to make. There's a crown and a bag on one side, see, and two people on the other. Bloke and a bird. Maybe the Thorn is holding somebody's kids for cash?"

"No," Colin said. He felt his chest tighten up, his mouth go dry. "They got somebody who matters to the Thorn, they want the money and merch that he took from them."

"Who do you think they got?" Hetzer asked.

"Blazes should I know, Hetz?" Colin snapped, but the image of that dark Napa girl came right to his mind. He figured that skinny piece of hairy college scrabble Veranix was always with was the bloke. "The rest?"

"Twelve bells on the bottom, and a fish. Tooser thinks that's the time and place for the drop. Twelve bells at a fish market. Didn't we hear the Thorn had some scrap with Fenmere's boys at a fish market in Denton?"

"The cannery on Necker," Colin said. "But this ain't a symbol for Fenmere or his boys at all. Or Red Rabbits." He pointed to the last image, the hand in a circle, done in blue ink.

"Yeah, Tooser didn't know nothing about that neither. Thought you might have a clue."

"Nah," Colin said. "And this ain't nothing of ours, anyway. This business with the Thorn has been too much trouble in the street, anyway."

"Trouble in Dentonhill, you mean." Hotchins had walked over to the table.

"Trouble in Denton means Fenmere gives trouble here," Colin said. "We don't need that kind of noise."

"Right," Hotchins said. "Last time Aventil made any noise, Fenmere rolled us all real good. We know how your father took that, Col."

"Don't you start on my father again, Old Man," Colin said, standing up, his blood boiling. "He did what he had to. Aventil gangs still survive at all because of that."

"I know it," Hotchins said. "I was there. Your father and your uncle, saints bless him, they did what they could. Did what they had to." Colin eased off. "I was just thinking, though, I was also in Quarrygate for a few years. You ain't been there, have you?"

"No, man," Hetzer said, shaking his head. Colin and Hotchins both stared hard at him, and he shrank away from the table.

"You do what you have to in Quarry," Hotchins said, "just to stay alive. Plenty of blokes in there bite their lips while the big dogs and the guards roll them."

"Even the guards?" Hetzer asked. "I'd thought they'd at least go after doxies."

"A lot of guards like the power of treating another man as a doxy, boy," Hotchins said. "That's the truth about Quarrygate."

"Listen, Hotchins," Colin said, "You don't need to tell us about this . . ."

"It's the truth," Hotchins said, his bald head turning red. Colin wasn't sure if it was with anger or shame. "It's what happens in Quarry. I never bit my lip, though. When they got me, it cost them in blood and teeth, every time. And in the Quarry, that gives you respect. They call you a cat. But it's what Fenmere's been doing to Aventil for twenty years, and it ain't cost him a thing. We're all scared mice."

"You saying we should start something?" Hetzer asked.

"I ain't saying that," Hotchins said, getting up from the table. "I'm too old to be anything but a mouse no more." He tapped the picture of the thorn on the paper. "But mice need to respect the cat." He walked away from the table.

Colin looked down at the satchel at his feet. The one the Napa girl had given him. Veranix wouldn't be able to trade anything, because he didn't have it to trade.

That Napa girl had counted on Colin to keep it safe. To keep Veranix safe.

That was the promise he had made when Veranix first came to Maradaine. That was a blood promise. To family and to Rose Street.

He grabbed the satchel and stood up, knocking the table and all its contents over in the process.

"Cap?" asked Hetzer, "What're you doing?"

"I ain't no mouse," Colin said.

"What are you gonna do? Be a cat? Hotchins just said . . ." Hetzer followed Colin down to the doors of the Turnabout.

"Not a cat," Colin said. He turned back to Hetzer and the rest of the bar. "Just a cousin, worthy of being called a Rose Street Prince. Come on." He walked out. Hetzer glanced back at the rest of the Princes in the bar. He gave a nod over to Hotchins, thumped his chest with his fist, and followed after Colin into the night.

Chapter 24

WILLEM FENMERE did not like what he saw.

Fenmere had spent most of his life involved in all sorts of unsavory things. He'd killed more men than he could count. He'd seen eyes gouged from their sockets. He'd seen men so messed from drink and drug that they lost control of every bodily function. He'd destroyed lives. He'd sold stolen children. He watched five men force themselves on a wailing doxy all at once, and then took her himself when they were done. His stomach was iron. He was a bad man, and he made no pretense that he was otherwise.

This Lord Sirath and his Blue Hand Circle made his stomach turn.

When they killed the rabbit, Fenmere thought that was strange, but not disgusting. He found it rather disturbing when Kalas started painting circles with the blood. The final thing that pushed him over the edge was Sirath wearing the dead animal as a hat. Sirath had already proven himself to be far more disturbing and petulant than any amount of money was worth. Their business and partnership was not something Fenmere needed, and it was no longer desirable, regardless of how many crowns they threw around.

The worst part, he felt, was that it was all in his own warehouse. The place would need to be scoured clean after this business.

No, he thought, *burned to the ground*.

The old professor and the dark girl were tied up, back to back, dangling on a hook over one of the blood circles. Kalas had also put a sack over the old man's head, and told Bell to hit him several times. That struck Fenmere as excessive, but Kalas and Sirath both said the professor was dangerous, so he let it go. The whole business was too absurd to complain about how the hostages were treated.

Gerrick was over by the door, shaking his head in disbelief. Fenmere knew just how his old friend felt. He walked over to him.

"Let's divorce ourselves of this whole mess," he told Gerrick.

"You sure?" Gerrick said. "I mean, I don't blame you, but . . . there still is the matter of the forty thousand crowns."

"Thorn won't come with the money, I'll tell you that much."

"You think?" Gerrick asked.

"I'm hardly convinced the old man and the Napa are people that matter to the Thorn, but even presuming they do, my gut tells me the Thorn isn't the type to let it go without a scrap. Remember what he did with Nevin. Or the Three Dogs. If they're his friends, he'll come get them."

"So what do you want to do, boss?" asked Gerrick.

"Get the blazes out of this place. Tell Bell to stay with a few boys. If the Thorn does come with the money, they can bring it back. Otherwise they can clean up after this mess. Saints know *Lord* Sirath won't do anything of the sort."

"Then we're going home?"

"Rutting yes, Gerrick. Unless you want to stay."

"Not a chance, boss," said Gerrick. "I'll let Bell know." Gerrick went across the room to talk to Bell. Fenmere looked back over at Sirath, who was now kneeling under the trussed-up hostages, muttering and tapping the floor with a knife. The dead rabbit still oozed blood down his face, and a few flies had already started buzzing around him.

The Thorn might be a pain in my side, Fenmere thought, *but I can at least respect that he's no freak.*

"You are a freak, Veranix. I want you to know this." Delmin said.

Veranix looked down at Delmin from the windowsill he had already climbed up on. Delmin stood down on the street, biting his lip to keep from laughing. He was alone down there. The streets of Dentonhill were eerily quiet. People had probably seen the paper job, and knew something was up, and chose to stay in. Even the Dogs' Teeth, down the way, was sedate this night. "What's that supposed to mean?"

"Besides the fact you can jump and climb like some kind of monkey?" asked Delmin. He chuckled.

"When did you ever see a monkey, Delmin?" Veranix asked.

"I . . . have read about them," Delmin answered, his face souring. "Why are you climbing up to the top of the shop?"

"Two reasons," Veranix said, holding up two fingers at Delmin to emphasize the point. "One, I'm armed and dressed for a fight. That looks suspicious, so best I stay out of sight. Two, if I'm too close to you, it's harder for you to track what you need to find. So I'll follow you from the rooftops."

"Fine, fine," Delmin said, shaking his head. "Freak."

"You're just jealous," Veranix said. He flashed a grin while jumping up to the lip of the roof and flipping himself over.

"Someday you're going to tell me how you learned all that," called Delmin.

Veranix leaned back over the edge of the roof. "Shh. Start tracking."

"Tracking, right," Delmin muttered. He started pacing around the road.

Veranix took a moment to stretch his legs and arms, get a sense of his body. "Before any show," his grandfather used to say, "you've got to have a feel for your tools. And your body is your most important tool."

"Big show tonight," he whispered absently. He felt solid, ready. The injuries he had taken to his shoulder and leg hurt plenty, but he wasn't going to let them stop him. He'd have time to heal after Kai and the professor were safe. He checked the straps on his belts holding his weapons on tight to his back. His father's bow and quiver of arrows were secure. The bow had felt wrong when he practiced with it before he left the campus. He had remembered it being harder to pull, being bigger in his hands. The last time he had tried to use it was two years ago. *Perhaps I wasn't ready for it then*, he thought.

He absently ran his fingers over the arrows, feeling for the one with the notches filed on the end. He had to know exactly where it was, and be ready to pull that one in a moment when he needed it.

His new staff was secure in its strap. The staff was one of Kaiana's garden tools, with the head sawed off. He mused that she would probably be angry that he wrecked it, but it was his way of honoring her.

He was wearing his old maroon cloak. He was annoyed with himself that he had abandoned it, thought of it as "old." He shouldn't have gotten used to the napranium cloak and rope so quickly. He had become cocky with them, thought himself helpless without them.

Not anymore. Tonight he was going in, muscle and bone, like grandfather used to say. His body was his tool, and he knew how to use it well.

On the street below, Delmin began to move in earnest, north, deeper into Dentonhill. Veranix kept him in sight as he ran to the edge of the shop. He launched his light frame into the air. No magic this time, just skill and training. Pure.

He landed on the next roof, his boots barely making a scuff as he kept going, not breaking pace

He had forgotten how good that felt.

He restrained the urge to let out a whoop of joy as he continued along the rooftops.

Look out, Lord Sirath, he thought. *Veranix the Thorn is coming for you.*

Hetzer was scared out of his mind. It was a good kind of fear, though; a fear that drove him. It kept him moving, kept him aware of everything around him. He had never in his life been this deep into Dentonhill before. Rose Street Princes almost never crossed Waterpath, and they certainly didn't go out to Necker Square. Colin seemed to know where he was going, though, and he walked with determined confidence. Hetzer mimicked that.

Hetzer also mimicked Colin in rolling down his shirtsleeves. Habit was to wear them rolled up, so everyone could see the tattoo of the rose and the crown on their right arms. In Aventil, they wore their brand with pride. Hetzer bristled at the idea of covering up, but as tough as he felt he was, he had no intention of taking on all of Fenmere's operation. He wasn't the Thorn.

Hardly anyone was on the streets, though. Everyone who walked past them did it hurriedly, eyes to the ground. Hetzer could sense it in the air, that feeling that something big was going to happen tonight.

"All right," Colin said as they approached the square. He pointed to a side alley. "You're going to wait in there with this, keep an eye on me." He handed the satchel to Hetzer.

"What are you gonna do?" asked Hetzer.

"I'm going to meet whoever is here for the trade. The merch for the bloke and bird. But we gotta run it smart, see? We don't give them nothing without seeing the people they got, see?"

"What merch?" Hetzer asked. He looked at the satchel in his hands. "What the blazes we got here?"

"We've got the most valuable thing in Dentonhill,

Hetz." He patted the satchel. "Now you got it. Something takes a left turn, you run home, got it?"

"This ain't the Thorn's merch, is it?" Hetzer asked. He couldn't believe the words he was saying. "Colin, cap, how the hell you get . . . sweet saints, you are the Thorn, ain't ya?"

"I ain't the blasted Thorn!"

"But you know who he is, don't ya? He is a Prince, ain't he?"

"Shush," Colin said, pushing Hetzer deeper into the alley. He looked around the corner into the square. "Not on his arm, he ain't."

"But then . . ." Hetzer started. Colin snapped his fingers at him, hushing him again.

"You listening, Hetzie? You hold onto that merch, and you watch. I whistle, you come. They lead me somewhere else, you follow, but don't let them see you. You're good at that."

"Blazes, yes," said Hetzer. "And if its sours, I run."

"You run like Ginny Thouser is waiting in your bed for a roll, get it?"

"Got it." He clapped Colin on the shoulder. "Just another merch trade, deep in Fenmere's country. Let's do this, aye?"

"Aye," Colin said. Without another word, he went out of the alley and walked across Necker Square. He stood in front of the cannery, where Hetzer had a clear view of him.

Hetzer glanced at the satchel. This was really the merch that Fenmere was going crazy for? This was what the Thorn pinched from him? He could hardly believe it. He snuck a quick peek in the satchel.

All he saw was a rope and some cloth.

Hetzer almost started to laugh. Colin was playing an angle here, he just didn't know what. There was no way there would be this much noise over junk like this. He trusted Colin knew what he was doing; that's why Colin was a street cap, and he wasn't. Some people thought it was because Colin was a Tyson, but Hetzer knew better. Blazes, he knew well how hard Colin needed to prove himself as a good captain, that he was more like his uncle than his father.

A strange thought crossed Hetzer's mind. What was it Colin had said back in the Turnabout? He had to be a cousin worthy of being called a Prince. That was rubbish, of course. There wasn't another man more worthy of Rose Street than Colin, as far as Hetzer was concerned. What's more, Colin didn't even have a cousin. For that to be true, then . . .

Then the Thorn would have to be the son of Calbert Tyson.

That was a ridiculous thought. Hetzer shook it out of his mind. He looked back over at Colin, who was still waiting at the cannery. Far off in the distance, church bells started ringing. Twelve bells for midnight.

This was the moment.

Hetzer glanced up at the sky. The blood moon was full, and it was moving close to the white half-moon. It was almost touching it, like it was going to cross in front. Hetzer had never seen anything like that before.

"You showed, scrapper," said a deep voice in the shadows. Colin saw someone walk out of the cannery. He was an older man, short hair and more than a few scars on his face. He looked like a man who had been in a lot of fights, and won most of them.

"You lose a bet or something?" Colin returned.

"Nah," the tough said. "Surprised you just walked up, instead of pulling some trick."

"Not tonight," Colin said. "You've got something to return to me, eh?"

"Gonna ask you that."

"You should know how to do a trade, tough," Colin said. "You think I'm gonna drop my merch for you without seeing my side?"

"Your doxy and the old man are safe, Thorn."

"Forgive me if I don't trust that," Colin said.

"Fair enough, scrapper," the tough said. "Come on, then." He started to walk off down one street. "Oh, two things first." He hauled off a sucker punch across Colin's chin. He stepped back as soon as he did it, making it clear to Colin he was only taking that shot. "That's for my table."

"Table had it coming," Colin said. He wasn't sure what else to say. This tough clearly had a grudge against Veranix, and if he thought Colin really was the Thorn, so much the better. "What's the second thing?"

"The guy with the crossbow has his eye on us," the tough said. "You remember him, no?"

"Who could forget?" Colin said.

"Well, he can shoot a tick off your balls from where he is, so don't think he can't put one through your heart. No rope tricks, eh?"

"Wouldn't dream of it, tough," Colin said. "Lead the way."

The tough winked at him, and walked off to the

northeast down Necker, deeper into Dentonhill. Colin walked behind the man, hoping whoever the sharp-shooter was, he was keeping an eye on him, and not seeing Hetzer. For Veranix's sake, for his friends, the last thing Colin needed was for this deal to take a left turn.

Chapter 25

MORE THAN ONCE, Veranix feared that Delmin had lost the trail. They had taken a desultory route, but there was consistent progress to the north and east. From his vantage point on the rooftops, he couldn't always see Delmin's face, but when he did his friend looked determined, certain. He also looked frightened out of his mind. Veranix took some comfort in that. Fear was probably the smartest thing to feel right now.

They were in the northeast corner of Dentonhill now, near Inemar. This part of the neighborhood was filled with warehouses, and Veranix figured most of them belonged to Fenmere. Veranix crouched low, leaning over the edge of a roof. Delmin had stopped in the street. He looked dazed and disoriented. Veranix swore under his breath. He shouldn't have dragged Delmin into this. He shouldn't have gotten anyone else involved. Especially not Kaiana. He wouldn't forgive himself if she got hurt or killed.

Delmin placed a hand on the wall of one of the warehouses. He stood there for a moment. Veranix prayed that no one would notice him. Delmin turned up and looked to the roofs above him. With a slight nod, he tapped on the wall of the warehouse, and then walked away down the street.

This was the place.

Veranix looked it over. There were two doors on this side of the building. One was a large double door for letting carriages and wagons in. The other was normal-size. The slate roof slanted at a steep angle. The stones didn't look very solid. His footing could easily slip if he made the jump for the roof. The slate would definitely come loose, alerting anyone inside to his presence.

Near the corner of the building, he spotted what he needed. A window. It was covered with an ironwork lattice, but it was still another way in besides the front door. There was no other way in that he could see from here. He'd have to go down to the street level to search further.

He heard a sound at the front door. Two men came out, with a third right behind them. He didn't recognize the two men, both older and well dressed, but the third was Kalas.

"It's only just after midnight," Kalas said. "Your man might be leading him here now."

"Might, might," one of the gentlemen said, waving a dismissive hand at Kalas. "Perhaps you're right. But I really don't need to see it."

"Lord Sirath will not—"

"Will not be pleased, yes," the gentleman said. "I am not pleased, Mister Kalas. You and Lord Sirath and the rest of your Circle have proven to be ill-fitting partners, and I want no more of it."

"You will regret this, Fenmere," Kalas said.

A chill ran up Veranix's spine. This was Fenmere. Veranix had never seen the man before. Here he was. No legend, no iconic tyrant. He was just an old man in an expensive suit.

Veranix hadn't even realized he had drawn an arrow until he was lining up the shot.

Right below him like this, it was an easy shot. Fenmere stood still, arguing with Kalas, looking more annoyed than anything else. His heart was clean in front of him, and he could send an arrow through it before anyone knew what happened.

That would be it. The man who had caused so much pain, sold so much death, both in Veranix's life and all of Dentonhill, would be dead.

Veranix faltered. If he took the shot, Kalas would raise the alarm. He'd cry out and Lord Sirath would react. He wouldn't be able to take them by surprise. Professor Alimen and Kaiana would surely be dead before he could get to them.

Kalas put his hand on Fenmere's shoulder, trying to coax him to return. Fenmere pushed it away.

"I'm leaving some men behind to clean up after your little . . . event, Kalas. They'll help you however you need." He brushed off his suit. "If the Thorn does arrive, they can deliver his dead body to me in the morning. But not too early, please. For once, I'd like to get some sleep." He turned down the road and walked toward a carriage parked at the corner.

Veranix held the aim on Fenmere as he walked. The shot would still be good, and the man would still be dead. He could still take it. The man who killed his father, ruined his mother . . . he would be dead.

The cost would be too high, though.

He relaxed his arm.

Tonight was not the night for Fenmere.

I have your face now, old man, he thought. Every line on his craggy face, the bulbous nose, the dark, deep-set eyes, the iron-gray hair, straight and pulled back, were all burned into Veranix's mind.

He lowered the bow.

A boot scuffed behind him.

"You should have taken the shot, mate."

He spun around, raising the bow again. He was ready to fire, but the other man already had a crossbow aimed at him. Veranix easily recognized the greasy, eel-faced man.

"Samael," he said, keeping his arm tense, ready to snap the shot. "Tonight is full of surprises."

"I'd say so," Samael said, grinning evilly. "I thought I was following you down there." He nodded his head down to the street. Veranix didn't dare glance away to see what he was referring to. Did he follow Delmin? Or someone else?

"I'd never make it that easy, chap," Veranix said. His shoulder, already injured, burned from the strain. He couldn't hold the bow back for too much longer, and as long as Samael was trained on him, he couldn't shoot without getting shot back.

"I should have guessed," Samael said. "All the better. They can keep the impostor. Since I've got the real thing all to myself, I can still collect my fee."

Hetzer hated keeping a tail on someone in a neighborhood he didn't know. Back on Rose, he knew which alleys he could slip into, which stores he could cut through, every crack and pass he could use. Here, on strange streets, on a quiet night, he couldn't hide as well as he wanted. He had to keep his distance, stay farther back than he'd like. He'd almost lost Colin and the other guy twice. It didn't help that this part of town had long north stretches with no side streets, just big, tight-packed buildings.

Someone else had been following them as well, Hetzer noted, from up on the rooftops. He would dash ahead of Colin and his guide, and then train his crossbow on them as they passed. Then he'd dash again, keeping the time Colin wasn't in his sights down to a minimum. Hetzer was impressed by the way the guy could move. There wasn't a rooftop racer like that in the Princes, or in all of Aventil.

Hetzer was glad that this one had been focused on Colin, not scouting the area around. No one spotted him, as far as he could tell.

They were led to a warehouse district in Dentonhill. Surely all owned by Fenmere, Hetzer thought, like everything else in this neighborhood. The guy brought Colin over to one building, where a stick-thin guy, dressed like a proper gentleman in a deep blue suit, was standing at the door, looking mad enough to eat the road.

"Oy," the guide said. "I brought the one."

Hetzer slipped into a crack between two buildings, close enough that he could hear. Best ears on Rose Street, he had.

"This one?" the man in the blue suit said. "He looks like street trash."

"Watch what you call trash, swell," Colin said. "You'll get what's yours coming."

"I'm sure, young man," the suit said. "There is something of mine which should be coming." He leaned in to Colin. "You don't have it, though. But you did."

"Yeah, yeah, you want your merch, swell," Colin said. "You want it, you've got to deal. You've got a bloke and a bird you're ransing?"

The suit looked at Colin, and then at the guide, then back to Colin. "I don't know what the blazes you're saying."

"The trade, mister," the guide said. "Your things for his friends."

"Right," the suit said with an evil smile. "The trade. You want your friends released."

Hetzer heard a whispered hiss. He looked across the street, and nestled in a matching crack between buildings was another bloke, looking right at him. This one was in the uniform of a Uni brat. He looked scared out of his mind, but he was pointing at Hetzer, and waving him over.

Whoever this crazy brat was, he clearly wasn't working for Fenmere or any these others. He was way off his block. This was the kind of Uni kid that any street tough could easily shake for some coin. What the blazes was he doing here, and why in the name of any saint did he think he could signal like they were friends?

"That's it," Colin said. "You want your merch, you can get it. But I got to see my people."

"Well," the suit said, looking Colin over like he was a roast lamb, and he was deciding which part to eat first, "you've clearly been in possession of my things. But I can't imagine someone as . . . unremarkable as you has been the source of all our misery."

The Uni kid was really freaked now, pointing at Hetzer as frantically as he could without causing any commotion that others would notice.

"I'm full of surprises," Colin said.

"Certainly," the suit said. "Bring him in." He went into the warehouse and the guide pulled Colin in with them. The door slammed shut.

The Uni kid took the moment to act. He dashed out of his crack over to Hetzer's. Hetzer didn't waste any time grabbing the kid and clasping his hand over his mouth.

"Shh," Hetzer said, "you on the *'fitte* or something?"

The kid shook his head.

"So why you trying to get us both killed, Uni brat?" he asked, keeping his voice a whisper. "This is some serious bad news going on here, and you want none of it. You hear?"

The Uni brat nodded. Hetzer noticed his eyes looking up to the roof across the street. He glanced over.

There was the rooftop racer, crossbow trained on another guy, who had his own bow aimed at the racer.

"Oh, blazes and saints," Hetzer said, relaxing his grip on the Uni kid. "That's the Thorn, ain't it?"

"You've . . . you've got the . . ." the Uni kid stammered, pointing to satchel. "If you have . . . and if I can sense . . . then they . . ."

"It's a trade drop, kid," Hetzer said, keeping one eye up on the racer and the Thorn. "We're helping the Thorn, get? Get his bird and bloke back."

"No," the Uni brat whispered. "Let him . . . let him . . . they can't get that stuff, you hear? If they get it, it's going to be . . ."

The loading door of the warehouse flew open. Two

young tossers, skinny and pale, came charging out. Both of them wore blue cloaks and hoods, and their hands were glowing.

"Oh, sweet saints," the Uni brat said. He grabbed Hetzer's wrist and pulled him into the street. "Run. RUN!"

Chapter 26

COLIN WAS DEEP in the thick of it now. He didn't fully know what to make of what was going on, but he realized that Veranix had gotten mixed up in something far stranger than he had figured. Just being a Rose Street Prince dragged into a warehouse on the far north side of Dentonhill normally would mean that he was a dead man. That was the least of his worries. He was still armed—he had two knives in his boots. These blokes hadn't even bothered to search him.

That either meant they were fools, or they didn't care if he had knives or not.

Looking at this lot, the second option seemed more likely.

There was the usual group of thugs that looked like Fenmere's men. That wasn't a surprise. It was everything else that made Colin's head spin.

The suit from the door was the most normal looking of the four who clearly weren't part of Fenmere's crew. There were two other young blokes, blond and dark-haired, in blue suits and fur-lined cloaks. They looked ridiculous. The two of them were busy drawing sym-

bols with chalk on the floor of the warehouse, all. centered around the two people trussed up and hanging
from the ceiling. They were Veranix's Napa girl and an
old man. Both of them were blindfolded and gagged,
and the old man looked like he was knocked out.

Then there was the one standing in the middle. He
was a redhead, wild haired, with a body that seemed
all skin and bones, covered in several strange tattoos.
He was wearing only a fur cloak and a dead rabbit on
his head—not a rabbit-skin hat, a dead rabbit, with
blood oozing down over his face.

He turned and looked at Colin.

"Is it him?" he hissed. He bounded over to Colin like
a wolf coming for a deer.

"Whoa, chief," Colin said. "You back the blazes off."
It was useless, the crazy man was right up on him.
Colin pushed him away. As soon as he did, the two
young suits came racing over.

"You dare?" one of them asked. Each grabbed one of
his arms, gripping him tighter than he would have
thought they could.

"Hey, hey!" Colin shouted. "You want your merch,
you don't be pulling any plays like this!" Both men
looked at him, and then looked at each other, puzzled.
They both then looked at the suit from the door.

"I don't know half of what he's saying either," said
the suit, shrugging.

The blond one looked him up and down. "He
doesn't have them," he said.

"No, course not," Colin said. "You all don't know
how a trade drop goes. You think I'd bring the merch
here in the middle of all you? What kind of fool you

take me for?" He looked over at one of Fenmere's heavies, standing off to the side. "Tell 'em, would you?"

"He's right," the heavy said. "You really think he'd just come and hand it to you?"

"Shut up," the dark-haired one said. He crouched down, examining Colin's hands and body. "He has been near the things."

The heavy moved closer, taking a good look at Colin. "You're not the Thorn."

"Did I say I was?" Colin said. "I just said I'm here to do a trade of the merch. You want to do a deal, you've got to drop the bird and the old man."

"Is he talking about the hostages?" the suit asked.

"He's not the Thorn?" the one who brought Colin over from Necker Square asked. "You sure?"

"Thorn's got a thinner chin, higher voice," the heavy said. "And he doesn't have the accent of Aventil street trash."

"Street trash?" Colin said. "You want to see some trash?"

"Enough," hissed the crazy man. "Where?" His question was not directed at Colin, but at the two holding him. The dark-haired one looked around, darting his eyes like he was watching smoke.

"There," he said. "Right outside."

The two young suits let go of Colin and stalked over to the loading door. With a breath and a snap of their fingers, the door blew open all by itself. *Mages,* Colin thought. *That's what this mess all is.* The two of them stalked out into the street.

Colin prayed that Hetzer had the good sense to run. Out in the street, a terrified scream said the same thing.

"So why not take the shot?" Veranix asked Samael.

"Simple," Samael said. "I can hold this crossbow up a whole lot longer than you can keep that bow drawn. It's just a matter of waiting you out."

Veranix knew he was right. His shoulder was screaming. The stitches were tearing open. He was sure that Samael could see the beads of sweat building on his forehead.

"I start to lose it, Sam, I'll just shoot."

"True," said Sam, edging his way closer to the edge of the roof, never taking his eye or his aim off Veranix. "But that's gonna be a sour shot."

"You think I'd miss a ten-foot shot even if it went sour?"

"We'll have to see," Samael said. "I know I've got you dead to rights. So you could save your arm and ease off."

"Ease off, sure," Veranix said. "That'd be real healthy. Listen, I have a big night planned here, so if you're going to shoot me, can we get it over with?"

"Always the smart mouth," Samael said.

Veranix's shoulder felt like it was going to snap. He didn't have much longer.

"You think it's easy thinking up clever things to say in the middle of a fight?" Veranix asked. "It takes a lot of work and most people don't—what is that thing?" He cried out the last part.

"Yeah, I'm not looking," Sam said.

"Had to try," Veranix said.

"Fair cop, totally," Samael said. "Anyone who falls for that trick deserves getting plugged."

"I agree, actually," Veranix said. "You know, I don't have the things those guys want anymore."

"Sure you don't," Samael said.

"Totally true." Veranix pushed down the strain creeping into his voice. "I would have clobbered you with the rope if I still had it."

"You lose a card game or something?"

"Girl broke my heart and took the stuff," Veranix said, doing his best to shrug without losing his aim. "What are you going to do?"

"It's a heartbreaking story. I'll cry in the beer I'll buy with your bounty."

"You know what your problem is, Sam, you have no sense of romance."

At that moment, there was a horrible wooden crunch below them. Then Delmin screamed on the street below, "Run! RUN!!"

Samael's eyes moved half an inch to glance in the direction of the noise.

Veranix let the arrow fly. In the same instant, he jumped back, going over the edge of the roof. Samael released his shot, but Veranix was already dropping. The bolt barely skimmed over his head. He had no idea if he hit Samael or not, but with only a few seconds until he hit the ground, he had bigger problems.

Especially since the two trackers from the Blue Hand were storming out of the warehouse, chasing after Delmin.

His right hand was free. Despite his shoulder being almost useless, he reached out and grabbed a gutter drainpipe on the side of the building and yanked himself over. He clamped his feet around the pipe, slowing his descent, but his weight was more than the pipe could take. It tore from its housing, bending out from the building.

He rolled with it, and with a graceless flip, landed on the ground, his feet and knees no worse off than his shoulder. They hurt like blazes, but he could keep going.

The two bloodhounds, Kent and Forden, were already charging down the street. Almost instinctively, Veranix reached for the marked arrow. He had to stop himself; that one was for Sirath, and no one else.

He couldn't see far down the street, not in the moonlight. He could chase these two, keep them off Delmin, but then he'd lose any advantage he had over the rest, lose the chance to save Kai and Professor Alimen.

He promised Delmin he'd be safe.

He drew an arrow and shot it at Kent. His shoulder cried out as he pulled back the bow, but the shot fired true. The arrow hit Kent in the back, and the mage dropped down. Veranix readied a second arrow for Forden.

He heard a sharp click above him.

Veranix spun on one heel and aimed up, to the top of the building he was just on. He let the arrow fly before even seeing what was happening, and drew another and notched it on his bow.

Samael had his crossbow cocked and ready, standing up on the edge of the building. The only thing keeping him from shooting was the arrow in his neck. After a moment of standing in shock, Samael fell forward, smashing headfirst onto the cobblestone. Veranix cringed away. Even when it involved a killer like Samael, he hated seeing someone die in front of him. Especially by his own hand.

Someone inside the warehouse snapped, "What's taking them so long?" Veranix glanced down the street. Delmin and his pursuer were out of sight. Kent was still on the ground, struggling to get up. The light from inside the warehouse spilled out into the street, and he could see shadows moving, people going to the door.

He fought down the urge to charge through the loading door, shooting at anything that moved.

Veranix was in the shadow, unseen by the people in the warehouse. He still had a chance to take them by surprise, but to do that he'd have to get the high ground. He'd have to know who was in there, where they were. He had to get in without them seeing him. He had to stop them while keeping Kai and the professor safe.

Every part of his body ached as he bounded up to the top of the doorframe, jumped to grab the lip of the roof, and swung himself to the second-floor window. It was large enough for him to get through, were it not for the iron lattice over it. He cursed silently. If he still had the rope, he could rip the thing out of the wall. Normally he could magic it off, but not here or now, not without spoiling everything.

"Muscle and bone," he whispered.

Shouts came from inside the warehouse. "You tossers don't know nothing! This ain't how a trade gets dropped! This is how deals go south!" He knew the voice. That was Colin.

What the blazes was Colin doing here?

Of course, Veranix thought, *Kaiana said we had friends in the street*. He pulled his staff out and wedged it under the latticework, as everything clicked together in his head like a puzzlebox being solved. Kai knew about

Colin, so that's how she hid the rope and cloak. Colin would know how to read the paper job as well as anyone on the streets, and he'd know what it really meant.

He came to save Kaiana for Veranix as well.

That meant the cloak and the rope were here. That meant Sirath could get them. Veranix couldn't let that happen. It didn't matter if Delmin's ideas about *numina* beasts were true or not. If Sirath got his hands on either one of those items, he'd be unstoppable.

Bracing himself as best he could, he prayed to every saint he could think of that he had enough leverage, that the iron was rusted, that the plaster housing it in the wall was weak, anything, anything that would let this work.

He pulled the staff down with every bit of strength he had.

Chapter 27

ETZER RAN, ran like Colin had told him. He didn't know which way he was going or where he was running to, other than away from those two cape-wearing suits coming after them.

He hated running from a brawl.

He glanced back when he heard something behind him. One of the suits had stumbled and fallen. The other one was still coming, pouring on the speed, catching up to them.

"Blazes," he muttered. This was going to be a fight either way, it looked like. Suddenly a bright blue light came racing over their heads.

"Keep running," the Uni brat gasped, half out of breath. "Don't stop!" Then the kid stopped. Hetzer faltered, turning back.

The one in the cape raised his hand, and another blue light came out, right at Hetzer. The Uni brat held up his hands, and everything shimmered in front of him. The blue light fizzled to nothing.

"Go!" the Uni screamed. Hetzer was shocked. This brat was protecting him?

The chaser stopped, shaking his head. "You're not even worth it," he said. He waved his hand dismissively. The Uni kid was knocked in the air, as if the chaser had swatted him like a fly. He crashed into the side of a building, and crumpled to the ground.

"You wanna brawl, freak?" Hetzer said. "I've got one for you, if you want one."

"No, you don't," he said. With another wave of his hand, Hetzer was knocked over. Hetzer remembered one time, when he was a kid, he had been grazed by a runaway cart. That had knocked the wind out of him and sent him to the ground. That was the only thing he had to compare what just happened to him, and this was ten times worse. He could barely breathe, barely move. He was still held down on the ground, pressed by something he couldn't see or grab. The chaser walked over to him and picked up the satchel, and then walked back down the street without giving either him or the Uni brat another look.

He was out of sight when Hetzer was able to move again, the pressure off his body as suddenly as it had arrived. The chaser didn't care about him, it was the satchel he wanted. That's what the Uni kid cared about as well, that's what he was protecting.

The kid was breathing still, but he was out cold. Hetzer had seen plenty of blokes and Princes knocked out that way in brawls, and they were always fine after a bit. He wasn't worried about the Uni kid.

He was surprised he cared that the Uni kid was all right. He smirked to himself. The kid might be a scrawny Uni brat, but he had the heart of a scrapper. He stood up and fought when it mattered.

That's what made a Rose Street Prince worthy of his name, and Hetzer respected that.

He rolled up his sleeves, showing his tattoo to the neighborhood and the world. Then he pulled out two knives from his belt. His street cap was in trouble, and it was time to show he was worthy of being called a Prince as well.

Colin hadn't seen a deal turn left like this since the Creek Trade last summer. That mess ended in three people dead and a bunch of merch lost in the creek. This time, Colin at least could rest easy that if anybody ended up dead, it would just be him. At least, that would be the case if these heavies didn't roll up his sleeves and decide to make a move on the Princes.

"Is it here?" screeched the scary one with the red hair. "Do we have it?"

"I think he's coming back," one of Fenmere's boys said, looking out the doorway. "Someone's coming, anyway." The rest of the heavies, except the one who'd led Colin to the place, all stayed back and away.

"All right, all right," Colin said. "You're getting your merch already."

"I just got it," the blue suit said. "Merchandise, that's what you're saying."

"Good, smart guy," Colin said. "How about you let the old man and the bird scatter now?"

"He means letting the girl and the old man go, Kalas," said the heavy at the door.

"Yes, thank you, Mister Bell, I figured that one out," the suit said. "But I'm afraid not. We need the old man for the next part of what we will do. As for the girl, she's not my usual choice of diversion, but I have varied tastes."

"That ain't how it goes, suit," Colin said, moving closer. Two of Fenmere's heavies approached him, but they didn't seem to want to be any closer to Kalas.

"Oh, please, you think you'll tell me what to do?"

"This deal already turned left, suit," Colin said. "I don't think you want to know how left it can turn."

"Is . . ." Kalas started, looking confused. He glanced at Bell. "Is that some sort of a threat?"

"Yeah," Bell said.

The two young suits came in, one of them supporting the other. The blond one had an arrow sticking out his back. The thing that really caught Colin's eye was the other one: he had the satchel.

"Got it," he said.

"You were shot?" Kalas asked as he came over to them. "Who shot you?"

"Don't know," the blond one said. "Came out of nowhere."

"It's the Thorn!" Bell said. "It must have been him."

"You come here with the Thorn, rat?" Kalas asked Colin.

"He's not part of my street," Colin said. "I never throw with him."

"He's here!" Bell said. He now pulled out a sword and was looking around.

"It doesn't matter," Kalas said. "We have what we need" He took the satchel and opened it, pulling out the cloak.

"That belongs to the Thorn, suit," Colin said. He

couldn't help but smile. "If he's got the stones to take on Fenmere, he won't worry about going for you."

"Let him come," Kalas said, holding up the cloak. "I'd like to see him try to take us on."

A sharp whistle sang through the air, and in the next moment an arrow was through his hand. He screamed and dropped the cloak.

Colin looked up. In the rafters, there he was. Veranix, standing tall, bow out, ready to take another shot, wild grin across his face.

"Happy to oblige, Kalas," he said. "Want to see my next trick?"

"Get him!" Kalas shouted to no one in particular as he dropped to the ground. All of Fenmere's men in the place looked stunned, unsure of what to do. The two Blue Hand bloodhounds stayed at the door, disdainfully looking at Fenmere's heavies, as if they considered getting Veranix a chore that was beneath them.

Sirath, on the other hand, was moving toward the cloak.

"Insect," he growled at Veranix.

Veranix grabbed the marked arrow and notched it. "Don't even think about it, Sirath."

"Bah," Sirath said, shaking his head. He stepped closer.

Veranix drew back. "Not another step, Sirath, or this goes in your chest!"

Sirath chuckled. "Threats from you? Pathetic mage. Petty thief." He took one more step.

Veranix didn't need another excuse. He let the arrow fly.

There was a rush of magic from Sirath, as he dismissively waved his hand at the arrow. The force shook the whole building, almost knocking Veranix off his perch.

It made no difference. The arrow was unaffected, just as Veranix hoped it would be. It flew true into Sirath's chest. Sirath screamed and fell to the floor, gasping and writhing. He flopped about violently, like a fish pulled from the river. Everyone else in the room was paralyzed by the spectacle.

"I am an excellent mage and a fantastic thief, Sirath." Veranix laughed as he snapped his bow back into its holder. "I just stole your magic!"

The arrowhead was dalmatium, filed down to a razor-sharp point. The arrow had then been rolled in the filed powder. Dalmatium dust was running in Sirath's blood now, tearing him up more than any poison would.

Veranix jumped down to the floor, controlling his descent with magic. He was no longer burdened by carrying the arrow, but he could still feel the dust on his gloves. Doing magic was like walking through mud. He stripped them off and threw them at the two bloodhounds as he landed. There was nowhere near enough of the powder to disable them, but it could confuse and disorient them for a bit. He drew out his staff.

Sirath was trying to get to his knees, arms flailing blindly, the look on his face pure agony. Veranix sprang past him, striking him in the face and knocking him back down. Fenmere's men drew weapons, but each of them seemed to be waiting for someone to take the lead. Two of them were between him and the cloak.

"Get the tosser!" shouted someone. Veranix realized it was Nevin. He had barely gotten the words out when

Colin moved, drawing two knives from his boots and tackling the dealer boss. That was all the excuse that the others needed, and they came charging over. No chance to grab the cloak.

Veranix leaped up to the rope Kaiana and the professor hung from. Holding on by one hand, he undid Kai's blindfold and gag.

"Miss me?" he asked.

"What—" was all she said as she looked around at the room. Fenmere's men were gathering below them. Kalas clawed for the cloak, Sirath writhed on the floor, and the two bloodhounds were furiously swatting at their own faces.

"Get ready to run," Veranix said, swinging around to the professor's side. He removed the blindfold and gag. The professor was out cold, a huge purple welt across the top of his head. This made things harder.

"Run?" Kaiana asked. Veranix swung back around to face her.

"You've got to get the professor out, Kai," he said. "I'll make a hole to the door."

"A hole, but—"

"Just get safe, Kai," he said. "I'm sorry for all this." He let go of the rope, touching it with a hint of magic as he did. It dissolved into ash and dust. He dropped to the ground, giving a hard blast of magic in all directions. It bowled over the group of thugs, and slowed the fall of Kai and the professor. She landed on her feet, grabbing his limp body.

Veranix felt a heady rush from that magic. He got more blast out of it than he had put into it. It was almost like when he used the cloak, but wilder, more out of his control. *Numina* was surging like a boiling pot.

The Winged Convergence. It must be doing something to magic right now. He could feel it, like ants crawling up his spine.

No time to think about it. He had to get Kai and the professor out.

Veranix went at two thugs who blocked the way to the door, and who were still reeling from his blast. He spun his staff about, clocking them both and keeping them from recovering. Kaiana lifted the professor over her shoulder like a sack of grain and made for the door.

Forden was there with the rope in his hand. The rope spun too fast to see; it was just a blur blocking their exit. "That is it!" he shouted. "I'll kill you all!" He stepped closer.

Veranix tried to reach out, take control over the rope, feel his original connection to it. This mage was too powerful, though; he held complete sway over it. They only had a moment before he tore them to pieces with it.

"Rose Street!" came a yell from the door, and someone—a Rose Street Prince, by his arm—came charging in, knives out. He tackled Forden, stabbing as he hit. The mage screamed out, and the rope responded reflexively, coiling back and wrapping around the attacker. The Prince cried out as well as the rope constricted around his chest, but he had wrapped his legs around Forden, and would not let go. He stabbed again and again, refusing to yield. "This! Is what happens! When you cross the Princes!" he gasped out.

"Go!" Veranix yelled, and Kaiana didn't delay, charging out the door with Professor Alimen.

Veranix saw Kalas grasp the cloak with his good hand. He dashed over and grabbed the other end of it. "No, you don't, Kalas."

"You ruined everything!" Kalas said. Veranix could feel the *numina* coursing through the cloak, through the both of them. Kalas was trying to tap into it, but Veranix was pulling on it as well. Neither of them could take control over the cloak's power.

"You'll have to wait another forty-seven years, then," Veranix said. With his free hand, he lifted up his staff and hit Kalas. Before he could swing again, the staff dissolved into dust. Kent was on his feet, pale and bleeding, holding his hand out as if he intended to strike again. He then cried out and dropped down again, a knife in his back.

"Don't touch him," Colin said, his hand still outstretched from throwing the knife.

Veranix grabbed Kalas by the throat. Kalas struggled for a moment, but then looked over at Sirath, barely breathing on the floor, futilely clawing at empty air like he was blind. Veranix almost felt pity for the man.

"I'm sorry, my lord," Kalas whispered. "I have failed you and the Nine." He drew the *numina* again, in a surge that took Veranix by surprise. Unable to pull on the *numina* Kalas had, he squeezed harder on his throat. Kalas didn't direct the *numina* at Veranix, though. Instead he focused on Sirath, who then vanished in the blink of an eye.

Veranix wrenched the cloak from Kalas's hand. Kalas dropped to the ground as soon as he lost contact. The *numina* poured into Veranix's body, and with that he was able to summon the rope over, which lay dormant around the two bodies by the door. It coiled up and undulated at his feet, like a tame snake ready to strike at his command. He turned to the few of Fenmere's men who were still standing. None of them looked like they wanted to be in the warehouse a moment longer.

"If you want to run, now's the time," Veranix said. All of them dropped their weapons and went for the door. Veranix recognized one of them, and wrapped the rope around him, lifting him off the ground.

"Hello, Bell," he said, bringing the man over. "I see Fenmere didn't kill you."

"Oh, let me go, Thorn," Bell said, looking as if he was about to start weeping. "I'm done, man. I'm done."

"You know, Bell," Veranix said. "I'm a man who believes in repentance. So I will let you go, trusting that you will give a message to your boss."

"Another message? Why me, Thorn?"

"Because I like you, of course," Veranix said. "Tell Fenmere that tonight was about stopping the Blue Hands, and he'd be wise to not involve himself in mystical matters anymore."

"Oh, he's done with them, chief," Bell said. "He doesn't want anything to do with them."

"Good," Veranix said. "He should consider the same attitude when it comes to *effitte*. And crossing Waterpath."

"He won't stop . . ."

"I know he won't," Veranix said. "Tell him I'm still here, and I'm going to be watching him. I won't stand for his junk coming into the University or Aventil. Let him know I'm not done with him."

"Yeah, sure," Bell said. "Just let me go, Thorn."

"Go, run." Veranix set Bell back on the ground by the door. Bell dashed off as soon as he was free.

Colin was over by the door, pulling the dead mage off the other man. Veranix went over.

"Colin, is he—" he started. The young man, a street tough, one of Colin's boys lay on the ground. He looked dazed, blood coming from his nose and ears. He wheezed and coughed.

"Easy, Hetzer," Colin said.

"Hey, cap." Hetzer barely got the words out. "We help the Thorn?"

"Yeah," Veranix said, bending over the dying man. "You did it." Hetzer looked at Veranix, his eyes finally finding something to focus on.

"It's you," he said, reaching up with a bloody hand. He cusped Veranix's head. "You're the one, Thorn. You show them."

"I will," Veranix said.

"He is, isn't he?" Hetzer asked Colin. "He's the one who should be—" He didn't finish his sentence. He stopped breathing or moving, his eyes still fixed on Veranix.

"Should be what?" Veranix asked.

"Ain't nothing," Colin said. He got up and walked away from Veranix, not looking at him.

"I can't believe you came here," Veranix said. "I . . . I don't know what to say."

"Ain't nothing," Colin said again. "I made your father a promise, and a Rose Street Prince always keeps his promises."

"His name was Hetzer?"

"Yeah," Colin said. "He died a true Prince."

"He did," Veranix said. "You need help taking him home?"

Colin shook his head. "I can handle it, cousin. You've got to look after yours, and I'll take mine."

"Thank you, Colin," Veranix said. "I wouldn't have been able to—"

"Yeah, I know," Colin said. "It ain't nothing, I told ya. Now get out of here. And let's keep to our sides of our streets for a bit."

"Sure," Veranix said. Colin still hadn't looked at him. Instead he went over and picked up his dead friend. He started to walk out down the street.

"Hey, cousin," he said after a moment. He looked back at Veranix. "He's right, though. You fought like a Prince tonight. Your dad would have been proud." With that, he went out into the dark street.

Chapter 28

VERANIX FOUND DELMIN sitting on the curb of the street, dazed and disoriented, but otherwise unharmed.

"Did we win?" Delmin asked.

"I think we did," Veranix said, holding up the rope.

"The Blue Hand Circle?" Delmin asked.

"Two are definitely dead," Veranix said. "I didn't check on Kalas after it all."

"No?" Delmin asked. He got up from the curb, rubbing his head.

"For one, I didn't feel like sticking around in the warehouse. And I'm not much of one for killing someone who's already helpless."

"That's a dog that'll bite you back, you know," Delmin said. He slowly started walking down the street, and Veranix kept pace with him.

"Could be," Veranix said.

"And Sirath?" Delmin asked. "Oh, excuse me. *Lord* Sirath."

"Pretty sure he's dead," Veranix said. He thought about it for a moment. "Though Kalas, he . . . what's the word? Where you make someone vanish and reappear somewhere else?"

"Teleport," Delmin said. He was definitely favoring one leg as he walked. Veranix got under Delmin's arm and helped him.

"Right. I think Kalas did that to Sirath. And he said something about 'he failed the Nine.' Mean anything to you?"

Delmin shook his head. "Kaiana and the professor?"

"They got out, Kaiana running like blazes with him over her shoulder. You didn't see them?"

"No," Delmin said. "We go on faith they got to safety?"

"I have faith in Kai," Veranix said. "She'd sort out where she was and how to get back to campus. She knows a lot of the neighborhoods around the campus, and, well, she knows how to run."

"And if she doesn't?"

"We'll keep an eye out for the two of them," Veranix said. "I need to get you back to campus as well."

Then Delmin looked over at Veranix, as something occurred to him. "There was a kid, like a street urchin type, and he had the cloak and the rope. How . . . why did he?"

"I'm not entirely sure," Veranix said. "But Kaiana hid the things away, and it got to the Rose Street . . . to one of the street gangs . . ."

"Is there a long story in here that I don't want to hear, Vee?" Delmin asked.

"Maybe so," Veranix said. "How bad is your leg?"

"It'll sort itself out in a bit, I think," Delmin said. "Nothing too bad."

"Walking back will take a while," Veranix said.

"Now that I have these back, we could go the faster way."

"No, we walk," Delmin said forcefully. "My leg may be hurt, but I prefer a route on solid ground."

"Fair enough," Veranix said. They walked for a while in silence. After another half block, Veranix said, "You know, last night I stole a horse."

"Walk!" Delmin snapped.

"Fine, fine." Veranix let the silence hang for a moment. "It is a nice night for it, you know. I mean, look at the moons. Winged Convergence. How often you see something like that?"

"Not often," Delmin said, stifling a laugh.

"I'm telling you, Del," Veranix said. "There's something magical about a night like this."

"Really, you have to shut up."

At nearly two bells after midnight, the Turnabout was empty of all but the diehard Princes. All boys Colin knew on sight, all loyal guys with ink on their arms. Despite the late hour, all of them jumped up to full attention when Colin came in, Hetzer's body draped over his shoulder.

"Blazes, Colin!" one of them said as soon as he walked in. "What happened?"

Colin laid Hetzer's body on the floor. Kint, behind the bar, didn't look happy, but he didn't say anything, either.

"I'll tell you what happened," Colin said, looking at all the gathered men who surrounded the body. "Tonight a Prince gave his life for Rose Street. Tonight a Prince fought for something that he believed in. Tonight a Prince was there to help us and ours."

"Who killed him?" another Prince asked hotly. "Where do we hit?"

"Don't hit no one, not tonight. Tonight's business is done."

"No, Colin, if Hetzer is dead . . ." Voices all started rising.

Colin whistled for the boys to hush. "Hetzer avenged himself, with his own hand. And he did more than that."

"What more?"

"Hetzer died saving the Thorn."

The room went quiet. One of the boys finally broke the silence. "You're kidding us, Colin."

"The Thorn hit Fenmere tonight, I'm telling you, and the crazy mess he was up to his neck in."

"What mess?"

"Mage circles."

The room filled with shouts and cries.

Colin shouted over the crowd. "I don't know all of what they were up to, but the Thorn knew it had to be stopped, and he stepped up. And Hetzer stepped up."

"Why were you and Hetzer there?" someone called out.

"Was it that paper job?"

"Did you know what that was about?"

"You know who the Thorn is?"

"Was Hetzer the Thorn?"

"You the Thorn?"

"Shut it!" Colin screamed out. The boys stopped talking, but the intensity on their faces burned into him. "I ain't the Thorn, and neither was Hetz, all right? Yeah, I saw that paper job, and Hetz and I decided it was in our interests to check it out."

"You saw the Thorn, though? You know who he is?"

Colin was about to snap at the person who asked, until he saw it was Old Casey.

"I saw him," Colin said. He didn't want to lie to one of the bosses. Not straight out, not over the body of a dead Prince. That wasn't right. "He ain't one of ours, or any other Aventil gang that I know."

"So what good is he to us?"

Colin chose his words deliberately. "The Thorn let Fenmere know to stay on his side of Waterpath. That he was going to hold him there."

"The Thorn can't hold the line," Casey scoffed.

"He says he can, and from what I saw tonight, I believe him."

"You believe in him now?"

"I didn't until tonight," Colin said.

"All right, then," Casey said. "We've got some work to do tonight, boys."

The collective sound from the group was less than excited. Colin knew damn well he wanted to get to a flop to crash, and everyone else in here probably did as well.

"We got to give Hetz a wake, boss?" Colin asked.

"That's part of it," Casey said. He walked over to the door of the Turnabout, looking out into the night. "But the real work is, we need a paper job, and I want it out there before dawn breaks."

It was half past two bells when Veranix and Delmin finally got to the campus gate. They had a long argument about how to get through and onto campus, which Delmin finally won by advocating the direct approach, walking straight up and waving to the cadets on duty. Veranix had put on the cloak and used it to mask his appearance, making himself look like he was wearing a school uniform like Delmin was.

"Evening, boys," Delmin said as they entered.

"Evening, right," one of the cadets said. "It's after two bells, you know."

"It's a Saint Day," Veranix said. "We've got to tell you guys, there were these girls, over at the Dogs' Teeth."

"Oy, you'll pox yourself blind with those girls," the other cadet said. "Look, mates, we know you had no classes, but—"

"No curfew on Saint Days," Delmin said quickly.

"We know it," the second cadet said, nodding. "Still, there's got to be limits."

Delmin looked to the second cadet, who appeared to have seniority. "Let's just say we were engaged in acts of penance, in deeply spiritual observation."

The second cadet shook his head. "Dogs' Teeth brew and girls, you'll be in penance later, that's for sure."

"Tonight's been a strange one," the first cadet said. "Tell them about the prof with the Napa girl."

"That's neither our business nor theirs," the second said.

"Right," Veranix said, laughing. He did his best to sound casually disinterested. "They look like they had a good night?"

"The prof looked like he had a rough one," the first said, laughing a little. "And she looked like she could give a rough one."

"Oy, that's enough," the second barked. The first slunk down, ashamed. The second turned back to Delmin and Veranix. "Anyway, I'm telling you, try and make it to gates before midnight in the future, you know? Even on Saint Days."

"I agree," Veranix said, nodding. "Really, I am opposed to coming through the gates this late, but it was one of those nights."

"Don't want to know," said the second cadet, laughing. "Go on, and get abed. Other cadets or prefects catch you walking about on campus, they might not take so kindly, hear?"

"We hear," Delmin said. He gave them another polite wave, and the two of them went as fast they could up the footpath to Almers.

"We should check on Kai and the prof," Veranix said, pointing over to Bolingwood.

"No way, Vee," Delmin said. "You heard those two. We know they're all right, and we have to get into quarters. We'll find out more in the morning." Veranix was annoyed, but he shrugged in assent. He certainly did need the sleep.

After all, he still had classes in the morning.

Morning came with a pounding on the door. "Ten minutes to the Walk!" Rellings shouted as he opened the door. "You hear that Sarren? Calbert?"

"Got it," Delmin said blearily.

"Ten minutes," Veranix said. Rellings scowled but said nothing more to them as he moved on. He pulled himself out of bed and started to get his uniform on.

"Blessed saints," Delmin muttered. "Is this how you feel every morning after one of your big nights?"

"This isn't bad," Veranix said as he pulled on his pants. "Blazes, I got over five hours of sleep tonight."

"Eh," Delmin said. He dragged himself from his bed and left the room for the water closet.

Veranix finished dressing, put on his cap and headed out into the hallway. Rellings was at the top of the stairs, lining people up to walk over to Holtman.

"Morning, Rellings," Veranix said with as big a smile as he could manage. "You know what they're serving today?"

"Don't know, Calbert," Rellings said. "I do know you won't be joining us, though." He looked far too smug as he pulled a note out of his pocket and handed it to Veranix. "Report to Professor Alimen's office at eight bells."

Veranix opened the note up and read it, though it said nothing more than what Rellings just told him. "How much time does that give me?"

"Five minutes, more or less," Rellings said. "Given your instructions, you are relieved from doing the Walk to breakfast."

"Always the gentleman, Rellings," Veranix said. He pointed to one of the underclassmen waiting in line. "Save something for me, you hear?" He dashed down the stairs, out the main door, and across the lawn as fast as his legs could naturally carry him.

The tower bells rang eight just as he reached the top steps of Bolingwood. Pausing for a moment to catch his breath, he knocked on the door to Professor Alimen's office.

"Come, Mister Calbert," Alimen called from behind the door. Veranix went in to find the professor setting a breakfast table with two plates. He appeared to be in good spirits, despite the bruises on his face.

"Very punctual, Mister Calbert," Alimen said with a

slight smile. "I dare say our little talk yesterday has had a positive effect on you."

"I did rest well last night," Veranix said. "And you, sir? How are you feeling?"

"Why do you ask, Mister Calbert?" Alimen asked as he placed a steaming dish in the center of the table.

"You seem to have . . . something on your head, sir," Veranix said, pointing at the bruise.

"Ah, yes," Alimen said, chuckling. "I had a bit of an adventure last night, though I must confess, I'm not totally clear on what all occurred. Please sit." Veranix sat down at the table. Alimen cut out a slice from the dish and put it on Veranix's plate.

"I wasn't expecting breakfast this morning, sir," he said.

"Yes, but I'm sure you appreciate it, regardless," Alimen said. "Pour yourself some tea."

"What is this dish, sir?" Veranix asked as he served tea for himself and Alimen.

"This is the traditional breakfast from the Plenin region of the Archduchy of Patyma, where I grew up," Alimen said. "You use old bread, cut into cubes, and you mix it with sausages and sheep's cheese, and then soak the whole thing in eggs and cream. Then you bake it and it's quite delicious." Veranix took a bite, and he had to agree with the professor's assessment.

"There's a similar dish in Oblune," he said. "But they use pork belly instead of sausages, and a sharper cow cheese."

"Hmm, yes," the professor said as he sat down. "I've had that before, and it's all wrong." He took a few bites in silence. "Anyway, last night I was abducted by our friends from the Blue Hand Circle, as was Miss Nell.

She was yet again the victim of circumstances, as I was having a word with her when they came."

"Is she all right?" Veranix asked.

"She is quite well," said the professor, "Though perhaps later you can go to her quarters and give her a kind word."

"Her quarters?" Veranix asked. That was confusing. "I thought Master Jolen had kicked her out."

"Well, let me continue," Alimen said. He took a few more bites before he did so. "I'm not sure exactly what the Blue Hand Circle was trying to achieve, but it seems they were convinced that I was somehow instrumental in regaining their stolen property. Which was ludicrous, but I think they had become quite unhinged. That Circle had always had something of an obsession with the more obscure and arcane corners of magical studies. Some of those corners can truly disturb the mind, Mister Calbert. Be aware of that."

"Yes, sir," Veranix said. "No arcane corners."

"Near as I can tell—as they knocked me out before they began whatever ritual they had planned—whatever they were doing went horribly wrong. Blew up in their collective faces. Miss Nell managed to get us loose and rescue me."

"Did she?" Veranix said, doing his best to sound surprised.

"Carried me back to campus herself," Alimen said. "Quite extraordinary girl, she is. Thus at sunrise this morning I went to Master Jolen and made it clear to him, in the light of such heroics, her employment at the University should not be terminated."

"That . . . that's amazing, sir." Veranix said. He shoved more of the food into his mouth to cover up his smile.

"Indeed, Mister Calbert, I had already checked into the school charters about the specific regulations, in regard to your fraternization with her. There is nothing in any rule preventing such liaisons between male students and female staff. In fact, somewhat disturbingly, the charter encourages the opposite in alarmingly specific detail." He coughed uncomfortably. Taking another bite he added, "The charter was written some centuries ago, and I suppose certain standards were different in those days."

"So she has her job back?" Veranix asked.

"Indeed she does," Professor Alimen said. He took a sip of tea. "That being said, Mister Calbert, do not think that means you should feel free to go sneaking off out of your quarters in the middle of the night. No matter how tempting or important the reasons might seem to you." He said this last part quite pointedly. "Am I clear?"

"Quite," Veranix said. "So, Professor, why exactly did you have me come for breakfast?"

"Ah, well," Professor Alimen said. "As I told you yesterday, it is clear to me you are in desperate need of greater academic discipline. Therefore, on lecture days, you will meet me here at eight bells to help me prepare the lesson. Every lecture day."

"That's not fair—" Veranix started. On the professor's withering look, he bit back the sentence and tried again. "That's not fair to Delmin, is it? He'll think I'm being groomed as a favorite."

"Well, that's the other part of my plan for you, Mister Calbert," Alimen said. "You will now also have double practicals. One with me, and one with me and Mister Sarren. I think he would benefit from working directly with you in those aspects. I'm also developing a plan on having the two of you work in a more hands-on manner with the first- and second-year magic students."

"You really intend to keep me busy, don't you, Professor?" Veranix asked, finishing the last bite of his breakfast.

"Whatever it takes to keep you out of trouble, Mister Calbert," the professor said. He cut another piece out of the pan and gave it to Veranix. "I plan to make you be the best you can be. Are you ready for that?"

"I'm ready for whatever comes," Veranix said, cutting into the second helping.

"Good," Alimen said, smiling warmly. "Now, first, perhaps you can help me find my sample of dalmatium. It does not seem to be anywhere."

It was nearly nine bells when Veranix came out of the tower, carrying a case full of gems and crystals for that day's lecture. Alimen walked ahead of him, humming tunelessly as he went. Veranix was of the opinion that the professor was enjoying himself a bit too much, but if this new arrangement meant regular breakfasts like that, he wasn't going to complain. Not too much, at any rate.

Just outside the lecture hall, Kaiana was pruning one of the fruit trees along the walkway. The spring blossoms were now in full bloom, so she was surrounded in a sea of deep pink, which accented her dark skin in a way that Veranix found surprisingly beautiful.

"Have a quick word," Alimen said. "But hurry in." He clapped Veranix on the shoulder and went into the lecture hall. Veranix approached the tree as Kaiana jumped down to the ground.

"So I hear you're the big hero," Veranix said.

"Best story I could come up with," she said with a shrug. "I am getting a bit tired of coming up with stories, though."

"I think you're done for a bit," Veranix said. "The professor has a plan to keep me very busy for a while." He looked down at the ground uncomfortably. "You really were, though. A hero, I mean. You did great last night."

"I just ran," she said.

"Ran like blazes," he said, laughing. "With Alimen over your shoulder, even. That's amazing."

She smiled warmly. "You were brilliant."

"Yeah, well," Veranix said, grinning back at her. "That's just what I had to be."

"Oh, shut it," she said. She bit her lip for a moment. She reached into her bag and pulled out a piece of paper. "These are all over the place outside the campus wall. Hundreds. I've never seen anything like it. What does it mean?" He took the paper from her. It showed a drawing of a canal—a waterpath—and both sides of it were lined with vines. Vines covered in thorns. A few crude sketches of men were on one side, getting stuck in the thorns and vines.

"Now that's a paper job," Veranix whispered. "Colin and the other Rose Street Princes are letting Fenmere know, anyone crosses Waterpath, then they'll get the Thorn."

"What does that mean for you?"

"It means," Veranix said, pocketing the paper, "that the idea of me should be enough to keep him at bay."

"So, is that it, though? You're not going after Fenmere at all?"

"Not yet," Veranix said. "I'll let him stew for a bit, at least until Professor Alimen grows tired of keeping the watch over me."

"But you will go after him," she said. It wasn't a question.

"Like fire and blazes," Veranix whispered, hotter and angrier than he expected. "As long as he's poisoning the streets."

"Good. I'll keep a lamp on for you when you do."

"Wouldn't have it any other way," he said. The bells started to ring. "I'll come see you later, but I've got to get in there."

"Go," she said, and went back to her trees.

Veranix picked up the case and went into the lecture hall. Today was going to be a long day, and he had plenty still to learn.

Satrine Rainey...

Former street rat. Ex-spy. Wife and mother who needs to make twenty crowns a week to support her daughters and infirm husband. To earn that, she forges credentials and fakes her way into a posting as a constabulary Inspector.

Minox Welling...

Brilliant Inspector. Uncircled Mage. Outcast of the stationhouse. Partnered with Satrine because no one else will work with "the jinx."

Their first case together
—the ritualized murder of a Circled mage—
brings Satrine back to the streets she grew up on, and forces Minox to confront the politics of mage circles he's avoided. As more mages are found dead, Satrine must solve the crime before her secrets catch up with her, and before her partner ends up a target.

Return to Maradaine in

A Murder of Mages

A Novel of the Maradaine Constabulary

by Marshall Ryan Maresca

978-0-7564-1027-8

DAW 212

Tad Williams
The **Bobby Dollar** Novels

"A dark and thrilling story.... Bad-ass smart-mouth
Bobby Dollar, an Earth-bound angel advocate for
newly departed souls caught between Heaven and
Hell, is appalled when a soul goes missing on his
watch. Bobby quickly realizes this is 'an actual, hon-
est-to-front-office crisis,' and he sets out to fix it,
sparking a chain of hellish events.... Exhilarating
action, fascinating characters, and high stakes will
leave the reader both satisfied and eager for the next
installment." —*Publishers Weekly (starred review)*

"Williams does a brilliant job.... Made me laugh.
Made me curious. Impressed me with its cleverness.
Made me hungry for the next book. Kept me up late
at night when I should have been sleeping."
—Patrick Rothfuss

The Dirty Streets of Heaven: 978-0-7564-0790-2
Happy Hour in Hell: 978-0-7564-0948-7
Sleeping Late on Judgement Day: 978-0-7564-0889-3

To Order Call: 1-800-788-6262
www.dawbooks.com

DAW 207